Seduced by Magic

Cheyenne McCray

St. Martin's Paperbacks

SEDUCED BY MAGIC

ISBN: 0-312-93763-6
EAN: 9780312-93763-8

Printed in the United States of America

St. Martin's Paperbacks edition / October 2006

St. Martin's Paperbacks are published by St. Martin's Press, 175 Fifth Avenue, New York, NY 10010.

10 9 8 7 6 5 4 3 2 1

Praise for CHEYENNE McCRAY and

Forbidden Magic

"Wildly erotic and dangerously sensual, this explosive paranormal thriller sizzles. McCray erupts on the scene with one of the sexiest stories of the year. Her darkly dramatic world is one readers won't mind visiting again . . . McCray knows how to make a reader sweat—either from spine-tingling suspense or soul-singeing sex . . . McCray cleverly combines present-day reality with mythological fantasy to create a world where beings of lore exist—and visit the earthly realm."

—*Romantic Times BOOKclub Magazine*

"McCray's paranormal masterpiece is not for the faint-hearted. The battle between good and evil is brought to the reader in vivid and riveting detail to the point where the reader is drawn into the pages of this bewitching and seductive fantasy that delivers plenty of action-packed sequences and arousing love scenes."

—*Rendezvous*

"*Forbidden Magic* is a spellbinding, sexy, superbly written dark fantasy. I couldn't put it down, and you won't want to either . . . [a] fabulous plot . . . [Cheyenne McCray has an] incredible skill at keeping readers engaged in every moment of the action. Long-time fans and newbies alike will be enchanted and swept away by this enduring tale of courage, love, passion, and magic."

—*A Romance Review*

"If one were going to make a comparison to Cheyenne McCray with another writer of the supernatural/sensuality genre, it would have to be Laurell K. Hamilton . . . *Forbidden Magic* definitely puts McCray in the same league as Hamilton. The book is a very sexy work . . . *Forbidden Magic* is dark and filled with danger at almost every turn. Magic and mystery abound in San Francisco, with a major battle between the forces of good and evil, and the outcome is always in doubt when it comes to demons."

—*Shelf Life*

More...

More...

To my husband, Frank Federici—
after twenty years, the magic is still there.

Acknowledgments

Thank you as always to the special people in my life. My mom and dad for their support, my children for giving me the space to write when under deadline, and my friends for being there when I need them. And thank goodness for coffee shops and bookstores to write in when I need to escape!

Thanks bunches to Peggy Phillips for help with reading tarot cards.

Special thanks once again to my editor, Monique Patterson, along with my wonderful critique partners—Annie Windsor, Mackenzie McKade, and Patrice Michelle. Couldn't have done it without you *all*.

One

San Francisco
Fifteen months prior

Copper Ashcroft moved through the fog-shrouded San Francisco night and shivered. Everything looked and felt exactly as it had in her dream-vision.

Rocks and twigs crunched beneath her running shoes as she made her way down the darkened trail to the sacred stretch of beach below, with only her wand light to illuminate the path. Tonight was a new moon and it was foggy as hell. But she knew her way and didn't pause.

Her arms strained as she gripped the carved wooden chest bearing the tools of her witchcraft at the same time she carried her wand. Her breathing came easy. She was fit from regular exercise, playing softball, and toned from working out at the health club. She'd been a track star and a mean softball pitcher in high school, as well as being the lead pitcher on the California Bears team at UC Berkeley during her undergrad years.

Copper stumbled over a root and almost tumbled down the path. She grimaced and steadied herself. "Bless it," she murmured. She'd known the root was there. "Too bad being fit and athletic doesn't make me any less clumsy."

Zephyr buzzed at her ear, but she ignored her honeybee familiar. She sensed Zeph's unhappiness that she was attempting this moon ritual alone, but in Copper's dreamvision she'd performed the ceremony with no one else around. For some reason the goddess wanted her to do this by herself.

She stepped from the dirt path onto sand when she reached the small portion of beach known only to the Coven of D'Anu witches to which she belonged. Her Coven was one of thirteen scattered across the United States. Many more Covens existed around the world, working to keep the cities they inhabited safe from dark magic. Descendents of the Ancient Druids, the D'Anu were powerful witches who used only white witchcraft.

Well, besides Copper and her sister, Silver. The sisters believed in utilizing gray magic to protect their world from the evils that preyed upon the innocent. If their father found out . . . they'd be in a world of trouble. Victor Ashcroft was high priest of the D'Anu Coven in Salem, Massachusetts, and he was a rather formidable man. Their mother, Moondust, was more an ethereal being, the calm in the storm. But she would agree with their father.

White witchcraft just wasn't strong enough as far as Copper was concerned. She was somewhat of a rebel when it came to choosing between white and gray, and she had no fear of the gray or ever slipping to the black.

With white magic, their skills were limited. Several of the D'Anu could affect the weather but they didn't dare tip the natural balance. Most could heal and work with animals, "talk through trees," and make plants grow like crazy—even fast enough to help them bind an enemy. Useful, but . . . not strong enough.

Sand shifted beneath Copper's jogging shoes as she heaved the chest higher in her arms and carried it across the small beach. Her jeans felt snug and comfortable and her cropped T-shirt allowed the coolness of the night to brush her flat belly. In the distance she could see a portion of the Golden Gate Bridge, its lights looping up and down in the darkness. A foghorn added to the eerie quality of the night, and despite the familiar sound, goose bumps prickled her skin and tiny hairs rose up on the back of her neck.

Copper remembered the old Grimoire she and Silver had used to learn gray magic. Mrs. Illes had given it to them before she passed on to Summerland, and Silver still had it. The ancient book looked harmless enough, but the spells inside—well . . . As Copper had found out when she tried to summon the tide and ended up almost flooding the city, gray magic had the potential to blow the natural order all to hell. Gray witchcraft could help a lot, but it could also cause indirect harm, like hurting a living creature or subverting a being's natural will.

If anyone of the D'Anu suspected that Copper and Silver practiced gray magic, the pair of them would be kicked out of the Coven. Even using the craft to track down criminals just wasn't allowed.

Besides, gray witchcraft carried heavy-duty risk to most witches, too. Many believed there was such a fine line between gray and black that gray witches could feel the incredible power that darkness offered. If a gray witch became too emotionally entangled—her own anger, want, need—her spells could lean close to the black. She could use her magic for personal gain and power instead of the general good.

Touching gray, Copper could sense the immeasurable and powerful flow and pull of dark magic. Yet Copper didn't fear it. She embraced gray magic. She had no doubt she wouldn't tip to the dark side no matter how deep her gray magic ran. Silver wasn't so sure and wasn't as strong a gray witch as Copper was.

A knot twisted Copper's belly as she allowed a brief flash of why she believed so strongly in gray magic. A childhood friend, Trista, had been murdered when Copper was sixteen. If Copper had been a strong gray witch at that time, she knew with every fiber of her being that she could have saved Trista.

Copper shoved the thought and the threat of tears away. When she reached her favorite part of the shore, she bent and dropped the chest. It made a dull thud that was almost lost in the sound of waves crashing against the shore. The wind off the water carried smells of fish and salt.

As she settled on her knees before the chest, she caught another scent that made her pause. Her skin prickled again. "Wolfsbane?" she murmured.

She shook her head, her shoulder-length copper-colored hair swinging with the movement. *Your imagination is on overdrive, girl.*

Holding her wand tight in one hand, Copper fumbled with the catch on the trunk using her other, but finally managed to flip the rusted latch open. "I really need to get that oiled," she muttered. It was one of those things that tended to be low on the priority list.

Hinges creaked as she opened the trunk lid and peered at the contents. Zephyr landed on the curve of her ear just as her wand slipped from her fingers and tumbled inside. She lost her focus and her wand light went out.

"For the Ancestors' sake." Her copper pentagram earrings swung against her neck as she rummaged around inside the chest until her fingers found her wand. She was never clumsy with her magic, but she tended to drop some things and knock over others.

The wand was made of copper and tipped with a round quartz crystal at one end and a pointed quartz crystal at the other. She gripped it tightly in her hand and frowned when the crystal did not immediately brighten again. She focused her magical energy on the wand. This time golden light glittered from the crystal and caused the pentagram on her thick copper bracelet to look as though it glowed against her wrist. She didn't know what she'd do without her wand—her magic was powerful, but only with her wand. Her hand magic wasn't so hot.

Copper mounted the wand in a corner slot of the trunk where it continued to spill its golden light across the sand, making the grains sparkle like Faerie dust.

She quickly stripped out of her clothing, tossing her T-shirt, bra, shoes, socks, jeans, and thong in a heap on the sand. Even though her witchcraft helped keep most of the coldness at bay, the chilly San Francisco wind whipped at her body, causing her nipples to tighten. She hurried to slip on a shimmering earth-colored robe she dug out of the chest and wrap it around her body.

Copper gathered her supplies, only dropping one candle and her incense burner as she strode a few feet away to where she would cast her circle. After she retrieved everything she needed, she placed each candle at the cardinal points—yellow for Air at the east, red for Fire at the south, blue for Water at the west, and green for Earth at the north.

She arranged her altar, careful not to spill her chalice as she filled it with purified water. As she reached for the cotton bag full of salt granules, her arm brushed the chalice, tipping it. Her heart raced as she dropped the bag to catch the cup before it could fall over and completely lose its contents. With a sigh of relief, she let go of her death grip on the cup and retrieved the cotton bag to pour salt to represent Earth into a small dish. *Almost done.* With her magic, she lit a black candle that represented both the new moon and Fire, and then she burned cinnamon incense for Air. Of course the filled chalice represented Water.

When Copper finished her preparations, she retrieved her glowing wand and returned to stand within the circle of candles. She took a deep breath. Everything she had just done was routine, yet it felt . . . different. It felt as her dream-vision had last night, and a sense of urgency filled her. Something wrong, terribly wrong, was going to happen in San Francisco—unless she found a way to stop it.

Copper prepared to cast her protective circle. "Goddess, I need your aid in learning as much as I can about the dangers I know the D'Anu will be facing." *I'll inform Silver and the Coven about my dream-vision once I have more to tell.*

She centered herself as she stared out at the ocean, breathing deeply and releasing all tension from her body. The wand was warm in her hand from the magic that filled it. The golden glow it cast looked like early morning sunlight sparkling upon the water's less than calm surface. It was time to cast her circle and perform the moon ritual.

In the ritual she would ask the goddess for aid in whatever evils were coming their way, and to show her a vision of what they were about to face. Copper was not a seer, she could only dream-vision as her divination talent. But sometimes—well, rarely, but still—the goddess would show her visions when she performed a moon ritual.

Copper breathed deeply, allowing all the night smells to fill her. There was definitely a difference between night and day scents, as if the moon cast its own delicate perfume over the world, even when it was shrouded.

Zeph crawled along the top of her ear as she prepared to cast the circle. Already she felt his magic mingling with hers. But she also sensed distress coming from the familiar. "What's wrong?" she asked, wishing he could speak aloud. But she could only feel his agitation, as if he were worried about something.

Refocusing her attention, she let the earth-brown robe slide down her shoulders and arms to land around her feet in a satiny mass, leaving her bare body to be buffeted by the wind. Sand trickled between her toes as she widened her stance to shoulder-width apart, leaving her bare sex to be stroked by the night breeze just as that same rush of air hardened her nipples. Her shoulder-length hair teased the nape of her neck and she shivered from the combined sensations.

Copper raised her wand to start casting her circle when

a sensation of dark power trailed down her spine; Zeph grew frantic, his wings buzzing. The scent of wolfsbane was strong this time, so very strong.

A presence behind her.

Someone . . . someone watching her.

Zephyr gave a buzz of warning. Copper gripped her wand tighter. Should she quickly attempt to cast the circle to keep evil away from her, or should she face whatever was behind her?

She was certain she didn't have time to close the circle. She whirled and raised her wand so that its light might blind whatever being had crept up on her, and to use the wand's magic if need be.

Copper's pulse began racing. Perhaps ten feet away from her stood a man. A breathtakingly handsome man with eyes as black as his hair, high cheekbones, and a cleft in his square chin.

Around his neck, on a thick chain, hung a stone eye that glittered in Copper's wand light and glowed a deep red. The sight of it caused her stomach to churn before the red faded away.

What captured her attention the most was the controlled power emanating from the man. A power so intense and dark that Copper nearly recoiled. But she stood her ground. With a tilt of her chin, she narrowed her eyes and faced what she was certain to be a ruthless, incredibly powerful warlock.

"Leave," Copper said, shoring up her magic at the same time. "This place is sacred. You don't belong here."

The warlock smiled, a smile as sensual as it was sinister. "Finally . . . a witch worthy of my time and my training." He paused and brought his hand to the stone at his neck, the red glow returning and bleeding through his fingers. He gave a slow nod, as if in response to some communication from the eye. "Yes. There is another—you have a sister whose power is as great as yours, and she rides the line of gray magic just as you do. Only she is more . . . vulnerable."

At the mention of her sister, a chill went through Copper and she straightened her spine. "Who are you?" She tried to ignore the bite of the wind as she stared the warlock down. This was the evil she had dream-visioned about. This was what . . . no, *who* she was to battle to save everything she loved.

She had to be rid of him before he destroyed what was good and pure. But how?

Zephyr gave an angry buzz and she sensed his desire to sting the man in front of her. "No," she murmured. "Stay."

The man raised his hand and beckoned to her. She felt the power of his touch on her naked body. It was as if his bare hand were stroking her, touching every intimate part of her. He took a step forward. "I am Darkwolf."

"Well, *Darkwolf,*" she said as the glow intensified from the pointed end of her wand tip. "Stop right there or I'll make you wish you'd stayed in the sewer you crawled out of."

"I think not." He moved closer and raised his hand so that his palm faced her.

She was certain she knew exactly what the goddess wanted her to do to keep them all safe. In a rush, Copper chanted.

> *Goddess give me power this night*
> *Send the moon's strength to help me fight.*
> *Ancestors bless this wand and make it a sword*
> *To send this evil to Otherworld!*

Light blazed from Copper's wand, so bright that it blinded even her. Power flooded her, power of the Ancestors, the goddess. But she needed more—the gray magic she held always at the ready.

She poured her gray magic into the spell with all that she had.

In the next moment something shimmered before her. Something alien. Something that couldn't have been just from the warlock.

From the eye?

Her spell struck the magical shield that was so strong her witchcraft rebounded. The spell shot straight back at her. Before she had time to form a spellshield, her own magic slammed into her and flung her high, into the air . . .

She was falling . . . falling . . . falling . . .

Into sunlight. Into the breath of spring.

She landed facedown, her bare skin upon the softest grass she had ever felt. The rich scent of it and dark loam filled her senses, along with the perfume of rose petals. Vaguely she heard the sound of Zephyr buzzing and the faintest music . . . Faerie song.

She tried to raise her head, but the Faerie music grew ever fainter. Light faded. Darkness came and swept her away on swift wings.

Two

Tiernan, a Tuatha D'Danann warrior and Lord of the House of Cathal in Otherworld, narrowed his gaze at the two human witches in Silver Ashcroft's apartment. He raked his fingers through his blond hair as both Silver and Rhiannon focused intently on fog now wafting from the pewter cauldron like smoke from a campfire.

Hawk shifted beside Tiernan and he sensed the man's unease. Hawk was also a D'Danann Enforcer who hailed from Otherworld. But Tiernan was nobility. Hawk was not.

The D'Danann were powerful winged Fae warriors, once ancient gods who had resided in Ireland before leaving to form their own Sidhe in Otherworld. The D'Danann were a neutral race of Fae who only answered calls of distress from Otherworlds if they believed it to be within the natural order. Fortunately for the city of San Francisco, the Chieftains had allowed the D'Danann Enforcers to travel to this place and assist the D'Anu witches in battling the Fomorii demons and the Balorite warlocks.

Just before Samhain, Silver Ashcroft had used a moon ritual to summon the D'Danann to aid her and all witches against the threat of the demons and the warlocks. Perhaps the Chieftains agreed to aid the witches in part because the witches served the goddess Anu, and the D'Danann were her offspring.

"Oh, my goddess," Silver whispered, drawing Tiernan's full attention as the fog began to take shape. Her silvery-blond hair fell over her shoulder as she leaned closer to the cauldron. "It's the Balorites and the Fomorii. They're in a chamber—a cavern. Opening a great door."

Tiernan unfolded his arms from across his chest and his breathing grew a little more rapid.

Rhiannon's face had gone from her normal fair complexion to an even paler shade. The witch, who had chin-length auburn hair and usually a feisty look to her green eyes, was not one to show fear. However, her expression this time made him uneasy, especially when she said, "They're not—they *wouldn't.*"

Tiernan started to stride forward, to see what the witches were observing, but Hawk held out his arm, blocking Tiernan. He could have forced himself past the warrior's arm, but he realized the wisdom of Hawk's action. The witches could not perform their task with interference.

"Balor." Silver swallowed, her throat working, as Tiernan watched, his muscles tense. "I see him and his great single eye. I see the Balorites—and other beings—freeing both Balor's body and his soul."

Tiernan's heart set to pounding despite the fact he normally held little faith in human witch divination.

Rhiannon braced her hands on the wooden table the cauldron perched on, her knuckles white from clenching her fists. Her face was so close to the fog that it caressed her cheeks.

Silver recoiled, her palm over her mouth, before she dropped her hand. "How can they? He was exiled far below Otherworld. Beyond Underworld, even."

Tiernan could not help the rumble that rose up in his

chest at the memory of Balor's exile centuries ago. From the corner of his eye he saw Hawk give him a disapproving look.

Rhiannon backed away from the table, but kept her eyes on the fog. "Somehow Darkwolf and the Fomorii will find a way to free Balor—if we don't stop them first." Rhiannon's gaze swung to Silver then back to the cauldron. "What—what's that?" She studied the foggy shapes above the cauldron. "No, *who* is that?"

Silver's shoulders began shaking and tears started rolling down her cheeks. "It's Copper—" Her voice came out in a strained whisper. "She's stretched out like she's a sacrifice."

"And she's bleeding," Rhiannon said, horror written across her face.

Tiernan's gut wrenched and he grew cold.

The fog diminished until nothing was left but a faint spiral and then it was gone, too.

In mere strides, Hawk had Silver in his arms. She gripped the front of his tunic in her fists and sobbed freely against his chest. "I've scried and scried to find Copper since she vanished and have seen nothing. But now, to see her like that? Oh, goddess."

Hawk held her tight as she continued to cry.

Tiernan clenched his jaw and turned to Rhiannon. "Tell me everything you saw."

The usually calm and collected witch visibly trembled as she raised her chin to look up at him. "You heard every word. The Balorites and Fomorii are searching for a way to free Balor."

He tried to keep his voice steady. "Are you sure this will happen? Or has it already happened?"

Rhiannon steadied herself by placing one hand on the table beside the cauldron. She closed her eyes and took a deep breath before releasing it again. For a moment the witch went still. Her breathing became heavier, her expression twisting to one of pain. Tiernan noticed her eyes were moving rapidly behind her eyelids, as if she were dreaming or watching a scene unfold within her mind.

Finally she opened her eyes. "My sight tells me it hasn't happened yet. Other beings are helping to search for the door that will free Balor. I have no idea how soon they will locate it, though."

"Copper." Silver sniffed and wiped the back of her hand across her swollen red eyes. "She was there, tied down in some kind of circle, and her eyes were closed. Someone, something was bleeding her."

Tiernan glanced to the frames sitting next to Silver's computer and saw one of the pictures of the laughing red-head. Every time he saw the pictures he found himself intrigued by the missing woman, almost to the point of obsession. For some reason the thought of something happening to her made him beyond furious, heat quickly chasing away the chill that had overcome him.

"You are certain it was your sister? You are certain your *vision* is true?" Tiernan asked in a harsh voice.

Silver's spine stiffened and her gaze snapped to Tiernan's. "There is no doubt in my mind."

Hawk glared at Tiernan, his jaw tense. "I do not care if you are a *lord*. You do not speak to my mate in such a manner."

Before Tiernan could respond, the door swung open. Alyssa and Sydney stumbled into the room. Both witches were flushed, as if from running.

"We divined where the Balorites and Fomorii are," Alyssa said in a rush. "But you need to hurry because they are leaving."

Tiernan eased around the corner of what appeared to be an abandoned building, his muscles tense and his jaw clenched. His senses were on full alert and his body prepared to unleash his wings and launch into the air at a moment's notice. He gripped the hilt of his sword tighter, where it rested beneath his long, black coat.

It was an unusually warm day for San Francisco, and sweat trickled along the side of his face and down his neck to his chest. He would have preferred the cover of darkness, but if the witches' scrying was correct the remaining warlocks and Fomorii demons were currently using this building as their base—if they had not yet fled. He was hoping for the former. What he wouldn't give to kick some demon ass right now. Capturing at least a few warlocks would make his day, too.

Other than the Elves, the D'Danann warriors were the only beings who could battle and win against the Fomorii. The D'Danann could unfold or hide their large feathered wings at will and had the ability to shield themselves from human or demon sight when searching the skies for signs of whatever beings they looked for. The D'Danann could wrench the head from an enemy and tear his heart out with one strike to the chest.

The warriors had been summoned to this Otherworld, Earth, by a D'Anu witch just before Samhain. Now, perhaps eight weeks since that time, they were no closer to finding the Fomorii queen or the warlock high priest. They had gone well into hiding, no doubt to regroup after a great many of the Fomorii had been sent back to Underworld on Samhain. Thanks to the D'Anu witches' divination talents, the D'Danann had come close to finding the Fomorii and warlocks. But for some reason they were always too late, a fact that puzzled the witches. It was thought that perhaps the Balorites had an exceptionally gifted seer who was able to warn the warlocks and Fomorii in time.

The Balorites were an especially sinister Clan of male and female warlocks who had originally summoned the Fomorii. The Balorites, led by the high priest Darkwolf, had employed the darkest of rituals to bring forth the demons.

They had sacrificed the lives of innocents and had used their blood.

Darkwolf wore a stone eye on a chain about his neck, and it was believed by the D'Danann to be a tool of the ancient god Balor. Somehow Balor was influencing the will of the warlocks to bring forth his minions.

Fomorii could inhabit another being's body, killing the host instantly while the demon took over the being's shell, virtually becoming that person or creature. In their natural state, the demons were of hideous shapes and colors. Some had one eye like the god Balor, while others had many. Their limbs were odd-sized or numerous, as well. They had long needlelike teeth and horrible claws. The Formorii had started tipping their claws in iron, which was deadly to Elves and Fae, including the D'Danann.

Even though he could not see his comrades just yet, Tiernan knew that Hawk and the other D'Danann Enforcers crept just as quietly around the building, and some of the D'Danann had flown to the rooftop to gain entrance. The witches who had insisted on accompanying them were, surprisingly, as light-footed as the D'Danann.

When Tiernan passed an open window, a whiff of rotten fish invaded his nose. Yes. The stench of the Fomorii. Only there was not more than a hint of it. No doubt the D'Danann and witches were too late; but he did not let down his guard.

Tiernan reached the steps leading to the door of the building and Hawk appeared around the corner, across from him.

"I fear they have left," Tiernan said in mind-speak to Hawk.

"Aye." Hawk gave a sharp nod of agreement, but held his sword at the ready, just as Tiernan did.

Part of the D'Danann magic was the ability to tread so lightly when they willed it that not even the slightest sound could be heard. Despite their size, their boots, and their muscled bulk, not a single step creaked beneath Tiernan's and Hawk's combined weight as they eased their way up the weathered stairs.

However, they could not control the squeak of the door-knob or the scrape of the rotting door as Tiernan opened it. The peeling paint was rough beneath his palm when he placed it against the wood and pushed it all the way open. At once he smelled dust and decay along with the demon stench.

They entered a narrow hallway and the smell of Fomorii grew stronger. But not strong enough. As they worked their way through the building, Tiernan and Hawk communicated with their fellow warriors using mind-speak and learned that the other warriors too had found nothing. From what Tiernan could discern, the building was apparently void of any furniture or other objects. It was stripped bare—it probably had been that way before the Fomorii had taken possession of it. The smell of rotten fish and the deep gouges in the floor and on the walls were the only signs the demons had been there.

Toward the end of their search, Tiernan came upon a scrap of old parchment that was out of place in this modern world. He found it in a cobwebbed corner of one of the rooms. He frowned as he retrieved the tattered paper that felt rough between his fingers. An ink drawing was sketched on its surface—a vertical rectangle with a circle beneath it. A smaller ring was within the larger circle, and strange runes were etched in the space between the two circles.

Hawk came up beside Tiernan and studied the drawing, as well. "I believe either you have found something of import," Hawk said, "or something meant to lead us astray. Perhaps Silver or one of the other witches can use their knowledge or their divination skills to determine its meaning."

Tiernan gently rolled the worn parchment and slipped it into the pocket of his black overcoat that covered his weapons. At one time he hadn't given much stock in human witches. Not until the D'Anu, with the assistance of the D'Danann, had vanquished a good number of the Fomorii and sent the beasts back to Underworld.

When they found no other clues, Hawk and Tiernan gave orders to return to their home base.

Damn the Underworld, the Fomorii were still one step ahead of them.

Tiernan folded his arms across his chest and focused his gaze intently on the witch Silver Ashcroft. She was standing, slightly bent over her scrying cauldron. The piece of parchment was still in his pocket. He intended to show it to the witches when Silver finished her second scrying attempt. The room carried the scent of Silver's lily perfume and some kind of citrus smell that she said she used to cover up the musty odor of the old apartment.

The witch, Hawk, and Tiernan were again in Silver's apartment within a building in the Haight-Ashbury district of San Francisco. The building was owned by Jake Macgregor, a Special Forces agent who dealt with paranormal crimes. After Silver was banished from the powerful D'Anu Coven she had belonged to, for using gray magic, several of her sister witches left with her to form their own D'Anu Coven. But this Coven was now entirely made up of witches willing to use gray magic.

Jake had offered a portion of the building he owned to the D'Danann and the D'Anu witches to use as a headquarters while they searched for the rest of the Fomorii demons and Balorite warlocks. Jake had inherited the building from a wealthy uncle and drew a steady rent income from residents, but fortunately he had several available apartments.

Silver drew Tiernan's attention as he looked back to her

cauldron where wisps of fog still rose in lazy spirals. "I saw Darkwolf, and that demon Junga when I scried," Silver said with a touch of anger. "I couldn't tell what they were talking about, but Darkwolf was looking over some kind of map."

Hawk rested his hand on Silver's shoulder and said, "Do you know where the bastards are?"

Silver sighed and shook her head, her long silvery-blond hair spilling over her shoulders with the movement. "Not yet." She glanced from Hawk to Tiernan, a determined look in her stormy gray eyes. "But I *will* find them."

"Were there any clues?" Tiernan rubbed his temples. "Did you notice anything about the place they occupied when you had this—this vision?"

Silver nodded. "I was just about to get to that." She pulled away from Hawk and paced the length of the apartment's common room, her heels clicking on the tile floor. Her silk blouse pulled against her breasts and her skirt reached to mid-thigh. Her apparel was much different from that of the D'Danann ladies of the court, who tended to wear long dresses with full skirts.

Tiernan actually preferred the clothing of Silver and of the D'Danann warrior women over that of the ladies of the court with their silks and satins. The D'Danann warrior women girded themselves in leather tunics and breeches, as did the male warriors. But it was not for him to say what the women of the court wore.

"I saw walls filled with books—rows and rows of them," Silver said. "It was like they were in some kind of library."

Tiernan raised an eyebrow and Hawk grunted. "There were also works of art and a large window."

Silver continued her pacing. "I believe it's a private library."

Silver sighed and paused in her pacing to glance at her desk in one corner of the room. She went to the desk and picked up a photograph. "I can't help but hope that once we locate that damned warlock Darkwolf, we'll be able to find Copper." Her voice caught and he could hear the tears in her voice. "Before something happens to her. That vision can't come true. It just *can't*."

Tiernan moved closer to Silver to view the picture of her sister and his heart set to thumping.

"Darkwolf." Silver's voice had an edge of anger. "When we battled the Fomorii and Balorites at Samhain, he alluded to knowing what happened to her. Maybe even having something to do with her disappearance."

"We will find her," Hawk said as he wrapped one arm around Silver's shoulders and squeezed her close to him.

Without asking, Tiernan took the photograph from Silver's hands. He studied the woman in the picture, his gaze taking in the face he had already memorized. Every curve of her Fae features, the sprinkling of Faerie kisses across her nose, her cinnamon eyes, her copper-colored hair. She was aptly named. It was one of many times he had studied the picture.

His heart clenched at the thought of this beautiful woman, missing for so long. Where had she gone to? Or where had she been taken? He refused to believe that this woman was dead. No, his gut told him she was alive, and by the gods, he intended to help find her.

Damnation. How could a simple picture make him want her so?

He tried to ignore the irrational stirring in his gut and his groin. He was to be mated with one of the women within the D'Danann High Court. His bonding with Airell of the House of Torin would bring together two powerful houses—there would be no room for trifling with other females for anything besides sex. Least of all a part human, part Elvin, witch.

He handed the picture back to Silver whose gaze was pinned on him as if she knew his thoughts. As if she were aware of the primal urges within him every time he looked at the picture of her sister, who smiled with such mischief in her eyes.

Irrational.

His was an ordered world. He was methodical and never impulsive. Such a woman would never be an attraction to him.

Silver placed the picture back onto her desk. "Why don't we meet up with the others at Enchantments?"

Silver, Hawk, and Tiernan headed out of the aging building to the store the witches had rented just a few doors down from the apartments. Over the past few weeks since Samhain, the witches, along with Jake, had combined monetary and physical resources—not to mention a good dose of magic and D'Danann muscle—to remodel and open the once boarded-up store. There were still things that needed to be done, but it looked remarkably well considering the short length of time the witches had had to put it together.

They had made it into a New Age café similar to Moon Song, a store/café that Silver had run for the D'Anu Coven before she was banished. They had named the new store and café Enchantments. It was in what Silver said was the most New Age and one of the most artistic parts of San Francisco—the Haight-Ashbury district.

All Tiernan cared about was the fact that Cassia cooked and baked the best food he had ever eaten in all of the Otherworlds. D'Danann were notorious for the amount of food they could consume. He was no exception.

Enchantment's kitchen was the main gathering place for the D'Danann and witches. It afforded more room than Moon Song had, which was an added benefit. The warriors could eat their fill with most of the witches cooking for everyone. The warrior women could match the men bite for bite, and still remain toned and muscular.

When they reached the kitchen of Enchantments, Tiernan's stomach rumbled. The kitchen smelled of spices and fresh-baked pumpkin bread.

Silver called to Cassia who was wiping her hands on her apron. The blue-eyed, curly-headed witch was part Elvin and had an ethereal glow about her now that her true identity had been revealed. Before she had let her true self be known, she had acted the part of a clumsy, inept witch to better protect Silver from the dangers she had faced before Samhain.

Tiernan grabbed a slice of warm pumpkin bread and Hawk scooped up a chocolate chip cookie.

As he ate the bread, Tiernan dug the piece of parchment he had found out of his pocket and handed it to Cassia.

"Where did you get this?" Her eyes widened. "I don't recognize these runes at all." She shuddered and goose bumps appeared on her forearms. "All I can tell is there's something very wicked about them. This paper is shrouded in evil."

Silver quirked an eyebrow at Tiernan. "What's that?"

He shrugged. "I do not know."

Cassia kept the parchment close as she drew out her black and gold rune stones. She tumbled them onto a clean portion of the counter and studied them. "The stones give no additional clues save that we are in grave danger."

"So what's new?" Silver sounded flippant, but her eyes held that same dark concern that had been present ever since she saw the vision of the coming of Balor and of Copper.

Cassia gave the parchment to Silver. Immediately the witch started shaking so hard the parchment trembled in her fingertips and she looked as if she might faint or throw up. Or both. Tiernan would have taken her by the arm to aid her if Hawk had not already been at her side. "This is the circle," Silver said in a hoarse whisper. "Copper was tied down in a circle just like this when I scried with the cauldron this morning."

Rhiannon took the parchment from Silver. The moment the witch's hands touched the parchment her face paled as it had earlier. As she held it tighter, she said, "I get the feeling of immeasurable evil." She inhaled and slowly let out her breath. "I see a door within a massive room. The circles are engraved into the floor with the runes scraped or carved into it."

Tiernan studied the drawing more closely. He could easily see now that the vertical rectangle could be a door, and the circles could be on a floor before it. A look of relief swept over Rhiannon's face when Mackenzie took it from her.

With an expression of distaste, the petite blond set the parchment on the kitchen table, then dealt her tarot cards into a Celtic cross. Among other things, the cards revealed grave danger and battles ahead, but also that a new friend would be taking a journey and an old friend would be returning.

After everyone had the opportunity to look at and evaluate the parchment, Tiernan left the store. He stood in the store's back parking spot and lifted his face to the sky.

At the same time he unfolded his great brown wings from his back, he shielded himself from sight. With a simple flap of his wings, he took to the sky in search of the damnable warlocks and the Fomorii.

Three

Otherworld
The present

It could have been days, months, years. All Copper Ashcroft knew was that she had to find her way out, her way back home. And something was telling her that it needed to be *soon*.

"What is wrong, witch?" Riona, the Faerie queen who was trapped with Copper, flitted from around the bushes that hid the Faerie mound in their Otherworld prison. "Are you homesick for this San Francisco you are always talking about?"

"Yeah. What's new?" Copper shrugged and shifted on the smooth rock beneath the apple tree. She'd never had a melancholy personality, but a girl could only be trapped so long without getting a little tired of it. "Goddess, how I miss everything—working in the shop with Silver, my classes at UC Berkeley." She'd been working on her masters in education, and also had a minor in Celtic studies and physical education.

"And then there's the city itself," she continued. "The smell of the ocean, the sound of a foghorn, the clang of trolleys." *Rock music. Dating. Restaurants. Department stores.*

Shopping! And sex. Definitely sex. She'd never dated anyone seriously. She had too much fun going out with different guys and enjoying the company of her friends. But she sure liked sex.

Riona landed on Copper's shoulder. Her perfect, naked, six-inch body was the color of cream. Her hair was long and midnight black, her eyes amethyst and her wings a pale purple. Every time she opened and closed her wings, Faerie dust glittered in the evening air and Copper caught the familiar scent of roses.

"Mostly I miss Mother, Father, and my older sister, Silver." Copper glanced at the Faerie queen. "I'm glad to have all of you for company, but I would love to see my friends and the D'Anu Coven of witches I belonged to—even that old crotchety high priestess, Janis Arrowsmith."

What she wouldn't give to have Janis glaring at her right now. She swore the high priestess was always glaring. Of course during the time Copper had been gone, a new Adept would have filled her place as one of the thirteen female and male witches that comprised the D'Anu Coven, all descendents of the Ancient Druids.

Riona crossed her dainty little legs at her knees and started swinging her foot. "It *is* your fault, witch, that we are all imprisoned."

"I just don't understand what happened," Copper said for the millionth time. Was it really her fault? Her magic had rebounded off something—some kind of shield—and she'd sent herself into this Otherworld place.

"You are a very powerful witch," Riona said softly, her voice like tiny bells in a gentle breeze.

Copper blinked. Riona complimenting her?

"I just know that spell would have worked if it wasn't for that shield," Copper said, deciding to go on. "I am *so sure* the warlock will be responsible for something terrible that's going to happen. I was so sure the spell would work." Thoughts of her sister, family, and friends being in danger and possibly being hurt or worse made Copper's chest burn. What if something *had* happened and she wasn't there to help?

Not only had she sent herself to Otherworld, but she'd ended up inside a magical shield that surrounded herself, a meadow with a rock wall on one side, a mini-waterfall and stream, a pine tree, and the apple tree—everything contained within the shield.

All of the creatures and beings trapped within this house-sized prison were apparently invisible to any being outside the shield who happened to be nearby. And none of the beings confined with her were happy about being held hostage. They blamed it on Copper's magic no matter what she said.

Riona patted Copper's shoulder, her touch as soft as flower petals drifting upon her skin. "Believe it or not, I have confidence that one day you *will* free us all."

Copper's eyes widened in astonishment as the Faerie queen flitted away to return to their tiny Sidhe, which was a mound, some bushes, and a garden of assorted flowers, not farther than a stone's throw away. Riona had never before expressed any faith in Copper. What was this little world coming to?

She looked up to the sky. It was an overcast evening with swirling dark clouds gathering overhead. Interestingly enough, they still had changes in weather, which meant that the walls couldn't be limitless and there was no ceiling. Yet none of the Fae had been able to fly high enough to get out.

The moon went through its usual phases, too, but no matter how she tried, her moon rituals wouldn't work and she received no visions from the ritual. She wasn't a seer of course, but in the past the goddess had sometimes been helpful during moon rituals.

Copper decided she might as well do something active instead of moping on the rock. She stood and grabbed one of the higher branches of the apple tree, gripped its rough thickness, and started doing pull-ups. She'd kept in shape by doing pull-ups, sit-ups, arm curls with rocks, and managed other toning exercises, as well as jogging around the circumference of their prison. She even practiced her softball pitching for amusement by throwing rocks at the shield, and sharpened her reflexes by dodging them as they rebounded back at her.

While she performed her pull-ups, her mind returned to the dream she'd had last night. It had been so freaking intense.

She'd been crawling along a recently made tunnel, the smell of fresh earth confirming it was newly dug. The walls had glittered with veins of ore and an occasional gem. She had squinted. Dark shapes loomed in and out of her vision.

In her dream a sudden chill had pricked her skin with goose bumps and she'd felt an icy wash of fear.

In the next moment she had dropped. She'd plunged through the blackness, screaming . . .

She thought for a moment she saw a dark being as she fell, a being with fire for hair, but it was only a flash before she woke. Her breathing had been heavy, as if she'd been running the circumference of the prison.

She'd woken with her heart pounding in her ears, feeling as if something horrible were going to happen. Even the thought of the dream made her stomach clench.

"Get a grip," she mumbled as she finished the last pull-up, then got down to the grassy ground and began doing guy push-ups. She used her upper body and the strength of her arms to do the push-ups as her toes dug into the grass, balancing her.

Her braid fell over her shoulder as she continued her workout. Of course the copper color of her hair was the reason her mother had named her Copper. Moondust had named Copper's sister Silver, after the shade of blond hair she'd been born with. Both were unique names that had caused a lot of teasing as the girls grew up. Neither one of them had minded—much. From a young age they had been encouraged by their mother to enjoy their differences, and that included being witches.

Copper finished her push-ups, feeling a little sweat break out on her skin. She picked up a good-sized rock, bent over, and braced her other hand on the rock beneath the tree and started working out her triceps.

She watched a pair of Faeries gathering nectar from a bright purple bloom in the waning light. Riona perched on a white flower nearby. Her arms and legs were crossed, her foot swinging as usual, her wings slowly opening and closing, while she watched the male Faeries putting the nectar into delicate bags made of leaves. All the Faeries were tiny with perfect naked little bodies and translucent wings that released sparkling dust of different colors, depending on the Faerie.

Several Faerie children played hide-and-seek among the flowers and the trees along with Zephyr, Copper's bee familiar. The Faerie children's sweet chatter sounded just like water trickling over the rocks at the spring on the other side of the meadow.

"Dammit. How did this happen?" Not for the first time she wondered why the Ancestors and the goddess allowed her and all these beings to be trapped. She switched arms to work out her other triceps.

When she finished working out her upper body, she started jogging around the confined space. She knew when she had reached a wall because it shimmered before her, taunting her. If she touched it, she would receive a shock that frizzed her hair. She wondered if it would become permanently bushy if she kept experimenting every now and again to see if the barrier would finally let her through.

She scowled at it as her bare feet pounded soft grass. "Freaking wall."

Her frown deepened as she thought of other dreams she'd had since she'd been in Otherworld. Her dreams were actually visions. She shivered as she relived dreams of horrible misshapen demons, of her sister and Coven under attack. And dreams of that damned warlock who was the reason she was here to begin with.

The feeling of needing to get back to San Francisco and her family grew more intense every single day, and she had a difficult time keeping herself from performing her rituals frantically. She needed to be calm and controlled, but it was getting harder every day.

Most of her thoughts concerned Silver. She knew that if Silver had to use her gray magic it would be hard on her, it would take its toll. Copper so firmly believed in using gray magic that she wasn't afraid of it. But Silver . . . she believed in it, but she still feared it.

Her dress rustled as she continued to jog around the meadow. The Faeries had fashioned a dress made of soft leaves and vines that never withered, never dried, and felt delicate and sensual against her skin. With every movement she made, it caressed her breasts, her belly, her buttocks.

For possibly as many days as she'd been stuck here, she wished a man had been trapped with her—er, not the warlock—but someone sexy, a guy who would really turn her on. With the proverbial apple tree, they'd be a regular Adam and Eve in this paradise—

Not.

What she wouldn't give for her jeans, T-shirt, and running shoes. She usually wasn't one for dresses, even though her preference had driven her father crazy. He thought witches should wear flowing dresses like her mother did. Silver *really* drove their father nuts because she wore such short and sexy skirts along with three-inch heels. The two of them would get an earful when Copper went out on the town. Copper wore a *killer* pair of thigh-high boots, and a short and sassy skirt.

Of course their father loved them no matter what. Even though he was gruff on the exterior, and had a hard time showing his emotions, Copper knew just how much he cared. Moondust had always shown her love easily. Copper's mother was gentle and kind—the type of person who could make you feel good with only a look, and the only person to calm their father when he was on a rant.

Copper rolled her eyes to the increasingly darkening sky, then shook her head. "There's got to be a spell that can get me and every other living being out of here."

She'd tried everything she could think of. Even the Faeries had attempted to help her with their magic. The Pixies, Brownies, an Undine, and Drow—they were no help at all. The Pixies preferred to tease and taunt, often stealing leaves from her vine dress when she wasn't looking. The Brownies bit her ankles when she wasn't careful where she stepped. The Undine preferred to keep to herself.

The Drow—bluish-skinned Dark Elves—kept trying to lure her belowground but she had no inclination to do so. The Drow king, Garran, had visited her one night—the Drow could only come out when it was dark. He'd made it clear he wanted her.

Even if he was tall and sexy—no, thanks. She wasn't about to take the chance that Drow magic would trick her into staying belowground and cause her to *want* to live with the Dark Elves.

He'd smiled and winked. "One day you will come to me."

Copper turned her thoughts away from the cocky bastard and back to her current predicament. A small spring tinkled down a rock wall several paces from the apple tree. Even though she'd been trapped, she'd been blessed with just about every convenience—if you could call them conveniences—that she needed. Often Copper wondered why that was so. It was as if the goddess or the Ancestors had planned this, and that there was some meaning to it.

What could that possibly be? She needed to be home, needed to be near her family and friends.

The copper pentagrams at her ears swung freely as she made another jog around the meadow. When she finished her workout, her skin was warm and a light coating of sweat covered her body. She was going to have to come up with some new exercises to get a better workout.

She knelt at the spring and washed her hands in the lower basin. When she finished, she scooped sweet water from the upper basin into her mouth with her hands. As always it was icy cold and the best water she'd ever tasted. But she'd give anything to be back in San Francisco and drinking city water, even with all its minerals and chemicals.

She sighed and picked at one of the vines on her dress. She wanted, *needed* to break through the shield and get the hell out of here. At this point she'd prefer being anywhere in Otherworld to being confined to this tiny space. Of course free, that was, not trapped. At least then she might be able to convince some being to help her get home. She'd always read that the Elves had doorways that led to Otherworlds.

Too bad the Dark Elves didn't have any such doors available belowground. Garran had said all their doors had been blocked, so they had no means of escape, either. They continued to dig downward, supposedly to find some way to get out.

Copper got to her feet and walked to what wasn't much of a shelter in the rock, but where she curled up to sleep at night on a thick blanket of dried grass, vines, and leaves. It was much longer than her, lengthwise, and its width was more than enough to keep her out of the weather. She could also sit up with room to spare. The leaf and vine dress kept her warm and comfortable, and she was sure that it helped make the bed softer, too.

She retrieved her wand that had thankfully crossed over with her, and gripped it tight. The wand warmed in her hand as she stepped through the short grass that tickled the soles of her bare feet. Rabbits and strange creatures that looked like a cross between a ferret and a toad kept the grass shorn so that it always looked freshly mowed. The ferret-toads made a *gruuupp, gruuuupp* sound when they were mating. It was particularly annoying.

No fair that everyone and everything else was getting laid and she wasn't.

Carrying her wand, Copper went to the center of the meadow, on the other side of the apple tree. Zeph zipped over to her, perched on the curve of her ear, and she felt the strength of his support.

"Have faith, little guy." She raised her wand and the pentagram sparkled on her bracelet. "The goddess must have a plan for us, and it can't be to stay in this place forever."

Zeph buzzed and Copper called out a simple circle-casting spell. After it was cast, she tried a new spell, hoping this would be the one.

> In this place on this sacred ground,
> Within this circle good shall be bound.
> With the light of my wand this place surround,
> May what is lost now be found.

The crystal at the end of her wand glowed through the evening, a brilliant gold that glittered off the walls of their prison. The light seemed stronger than before and she felt tremors through her hand. She focused on the wand, and poured her gray magic into it. Silver wouldn't have agreed to use it so freely.

No, it's too dangerous, Silver would say. *You should only use it in dire circumstances.*

Whatever.

Copper gathered her focus and her gray witchcraft and concentrated on the spell she'd just spoken aloud.

Nothing.

She chanted it again, louder this time, pouring more gray magic into the spell.

The light from her wand dimmed and began to retreat, as if withdrawing back into the crystal.

Copper held her breath for at least ten seconds and then she heard what sounded like a collective sigh around the meadow.

Disappointment rushed over her, but then a feeling of hope, too. That was the most her wand had ever glowed during one of her chants since coming here. Maybe she was getting closer. Getting stronger?

Since she'd been trapped here, she'd tried tapping into every bit of witchcraft she had, including her deepest gray magic.

After yet another failure, she placed her wand in the shelter. Copper stripped out of her dress and stood by the small pool of water created by the stream. There was an upper basin that she used to drink from, and a lower basin that she used to cleanse herself.

With shampoo, soap, and a soft grass sponge the Faeries had given her, Copper first undid her braid and washed her hair, then soaped her body. When she rinsed in the icy cold water, she shivered and wished for a nice thick towel. Once a week she used a cream that the Faeries had supplied that allowed her to remove hair from her underarms and her legs. She'd never been much for hairy legs, or armpits for that matter.

After she ate a filling seedcake the Faeries had left her for dinner, Copper brushed her teeth with Faerie toothpaste that tasted like berries and a twig and grass toothbrush. Refreshed, she slid into her shelter and relaxed on the now overly familiar cushion of the dried vines, leaves, and grass.

Instead of falling asleep right away, she stared up at the rock ceiling of her shelter and listened to the chirrup of crickets and other night sounds. She couldn't really see the ceiling because it was now dark outside. An ache rose deep inside her. She missed her family, and both human and witch companionship.

And she *really, really* needed to get laid.

Right now any man would do. Well, not any man and not just any being. She could have had one of the sexy Drow, especially the king, but she didn't want to go *there*.

As a witch, she might be immune to Drow magic, but she didn't want to take any chances.

But she could certainly pick a dream man.

She'd always had a thing for blonds. She could imagine a man with her, his naked body between her thighs, his chest pressed to hers.

At the thought, she pushed up her vine and leaf dress just enough to bare her pussy. She cupped her mound, then slipped her fingers into her wet folds.

Copper gave a soft sigh as she closed her eyes and the man's image came clearly to her. She'd be naked, too, and the man would suckle her nipples, biting them as hard as she liked it. He'd caress her, touch her in all of her intimate places, tease her into a frenzy. Then he'd place the head of his cock at her entrance and plunge deep inside of her.

As she imagined her mystery man fucking her, she widened her thighs, plunged two fingers into her channel and gave a little moan. She pinched one of her nipples through the dress while she slipped her fingers out and began to circle her clit.

Yeah, that was it. He'd take her so hard she'd cry out with every thrust.

Her fingers circled her clit faster and faster as she continued to imagine the man. Oh, yes. He'd drive in so deep she'd feel him all the way to her belly.

Sensations built up within Copper and her thighs began to tremble. She was so close. So close. And he was fucking her and calling out her name. Harder. Faster. Harder. Faster.

Copper's orgasm swarmed throughout her body like tiny fireflies that sparked in the night. She moaned soft and low while her core continued to contract, adding to the intense sensations.

After her orgasm finally melted away, Copper smiled, tugged down her dress, and rolled onto her side. She rested her head on one arm, using it for a pillow, then drifted away into a satisfied sleep.

four

San Francisco

The Balorite high priest Darkwolf studied Sara, the warlock seer, who stood before him. Sara was brown-haired, slight of build, lovely, and she had a sweet jasmine scent. She wore snug jeans and a tight-fitting, low-cut shirt that molded her small but perfect breasts and gave him a fine view of her cleavage. Her brown eyes held a hint of something that made him wonder if she had her own agenda.

Beside Darkwolf, Elizabeth Black perched on the edge of the mahogany desk, her elegant legs crossed, her arms folded across her chest, and a scowl directed at Sara. Darkwolf never forgot that inside Elizabeth's beautiful shell resided a demon queen—Junga. And he never let her forget the sexual power *he* held over *her*. Just the thought of bringing this demon to her knees was heady. She was extraordinarily powerful, but it gave him incredible satisfaction that he knew her weakness—being sexually dominated.

Darkwolf, Sara, and the demon-woman were in the private library of a wealthy and influential man who had once owned the mansion they now used for their lair. After they had fled the abandoned building they had been using temporarily, Darkwolf had picked this location as the perfect place for the warlocks and Fomorii to use as their headquarters.

One of Junga's demon underlings now controlled the wealthy former owner's body, his shell. Junga ruled the Fomorii with such an iron will that none of the demons dared to defy her. She was queen, and Darkwolf had no doubt that not one of the remaining demons would even think of challenging her. They quavered when she was nearby and immediately took to whatever task she ordered them to perform.

The library smelled of leather, cherry pipe tobacco, and lemon oil. At his insistence, before they entered the home, the Fomorii had remained in their human forms, so he didn't have to smell the demons' rotten fish stench. They'd been lucky the seer Sara had foretold the coming of the D'Danann and she had suggested this manor as their refuge. He couldn't have asked for better accommodations than what they now commanded.

Elizabeth-Junga flicked a speck of lint off her clothing. She was of course wearing a fitted suit in her favorite color, blood red. And beneath that skirt—at his orders—he knew she wore only garters holding up her sheer stockings. Just the thought of her bare pussy made his cock ache.

Elizabeth's gaze immediately returned to the warlock seer. Darkwolf saw the jealousy in her eyes, and it almost made him smile. He wanted Sara, and Elizabeth knew it.

Darkwolf focused on the seer. He leaned his hip against the desk and crossed his arms over his chest. His blue T-shirt stretched taut with his movement. He wore black boots and faded blue jeans and his dark hair curled slightly at his nape.

The warlock seer's gaze moved to the stone eye resting on his chest and he saw the hint of a smile curve the corner of her mouth. This one was special—she always seemed intrigued by the eye, rather than fearful.

Sara was new to his Clan, a former D'Anu apprentice he

had seduced into his fold. Darkwolf had every intention of initiating her further by fucking her, making her scream with her orgasm, and begging him to fuck her again. He took what he wanted, when he wanted, and made sure the women enjoyed every minute of it.

Darkwolf knew Sara wanted him, but he had drawn out the wait, intending to make her desire him so badly that when he finally took her it would be a fuck beyond her wildest dreams.

The seer had been somewhat of a surprise. When he had first persuaded Sara to join his Clan, he had thought her to be somewhat meek. But she had proved to be a much stronger woman than he had anticipated, and she showed no fear of him or the demon queen. He found that intriguing . . . and arousing.

The stone eye at Darkwolf's throat warmed and he sensed Balor's presence in his mind. A sharp pain shot through his head as it often did from Balor's intrusion and Darkwolf gritted his teeth. He never showed any outward emotion at the pain. He must always give the appearance of control, confidence, and dominance.

Ever since he had found the stone eye on the shores of Ireland, the ancient sea god's essence had possessed Darkwolf, driving him to do the god's bidding.

At times Darkwolf had flashes of his old life, when he was simply Kevin Richards, a white witch. And sometimes he wondered if there was a way to turn back time. A way to take off the eye and set himself free.

But no. That white witch was no more. Blood stained Darkwolf's hands and black magic stained his soul. Balor's possession of him had changed his life forever.

"Tell me what you saw," Darkwolf finally said, drawing himself back to the moment.

The stone eye against his chest began to glow deep red with Balor's power and Sara smiled, almost as if she knew something about the god that Darkwolf didn't.

"I saw the witches and the D'Danann." Sara's eyes appeared unfocused for a moment, as if she were recalling the images. "They found a piece of parchment at the place we just left." She paused and glanced at Elizabeth whose scowl deepened. The seer gave a smile that could almost have been described as catty. She returned her gaze to Darkwolf. "The parchment had a rectangle and a circle within a circle on it. Silver Ashcroft used her cauldron to scry, and I believe she learned a great deal of what you have planned." She cocked her head. "I also think she may have found clues to where we are—but nothing that would give us completely away. Not yet."

The sharp pain in Darkwolf's head intensified, but he ignored it. "Thank you, Sara." He gave her his most sensual smile. "You will be rewarded well for your service to Balor."

Sara gave him a slight bow before her eyes met his again. Her tongue darted out to touch her lower lip. "Thank you, my lord."

Every time she said *my lord,* his cock hardened. He reached out and took her small hands in his, keeping his gaze focused on hers. "I thank *you,*" he said, before drawing her fingers to his lips and kissing the knuckles of each hand. Sara's eyes seemed to turn a deeper brown and her expression was more than seductive.

Sara cast a sly glance at Elizabeth who gave what sounded like a low growl. Darkwolf smiled at the woman's—demon's—jealousy.

"Return to your duties," he told Sara, "and I trust that you will come to me the minute you have another vision."

Sara's eyes held his for a moment. She gave a small bow of her head. "It is my pleasure to serve you in any way . . . my lord." With a final look into his eyes, she turned and walked out of the library. Darkwolf couldn't resist watching the sway of her ass, the way the jeans molded her perfectly. He could imagine driving into her tight hole or her pussy and the thought made his cock swell even harder.

When Sara was gone, the library door closed with a thump as Darkwolf gave a flick of his fingers, using simple magic. For a moment he stared at the double doors. The stone eye against his chest cooled and the sharp pain in his head receded.

"Must you fuck everything that walks?" came Elizabeth's voice—Junga—from beside him.

He slowly turned to look at her, giving her a cool stare. "I fuck you, don't I?"

Junga literally growled. Her fingers elongated into claws, her teeth grew longer and sharper, her voice deeper. "Watch what you say, warlock."

Junga was far from intimidated by him. Except when it came to sex. Then she took all that he dealt out to her. She couldn't get enough of his sexual domination. She loved to be spanked, flogged, and reveled in other forms of sexual pain.

Except for sex, she was the proud warrior queen. She consistently went against his will. Despite his orders that for now they remain as low profile as possible, she insisted that her demons feed on human flesh and had them take over the shells of more influential, powerful people.

Darkwolf gave Junga a dismissive wave. He knew her weaknesses, the power he held over her. He had no fear of the demon that resided within the beautiful woman's shell. At times he thought about the fact that the woman he fucked was a hideous-looking demon when in her natural form, but he chose to ignore it and preferred to dwell on his ability to control her.

He kept his amusement from his expression as he rounded the desk and once again bent over the map of Otherworld and its barrier to Underworld. "The door . . . surely the Dark Elves will reach it soon."

His gaze met Elizabeth-Junga's. She had retracted her claws, her teeth were returned to normal proportions, and she was once again the bitchy but beautiful woman. "Do you—"

Junga paused and the expression on her features shifted. Concern? Fear? "Do you think it wise to release creatures other than the Fomorii, and such a powerful being as Balor?"

Darkwolf managed to control his surprise and attempted to keep the Fomorii god, Balor, from reading his thoughts. It would not do to have him mistrust Junga when Darkwolf needed the queen. "Balor would not be pleased to hear what you've said."

The Fomorii queen gave what could have been taken as a casual shrug, but he knew it was not so casual. "How do you know we will not all be destroyed by these beings?" She looked away from him for a moment before returning her gaze to his. "Will Balor sacrifice us in order to regain his rule?"

At this Darkwolf hardened his expression. "We serve Balor. We do as he commands through the essence in his eye. You know such a great god would not so casually strike down those who serve him." He met Junga's gaze head-on and wouldn't let it go. "Will you continue to serve him?"

"Of course." Junga pushed herself from the desk. "Are you certain he will grant the Dark Elves' request for their part in finding the door?"

"Yes." Darkwolf tossed the map aside. "Balor will not forget the Drow as long as they serve him well. He'll allow them to live aboveground again, so that they can walk in sunlight."

Junga paused as if considering what he'd said. "When will the Drow king return?"

Darkwolf scowled. "We're to meet him at the pier in two days' time."

Junga clenched her fists—she had often expressed her distrust of the Dark Elves. "If the parchment with the symbols had not been lost, we would eventually have had them deciphered. Surely this Drow would have found us an interpreter."

Anger flashed through Darkwolf and the pain in his

head grew sharp enough that he could barely keep from wincing. The map keeper had paid with his life for losing that scrap of parchment. The lost paper had accidentally been torn from a page of a brittle, ancient spellbook.

Darkwolf had been directed to the spellbook when Balor first took over his body and mind in Ireland. He had found it in a cave so old and dank that it had been beyond eerie. He hadn't known the importance of the parchment or spellbook until recently when Balor had revealed the information to him through his thoughts.

It was the drawing of the runes that, with the right ceremony, would open the door to Underworld. Not only would more Fomorii be freed, but other creatures that would answer to Balor.

The loss of the piece of parchment didn't matter. Balor would tell him what they must do.

His cock hardened as he studied what was currently a beautiful woman standing beside the desk. Her black hair lay softly about her shoulders. It was easy to forget she was a demon—a hideous demon—within that shell. The fact that he could dominate her in this form gave him a sense of power that made him afire with it.

"Get over here," he demanded.

Elizabeth—Junga—gave him a fierce look. "You do not order me around, *warlock.*"

Darkwolf had to remind her who was in control. He strode over to her. Immediately he palmed her full breasts. He knew the moment he touched her in her Elizabeth shell, she would give in to his dominance.

Elizabeth tilted her head back and moaned while she reached down and rubbed his cock through his jeans. At Darkwolf's command the demon-woman unbuttoned her fitted suit jacket and tossed it aside, baring her breasts as she wore no bra, something that he insisted upon and that she enjoyed. The body of the woman she now inhabited was delicious and his erection swelled even harder at the sight of her large breasts, sensual curves, and the full lips that he enjoyed having slide over his cock.

After dropping her skirt to the floor, she was naked save for the garters and high heels.

Darkwolf gave a sound of satisfaction as he unfastened his jeans. "On your knees in front of me."

Junga obeyed at once, kneeling on the hardwood floor. She widened her mouth and took his thick cock deep in her mouth. He grabbed her by the hair and began pumping his hips, his flesh smacking against her face.

When Darkwolf climaxed, the power he felt over her was even greater. Red flamed in his mind, and he felt Balor's enjoyment of the moment. After Darkwolf's semen filled Junga's mouth, he thrust his hips forward a few more times. He was certain the power of Balor was what rushed through his cock, making it fully erect again.

Darkwolf didn't give her a chance to catch her breath, even as she swallowed down his seed. He motioned for Elizabeth to stand and go to the desk. "Hands braced on top," he commanded. "Bend over so that I can see your ass."

Shivering, Junga obeyed. Her naked body glowed in the soft library lighting and from the side Darkwolf saw that her nipples stood out like ruby stones.

Darkwolf moved behind Elizabeth and grabbed her hips. Without ceremony, he drove his cock into her pussy. Her cry echoed through the room. "Yes," she murmured. "Fuck me like that."

He thrust himself in and out of her pussy rough enough that her breasts rubbed against the hard surface of the desk. As hard as he could, he slapped one side of her ass with his palm. Elizabeth gave a loud cry. "You *will not* question Balor ever," he commanded. She whimpered and he slapped her other ass cheek just as hard, causing her to shout again.

Her long manicured fingernails dug into the wood of the desk when he slapped her again and again. He knew she loved the pain, and he gave it to her with everything he had. Her ass cheeks grew hot beneath his palm and her cries grew louder.

"You are here to serve Balor, do whatever he commands," he said as he continued to spank her. "Do you understand, bitch?"

"Y-yes!" she shouted at the same time her orgasm ripped through her. Her entire body bucked and trembled. He slapped her ass cheeks again, causing her to cry out and her pussy to squeeze his cock.

He grabbed her by the hair, twisted her around, and forced her down to her hands and knees on the floor, so that her ass was facing him. Without allowing her to catch her breath, he knelt behind her and drove his cock into her ass, his favorite place to fuck the demon-woman. It was tight and clamped around him, giving him ultimate pleasure.

Junga moaned and it pleased him that the nonlubricated invasion most likely hurt her. He knew she liked pain, and that only made him thrust into her harder.

"Like that, Darkwolf!" she cried. "Just like that."

He slapped her ass as hard as he could, causing her to shriek. "No one fucks you like I do, isn't that right?"

The demon-woman's words came out in a pant and she squirmed beneath his thrusts. "No, Darkwolf. Only you."

With one more smack of his hips against her ass, Junga shrieked with another climax and he came in a rush. All his pleasure centered around his cock and balls.

Darkwolf grinned in satisfaction at these moments of complete dominance over her. He tucked his cock back into his jeans as he stood and said, "Get up, bitch, and get dressed."

For a moment Elizabeth stayed where she was—either in defiance or because she was out of breath, he wasn't sure which. She slowly got to her feet and turned to him. She was a goddess in Elizabeth's form, her naked body near perfection.

Control and dominance. That was the key to keeping every being within his power in line.

five

Otherworld

Tiernan gasped for breath the moment he walked through the veil to Otherworld. His chest seized and his vision blurred. He wanted to claw at his throat. His eyes felt as if they were bulging from their sockets—

He could breathe again.

Tiernan leaned over, his hands braced on his thighs, and he fought to steady himself. Even before he raised his head he knew he was home just from the sweet scents of pine and wildflowers, as well as the sounds of Faerie song and grumbling Dwarves in the distance.

When he finally did straighten, he realized Cassia, the Elvin Witch who had escorted him through The Veil, was no longer by his side. He whirled to look behind him and saw only a great mound of earth, as well as the bushes, trees, and flowers of his homeland. Cassia and the bridge had vanished.

Tiernan faced the direction of the village. He breathed deeply of the scents of rich earth, moss, and unpolluted air. He unfolded his wings and took to the sky.

It was not long before he landed in the village and

folded away his wings. Peasants simply nodded to Tiernan, murmuring such things as, "Good day, my lord." As soon as the peasants acknowledged him, they continued with their tasks. It wasn't their place to converse with him. Only gentlemen and ladies of the court could do that freely— and the ladies would never be seen in such a common place as the village.

Only the warrior class could move freely between those very separate worlds, and he was that rare Fae—a warrior, but also of the court.

He generally liked the village and enjoyed being with other D'Danann warriors, drinking ale and eating trenchers of beef or pork while sopping up the juices with freshly baked bread. He also enjoyed observing the vendors as they hawked their wares, the smell of smoke from the forge, and smells of roasted meats and vegetables coming from many a cooking fire. He had quite often slaked his desires in the building at the far end of the village, one of the well-kept Pleasure Houses, where he had spent much free time fucking one beautiful woman after another.

His thoughts turned back to the disparity between classes. A warrior's life he lived, yes, but there was always a sense that he did not fully belong in their world.

Tiernan strode with purpose past the Chieftans' large gathering chamber at the far end of the village. Behind the chamber stood enormous black gates that kept out all but the D'Danann hierarchy. Manor after beautiful manor was ensconced within the brown walls that blended in with the forest.

Guards at the massive entrance bowed as they opened the gates to allow Tiernan to pass through. He scarcely gave each guard a nod and barely noticed the surroundings that had been a part of his life for centuries. Beautiful gardens, flagstone paths, and natural waterfalls he had known since the D'Danann left Ireland to form their own Sidhe. Sounds of water roaring over rock and crashing to great pools, and the chirp of birds met his ears. And if he was not mistaken, he heard Faerie song as well.

A burst of energy surged through him. It felt good to be home after spending much time in San Francisco of the Otherworld called Earth he had been summoned to, and a sense of pride in his homeland thrummed through his veins. Yet urgency coursed through him as well—he could not stay long as he must return to San Francisco to aid his fellow warriors in stopping the warlocks and Fomorii. But he had a task to perform here before he could leave again.

When he reached his family's manor, he strode up the stone steps of his home. One of the many servants of the House of Cathal welcomed him as he opened the door and let Tiernan into the manor made of granite and the finest woods the Dryads would allow to be taken.

"Tiernan!" Cian's voice came from the top of the stairs. His mother picked up her apple-green skirts just enough that she wouldn't trip over them. White petticoats swirled around her ankles as she descended the stairs to greet him. Her hair was the same shade of blond as Tiernan's. She was of full figure and had a smile that could light up the darkest of rooms.

"Mother." Tiernan's heart warmed as he took her hands in his when she reached him, and he kissed each of her cheeks. As always, the faintest hint of lilacs surrounded her.

"My son. Right on time for your handfasting in two days." She squeezed his hands. "Airell is all aflutter. I think the poor maid is having prejoining anxiety."

Tiernan swallowed a sigh.

He had known from the time he was a child many centuries ago that the family legacy was his to bear. As a lord and the only heir to House of Cathal, he would be expected to strengthen his house with a good union and continue the line. But no suitable bride from a powerful house had been born until eighteen years ago.

His parents, too, had only married to make their houses

stronger, and they had borne their first son. However, that son had been killed in one of the old battles. Therefore his parents sought to produce another son, and Tiernan was the result. The task of bringing forth new heirs and ensuring the continuation of his family's lineage rested squarely on his shoulders. As he had from childhood, he only wished to please his parents and live up to his many responsibilities. Duty and honor were more than words to him, more than court games or gallant speeches.

The reason for their handfasting was to produce an heir. A strange sensation jerked at his gut. He was of the same mind as Airell and had no wish to mate with her as she was so young compared to him. Merely eighteen years of age while he was centuries old. But their families expected them to join and produce a son. And that was what he would ensure they would produce, a son. No matter how many joinings it took.

The thought of a child of his own made him smile. The one thing lacking from his life, that he had always wanted, were children. A son or daughter—to him it mattered not. Even better would be two, three, or four.

However, he had never had intercourse with Airell simply because she did not wish it before their handfasting, and she preferred that he seek his pleasure elsewhere. It was perfectly acceptable among the members of the court for lords and ladies to relieve their needs with many of the Pleasure Partners in the village whose job it was to satisfy all comers. Tiernan was no exception—his needs were great, sometimes insatiable.

His mother slipped her arm through his and he patted her hand as his thoughts returned to the moment.

"What troubles you, son?" Cian asked.

"Nothing, Mother." Tiernan smiled as he looked down upon her. "I am simply pleased to be home."

"Your father will be delighted to see you, of course."

Cian guided him to his father's chambers, where the man spent most of his time when they were not entertaining.

Artan was reclining in the leather chair behind a table made from the special wood provided by the Dryads, the tree Faeries. He had contracts spread out upon the surface, and his forehead was wrinkled in concentration.

Along the walls were shelves of books, works of art, including oil paintings of the family, the House of Cathal's shield, and a collection of swords. It was interesting that his father collected such instruments even though he had opposed Tiernan's decision to become a D'Danann warrior all those centuries ago, rather than a legal counselor like him. He had said he did not want to chance losing another heir to battle.

"Ah, my son." Artan pushed his chair away from his desk. "I was just going over the contract of your impending nuptials with Airell."

Tiernan shook hands with his father in the hand-to-elbow grasp common to his people. He smiled at his father, from whom he had inherited his blue eyes and strong features. The redheaded Artan gave Tiernan a hearty pat on the back before returning to his desk and leaning back in his chair.

"With your handfasting just two days away, you must be thrilled," Cian said with one of her brilliant smiles. "I am so proud of you both. You will make a perfect couple and make the House of Cathal even stronger and more powerful."

What his mother said was true. Torin and Cathal were two of the most powerful houses in all the D'Danann court. From the moment Airell was born, she had been pledged to handfast with Tiernan when she reached her eighteenth birthday. Yet he was over two thousand years old, countless lifetimes older than she.

"We will make you proud." Tiernan looked from his

mother to his father. "We will carry on the honor and integrity of both houses."

"My son." Cian hugged Tiernan, and he embraced her in return. When she pulled away a single tear rolled down her powdered cheek. "No matter what, just know that we shall always be proud of you, Tiernan."

After a lunch of many portions of roasted fowl and vegetables followed by puddings and a rich fruit trifle, Tiernan left his home, intent on having a few moments alone with his betrothed. Spending time with his family, seeing the pride in his father's and mother's eyes had driven home the importance of carrying on both their lines.

The thought of being bedded by a man might seem distasteful to a young maid, but once they were joined he could show her the joy of such intimacy. With their handfasting so close, perhaps now she would be receptive to experiencing such pleasures.

When he reached Airell's family's mansion, he was informed by a servant that Lady Airell had gone for a walk in the forest. The servant gestured in the direction Airell had taken. Tiernan bowed his thanks and followed the tree-lined path.

A sense of peace filled him at being in his own world once again. He breathed deeply of the forest smells of rich earth and of the trees tended by the Dryads. No breeze stirred the air, yet he caught the scent of something familiar, something that did not belong. A powdery perfume. He sniffed. Airell's, of course. She had come this way.

Nary a leaf crunched under his boots as he made his way through the forest. Sunlight slanted through the trees and he felt the warmth on his arms whenever he came out of shadow into the sunlight.

He began to wonder how far the maid had traveled when he heard voices coming from behind a line of towering bushes ahead. Knowing the forest so well he could map every tree and stone if required, he knew there was a small grassy clearing on the other side of the bushes.

Airell's laughter rang clear through the forest. With a smile he started toward the clearing. He reached a gap in the bushes and came to a full stop.

Blood rushed in his ears. He could not move.

Airell was on her back, her blond curls splayed across the thick grass. Her bodice had been pulled below her breasts so that her creamy mounds and light pink nipples were exposed. Her long blue dress was pushed all the way up to her waist, exposing the fair hair of her mons, and her knees were bent, her thighs spread wide.

Lowering himself between her fair-skinned thighs was Urien, a brown-haired, brown-eyed young man that Tiernan knew to be of Airell's age. His breeches were untied and he guided his erection toward Airell's center. Her folds gleamed with wetness in the sunlit clearing.

Urien thrust into Airell. She arched her back and cried out before putting her hands on her breasts and pinching and pulling her nipples as he fucked her with long, sure strokes. Just her actions of pleasuring herself while she was being taken told Tiernan this wasn't the first time she had enjoyed sex.

Heat rose up within Tiernan and he ground his teeth. No wonder Airell had insisted he enjoy the women at the Pleasure Houses. Despite the fact she had claimed to not want to be touched by any man, she had been fucking one of the lesser members of the court.

Hands fisted at his sides, he prepared to make himself known. Arranged marriage or no, Airell was his betrothed.

Just as Tiernan was about to step forward, Airell's body shuddered and she cried out, "I love you, Urien!"

"Gods, but I love you, too," Urien said as he stared into Airell's face while she trembled with her orgasm. A few strokes more and he groaned his own release.

The two were tightly entwined when Tiernan strode into

the clearing. "Get up!" he ordered, his voice bellowing through the forest.

Airell screamed and scrambled to yank her bodice up and over her breasts, and Urien slid from between her thighs, jerked her dress down to cover her, and pushed himself to his feet. He hurried to tuck his cock into his breeches and tie the lacings before taking Airell by the hand and drawing her up with him.

Red blossomed on Airell's cheeks and Urien's face was flushed. She clung to Urien, her head turned away from Tiernan as if afraid of what he might do. Leaves and grass clung to her hair and her dress was wrinkled.

It took all Tiernan's control not to slam his fist into the younger man's face.

"Look at me," Tiernan demanded, his gaze moving from Urien to Airell. As she slowly turned her head, her bright blue eyes met his, and he saw her cheeks stained with tears.

Godsdamn. Why did she have to cry? He could not bear it when a woman cried.

"Please do not tell my parents." Airell's lips trembled. "And the court. Gods, please do not tell the court," she added in a hoarse whisper. "I would be marked, thrown from my home and all that I know and love. None of the Fae would aid me in any way."

She looked up at her lover who still held her close to him, his stance rigid. "And Urien—he would be sent to serve those horrible Dark Elves, forever banished below-ground."

Tiernan took a deep breath. "Go home." His voice was still sharp as his eyes rested solely on Airell. "We will discuss this when I am finished with Urien. Await me at your house."

Her grip on Urien's arm tightened. "Do not hurt him. Please, Lord Tiernan."

He let out a low growl. "Get home *now*."

Airell did not look at either of them as she pulled leaves from her hair and ran past Tiernan. The sound of a sob reached him and he almost sighed. Damn women.

He focused directly on Urien. The young man stood with his back rigid, his hands clenched at his sides, a spark to his brown eyes, his mouth in a tight line, and his chin high.

No matter how hot the blood surged through Tiernan's veins, no matter how much he desired to slam his fist against Urien's jaw, he would not.

"Have you no sense of honor or pride?" Tiernan took a step forward, his hands fisted at his sides, as well.

Urien cleared his throat. "Airell and I are in love."

"That matters not." Tiernan ground his teeth. "It is I she will be wedded to in two days' time."

Urien's chin rose a notch at the growl in Tiernan's voice. "I am the one she wishes to handfast with."

"As I said, it matters not."

"She doesn't want to." Urien's throat worked as he spoke. "She only does so because her family promised her to you."

"Exactly." Tiernan took a step forward, so close to Urien that he could see sweat beading on the younger man's forehead. "You cannot dally with a lady of the court when she is promised to another. You can fuck all the women that you wish to in one of the Pleasure Houses."

Urien's shoulders shook despite his bravado. "She is allowed to seek her pleasure with a man from a Pleasure House, but she chooses me."

"It is not allowed and she is my betrothed," Tiernan said. "And what if you were to impregnate her?"

Sweat rolled freely down Urien's forehead. "We have gone by the moon cycles. We have been very careful."

Tiernan let out a low, menacing growl. "This is something you have done many times?"

At that Urien's face went from red to a paler shade. "We are in love," he repeated.

"You do not have the means to raise your house high enough in the court to be allowed to wed her," Tiernan said. "The House of Brend would need much gold."

Urien lowered his eyes and his voice cracked as he said, "True. I will never have the means to marry Airell."

"Look at me," Tiernan demanded, and Urien's gaze snapped back to meet Tiernan's. "You will no longer have relations with my betrothed—unless you intend to lower your status altogether and become a Pleasure Partner."

Urien's jaw clenched and unclenched, but he said nothing.

Tiernan lowered his brows. "Return to your manor."

Urien gave a bow from his shoulders. "Yes, *my lord,*" he said before walking past Tiernan and into the forest.

Tiernan raised his face to the sky, closed his eyes, and took a deep breath, trying to relax the tension from his shoulders and neck. He opened his eyes and leveled his gaze on the trunk of an ancient tree near him. He raised his fist to slam it into the tree but jerked his arm back when a face, then a body melted from the aged wood.

"Hit me or any tree and pay the consequences," the Dryad said as she stepped fully from the tree. "As you know, the consequences are dear, indeed."

Tiernan lowered his fist and gave a low bow from the shoulders. "My apologies, Simone."

The Dryad cocked her head, her chestnut-brown hair flowing around her shoulders with the movement. Her bare skin was the color of dark brown silk, and her eyes were a shade of warm oak. "You choose to keep these lovers separated."

He ground his teeth. "There are no choices. These decisions were made long ago. It is up to Airell and me to carry on the honor and tradition of our houses."

"Honor and tradition." Simone's voice had a mocking edge to it. "Is that all that matters to you?"

"Is there anything else?" Tiernan said.

"Love." The Dryad's word carried on the wind like a single sweet chime from a bell.

"Love has nothing to do with such matters." He kept the scowl from his face and bowed at the shoulders again. "I must leave to discuss this matter with my betrothed."

Simone smiled. "Of course. But remember, there are always choices. Destiny is what we make of it."

Tiernan ignored her last comment. He gave a brief nod, strode away from the clearing, and headed back to the House of Torin to confront Airell.

When he reached Airell's family manor, he barely took in its beauty. The House of Torin was reminiscent of the palaces of ancient Roman times, yet it still managed to blend in with the other great manors of the court.

The same servant who had given Tiernan the whereabouts of Airell earlier opened the great doors. When he asked for her, the young servant led him through the enormous mansion with its great columns and sheer, colorful drapes that gently billowed as a breeze swept through. Tiernan and the servant reached the open doors that led to the gardens. In the distance he saw Airell from the back, and she was perched on a marble bench by a fountain. The servant bowed and retreated as Tiernan walked outside and into the gardens.

Airell had changed clothing, and now wore a pink gown. Her shimmering blond hair had been pinned in a conservative knot at the base of her slender neck.

He finally reached her and looked down at the young woman, who refused to look at him. Beside them the fountain made of marble Faeries bubbled musically and the smell of fresh cut grass and flowers drifted in the balmy air from the enormous gardens surrounding them.

Without waiting for an invitation, Tiernan sat next to Airell on the marble bench. Her rose-pink gown shifted with a light wind and a tendril of her hair escaped.

"Look at me." His tone was commanding. This was no

time for gentleness. He must deal with the situation and be done with it.

Airell shifted on the bench to meet his gaze. Her blue eyes looked glossy, almost as if she were ready to burst into tears again.

Not tears. Not the godsdamn tears again.

He kept his gaze focused on hers. With their blue eyes and blond hair, they were sure to have children of the same looks. Yet he could not imagine having a child with Airell. She was too young, too frail-looking.

But definitely not too innocent.

At that thought he ground his teeth. Finally he said, "Your dallying with Urien needs to be dealt with at once."

Airell's lower lip trembled and he saw the tears threaten to trickle from her eyes.

Shit.

He wanted to look away from the tears that were surely about to fall, but he needed to keep his features stern so that she would be clear on his intentions and on his words. "If you do not wish to engage in sex with me at this time, then you can choose a Pleasure Partner from the village or you may abstain. I will not risk your getting with a babe with Urien."

The tears started rolling down Airell's cheeks, but he did his best to ignore them. "When we are handfasted, we will attempt to produce an heir, no matter how many times we must join. After that you may have sex with any Pleasure Partner you wish to, but you will *not* dally with Urien or any other man of the court for that matter."

"I am with child." The words came so softly from Airell's lips that at first he thought he had misheard her. When it sank in, his body went rigid with shock. Her tears continued to run in rivers and all Tiernan could do was stare. A babe? Urien's child?

Airell looked away from Tiernan and down to her belly where her hands were now clenched. "I have not told him."

"A child." He spoke harshly as his temper flared. He had always wanted children, yes, but he did not want to raise another man's child, knowing that he was not the true father. "Godsdamn, Airell."

He pushed himself from the bench and began pacing.

"What will happen to me?" Airell looked up at him, her eyes red and swollen, her voice cracking with every word. "To Urien?"

Tiernan shoved his fingers through his hair. His mind raced. He could not allow Airell to face the humiliation of being marked and the horror of being cast out of the Fae realm. But neither could he marry a woman who carried another man's child. He could do many things for duty, for honor, but raising another man's child when all he longed for were his own? Must all his dreams be set aside for the sake of others?

"Urien and I could run away," she said, a hopeful tone to her voice. "We could be together then."

"You would be found within hours, if not minutes." Tiernan stopped his pacing and rested his hands on the hilt of his sword. "The forests are filled with Fae. You could never escape, Airell."

She hiccupped and lowered her head. "There is nothing I can do, then. I will be marked and cast out."

Tiernan's body was so tense he felt as though he was being stretched between two bars. He sank back down on the bench beside Airell. He released a sigh that came deep from his belly and leaned forward, his forearms braced on his leather-clad thighs.

He looked away from her and stared into the trees at the foot of the gardens. "I would never want to humiliate you, Airell. As I would not want Urien to face a more serious fate."

When he looked at her again, she was dabbing at her eyes with a kerchief she must have drawn out from a pocket in the folds of her skirt. "You would marry me still?"

Tiernan slowly shook his head. "I cannot be joined with you knowing you carry another man's child."

Airell's features crumpled once again, and the tears came harder and faster as she stared at her hands in her lap.

He reached over to her and laid his large tanned hand on her pale and dainty one. She was so small, so fragile.

Tiernan squeezed her hand and she looked up at him. "What happens now?" she whispered.

"I will find a solution." He took her fingers in his hand and brought them to his lips and gently kissed them before releasing her. "Give me time. I will tell our parents we are postponing our handfasting for six weeks. In that time I will find a way." Though he had no idea what way there could possibly be. He swallowed hard. "I will not allow you to be humiliated. Rest assured of that."

"Thank you," Airell said as she met his eyes. "You are more than kind, Lord Tiernan."

He stood and gave her a low bow. "My lady." He turned away and strode back along the path to the manor.

Six

She was in the tunnel again. The air smelled of sulfur, rotten fish, and earth, and the ground looked like it had been freshly dug. She squinted. Shapes ahead, moving through the unlit tunnels. Copper raised her wand, but the light was absorbed by the darkness, sucked up until she could barely see.

Her heart started pounding as she continued through the tunnel.

The ground dropped from beneath her feet.

She screamed as she tumbled through brilliant light so white it was like falling through a star. Wind rushed against her face and her heart felt as if it were on fire, that it would burn a hole through her chest.

With a thud she landed so hard on her feet she jarred her teeth.

Shaking, she blinked to regain her vision. Her wand light glittered off damp stone walls. When her heart didn't feel like it was going to explode, she realized she was on another dark pathway—a tunnel even farther belowground.

She was alone.

No—no. There were the shapes ahead. Familiar? She couldn't be sure.

She shivered in the damp air that smelled of ancient dirt and heard the steady *plunk, plunk, plunk* of water coming from somewhere ahead. And rotten fish again. Yes, she definitely smelled rotten fish.

Copper woke late with a strange feeling in her belly. It was gloomy outside, the air cool and moist with an oncoming storm.

For some reason the dreariness of the day and her dream didn't dampen her mood. She felt as though something special were going to happen.

"Maybe today's the day," she said aloud. A spell had been churning in her mind. Perhaps it was a spell that would set them all free. Something inside her told her she *had* to return home. These dreams, this feeling—they had never been so intense before.

Fully awake, she scrambled out of her shelter, got to her feet, and finger-combed her hair so that it lay in a wavy mass over her shoulders. She placed her hands on her hips and looked around the meadow. Ladybugs moved up the branches of the flowers and a grasshopper bounded across the clearing. The Faerie children were doing their chores and gathering fresh grass and seeds. The Pixies were playing their version of tag around the rock outcropping, and the Brownies were nowhere to be seen. That fact gave her little comfort. Where were those nasty little goons?

The Fae hadn't left Copper anything for breakfast—which meant they were in a fickle mood—so she headed for the apple tree, reached up, and plucked the reddest one she could find. The tree always had plenty of apples. It was as if any that were taken were replaced overnight, and it had fruit year round. She especially enjoyed the times when the perfume of the tree's blossoms mingled with the scent of apples.

When she'd perched on the rock at the foot of the tree, she took a big bite of the apple with a loud crunch. Sounds of Pixie laughter made her grin as she chewed. They were mischievous as hell, but they were fun to watch and listen to—if she wasn't on the receiving end of their mischief.

The Faerie Queen Riona appeared from around the tree and landed on her butt on Copper's shoulder. The tiny being braced her hands on either side of her and tilted her face to the sky.

"Good morning," Copper said between apple crunches. "What's going on with you today?"

Riona's lips twitched, whether with concern or amusement, Copper couldn't tell. "The Drow," Riona said. "They are up to something."

Copper raised her brows and stopped right before biting the apple again. "What do you mean?"

The queen gave a shrug of her tiny shoulders as she leaned forward to clasp her arms around her knees. "I have heard rumors. The Brownies say they dig deep, perhaps too deep . . . and are up to something else I cannot determine." Her mouth twisted into a frown. "I do not like it when I know not what they are doing."

"From what I remember of their history, the Drow are always up to something." Copper settled her hand in her lap, her partially eaten apple still in her grasp.

Riona nodded. "That is true. However, I cannot help but feel this is somehow different. And that they have been engaging in activities that I am not aware of."

Copper was surprised that the queen was actually confiding in her. "How can we find out?"

The Faerie queen's tiny lavender eyes met Copper's. "Perhaps you can go below and visit Garran. I cannot. Other than the D'Danann, Fae cannot tolerate being deep within the earth. It would kill us."

Copper's eyes widened. "Me? What if they don't let me go?"

With a smile, Riona said, "I have confidence in you."

A groan rose up inside Copper. "I can't believe I'm even considering this."

Riona pushed from Copper's shoulder to hover beside her. "Stomp on the Drow door five times. No doubt they will know it is you. They have strong magic."

Before Copper had a chance to discuss it further, to refuse even, Riona fluttered away. Copper sighed and shook her head. Even though she'd never been in the Drow realm, she knew this wasn't going to be easy.

After she finished the apple, she left the core on the rock for the Brownies who loved them. She forced herself to grab her wand, then walk across the soft grass to make her way to the side of the rock outcropping that she normally avoided.

"A girl's gotta do what a girl's gotta do," she murmured to encourage herself.

When she was behind the rock wall and saw the stone door, she paused. The door was flat upon the ground and surrounded by dirt, as if no grass would grow there. A pine tree stood beside the rectangular stone, the tree's shadow darkening the door and making it seem ten times more foreboding. The door was as long as a man and twice as wide, with strange markings all around the stone frame. There were no handholds, no way to open the door without Drow magic.

She took a deep breath, gripped her wand tighter, and stomped five times on the dusty stone with one of her bare feet. For a long moment she waited, half hoping the door wouldn't open.

A rumble cut through the air and then a sound like nails scratching a chalkboard as stone scraped stone. Copper winced and goose bumps pricked her skin.

When the door was fully open, she sucked in a breath of damp earth and minerals, and stepped onto the stone staircase that led down to the bowels of the home of the Drow, who had been banished to live underground countless centuries ago. They were not beings to be trifled with. But because of Garran's promise to her that night he came to the surface—that she would remain untouched by any of his warriors without her consent—she didn't really fear any of the Dark Elves in his kingdom.

Well, maybe a little.

The stairs were covered with coarse dirt and rock that felt rough to her bare feet as she walked down the stairs. A rush of cool air swept up and under her vine and leaf dress and she tugged on it. Damn the jerks, anyhow. They had probably done that on purpose.

After she was far enough down the stairs, the stone door scraped closed above her. Once again, that awful feeling ran along her spine at the sound. She blinked in the sudden darkness, but then torches sputtered to life along the walls hugging the stairs and she could see again. She waited for her eyes to adjust, then began her descent once again.

What could she possibly find out that would alleviate Riona's concerns—or confirm them?

Copper only hoped there wouldn't be too big of a price to pay for visiting the Drow. They enjoyed extracting payments. An eye for an eye and all that. She'd been an apt student of Mrs. Illes and knew the Fae and Elves well enough.

At that moment she realized she'd forgotten to bring Zephyr with her and she silently cursed. He was always good in a tight spot, and she could probably use him now.

When she reached a great circular hall, two Drow met her, looking as if they'd been expecting her. Copper sighed. They probably had been.

Torches sputtered to life around the room, surely for her benefit. The Drow needed no light to see in their dark world.

She allowed each Drow to take one of her arms to guide her across the great hall, their earthy, mossy scent sweeping over her. They were remarkably good-looking, rivaling

the sexiest of men. Their smooth skin was a bluish shade
that suited them. They had well-defined, muscular bodies,
long hair that hung loose around their shoulders or was
drawn back and fastened at their napes. Their hair color
tended to range from black to steel gray to silvery blue,
and most Drow were close to six feet tall.

Instead of shirts the Drow men wore shoulder and
breast plates made of the finest metals and snug breeches
of dark gray or black. At their backs were quivers with arrows, the shafts made of pewter and the heads of indestruc-
tible diamonds—that magically exploded when entering
an enemy's flesh, from what Riona had once told her.

The carvings of male warriors around the circular
walls glimmered in the light from the torches scattered
around the great room. From what Copper had learned,
Drow women were subservient to the males. That tidbit
was backed up by images of the women on their knees
looking up at the warriors.

"It is good to have you join us, fair one," the Drow
called Naal said as the two warriors' boots rang against the
polished granite floor.

She drew her gaze away from the images and glanced at
Naal to see him wink. He was Garran's younger brother,
the next in line for the throne, and she had met him the
same night Garran had visited her aboveground. Naal was
a good head taller than her, and if she was inclined to take
on Drow lovers, he would be one, as would Garran. But she
had no intention of doing any such thing.

And she hoped to the goddess that she would make it
out of here and soon. Surely Riona wouldn't have sent her
on a mission that would prove to be too dangerous.

The arched doorless opening ahead was one of many
doorways that led from the circular great room. "So, how's
Garran?" she asked as they neared the throne room.

Naal chuckled. "Missing you, I am certain."

Copper groaned. The closer they got to the king, the

more she realized it was going to be hard as hell to get back out.

The throne room took her breath away. The chamber was like a geode cut in half, every wall sparkling like cut crystal. To the back was an obsidian door that was just closing as she walked into the room. To the left stood a black granite table surrounded by granite benches. At the center of the room was the huge, black granite throne with a padded back, and to one side of it was a matching smaller throne.

Reclining on the larger throne was Garran, the Drow king. He was a powerfully built being with sculpted muscles, a massive chest, and a handsome face. He had one elbow resting on the arm of the chair and an amused expression on his face.

Gem-studded metal and leather straps crisscrossed his bare chest, and he wore elaborate shoulder plates. He had an ornate belt fastened at the top of his black breeches that were tucked into high leather boots. His long silvery-blue hair was loose around his shoulders, but she could still see his pointed ears. He was an incredibly handsome Drow, more so than the guards who had accompanied him to the surface that night—other than Naal, that was.

Naal and the Drow on the other side of her bowed and retreated to the doorway. Copper took a deep breath and stepped forward, the smooth, black granite floor cool beneath her bare feet. The slide of her vine dress against her skin reminded her of how vulnerable she was. When she reached the throne she didn't kneel or bow. Instead she kept her gaze fixed on Garran's liquid silver eyes.

"I am most pleased to see you." His voice was so deep it almost seemed to contain the rumble of thunder. He leaned back, crossed his boots at his ankles, and laced his fingers at his washboard abs. "Have you returned to take me up on my offer?"

Copper cleared her throat. "I simply came to—to visit."

She shifted from foot to foot. "I have never been below-ground as long as I've been in Otherworld." As his intense gaze studied her, she hurried to add, "I'm bored. I need something to distract me."

Garran pushed himself from his chair and she took a step back. "I can most certainly distract you, little one." He towered over her and her heart began to beat and her throat grew dry. What had she gotten herself into?

She took a deep breath and raised her chin. "So show me around."

He smiled, a rogue's smile, and reached out to stroke the side of her face. "I can think of many ways to 'show you around.'"

Copper took another step back, and he let his hand drop to his side. "I'm not here to get intimate with you, Garran. I just need something to do. Something to get my mind off the fact that we're all trapped here."

A flicker of something flashed in Garran's eyes, but then it was gone. No doubt he was none too happy at being imprisoned.

"Come." He took her hand in his and she felt the warmth of him straight to her toes. She drew away and he let her fingers slip from his. In her other hand she gripped her wand tighter.

Garran started by showing her around the throne room. The smaller throne was for his future queen. He made a point of looking at her when he said that and she snorted. He led her to the oval granite table and padded high-backed granite seats where he held council with his warrior leaders, as well as showing her other things in the room such as free-form carvings of great Drow warriors.

"Where does that lead to?" she asked, pointing to the black obsidian door.

Garran pushed his long silvery-blue hair over his shoulders. He truly was a sexy Drow. "A storage chamber of sorts."

She raised her brow, but he took her out into the great circular hall and pointed to the fine carvings of the warriors and their subservient women. Many of the Drow women had collars around their necks and a warrior held the chain connected to them.

Garran glanced down at her and grinned. "Would you not like to be my queen and share in our way of life?"

"You're kidding, right?" Copper shuddered. "I'm no man's slave-toy, thank you very much."

The king studied her for a long moment as they stood in the center of the hallway. "That is true. You have spirit—fire that our women do not." He focused intently on her. "I have never known a female as powerful and strong-willed as you. We would make a good match."

"Hmph." Copper shot him a look. "No doubt you don't give your women a chance."

Garran shrugged. "It is their wish. They enjoy their way of life."

"Give me a break," she said under her breath.

He laughed and proceeded to take her through several of the doorways off the great hall. She saw the beautiful banquet room as well as an underground city where goods could be bought and sold. There she finally saw Drow women who walked naked through the village, their bluish skin soft and supple in the gentle lighting that came from lichen growing on the ceiling. They giggled when they saw Copper with Garran, but otherwise smiled, chatted, and laughed among themselves, despite the fact that almost all of them wore collars. Garran explained that every woman who wore a collar served a master.

Just the thought irritated the hell out of Copper.

One of the chambers that Garran led her to was obviously his bedchamber. It had a huge bed in the center with a soft-looking mattress placed within what appeared to be half of a round carved-out piece of black granite. The room was enormous and lavishly decorated.

As she looked at the bed she wondered what it would be like to have Garran as a lover. He was handsome and powerful . . .

Even if it was a possibility, there was something missing. Almost like her heart was waiting for somebody she would probably never meet.

"This is where you belong," he murmured in her ear, and she shivered.

"As if," she responded and raised her chin.

He laughed as she started to back out of the room. But something caught her eye. Without consciously realizing it, she moved toward a table at the foot of the bed and Garran followed.

"Have you changed your mind, sweet one?" Garran said from behind her.

"Keep dreaming."

On the table was something that was most definitely not of this world. It was a brown plastic clock with the day of the week and big, illuminated, green numbers. According to the clock it was nine in the morning on a Wednesday.

Copper's gaze swung back to meet Garran's. "Where did you get this? It's from Earth, not Otherworld."

"There are many Otherworlds, sweet one. Earth is merely one of them."

Copper picked up the clock and looked at the bottom of it before placing it back on the table. "Made in China? Give me a break, Garran."

The Drow looked unconcerned, an expression that seemed forced. "It was a gift from a human. Long ago."

Hair prickled at her scalp as she picked it up and checked the battery compartment. "How is it that the batteries are still working?" she asked as she set it back down, her gaze meeting Garran's again. "Why does it look brand-new?"

Garran gave a shrug of his great shoulders in an obvious effort to look nonchalant. "Drow magic." He went to her, put his arm around her shoulders, and guided her from the chamber. "Now I will show you where we mine."

Copper didn't want to let him off that easy, but she was pretty sure she'd get nowhere with him. Where could he have gotten the clock? What human would he have met, and when? And why would he even begin to need one?

She set aside her questions after he guided her out of his bedroom to the Drow mine. They entered a tunnel that smelled of dark earth and minerals. When they walked out of the passageway, she had to blink until her eyes adjusted to the dimness of the place—then she caught her breath in surprise.

It was like they stood on a platform in the middle of a huge crystal-gray cavern—the dirt actually sparkled and it was studded with veins of gemstones and ore. Overhead hung stalactites that shimmered in the low lighting of the mine. The lighting was created by some kind of lichen on the stalactites and stalagmites.

Her scalp prickled and goose bumps broke out on her arms. "It's so dark," she murmured as she took in the view. *And creepy.*

"We have little need of light," Garran said from behind her and a shiver trailed down her spine.

A pathway had been carved along the walls of the mine so that the trail circled lower and lower until finally reaching the floor of the cavern, which Copper could barely see. When she squinted she saw more stalagmites springing up from the cavern floor.

Drow were working around a hole at the very center of the great chamber. The hole looked relatively small from where she was standing. Huge mounds of earth, gemstones, and ore were piled throughout the expansive cavern, some so high they were like mountains. She saw some Drow sifting the gemstones and ore from the excavated earth. Against one wall stood multiple pickaxes along with buckets and what looked like shovels.

Copper glanced up at Garran. "What do you dig for?"

He reclined against the side of the tunnel they had walked through, his arms folded across his broad chest. "It is what we do."

She turned back to the mine and the Drow busily pulling up bucketfuls of earth. "What do you do with all the gems and stuff?"

Garran gave what sounded like a humorless laugh. When she met his gaze again, he said, "Before we were trapped, we traded with the Fae, Shanai, Mystwalkers, and Elves." He had a faraway look in his eyes when he added, "Now we dig for other reasons that you would not understand."

Copper raised one eyebrow. "Trust me."

This time his laugh was more genuine. "Come, sweet one, it is time for you to entertain me."

She scrunched up her nose as she followed him out of the cavern and through the passageway. What on earth did he mean by that remark?

Copper found out soon enough. It took a while, but she finally negotiated her release. All it had taken was one sexy dance and spell-mending some of their broken drilling tools with her wand. Boobs and hardware—men were easy, no matter what the species.

Yet the trip had given her a feeling of something being off—not right. Especially because of the clock. And then there was Garran's comment—that they now dug for reasons beyond her comprehension. That little remark certainly had not set well with her.

When she'd shaken off the eerie feelings her trip had given her, she spoke with the Faerie queen and shared with her all that she'd learned. It fascinated Copper to now know what lay in the realm beneath her feet.

Riona listened, her perfect features expressionless. "I will have to think on this," she said when Copper finished talking. And with that she fluttered away, back to her Sidhe.

Copper shook her head. Wand in hand, she headed to the center of the meadow. It was time to try again.

She took a deep breath and stood with her feet shoulder width apart. She gripped her wand tightly in her fist and the pentagrams at her ears swung in the breeze that continued to grow stronger and stronger.

Something about this moment was special. She could feel it in her gut.

Mist began to form around her ankles, obscuring the grass that felt cool and damp beneath her bare feet.

Her heart pounded a little harder. She'd never had mist gather around her when she'd gotten ready to perform a spell. She'd done hundreds of spells—at least—over the time she'd been in this Otherworld prison. Every day, at least once a day, she tried a new spell. Any more than one a day seemed to drain her and make the next spell more difficult.

Copper took a deep breath and gripped her wand tighter as the clouds roiled overhead and the breeze lifted her hair from her shoulders. The air smelled of the oncoming storm and apples from the nearby tree.

This was it! She knew it had to be. This would be the magical time she could return home. Her scalp prickled and goose bumps rose along her forearms.

Zephyr zipped around her head before landing on her earlobe. Positive vibes came from the familiar that added to her elation. She quickly cast a circle, thanking the goddess for her assistance. She called to the Ancestors and the Elementals, asking their aid in freeing her and every other being trapped within their Otherworld prison.

When she finished her preparations, she closed her eyes and raised her wand to the east. She slowly turned clockwise in a full circle, keeping her eyes closed. A spell spilled from her lips that she hadn't practiced before.

God and Goddess, hear my plea.
Heed me, Elementals of earth, fire, air, and sea.
Use your great powers to bless this spell.
Ancestors, grant my request and wish me well.
I conjure with my magic thanks to thee.
For the good and true, so mote it be.

Copper held her breath as she kept her arm straight, the wand pointing again to the east. Her mind spun, her skin prickled, and she could see a bright red glow through her eyelids.

She opened her eyes and gasped as brilliant gold light flooded the meadow, blazing from the end of her wand. She held her hand steady as the light blossomed so brightly it nearly blinded her.

Copper's blood thrummed in her ears. Zephyr gave a distressed buzz. She started to shield her eyes with her forearm.

Yes. Yes. This was it. Wasn't it? Please. Please!

She held her breath, praying she was right.

Something large and powerful came through the light.

It slammed into her and she whirled through the air.

Seven

By the time he had spoken with Airell's mother and father, and his own parents, Tiernan's head ached and his muscles were tense. To keep Airell and Urien from facing judgment and subsequent punishment, Tiernan had simply stated that his obligations in the San Francisco Otherworld would detain him. The handfasting date would need to be rescheduled for another six weeks. Neither his parents nor Airell's had been pleased by his announcement.

Once he finished his immediate tasks, Tiernan found himself in the forest again. The ground was damp and the air smelled of recent rain and pine trees. His stride was long and purposeful as he headed toward the transference point where he was told the Great Guardian would aid him in returning to San Francisco. He *must* return at once to aid his fellow warriors in stopping the Balorites and Fomorii from releasing Balor's body and soul.

He still had difficulty pushing the image of the two lovers from his mind. Somehow, someway, he would come up with a solution.

A minuscule spark of light flickered in the forest, catching Tiernan's attention. It was directly in front of him. The Great Guardian's essence, perhaps?

No . . . He frowned as the spark hovered in the forest. It was unusual in its energy patterns—neither Fae nor Elvin created. As he watched, it grew into a small bubble of golden light, suspended over the leaves and dirt of the forest.

Tiernan pushed his long coat aside and rested one hand on the sword sheathed at his side. He moved closer to the now dancing glowing orb. It glittered, causing leaves to sparkle and surrounding rocks to glow.

He approached the orb slowly and his gaze narrowed. He didn't know why he had to get closer to the golden light, except that his gut told him to.

A sudden flare nearly blinded him.

Tiernan stumbled toward it—as if something shoved him from behind.

He struggled to regain his balance and back away, but the light surrounded him, gripping him tight like a lover's arms.

With a jerk it yanked him forward and snatched him from the forest.

A mind-bending sensation shot through Tiernan. He was flying faster than he could have imagined. He saw flashing colors in brilliant shades of the rainbow.

In the next moment he was flung into stormy skies.

He found himself hurtling through the air—toward a petite figure at the other end of the light.

Tiernan braced himself for the impact.

He grabbed the being in his arms who gave a cry as he slammed into it. He twisted in the air and came down hard on his back. Air whooshed from his lungs and his head struck the ground. But he maintained his grip and managed not to roll over again, despite the power of his momentum.

When he could focus his gaze he took in the being on top of him—the woman in his arms—as she raised her head. Shock coursed through him like wildfire as he recognized her.

"Ask and you shall receive," she murmured before he could say a word. "I wished for a gorgeous man and I got one." She rose and sighed as she straddled him. "Sorry to break it to you, but I really would rather have gone home."

"Copper Ashcroft?" Tiernan managed to get out despite the fact that the air had been knocked from his lungs.

The woman placed her palms on his chest, pushed herself out of his arms, and scrambled off him. "You know me?" Her cinnamon eyes were wide and disbelieving. "Who *are* you?"

Tiernan eased himself to a sitting position so that he was looking directly at Copper. Her hair was mussed and her Faerie kisses stood out against her now pale complexion. She looked dizzy, as if she might faint.

He steadied her by grasping her shoulders. For a moment he couldn't speak, and she remained silent, with her lips parted. She had an amazed and shocked expression on her features. She looked almost exactly like her picture except that her hair was longer and she was even more beautiful—the picture had truly not done her justice. She smelled of apples and cinnamon.

"Okaaaaaay." Copper's heart pounded so hard her breasts actually ached. "Try telling me what's going on. And who are you?"

The man's grip was so tight on her arms that she was sure he was going to leave bruises. "Tiernan," he said in an Irish brogue, his features composed as if he slammed into women every day. "I am Tiernan of the Tuatha D'Danann."

The extra jolt of her heart sent blood rushing to her head and she wondered if maybe her magic had backfired so badly that she was imagining things.

"D'Danann? The Fae warriors?" She shrugged away from his grasp. "This is nuts. Where did you come from?"

She tried to catch her breath as Tiernan held up his hand and gave her a sign to slow down. She took a deep gulp of air that somehow didn't want to move past her pounding heart.

"I know your sister," the man called Tiernan said. "Silver has a picture of you that she keeps in her home."

Copper couldn't stop another rush of questions. "Is she all right? What's happened? Ohmigoddess . . . did she summon you? Why would she take such a risk? Where is—"

Tiernan put his finger to her lips and shushed her. "There are only so many questions I can answer at a time."

Copper nodded and bit her lower lip, trying to keep from grabbing him, shaking him, and begging him not to talk so blessed slow.

"Your sister is doing well," he said, his deep blue eyes focused intently on her. "Silver summoned me and my brethren to assist her and the D'Anu Coven in battling the Fomorii."

On hearing this, she couldn't keep her mouth shut. "The ancient sea gods? The demons sent to Underworld?"

The infuriatingly calm man gave a single nod. "There has been a battle—or better to say several battles—in your city of San Francisco." When she nearly busted out with more questions he held up his hand and she bit her lip again. "But we defeated a good number of them."

"I had dreams," Copper let spill out. "Of what must have happened. I didn't know for sure if they were just dreams, but they must have been visions."

Tiernan wondered just how much information he should give her. Copper's mother was dead, and no doubt that was something she didn't know. It should be up to Silver to tell Copper once they returned to San Francisco. News like that should come from a family member with those Copper loved surrounding her.

Buzzing came from around Copper's head and Tiernan caught sight of a honeybee. He swiped at it, trying to knock it from the air.

"What are you—" The bee landed on her nose.

Tiernan raised his hand to flick it off, hoping it wouldn't sting her.

But instead Copper's eyes nearly crossed as she looked down at the honeybee on her nose and she smiled. She brought her finger up to the bee, which crawled up and onto the back of her hand. "This is Zephyr," she was saying. "My familiar."

He frowned. "A bee familiar?"

"Yup." The bee flew off her hand and buzzed angrily around Tiernan's head before flying to her and coming to a rest on the curve of her ear.

She wrinkled her nose as she looked at Tiernan. "He's a little ticked at you right now."

"Great," he muttered. "But if he stings me, he'll die like any other bee."

"Ah, that's where you're wrong." Copper pushed her hair back behind her ear, and Tiernan could see the bee more clearly now. If bees had an expression, the damned thing wasn't too happy at this moment. "As I said, Zeph's a familiar," Copper continued. "Familiars always have some kind of magic. He can sting multiple times, and he never loses his stinger." She gave Tiernan an impish grin. "It's best not to piss him off."

"Terrific." A fat raindrop splattered on Tiernan's face and he looked up at the swirling clouds overhead. "Do you have shelter?"

"More or less." Copper pushed herself to her feet and tugged down a strange tunic that reached her thighs. It appeared to be made of vines and leaves, and caressed and clung to her body in ways that made his cock swell almost painfully against the leather of his breeches. "But I have to take down the circle before we go anywhere."

He forced himself up to a standing position as more raindrops splattered both their faces and their bodies. She looked up at him and he realized how petite she was—more so than even Silver.

Copper picked up a copper and crystal wands then pointed it as she moved counterclockwise in a large circle around them, murmuring a short, singsong chant. After she reached the point where she had started, and finished her chant, she grasped his hand with her free one and led him toward an outcropping of rock. "Come on."

The instant her hand touched his, he felt warmth spread throughout his body and a tingling sensation that went from his head to his toes.

The witch didn't seem to notice as she tugged on his arm, and he followed her to a low shelf. He frowned at the sight of it, unsure whether his bulk would comfortably fit beneath the overhang.

"It's all I've got, but it's been home for what seems like forever," she said as they reached the meager shelter. "Come on."

She crouched down and crawled beneath the overhang and he almost groaned at the sight of her ass that was barely covered by the vine and leaf tunic. What in the gods' names was wrong with him? He had just shot through the Veil to Otherworld, found Silver's sister, and he was having erotic thoughts about her?

Fat raindrops splattered on Tiernan's head as he shrugged out of his long black coat and shoved it into a corner of the shelter. He unfastened the sword belt that held both his sheathed dagger and sword. Gripping his belt, he did his best to crawl in beside her. He banged his head just hard enough that a sharp pain shot through him.

"Gotta be careful in here," Copper said as she set her wand in a corner of the shelter and they both settled into the space.

Zeph zoomed around their heads, then perched on a rock that jutted out in a corner of the shelter.

Tiernan's head brushed the top of the rock and he knew if he moved too quickly in any direction he would surely thump his head again.

Grass, leaves, and vines rustled beneath him as he settled himself. He placed his weapons belt beside him, out of the rain. He and Copper both sat cross-legged, facing each other. It was the best they could do.

For a long moment they studied one another, and Tiernan couldn't think of a word to say.

The pounding of Copper's heart had slowed, but her limbs still trembled. She felt tremors of excitement and incredulity throughout her.

The man she gazed at was one of the sexiest she'd ever remembered seeing. His blond hair fell to his shoulders, and his eyes were a piercing blue. And his build—it was amazing that he had been able to fit into the shelter at all. Now that he'd taken his coat off, the sleeveless leather shirt he was wearing allowed her to view the carved muscles in his biceps. His powerful thighs flexed beneath his leather pants. He was so damn hot, and she'd been without a man for so long. If she wasn't so worried about everyone she'd left behind, she'd jump him, stranger or no. He'd be in for one helluva ride.

Outside the rain began to pour down in sheets. Drops splattered inside the shelter, leaving a slight chill on her skin. She leaned forward and her pentagram earrings swung at her ears.

Tiernan cleared his throat. "How did you get to this place, Copper?"

She twisted her lips in a grimace. "Some warlock named Darkwolf came up on me on the D'Anu beach. I— well, I tried to send him to Otherworld. My spell hit some kind of shield . . ." She gave a shrug that was lighter than she felt. "I ended up here."

"Darkwolf," he growled. "I have seen and know of the bastard."

"You do?" Surprise shot through her and then her scowl met his. "If not for that shield, I wouldn't be trapped here." She sighed. "At least I didn't end up in Underworld."

Tiernan braced one hand on the floor of the shelter. "The Fae . . . perhaps even Mystwalkers or Shanai—any one of those beings could have assisted you in getting to the Elves, who would most likely have returned you to your home world."

Copper wasn't sure what his reaction would be when she told him that she was pretty sure she was still trapped, and he was trapped with her.

Well, at least she wouldn't be alone.

She tried to push away the selfish thought. "There's some kind of barrier," she said in a rush. "It's like an invisible electric shield that keeps us inside and I think keeps anyone outside from seeing us, or we them."

Tiernan narrowed his focus. "Us?"

Copper gestured outside toward the pouring rain. "There are Faeries, Pixies, Brownies, an Undine, and Drow that are stuck here with me." She brought her hand down to caress the soft leaves of her vine dress. "Somehow we all have been trapped here for goddess knows how long."

For a long moment Tiernan couldn't find words. Then very slowly he said, "We are contained within this meadow."

She nodded and brought her gaze resolutely back to his. "We're stuck. Good and stuck."

Tiernan refused to believe there was no way out. "Perhaps my arrival has broken through the shield you speak of."

Copper brightened at once. "That would be too cool."

He cocked an eyebrow. "Cool?"

Her voice was lighter. "When it stops raining we can check."

"How did I come to be here?" he asked.

Copper bit her lip again in a way that he found innocent yet enticing, and that somehow managed to distract him from what could be a disastrous situation.

"Well," she started, "I was performing another spell to try and get out of here. For some reason it brought you here instead of letting me out." When he narrowed his eyes, she hurried to add, "I didn't mean to, really, I didn't. I wanted out." She gave a half-smile. "I know, I know." Her eyes met his head-on. "I said 'ask and you shall receive.' But I was joking." Then under her breath, "Sort of."

Tiernan started to rake his hair in frustration, but his knuckles rammed into the sharp rock above his head. He hissed in a rush of air and shook his fingers.

Copper took his hand and he felt that same flood of heat that he had experienced earlier when she had led him into the shelter.

She examined his knuckles. "You're bleeding."

He pulled his hand away from hers and rubbed his knuckles on his breeches. "I have experienced far worse injuries."

"I'll bet you have." She turned to look out into the rain that was coming down harder. "One thing about this place is that there are no bad guys to worry about—unless you could consider the Drow bad."

She turned her head and gave him a teasing look. "Unless you're a bad guy."

He did not know where it came from, but he said, "With you I could be, Copper."

It was one of those moments where they silently studied one another.

Finally she said without a smile or hint of emotion, "I bet you could be."

Tiernan shifted, uncomfortable from both the cramped quarters, and the heat that had just flamed between the two of them.

"How have you survived here over a year now?" he asked.

She gave a little gasp. "It's been over a year? You're kidding, right?" He didn't answer and her eyes widened. "I can't believe it. Time—it's passed so strangely here. I didn't know how long it'd been, but I really didn't believe it had been *that* long. My parents and sister must be worried crazy about me."

Tiernan remained silent, feeling a twinge in his gut at what was sure to come. He wanted to put it off as long as possible. He truly did not wish to be the one to deliver the news of her mother's death.

"Wow." She braced her elbows on her knees and her chin in her hands. "A whole year. I've missed so much."

"That you have," he said quietly, then found himself somehow glad that Copper had not been in the fight against the Fomorii, even if it meant she had been trapped in this prison in Otherworld.

"So tell me everything," she said, drawing his attention back to her. "I'm dying to know what's going on."

Tiernan's body tensed as his thoughts returned to his urgent need to hurry back to the San Francisco Otherworld. "The Balorite warlocks and the Fomorii demons are attempting to free Balor's body and soul."

Copper's eyes went incredibly wide. *"No way."*

"Your sister and Rhiannon scried this," he said, "and we believe we found evidence to support it." He explained about the parchment and the shapes upon it that could be a doorway and a sacrificial circle. What he did not tell her was that Silver scried that Copper was the sacrifice. "We believe they, or with the aid of other beings, are digging deep below the surface of otherworld."

"Oh, my goddess." She slowly shook her head. "This can't really be done, can it? Balor's body and soul released?"

Tiernan clenched and unclenched one fist. "It is possible."

"Shit." She looked at him with both disbelief and anger. "I've got to get home and help Silver!"

"As I need to return to assist." Tiernan explained how the D'Danann Enforcers were working with the San Francisco Paranormal Special Forces and the Coven of gray witches.

Copper blinked. "Coven of *gray* witches?"

Tiernan could not help but feel restless and impatient to leave. However, he forced himself to slow down and explain how the gray Coven came to be.

She rubbed the heel of her hand against her forehead. "I don't believe it. Silver kicked out of the D'Anu Coven? Rhiannon, Mackenzie, and the others leaving? This is all so surreal."

"Much has happened over the past weeks."

"What I really need to know," Copper said, "is everyone okay?"

He sighed. "No. A couple of witches from the D'Anu Coven were murdered by the Fomorii, as were law enforcement members led by the human Jake Macgregor, and some of my kinsmen. A few witches and apprentices went to the dark."

Copper's expression changed to one of horror. "Who—what—how?"

"I do not know the names of all of the dead." Fury seared his veins at the thought of those who had been taken from her world and his. "Many of the demons responsible have been sent back to Underworld." He clenched his fist. "But not before we destroyed as many as we could. Unfortunately, a fair number did escape."

"The D'Anu don't believe in killing." Her face twisted with obvious anger. "But right now I can't help but think the Fomorii deserved it."

She leaned forward and placed her hand on one of his knees, her expression intent, serious. "What about my sister? My mother and father?"

He paused, finding it difficult to tell her the truth.

Copper's whole body began to shake as she waited for Tiernan's answer. He was taking too long to respond and fear clawed her throat. "Tell me!"

He took both her hands in his and held them tight, and her fear rose. "Silver and Victor are fine."

"My mother?" Copper felt as if her head were going to explode. "Tell me she's okay. Please."

He cleared his throat. He could not evade such a direct question, and he knew it. "She was mortally wounded."

"Mortally wounded?" Copper's voice came out hoarse, disbelieving. She snatched her hands from his and clapped one over her mouth, holding back a scream. She hadn't heard right. Moondust wasn't dead. She wasn't.

"No." She dropped her hand and shook her head. "She can't be."

"You have my greatest sympathy," he said in a low voice. "I am sorry."

Copper scrambled out of the shelter, into the pounding rain, and screamed. When she reached the apple tree, she clenched her hands. She hit it with one fist, then the other, and then again and again as she continued to scream.

Tears poured down her face, washing away with the rain. Heat then chill, heat then chill.

She was beating her fists so hard blood began to stain the trunk of the tree.

The next thing she knew, her arms were pinned to her sides by a strong embrace, and she fought to get away. She screamed and screamed, her cries never ending as she kicked back with her bare feet at the same time she continued her struggles.

"My mother isn't dead!" She fought him harder. "My mother isn't dead!"

The man holding her said nothing, but didn't let her go. She fought and fought him.

Finally, after what seemed forever and no time at all, when she had no more strength left, she sagged in his embrace. Her legs refused to support her anymore.

Tiernan turned her around and scooped her up into his arms. He cradled her, whispering soft words in Gaelic, a language she'd heard but didn't understand. The words soothed her, yet they didn't. Nothing would calm the pain eating away at her heart. Nothing she did, nothing he did, could bring back her mother.

Rain continued to pound down upon them. Copper's hair was drenched and tumbled across her eyes. Her face, arms, and legs were wet, but the vine and leaf dress remained dry, as the Faerie magic shielded it. Tiernan continued to speak in the strange tongue as he gently stroked hair away from her face.

She found herself gripping his wet leather shirt, burying her face against him, and crying so hard she thought she'd never stop.

Tiernan's heart ached for Copper, and it was almost as if her pain were his. He felt every scream, every sob, to his very bones.

Eventually Copper collapsed from exhaustion in Tiernan's arms. Her grip on his shirt lessened and cries no longer spilled from her lips. Her body sagged and her eyelids fluttered and closed, but her body continued to shake.

He carried her through the endless rain to the small rock shelter. Her skin was cold against his chest, and he knew he needed to give her what warmth he could. He settled her on her side in the shelter so that her back was facing him, and he crawled in after her. He took his coat and covered her with it. He wrapped his arm around her waist as he molded his body to her length, tucking her head under his chin and holding his arm tight around her belly.

He held her, wishing there were some way to take away her pain.

When Copper woke, her eyelids felt heavy and swollen. Her head ached and pounded as if her heart beat inside it. Pain shot through her fists as she moved her arms, and her whole body felt as if she had been running and running for days.

For a moment she felt disoriented, as if she'd had a bad dream that she couldn't quite remember.

Then everything came rushing back to her.

Her mother was dead. Dead.

Pressure built behind her eyes, but no tears would come, as if she were beyond crying. Her pain was so intense that she was aware of nothing else. Numbness and disbelief at losing her mother made her heart ache in her chest as if it were actually breaking. It took her breath away and it felt as though she couldn't inhale. She was so swamped with an emptiness, a hollowness she knew would never go away.

Anger rose up so deep inside it felt like evil tingling through her limbs. At that moment she hated the Ancestors, the gods and goddesses, and everyone else in all the worlds. She felt forsaken, alone, cheated.

Something stirred behind her and she stiffened. She felt a firm body melded against hers, and something unfamiliar draped over her. When she glanced down she saw a man's arm wrapped around her belly.

Tiernan. The man she had somehow summoned. The D'Danann who had given her the news of her mother's death. A part of her felt relief that her sister and father had lived, but the pain of Moondust being taken from her was so great she could barely think of anything else.

She turned over, her muscles protesting with her movements. When she faced the man, she found his eyes open, his expression one of concern.

Tears she didn't think existed washed down her cheeks and she buried her face against his chest again and cried.

When her tears would no longer come, she let out a long shuddering sigh. She felt warm, cared for in his strong arms, even though she didn't know him. His scent of leather, male, and rain somehow comforted her, too.

She drew back a little in the cramped quarters and wiped the back of one of her hands across her eyes. "Thank you."

"There is nothing to thank me for," he said in that deep Irish brogue. "If I had acted sooner . . . perhaps she would have lived."

Copper stilled, and her throat nearly closed off. She forced herself to swallow. "I would like to get up, please."

Tiernan rolled away from her and into the early morning sunlight. He crouched and extended his hand to help her out of the shelter.

Copper allowed him to assist her in getting to her feet, but then she mumbled, "I need a few moments alone." After she shrugged off the coat and tossed it into the shelter she walked around the long outcropping of rock and went to the location she used to relieve herself. She always buried her remains. The Fae cared for the place with magic and it never smelled or looked bad. It simply appeared to be a clean patch of earth.

When she returned, she avoided Tiernan's gaze and cleansed her hands in the portion of the stream that flowed into the lower basin. Water dribbled over that basin and vanished into the ground, between rocks and the earth. The water felt cold and bracing, and seemed to reduce the pain in her hands from slamming her fists against the tree. Her knuckles were swollen and raw and it was hard for her to even open her hands.

She splashed a large handful of water on her face. The swelling of her eyelids and the ache in her head seemed to lessen as she splashed handful after handful of water onto her face.

When she thought she could look at him without bursting into tears again, Copper turned to Tiernan. He had simply stood and watched her, waiting for her to finish.

She almost threw herself back into his arms, needing to feel that human closeness to comfort her. Even though he wasn't human. Even though she really didn't know this man—this D'Danann.

Instead she shook the water from her hands and looked toward the apple tree. Her voice sounded rusty and unused as she spoke. "That's your breakfast unless the Faeries are in a particularly good mood."

He didn't say anything, just looked to one of the flatter rocks on the outcropping. She glanced at it and saw more

food than the Fae had ever left her before, and she almost
burst into tears again. They must have felt her pain, must
have offered the food as a way of expressing their sorrow
for her.

All were foods now familiar to her, but the Fae had
never given her so much at one time: a pile of pine nuts;
seed cakes; apple chews; bread made from roots that tasted
like pumpkin, along with a flower petal butter to spread on
it; and wild berry tarts with the shell made of grass blended
with seeds and nectar. It didn't sound very appetizing, but
the Fae had a way of making it taste delicious.

Some kind of creamy Fae salve that smelled of
marigolds was on a large leaf from the apple tree, and she
knew it was meant to apply to the wounds on her fists. The
first thing she did was spread it across her knuckles. At
once the swelling lessened and the pain and cuts vanished
so that her knuckles looked normal again. As she was a
witch, her wounds generally healed faster than normal, but
this salve was amazing.

Copper took Tiernan's hand, where he had scraped his
knuckles last night, and applied the salve to his almost
healed scrapes, then let his hand go.

She wasn't hungry, but she didn't want to insult any of
the Fae, so she moved to their offerings and picked up a
wild berry tart. Tiernan came up beside her and took one
of the tarts and bit into it while he watched her. She nib-
bled hers and felt a burst of comfort and warmth, as if the
Faeries had put into the food some kind of spell that would
soothe the ache inside. Likely they had.

Zephyr buzzed out of the shelter and onto her ear as she
ate from each offering. She felt stronger with every bite,
more able to face what would come next. The food and the
sense of comfort her familiar was channeling through her
made Copper feel as if she could better face the truth.

Her mother was gone.

She ground her teeth. Somehow she had to get them out

of there and find her mother's killers. But first she needed more information from Tiernan—yet she wasn't sure she was ready to hear it.

After they each finished their more than healthy breakfast, she settled on the wet grass at the base of the apple tree and hugged her knees. Zeph was flitting from one brilliant flower bloom to another by the Faerie mound. The air smelled of rain, apples, and early morning sunlight. Through the leaves of the tree she could see the sun beginning its rise in a now cloudless sky.

How could this day be beautiful when her mother was dead?

Copper felt so, so empty inside. Moondust's passing had created a huge void that would never be filled. She knew her mother would not want her to be sorrowful. Moondust always said to rejoice for those who went on to Summerland.

Copper let out a deep shuddering sigh. Rejoice. Right.

She choked back more tears and waited for Tiernan to join her. He hadn't said a word since he had told her he felt some responsibility for Moondust's death.

"Tell me what happened," she said when Tiernan sat beside her.

He was quiet for a while before he began the story of her parents coming to aid Silver in the fight against the Fomorii. How they were kidnapped, how they refused to turn to black magic to assist Darkwolf in conjuring more Formorii.

He didn't go into detail when he told her that her mother had been murdered by the Fomorii queen on Samhain, and she was glad for that. She didn't think she could take what were surely grotesque details of her mother's death.

He also told her why he felt some responsibility for her mother's death. Silver, Hawk, Cassia, and Mackenzie had been trapped by the Fomorii during that battle on Samhain.

Tiernan and the other D'Danann could do nothing for fear
of the four of them being murdered by Darkwolf and the
Fomorii. They had to wait until the right opportunity to
strike, and that was too late for Moondust.

Copper couldn't find it in her to blame him for anything. It wasn't his fault, even if he thought he could have
better protected her mother.

When he had finished explaining all that happened,
Copper couldn't speak for a long time. She leaned her head
back against the damp trunk of the tree and water leaked
from the leaves above to splash on her upturned face. She
didn't mind. It somehow made her feel more connected
with the world she now lived in.

Guilt stabbed at her like angry knives. If she hadn't
been banished to this place, she would have been in San
Francisco to help Silver fight the Fomorii. Between the two
of them they could have saved Moondust.

"If I had just been there," a voice said, and then she realized it was coming from her. "I could have helped. Could
have kept her from being murdered."

Tiernan placed his hand on her knee and squeezed. She
turned her head to look at him and met his blue eyes.

"Do not blame yourself." His eyes held a world of caring. "You had no choice. You could not go to your family."

"But if I hadn't been so *stupid*." She banged the back of
her head against the tree trunk. "If I hadn't followed my
dream-vision and gone to the beach that night . . . if I
hadn't tried to banish that warlock . . . I would have been
there for them."

Her breath caught and she stared straight ahead, seeing
nothing but a memory of Moondust. "At least I could have
said goodbye to my mother."

Eight

It was afternoon and Copper was again leaning in her favorite spot against the apple tree after a lunch of what had been leftovers from the large breakfast the Faeries had provided. She picked at a leaf on her vine dress while she watched Tiernan approach the barrier of their prison. Zephyr was off playing with the Faerie children in the flowers.

The Faerie queen appeared out of nowhere and perched on Copper's shoulder, and Copper caught the scent of roses. She glanced at Riona and saw that the Faerie had a wicked glint in her lavender eyes.

Riona twisted a lock of her black hair with one finger and her pale purple wings opened and closed, sprinkling iridescent dust on Copper's shoulder. "This should be fun," Riona said in a small but sensual voice.

Copper's lips quirked as she turned to look at Tiernan. The Fae certainly had their fun laughing at Copper every time she had tried to get through the barrier.

She glanced around the meadow and spotted the Undine poking her head above the water basin, Brownies lying in wait—no doubt to bite Tiernan's ankles if he got too close—and Pixies flitting about like gigantic butterflies, just waiting to perform some kind of mischief. The Pixies were no larger than a human hand, but their bodies were as round as Copper's upper arm. They had tiny green eyes, green and yellow butterfly wings, pale green skin, and malicious grins.

Of course there was no sign of the Drow because they could not tolerate sunlight.

Riona leaned forward, her elbow on her knee and her chin in her tiny hand as she watched the D'Danann warrior. Tiernan approached the invisible wall and stood there for a moment, studying its shimmer. His shoulder-length blond hair lifted from his shoulders in a light breeze, and he had an intense look on his features, as if he could will the barrier to vanish.

He brought his hand up and placed it against the wall.

The moment he touched it, a jolt shook his body. His hair frizzed and stood on end. He shouted a curse, snatched his hand away, and stumbled back a few steps.

Riona burst out in a fit of Faerie giggles and Copper snorted, trying not to laugh. But when Tiernan wheeled around, his hair looking like a long blond Afro, she couldn't hold back her own giggles. He had such an angry expression on his face. And his hair! Goddess, how could she not laugh?

All around them tiny gales of laughter sang from the treetop, rocks, grass, and the bushes.

"What?" he shouted, tossing a look from Copper to the Faerie queen, who was nearly doubled over.

Copper bit her lip, trying to hold back one last giggle of her own. "Your, um, hair."

Tiernan raked his fingers through his hair and his expression grew even more furious when he touched it. He used both hands, trying to get his hair to stay down, only to have it pop up again.

As soon as he marched back to the barrier, two Pixies flitted above his head and started weaving lattices, like connected rope ladders, in his hair, and tied little flowers on the many peaks as they stuck straight up with the rest of his hair.

Riona managed to flit away before Copper rolled over from laughing so hard. Her stomach hurt and moisture dampened her eyes. It felt good to laugh after all the sadness she'd experienced since yesterday.

When she could keep a straight face, Copper righted herself. "The Faeries gave me some dandelion shampoo that you'll have to use to get it to go back to normal." He glanced over his shoulder, narrowed his gaze, and she tried to look serious. "You might as well do all the checking you're going to do with your hair the way it is, 'cause touching the barrier is going to do that every time."

Tiernan gave a curse that came out as a low growl. She knew that like her, he was feeling an urgent need to get back to her city—there was so much on the line.

Goddess. Balor, set free?

Tiernan glared around the meadow as if daring any other being to laugh and growled again when little sniggers came from various parts of the meadow. When he stalked off toward another side of the invisible wall, he stooped down to draw his sword from where he had left his belt draped over a rock. Copper called after him. "You should probably leave your weapons. Metal of any kind only makes it worse." He grumbled and set the sword belt back down. At least in that he was listening.

She had firsthand experience. When she'd touched the end of her wand to the wall, trying to spell it away, she'd been thrown back at least ten feet from the shock of it.

A shout and a curse cut her attention back to Tiernan, who stood beside another portion of the barrier, his hair frizzier than ever with lots of flowers poking out of the mass. Muscles worked in his jaw and there was absolute fury combined with determination on his expression.

He held his hand out and began to run his fingers along the invisible wall, his arm jerking with the force of the electrical shock he was experiencing. But he didn't stop. He kept on going, stomping through grass and bushes along the way until he had circled the entire meadow and come back to where he had started. By the time he got back, two Brownies clung to each boot and had shimmied up high enough to bite his knees through his leather pants.

"Damn!" he shouted and kicked each foot so that Brownies went flying through the air, only to land safely on their little gnarled feet.

Brownies were ugly things—brown as the bark of a tree with pointed wrinkled faces that made them look like old women eating something extremely sour. Their bodies were bare, their joints knobby, and their hands just as gnarled as their feet.

After the last Brownie went sailing, Tiernan turned and glared at Copper. His hair was downright curly now, still standing on end, and the Pixies had made no less than six connected lattices that stuck out like thick blond flower stalks with bunches of blooms at each end. Copper had the hardest time not bursting into laughter again.

In the next moment Tiernan unfurled his wings. Huge, brown wings the color of milk chocolate. Copper's eyes went wide. She'd known he was Tuatha D'Danann, but this was the first time she'd seen the true proof of it. He flapped his wings once, twice, three times, stirring the air, and her hair fluttered around her face.

Tiernan rose from the ground, his eyes focused above him, his face into the breeze. Copper watched in amazement as the powerful wings carried the large man up, up, up into the sky. He circled above the meadow and Copper didn't know if she'd ever seen such an incredible sight. He was magnificent.

Tiernan soared higher, until he looked no bigger than a bird. As he neared the barrier, Copper held her breath.

None of the Fae in the meadow had ever flown so high. Could Tiernan find a place where he could break away to freedom?

She watched him draw closer to where the wall should be. He touched it with a wing.

He gave a loud cry as he was flung back.

And then he was falling. Tiernan was falling. End over end.

Copper shrieked, her heart pounding and her mouth dry. She scrambled to her feet, never taking her eyes from the figure plunging through the air, getting larger and larger as it approached the ground.

Instinctively, Copper used her witchcraft to fling up a spellshield and prayed to the goddess that it would catch Tiernan. This was the only hand-magic she'd ever performed without her wand, and she hoped it would work and she wouldn't get squashed flat. Damn, if her wand weren't in the shelter, it would have helped her make the shield stronger.

She concentrated with all she had, holding her arms up high and feeling the weight of the shield on her hands. She couldn't drop him. She couldn't!

The figure hurtled directly at her. She didn't dare move for fear of breaking the spell that held the glittering gold shield above her.

She clenched her teeth as his body grew close. When he was inches away from the spellshield she doubled the power of her magic.

And felt him slam into the shield.

The force of his landing knocked Copper to the ground, flat on her back. The power of the fall made her head spin and her back ache. But she kept her hands up, balancing him several feet above her. Sweat broke out on her skin and her arms trembled.

He was unconscious, that much she could tell. He had landed facedown, his wings resting on his back. His cheek was pressed to the shield, making him look as if his face were smashed up against a window.

Her arms trembled so badly now that she didn't know how much longer she could hold him. She had to move him so that he wasn't directly above her, but she was afraid she might break the spell and he'd slam into her. His bulk was so great, and she was so small.

The pressure on her arms began to lighten. Copper turned her gaze just enough to see Riona and several of the other Faeries with their arms outstretched and Faerie dust rising up from their wings. They were helping her.

Slowly they eased Tiernan away so that he was no longer above Copper.

Her shield failed. Tiernan dropped a good three feet. He landed facefirst into the grass with a loud thump.

Her heart pounded a little harder as she moved to her knees and pressed her fingertips to his neck. His pulse beat, sure and strong.

She looked at Riona. All the other Faeries had vanished. "Why did you let him fall the rest of the way?" Copper asked.

The Faerie grinned. "Deserved it, didn't he?"

Copper frowned. "How?"

Riona waved her hand around their prison. "He showed no respect for the Fae as he stomped around our home."

"He's Fae, too." With an exasperated sigh, Copper shook her head. "He was just trying to help us."

The Faerie flitted so that she was above Tiernan. "But he's arrogant and so awfully grouchy." She gave a little shiver of her wings, and Faerie dust sprinkled onto his face. Immediately he groaned and stirred. "You will have your hands full with him. Yes, that you will," she said before disappearing in a flash.

Copper stroked Tiernan's frizzed hair and part of a lattice as he groaned again. He smelled of sunshine, wind, and leather, and of the flowers twined in his hair. His wings began to fold away and she watched in fascination as they disappeared behind the leather of his shirt as if they had never been.

He pushed her hand away, then slowly got to his knees to sit on his haunches. "What happened?" he said in a voice so gruff it surprised her.

"You blacked out and fell." She glanced in the direction Riona had disappeared to. "I threw up a spellshield to keep you from hitting the ground, and the Faeries helped me get you safely down."

"Thank you," he said, but he didn't sound pleased. More like pissed. Probably from his failure to get out of their prison.

His chest rose and fell as he took a deep breath. Grass stuck to his cheek and his clothing, dirt smudged his face and sleeveless shirt, and his forehead glistened with sweat.

As if reading her mind, he jerked his black shirt over his head and wiped the sweat and dirt from his face. Copper watched in fascination as the muscles in his arms flexed. Her gaze traveled over his well-defined chest and abdomen. Wow.

He flung the shirt aside and glared at Copper. He looked as if he was furious with her.

She blinked. "What'd I do?"

"You brought us to this damnable place and there's no way out." He pushed himself to stand and continued to glare at her.

Heat crept over Copper's face and her stomach clenched. "Do you think I did this on purpose?"

"You're a witch." He waved his hand as if to encompass the meadow. "Get us the hells out of here."

She got to her feet and balled her hands into fists. "I've tried. And tried and tried."

"Try harder." He turned away and strode to the stream tumbling over the rocks.

For a moment Copper just stared at him as he stomped

away from her. She wanted to blast his butt with spellfire so badly she could taste it. Damn. Where was her wand when she needed it?

But then her stomach sank. It was her fault he was here. The weight of everything crashed down on her so hard that her shoulders ached with it. Copper moved to the other side of the great apple tree, away from Tiernan, where she could no longer see him and where he couldn't see her. Goddess, she needed some space. She slid down its trunk with her knees bent nearly to her chest. She leaned forward and buried her face in her hands.

The range of emotions made her feel like she was in a vortex, spiraling out of control. Grief from her mother's death; the brief respite of laughter as she and Riona watched Tiernan; fear when he plunged to the ground; anger at him for what he'd just said; and sadness beyond sadness again at the thought of her mother's death. She wanted to throw up, scream, and cry all at the same time.

And she wanted to punch Tiernan so, so, so bad. It didn't matter that he'd told the truth, that it had been her fault he was trapped here. She wanted to lash out at something—someone.

She barely noticed Zephyr racing past her with an angry buzz.

Tiernan stomped to the small stream at the rock outcropping. Just as he started to bend over to slip his hands beneath the trickling stream, he heard a loud buzzing.

A sharp pain buried itself into one side of his ass and he shouted.

Heat burned through his entire backside.

It took only a second for him to realize what had happened. Zephyr zoomed around his head, around and around, with a furious buzz.

"Damned bee," Tiernan started to say, but cut himself off. No doubt the thing would attack him again if he didn't watch it. He sucked in a breath of relief when the familiar zipped away.

Ass burning like it was on fire, he knelt, scooped large handfuls of icy cold water, and splashed it on his face. The water dripped down his neck to his bare chest, cooling him and his temper. A bit. Why the hell had the damned thing stung him?

He splashed more water on his hair, trying to flatten it. Only there were long tangles in his hair—no, wait. Things that stuck straight up like wheel spokes all over his head.

He groaned.

When he finished washing his face and wetting his hair, he stood and raked his hand through his hair, only to get his fingers tangled in the braid creations. He snatched up his shirt from the grass where he'd tossed it, and took the leather lace out of the neck opening. He caught his hair and tied it all back with the lace so that it wasn't sticking straight up any longer.

Tiernan glanced to where Copper had been standing. She wasn't there. But he thought he saw the hint of her vine-and-leaf dress from the opposite side of the apple tree.

His gut twisted. Damn. He'd acted like a total ass. He *was* an ass.

She had saved him from a nasty fall, and even then, after all she'd been through, he had taken out his frustration on her. What kind of man was he?

Shit.

No wonder Zephyr had stung him.

He wiped water from his face with the back of his hand, strode to the apple tree and around to the other side, his buttock burning with every step.

When he rounded the tree he saw that Copper had her face in her hands and her body shook with silent sobs.

She was crying.

Gods. He deserved to be strung up by his toes from the topmost branch of the apple tree. He winced. No doubt the first chance they had, Copper's Fae friends would be delighted to do just that, and Zephyr would help.

Tiernan sat down next to Copper, his thigh touching hers. She jerked her leg away as if he'd burned her. What should he do now? Hell, once again he didn't know what to do with a crying woman, especially when he was the reason she was crying. Last night had been different. He had held her because she had needed him.

Did she want him to hold her now? Would she let him?

Zephyr gave another angry buzz from where he perched on Copper's ear.

Hesitantly, Tiernan reached out a hand and held it above her back. He slowly lowered it until his palm rested on her vine-and-leaf dress. She flinched beneath his touch.

That ache in his gut was as heavy as a rock quarry. He wrapped his arm around her shoulders and pulled her in tight. "I apologize." He breathed in her apples-and-cinnamon scent and his belly twisted even more at what he had done to her. "I should not have taken my anger out on you." He rubbed his thumb in a slow circle on her shoulder. "Will you forgive me?"

There was a long pause. Finally, Copper raised her head, but she didn't look at him. Her eyes were swollen and red again, and he felt even more like an ass.

"Whatever," she mumbled, still not looking at him.

He grasped her chin and forced her to look at him. "Please?"

Copper's throat worked as she swallowed. Her eyes met his and for a long time he held her gaze. She took a deep breath, let out a long exhale, and said, "Okay."

Tiernan almost couldn't catch his own breath as he studied her face. Even with her eyes red and her face streaked with tears, she was beautiful. When he had seen Copper's picture in her sister's home, he had memorized her features down to the sprinkling of Faerie kisses across her nose.

Why it had seemed so important to him then, to find her, he didn't know. But here she was. Here he was.

Copper wiped away her tears with the heels of her palms and took another deep breath. She reached up and touched his hair and gave him a small smile. "I like the way you've pulled it back. The bouquet of flowers at the end is an especially nice touch."

He rolled his eyes and she laughed.

She had a beautiful laugh.

"Come on." She grabbed his hand as she stood, and tugged at him until he got to his feet. "Let's get rid of those braids and that Afro."

Copper's hand felt good in his as he allowed her to lead him to the water basins. "Sit," she ordered. He raised an eyebrow, but obeyed.

Tiernan plopped himself onto the grass, one knee bent with one forearm resting on it as he watched her turn away and head toward the shelter. His groin tightened as she got onto her knees to scoot into the shelter, and he had a nice view of the upper part of her thighs, close to her ass cheeks. Just a little more . . .

He groaned as she disappeared into the shelter, then shook his head and smiled. He was acting like some young warrior who had never bedded a woman before. When she slid back out into the sunshine, she was carrying a wooden cup and a wooden container with a lid, and her wand. By the patterns on the wood he knew the cup and container were Faerie-made.

"Okay, now how's the best way to do this . . . ?" Copper kneeled beside him and eyed his hair critically as she set the cup, container, and her wand down on the grass. "Those little buggers sure had their fun with you."

Tiernan grimaced, but as Copper reached up to touch his hair, he went stock-still. Her vine-and-leaf-covered breasts were directly before his eyes. They swayed with her movements as he felt her begin to undo what the Pixies had done to his hair. His gaze was fixed on her as she removed the tie from his hair, and he swore he saw hints of her nipples and the soft white flesh through that skimpy dress.

"Ooooh, they got you good." Copper leaned forward, getting so close he could move just a bit and suck the nipple through the dress . . . "It's going to take me a while to get these all out," he faintly heard her say.

His cock was so hard beneath his leather breeches and was only becoming more painful by the moment. As she worked on his hair, flower petals from the Pixies' handiwork drifted to the grass beside him. The perfume of the petals blended with Copper's own unique scent.

"So tell me about your home world." Copper's fingers stroked through his hair when she freed it from one of the lattice braids. Gods, he hoped it took her a long time to finish.

"Um, Tiernan?" He looked up to see her looking down at him, mischief in her cinnamon eyes. "Did you hear me, or are you too busy staring at my boobs?"

"Boobs?" he said, narrowing his eyes and shifting so that he could relieve some of the ache in his cock.

Copper had the hint of a grin on her face as she settled back on her haunches and cupped her breasts. "These."

Tiernan groaned out loud to see her holding herself.

When his eyes met hers again, her grin widened. "Thought so."

The heat in his groin was so intense, he was ready to pull her to the ground now and fuck her. At that moment, he could not think of one reason not to. "Watch it, little fire," he said, his voice low and gravelly.

Still with that quirky grin on her face, Copper released her breasts and moved so that she was behind him, her fingers in his hair once again. "So you're a breast man."

Said breasts rubbed against his bare back as she moved close to work on his hair. Tiernan swallowed hard. The woman was teasing him—and she probably had no idea what he would do to her if she continued.

"I asked you a few moments ago," she said as she worked on his hair, "to tell me about yourself."

He cleared his throat. "I am a D'Danann Enforcer, a warrior of my people."

"Yeah, yeah." She tugged at one particularly stubborn knot. When she couldn't get it untangled, she grabbed her wand and gently zapped it free. When she set the wand aside, she said, "I mean tell me about *you*. Like how old you are, what your parents are like, where you live, what you do when you're not being a he-man, what's your favorite color . . . those kinds of things."

Tiernan took a deep breath and shifted again to ease the ache in his groin. "I am over two thousand years old."

Copper's hands paused in his hair and she pressed closer to his back as she peered around him to look at his face. "No shit?"

He grinned. "No shit."

"Well." Copper went back to working on his hair. "I should have figured that since you all were former gods before you left to live in Otherworld. It's just a trip actually hearing you say it." This time her tug at his hair was hard enough to make him wince. "Sorry. Tell me more."

Tiernan paused for a moment, trying to decide exactly what to tell her. "I am a lord of the House of Cathal in the D'Danann court. My mother and father are ready to retire from their responsibilities and wish for me to take them on."

"A lord, eh?" She finger-combed part of his hair. "Do you want to? Take over the responsibilities of your house?"

"It is my duty," he said automatically.

Copper attacked what he hoped was the final Pixie braid creation. "But do you *want* to?"

"Of course." That was his destiny. It always had been. But right now he didn't want to think about his destiny or duty.

"Okay, so what's your favorite color?"

He turned just enough to grab one of her wrists, forcing her to stop and look at him. "Cinnamon eyes and copper-colored hair."

Her throat visibly worked. "You are the charmer," she said in a low voice.

"Right now that is all I see. All I want to see."

Copper's heart started pounding and her belly tingled straight down to her pussy. She took a deep breath. Oh, boy, was she playing with fire. She looked away from him and extracted her wrist from his hand. "I'm almost done with your Pixie braids," she said, trying to keep her voice light. Suddenly she wasn't so sure she wanted to move this fast.

But she wanted him. Goddess, did she want him.

Nevertheless, she hurried to finish the last braid. Without warning him, she took the wooden cup, filled it from the lower basin with ice-cold water, and poured it over his head.

That should cool things down a little, she thought, as Tiernan sputtered and turned to glare at her.

She gave him a sweet smile and dumped another cup, then another over his hair as the chilly water ran down his wonderful naked back, that incredible chest, along that flat belly straight to—a very hard erection beneath his leather pants.

Copper hurried to finish wetting every bit of his hair, which was still sticking up despite being wet. She took the lid off the wooden container and tossed the lid aside before using her fingers to scoop out some of the special shampoo the Faeries had made for her own frizzy occasions. The pentagram on her thick copper bracelet glittered with her movements.

As she washed his hair with the shampoo and the frizz died down, Tiernan cleared his throat. "Tell me about your life, Copper."

"Turnabout's fair play, I suppose." She gave a shrug as she soaped his hair. To keep it from staying curly, the shampoo had to be worked in thoroughly. "You know about my family." Her voice caught as she thought about her mother, but forced herself to go on. "You know I'm a witch and I have a honeybee familiar. I'm trapped with a whole bunch of pissed-off Fae, who think this is all my fault, in some kind of bubble." She scooped up water in the tumbler. "Close your eyes because I'm going to rinse the soap out now."

He leaned over to keep the soap out of his eyes. "What else?" he asked even as he shivered from the cold water.

"Hmmmm . . . I pitch a mean game of softball, I could probably give you a run for your money. And I majored in education at a university."

"How old are you?" he asked as more soap ran down his face and body when she poured another cup of water on him.

"Oh, probably what would be a nanosecond in your lifetime." She was almost finished. She squeezed out the excess water, then finger-combed his hair as he rose back up. "Twenty-six. I went to the university for four years, took some night classes for a couple of years, then went back to get my masters."

"You teach?" he asked, as she moved around to face him so that they were eye to eye.

"Not yet, but I plan to." She pushed her hair behind her ear and wondered where Zeph was. "I've been taking it slow. So much was going on with my Coven, including my becoming an Adept. I was also helping Silver run the Coven's store and taking one night class each semester."

Their eyes met and held. She was sitting so close to him that her thigh brushed his. "Blue," she whispered.

He raised an eyebrow. "Blue what?"

"My favorite color today is blue." She drank in the sight of him. His incredible physique, the intense look on his well-defined features, his wet, blond hair that now fell straight back behind his broad shoulders. And those eyes . . . "You have the most beautiful eyes I've ever seen."

Tiernan moved so fast he caught her by surprise. One second she'd been sitting, the next she was lying on her back staring up at him.

Nine

Flames burned through Copper like wildfire as Tiernan braced his knees on each side of her legs, his hands on either side of her head, her back pressed against the soft grass. His musky male scent blended with that of the dandelion shampoo she had just used on his hair. His mouth—she couldn't take her eyes off his firm lips. Sexy and so very masculine.

His features had an intense look and her belly went straight to her toes as he dipped his head down. When Tiernan's lips met hers, it was hot, fiery, passionate. He held nothing back, his mouth moving over hers, his teeth nipping at her bottom lip, and his tongue thrusting into her mouth.

Copper moaned and writhed beneath him as she reached up to slide her arms around his neck, beneath his wet hair. She brought him tightly to her and at the same time she pressed her mouth harder to his. She matched his passion, tasting him, biting at his lower lip, and moaning into his mouth. It was the most incredible kiss she'd ever experienced in her life.

Tiernan's wet hair fell forward to slide over her neck and her breasts. He groaned and drew away from her, his beautiful eyes meeting hers and holding her gaze with such an intense look she couldn't have turned away if she wanted to. His breathing was hard and she felt the warmth of it against her cheeks.

Her own breathing was just as harsh and the sensations in her body were nearly out of control. Her blood pounded hard in her ears and she felt a zing in her belly that made its way to her damp pussy.

"Little fire," Tiernan said in a low gravelly voice, "I do not think you know how close I am to fucking you. Now."

Copper slipped one of her hands from his neck, and his abdomen tensed beneath her fingers as she trailed them down, down to his pants. She cupped him by the balls and his eyes grew dark and stormy. The arms he had braced to either side of her head trembled and his jaw tightened.

"Don't wait." She squeezed his erection and brought her hand up to tug at one of the ties of his tight leather pants. "Fuck me now."

"Copper . . ." His growl grew deeper as she released his cock and ran her small hand up and down its length.

"I mean it." She tugged at his cock, forcing him to lower himself closer to her wet pussy. "I *need* this. I need it so badly I can hardly stand it."

Tiernan moved so that he was between her legs, forcing her thighs wide apart. Sweat had broken out on his brow from the effort to hold himself back.

Copper released his erection to tug up her dress, baring her pussy. The scent of her juices combined with his masculine musk made her heady.

She wrapped her legs around his hips, forcing him lower so that his cock pressed hard against her mound.

"Goddamn it, Tiernan." She reached up and kissed him hard. "Fuck me," she said against his lips.

He raised his face to the sky and with a pained expression he rocked his hips so that his cock rubbed from the curls of her mound to her now bare belly. But not where she wanted him. She slipped her fingers around his erection and started to guide it to her pussy.

"No." He had a tortured look on his face when his gaze met hers again. "You could get with child."

"Uh-uh." Copper reached up to kiss him hard. "I'm a witch. Even without my wand, I can conjure a magical shield within me that protects me from everything." She brought the head of his cock to her channel. "Consider it conjured."

Tiernan gave a growl. Copper raised her hips so that he slid a fraction into her channel.

"Hurry," she begged. "I need you now."

With one thrust, he buried his cock deep, deep inside her.

"Oh, sweet goddess." At that moment she couldn't imagine anything else feeling so good. She clenched her legs tighter around him, her body adjusting to the length and girth of his cock. "Don't move."

Immediately he looked concerned. "Did I hurt you?"

"Um, no." She raised her hips so that his groin was hard against her mound. "You just feel so damn good."

A droplet of sweat rolled from his forehead onto her cheek. "I cannot hold back much longer."

"Don't." She began moving her hips up and down. "Fuck me harder than you ever have fucked anyone before."

Tiernan took her at her word and rammed into her and she cried out at the incredible feel of it. He thrust so hard, his hips slamming into hers, that she knew she was going to be bruised. She reveled in it. Goddess, but she needed this. He felt so good, the head of his cock hitting that sweet spot deep inside her, his leather pants rubbing against the inside of her thighs, her dress bunched up around her waist.

Her body trembled and a sensation swept through her like a thousand tiny pinpricks from her scalp to her toes. A flush of heat followed the prickling sensation and her mind began to whirl. She imagined tiny golden bubbles sparkling around them just as her orgasm burst through her.

Copper couldn't help the cry that tore from her throat, no more than she could stop her body from trembling, shuddering with every wave of her climax.

Tiernan kept thrusting in and out, harder, harder, harder, drawing out her orgasm. Moments later he gave a shout that sounded like triumph, a pure male cry that made her channel convulse even harder around his cock as he throbbed inside her. They were both sweaty and out of breath.

He stopped and pressed his hips tight to hers as he looked down at her. "Godsdamn, woman."

She gave a smile of satisfaction as he rolled onto his side, bringing her with him so that they were pressed chest to chest, his thigh pinning hers down, his cock still inside her. He traced his finger over her nose. "Such sweet Faerie kisses."

"Freckles." Copper kissed him, moving her mouth gently over his, before drawing back and looking into his intense eyes. "Ready for another round?"

Words failed him as the beautiful woman untangled herself from his arms and stood so that he was looking up at her. The sweet curls of her mound glistened with her wetness, her musk nearly driving him mad.

A sexy smile curved the corners of her mouth as she reached down to grab her dress from where it bunched at her waist. She tugged it over her breasts and over her head in a lithe movement. He could not take his eyes from her full breasts. She was right—he apparently was a "breast man," and hers were perfection. Her nipples were taut, and when she reached up and pinched them between her fingers, he groaned. Copper groaned, too, and tilted her face to the sky as she kneaded her nipples and her breasts.

Tiernan pushed himself to his knees and grabbed her by her hips. "This time we do it my way," he said in a voice husky with lust. "And right now I must taste you." The moment he buried his face against her mound, Tiernan thought she gave the sweetest cry he had ever heard.

Copper never remembered feeling anything like this in any of her sexual experiences. His tongue—goddess, his tongue did wonderful things to her clit. Incredible. He repeated the same motions and he gave low growling sounds as if he were staking his territory.

She couldn't help but watch him as he rubbed his face against her mound and buried his tongue in her folds. His stubble was rough against her soft skin, adding to the intensity of what he was doing to her. Sensation shot from her nipples to her pussy as she continued to pinch and pull them hard. She liked it hard. Liked everything about sex to be rough. Hard and fast.

He paused to look up at her, his face damp with her juices. "I do not think I have tasted anything so fine as you."

"Then don't stop." She dropped her hands from her breasts and slipped her fingers into his still damp hair and pressed his head tight to her tingling flesh. "Dammit, don't stop!"

Tiernan must have sensed her need for roughness because he rubbed his face hard against her pussy and thighs and thrust three fingers into her channel.

When he nipped her clit her climax nearly made her drop to her knees. Her legs wobbled and she had to fist her hands tighter in his hair. Only his firm grip on her hips kept her from falling as her orgasm melted every bone in her body until she felt like a rag doll. He didn't stop licking and sucking until she begged him to. She was barely aware of golden bubbles of light floating around them.

He got to his feet and caught her as she collapsed against his chest. His skin felt hard and warm beneath her cheek and it took a moment to gather herself. When she finally raised her head, he immediately took her mouth, kissing just as roughly as he had licked and sucked her pussy. She tasted herself on his tongue, smelled her juices on his face, and the tingle in her belly magnified, giving her renewed strength. She felt as though she could actually stand on her own two feet.

Copper drew away from him and skimmed her fingers down his chest to his cock. To her satisfaction it was as hard as it had been the first time he'd taken her. She grabbed the waist of his leather pants and tugged them farther down so that his pants rode low on his hips. "I need you out of these."

He cupped her cheek and rubbed his thumb along her jawline. "Godsdamn, you are beautiful."

"The pants." She gave another tug so that they were down around his ass. "Don't try to distract me."

Tiernan backed away and shucked off his boots as she watched. Goddess, was he a cliché. Perfect physique, broad shoulders and chest, and long blond hair that went a little beyond his shoulders. Trim hips and an ass she just wanted to bite—not to mention a cock that had just filled her so well she didn't think she'd ever be satisfied with another man—unless he was hung and built like Tiernan. His thigh muscles worked as he kicked off his pants and she sighed. "Damn, but a guy like you could ruin a girl for other men."

His look was heated as he stepped away from his clothing and brought her up against him. The feel of his flesh against hers, his chest to her breasts, his cock to her belly, his thighs against hers—she thought she'd melt all over again. He kissed her hard before she slipped out of his grasp and slid down his length to her knees.

Tiernan had never met a woman like Copper. He had never wanted a woman as much as he wanted her.

The moment she took his cock and wrapped her fingers around it, he groaned—and when she slipped his erection deep into her mouth he thought he had never felt anything so exquisite in his life.

"Gods, little fire." He fisted his hands tighter in her hair as she moved her mouth and one hand along his length, while using her other hand to stroke his balls. "I am certain I could fuck you all night long."

Copper responded by meeting his gaze with hers and flicking her tongue around the crown of his cock in a slow, sensual movement. Her eyes sparkled with a hint of mischief as she let his erection slip from her mouth and blew softly on the head.

She was going to kill him.

When he growled and brought her face closer to his groin, she gave a soft laugh before taking him deep into her mouth again, as far as she could. She began sucking him in earnest, moving her hand up his shaft at the same time she slid her mouth down him, while fondling his balls. She gave a gentle squeeze as she scraped her teeth along his erection and he almost climaxed.

Tiernan gritted his teeth. The oncoming orgasm was traveling through him like a storm.

The storm broke loose.

Lightning flashed in his mind as his seed shot down Copper's throat. He groaned his release, his hips jerking against her face as she continued to suck him.

With his body still shuddering from his orgasm, he forced her to stop by pulling back at the same time he tugged at her hair to draw her away from him. If she did not stop he was going to collapse into a heap—rather undignified for a warrior.

She gave him a knowing grin before rising. "That good, huh?"

He growled and released her hair to take her by the shoulders and help her stand. "Your teasing will only lead me to fuck you again, woman."

"I damn sure hope so." She tilted her head and he kissed her, a hard kiss full of the insistent desire that would not release him.

He wanted to be gentle with her, but he could not. Just kissing her slammed him with more need and desire than he thought could ever be quenched. How could he feel this way with one woman, a woman he had just met?

But it already felt as though she were a part of him.

Copper woke the next morning with her face against Tiernan's chest, her head tucked under his chin. They were still naked and she reveled in the feel of his bare flesh against hers. His thigh was slung over her hip and, if she wasn't mistaken, he had a full-on morning erection.

She was so sore and it felt so damn good. The man's stamina was incredible—they'd fucked three more times after she'd given him head. She smiled. Maybe it was because he wasn't human. He was a man, but he was a Fae warrior and that obviously gave him more sexual endurance than any man she'd ever met.

Copper breathed deeply of his scent and the incredible sex they'd had. It could be due to the fact she hadn't had sex for over a year, but she had a feeling it was everything about him that made her want him so badly.

What had been really strange was that every time they reached orgasm, it seemed as if some kind of wild magic rocked her world.

Sex magic?

Sex magic could be incredibly powerful, she'd been told. She'd read that in Mrs. Illes's Grimoire, too.

Still cuddled in his arms, Copper skimmed one of her hands down his muscled chest to his taut abdomen, all the way to his cock. He felt so good beneath her palm. She loved the feel of the soft skin of his erection and the steel beneath it.

As soon as she wrapped her fingers around his length, he let out a sleepy groan. She smiled and pushed at his shoulder until he was lying on his back and she was straddling him. There was just enough room in the shelter that she could ride him without bumping her head. With no hesitation, she took his cock and slowly sank onto it and sighed with pleasure.

"Woman, you are all fire," he said as he grasped her small waist with his large hands while she rose up and down on him, taking him deep.

"With you, definitely." She continued riding him in a smooth and steady rhythm as her gaze met his blue eyes. "All I want to do is feel you inside me." She groaned as she felt her climax start to build within her. "And orgasm. Yeah, definitely orgasm."

He gave what looked like a pained smile as his hips bucked up to meet hers and she rode him faster and harder until she gave a cry of sheer pleasure. She saw those golden bubbles in her mind as she climaxed, each one sparkling with every throb of her pussy.

Tiernan gave one last thrust of his cock and groaned as he pulsed inside her. She leaned forward and kissed him before snuggling against his chest, just enjoying the moment. Yes, what she felt with him was magic. Golden bubbles and all.

"Guess we'd better get up," she finally said.

"Must we?" he asked in a teasing tone and Copper gave him another sound kiss.

Her belly rumbled and she laughed. "See? All this sex has made me hungry. We didn't even stop to eat last night."

"Truth be, a D'Danann warrior cannot go long without food." Man, did she ever love his sexy Irish brogue. He helped her roll off him and they climbed out of the shelter into the early morning sunlight.

After they both washed up with the chilly water in the basin, they slipped into their clothing. Fortunately Copper had thought to tuck them into the shelter before they slept or surely the Brownies or Pixies would have stolen them overnight.

To Copper's pleasure, the Faeries had left another large

breakfast that would tide them over for the afternoon, too. Just as she took a bite of an apple tart and Tiernan stuffed a piece of root bread that tasted like pumpkin into his mouth, Riona fluttered around the rock outcropping and landed on the shelf beside the food. Her long hair covered her breasts, but the rest of her was completely bare as usual.

"What's the special occasion?" Copper asked, gesturing to all the food.

The Faerie queen gave a mischievous smile. "The performance last night. I do not think we have seen anything like it in millennia."

A hot flush crept up Copper's neck to her face and she heard Tiernan choke on his bread.

"I can't believe you watched." Copper set her tart down and braced her hands on her hips. "Can't we have a little freaking privacy?"

Riona laughed. "I do believe that yesterday the Fae enjoyed more pleasures than they have since we have been trapped here."

The heat in Copper's cheeks grew as she glared at the Faerie. Before Copper could say anything else, Riona flitted away, leaving behind a small cloud of Faerie dust.

Tiernan snorted back what sounded like laughter and Copper elbowed him. "Just eat, you big lug."

When they finished eating, Copper did her morning workout. Tiernan watched with an expression that said he was either amused or impressed. He leaned against the apple tree while she did her pull-ups using one branch of the apple tree.

"Is this what you have done while you have been in this place?" he asked.

Copper tried not to look at him because he was just too distracting with all that blond hair and those muscles. "I had to stay in shape somehow." She didn't even pant she was in such good shape. She had to keep adding reps just to benefit from the exercises, and always tried to change her routine a bit.

When she finished her pull-ups, she landed lightly on the grass. "Let me guess. All you warriors are built that way and you don't even have to work at it."

He shrugged the shoulder that wasn't against the tree. "We train and spar regularly on the training grounds. The peasants and the lords and ladies of the court do not perform the same activities as the warriors and do not have the same physiques. Very few of us who are of the court are also D'Danann Enforcers."

"Peasants?" Copper picked up a big rock and started doing arm curls with it. Her biceps were well sculpted for a woman, without being overly muscular. She frowned at his comment. "You actually call people *peasants*?"

"Of course." Tiernan pushed away from the tree as Copper switched hands and started working out her other bicep. "That is the way of this Otherworld."

"So you're a lord, are you?" Copper grunted from the strain of working her muscles. "How did you become one?"

Tiernan folded his arms across his chest and widened his stance as he looked thoughtfully ahead. He looked so damn yummy in all that black leather. She especially liked that he wore a sleeveless shirt so that she could see his biceps flex with his movements.

"I was born into the House of Cathal," Tiernan said. "My father has been lord of the house for centuries, and once I am wedded, it will be my responsibility to carry on the family name."

Copper switched arms and started working her other bicep again. Intrigued by the differences in their worlds, she said, "Tell me more about the part of Otherworld where you live."

Tiernan started out by telling her about the D'Danann warriors and how they were a neutral race like the Drow, only the D'Danann were neutral-good, while the Drow tended to be neutral-evil. He frowned at that piece of information.

Copper paused in her exercise. "The Drow, evil?"

"Not exactly," Tiernan said. "They side with whoever, whatever they can benefit from the most."

Copper started working out her left arm again. "Neutral-good, neutral-evil—what does that mean?"

"As far as the D'Danann are concerned," he told her, "the Chieftains will only allow our warriors to assist other races if they believe it is the natural order of things. In the case of the Fomorii in San Francisco, the Chieftains agreed that the D'Danann Enforcers could assist the witches who fight the demons and the Balorites."

"So the Drow tend to assist the side that is evil?" Copper twisted her lips. "I can't imagine Garran and his bunch doing that."

"Possibly," was all Tiernan said in response.

When she asked more about his homeland, he explained how the Dryads had allowed many of the D'Danann to live in the trees, creating huge homes within the enormous tree trunks. The peasants tended to live in huts while the members of the court lived in mansions on the forest ground.

When she asked about the village, he smiled and told her about the vendors, the stores, the pub, and the Pleasure Houses.

At that Copper paused in her biceps exercises. Still holding the rock, she cocked her head. "Um, Pleasure Houses?"

He gave another casual shrug. "It is a place where D'Danann warriors and members of the court can enjoy pleasures of the flesh."

Copper cleared her throat, not sure how she felt about that. "So you've been there a few times."

"Many." He looked so casual, yet a frown furrowed his brow as he added, "My betrothed preferred that I relieve my needs at the Pleasure House rather than with her."

Copper's whole body began to tingle and she felt light-headed. Had she heard him right? "Your *betrothed*?"

Seemingly oblivious to the anger flooding her, Tiernan continued, "Airell and I were to be wed today." He sighed. "However, I postponed the date as a difficult situation has arisen, and I must come up with a solution." He glanced around the meadow. "It is not something I can speak freely about here."

Copper was on fire. Fury surged through her so hot and molten that she almost couldn't see straight. "So you fucked me even though you're supposed to marry another woman," she stated.

The bastard actually looked puzzled. "I—" he started.

"Don't even speak to me." Her arms trembled and she clutched the rock tighter. Goddess, how she wanted to deck him.

With all her might, Copper flung the large rock at the shimmering barrier of their prison. The rock exploded and pieces rained down around them.

After one glance at the look of surprise on his features, she turned her back to him, fisted her hands at her sides, and marched away, trying not to cry from anger. Her piss-off meter had just gone off the charts. If she'd had her wand, Tiernan would be across the meadow, smack up against the bubble's wall.

A thought intruded on her anger. Where was her wand, anyway? She hadn't seen it since she'd washed Tiernan's hair last night.

She almost screamed at that thought. The intimacy, the things they had shared. The sex they'd had.

And the bastard was fucking going to marry some woman in a few weeks.

Tremendous satisfaction filled her as she heard Zephyr's buzz and Tiernan's howl of pain as her familiar had hopefully stung him in the ass.

She hoped it was multiple times and that he couldn't sit for a week.

◆ ◆ ◆

That night Tiernan slept out on the grass and every now and then she heard him give a shout, and she was certain it was the Brownies nipping at him. She hoped the Pixies attacked his hair, too.

The son of a bitch.

He'd tried to talk with her all day long yesterday, but she'd merely given him the finger, a lot of good that did. By the bewildered look on his face he didn't even know the meaning of the offensive gesture. Still she avoided him, as best she could in the freaking confined space.

Copper rolled onto her back and stared up at the rock ceiling of her shelter. It was early morning and she was fighting not to relive the memories of their union.

She let out a shuddering sigh. Was that all it had been to him? A warrior just wanting a good fuck? Of course, she'd more than encouraged him.

She knew she meant nothing to him—they hardly knew one another, for the goddess's sake. They'd only met the day before she'd teased him—and wanted him.

He hadn't made the advances. He'd warned her, and she'd ignored him.

Still, that didn't make it right.

Her gut twisted and she forced those thoughts away. Instead, she recalled her conversation with Riona yesterday and grimaced.

When she had gone to search for her wand by the stream, while ignoring Tiernan, Riona came up to flutter beside Copper. "What are you looking for?" the Faerie queen had asked.

"My wand." Copper had sat back on her haunches and gazed around the meadow. "I left it here yesterday."

"Good luck," Riona had said as she flew back to the clump of flowers and bushes that shaded the mound where the Faeries were currently living. "Garran would like to get you belowground again . . ."

Copper returned to the present and groaned at the thought of what the Faerie queen had insinuated. Garran had her wand. "Great. Just freaking great," she muttered, as she stared at one particularly jagged rock in the ceiling of her shelter.

A shadow briefly blotted out the morning sunlight and immediately she saw that it was Tiernan. He lowered himself so that he was settled with his back against one end of the shelter entrance, his long legs stretched out in front of him, crossed at the ankles, and blocking the doorway. He folded his arms across his chest and stared at her with an unreadable expression.

Copper gritted her teeth as she pushed herself to a sitting position. "I thought I made it clear that I don't want to talk to you."

He studied her for a long moment, his blue gaze captivating hers.

Damn those sexy eyes.

Finally, he said, "I had no intention of hurting or upsetting you."

"I'm not hurt." She raised her chin a notch. "I'm pissed." Okay, so she *was* hurt, she just wasn't going to let him know that.

"You did not allow me to finish, and you have refused to listen to me." Tiernan shifted and crossed his ankles the other way. "We will remain here until I have had my say."

Copper pushed herself up and sat Indian-style. She crossed her arms over her chest. "Get it over with."

"Yes, I am betrothed to a woman of the D'Danann court." He held up his hand to shush her when she opened her mouth to let him have it again. She bit down on her tongue just in time for him to say, "However, I just learned that Airell is carrying another man's child."

Copper's jaw dropped. "Some other guy knocked her up?"

Tiernan gave her a puzzled look, but continued, "When

I first told you of Airell, I did not wish to explain such a matter before the Fae. I do not want her to be humiliated." He leaned his head back against the rock wall behind him and stared into space. "I must find a way to keep her from being marked and cast out of the Fae realm. And a way to keep her lover from being sent to serve the most evil of bastards."

Despite herself, Copper was beginning to soften toward him. "You would do that?"

He sighed so deeply that his shoulders rose and fell with the inhale and exhale. "I do not wish to be wedded to a woman heavy with her lover's child. But neither will I allow the alternative to happen." He still had a faraway look to his gaze. "Somehow I must come up with a solution that will please the court, make Airell and Urien happy, and release me of my vow."

"Do you love her?" Copper asked softly.

Tiernan plucked a thick blade of grass from outside the shelter, held it up, and twirled it between his fingers. "I am over two thousand years older than Airell. I have known her since she was a baby swaddled in blankets and held to her mother's breast." He flicked the grass from his fingers and looked at Copper. "The joining was arranged by my parents and hers when she was born. It was deemed I would wed her after she turned eighteen."

"But do you love her?" Copper asked again. She wasn't sure why she needed to know, but she did.

"Not as a lover or husband would." He pushed his fingers through his blond hair. She noticed a couple of welts from bee stings on his biceps, and she winced at the sight. "I care for her, yes. But I do not love her."

"Then why were you going to marry her?" Copper rubbed the thick bracelet on her wrist.

"Shortly before Airell's birth, the House of Torin had just risen to wealth and power," Tiernan said. "My parents and hers chose to combine forces to become one house.

Together our houses would be powerful enough that they would have the greatest voice on the Council and influence with the Chieftains."

"What about you?" Copper asked. "What did you have to say about all of this?"

He fixed his blue eyes on her. "It was not my decision to make."

"Bullshit." Copper met his gaze head-on as she un-crossed her arms and braced her hands on the grass-and-leaf bedding to either side of her. "You aren't the type of man to be told what to do. Even I can see that."

"It was my duty, my responsibility." His jaw hardened. "I made the vow to join with Airell at my parents' request. To break that vow would be dishonoring Airell and her family, as well as my own."

He rested his head against the rock again. "That is why finding a solution to this situation will prove most difficult. There is no single way that all will be appeased. Someone will be hurt by the choice that I make." He sighed. "If we wed, neither of us will be happy. She loves Urien and I will be raising another man's child. If I refuse to wed her, and it is learned what she has done, she will be marked and banned from the Fae realm, and Urien sent belowground to serve the Drow."

For a moment neither of them said anything. Finally, Copper said, "Sounds like you're stuck between a rock and a hard place."

"That would accurately describe it," he replied after a moment.

Out of habit, Copper started picking at the hem of her vine-and-leaf dress. "So you . . . I was just like one of your pleasure partners."

Tiernan reached forward and cupped her cheek. She wanted to lean into him, oh, how she wanted to. "You will never be that to me," he said softly. "From the first time I saw your photograph I knew you were special."

Copper felt weighted down. Pressure built in her head. She pulled away from his touch and rested her face in her hands so that she couldn't see him.

But he didn't stop touching her. He gently caressed her hair away from her face and she couldn't help an involuntary shiver.

"Copper, let us at least be friends." The way he said her name sounded like a caress. "I want more from you, but I will not take what you do not wish to give."

She raised her head and his fingers trailed down the curve of her neck. "Sex, you mean."

Tiernan let his hand slide down her arm until he no longer touched her. "That and friendship is all I have to offer. All I *can* offer."

One rule of thumb was to never get involved with an engaged or married man, and she'd always followed it. Why, then, was she even thinking of taking him up on it even if he was trying to find a way out of the situation? Sex and friendship. No commitments, just sex and friendship, both sides knowing exactly where they stood.

Copper took a deep breath. "I'll take you up on the friendship thing, but sex . . . you're on your own, buddy." Damn, it killed her to say that.

Ten

San Francisco

To Darkwolf's irritation, Garran, the Drow king of a faction of Dark Elves, smirked as he reclined against a massive wooden leg, called a pile, one of the many pilings supporting the pier. They stood on the rocky shore of the bay, at the base of the abandoned pier where centuries ago the Drow had created an entrance from Otherworld that was hidden from any eyes but their own.

The wind was mild yet chilled, and it carried to Darkwolf the earth-and-moss scent of the Drow king, mixed with Sara's jasmine perfume. Junga and Sara both stood off to the side, watching. Sara had a satisfied expression on her face, while Junga looked surly.

"Are you certain Balor will give us what we want in return for our service?" the king asked, an arrogant tone to his voice. "We wish to once again walk in the light."

Heat rose in Darkwolf's chest like fire and his head ached with Balor's invasion in his mind. The sharp pain was even more intense than usual. The insolent bastard of a Drow would pay one of these days if he continued to express his doubt of Balor. Outwardly, as always, Darkwolf kept his expression unreadable, his emotions hidden.

Junga looked from the warlock to the king, one eyebrow raised as she watched the interplay. Due to the nip in the air, she was wearing form-fitting jeans, a snug sweater, and her hair hung loose about her shoulders. Sara was dressed similarly, but where Junga had a haughty, bitchy look, Sara's was one of confidence—and perhaps a little deviousness, too.

Garran had the bluish-gray skin of the Dark Elves, and silvery-blue hair that reached his shoulders. He wore leather straps that crisscrossed his bare chest, a dagger and sword on a belt slung low about his hips. He was as tall as Darkwolf, but larger in build.

"You shall have it," Darkwolf said. "However, you must deliver the witch, Copper, as well. Balor has relayed to me that he requires her services." *Her blood.* Balor cared only for the powerful witch's blood.

Garran's expression grew fierce. "Copper is *mine*. When all is said and done, I will claim her. I wait only for the door to be discovered and opened, and for her to come to me willingly."

Darkwolf chose not to answer. He also needed Copper to lure the witch Silver to him, but he didn't have time to argue with the Drow. Balor had conveyed to Darkwolf that he needed Silver's or Copper's blood, but Darkwolf refused to kill Silver. He would make use of Copper instead.

Garran's gaze drifted slowly over Junga and Sara. "I have yet to fuck a human. These are both particularly exquisite."

Sara gave a sensual smile.

Junga clenched her human fists at her sides and Darkwolf could tell she wanted to erupt into the powerful demon she was.

"You would be wise to keep your tongue, Drow," she said in a low growl.

The Drow king smiled and a spark literally flashed in

his dark eyes. "A being who is not what it pretends to be, I see." He swung his gaze to Darkwolf's. Junga gave another low growl and Darkwolf saw the demon wavering again, wanting to crawl out of its human shell.

Sara gave a seductive smile and walked up to the king. She ran one finger from the hollow of his throat, over his chest and the leather straps, down to his waistband. "You can fuck me all you want. Take me with you if it pleases you."

Garran laughed and pushed her hand away. "A spy, no doubt."

Sara gave him a little pout. "You would have had the best fuck of your life."

The Drow king grinned and cast his gaze back to Darkwolf. "I will seek you out here on the arranged date." He gave a mock bow before he disappeared into the darkness beneath the pilings of the pier.

Anger burned in Darkwolf at Junga's and Sara's interruption of their meeting. Although Junga was the Fomorii queen, *he* bore Balor's eye. And Sara—he could not believe her insolence . . .

Yet perhaps the warlock seer was even more devious than he had thought. Perhaps she *had* been angling to be a spy, an inside source for Darkwolf once the Drow neared the door.

Darkwolf barely held back a smile. Sara was proving to be far more interesting than he had expected.

Eleven

Otherworld

The still air was almost suffocating as she walked through the dark tunnel again. Yet . . . things were different. Bile rose in her throat and she felt as if she couldn't breathe. Fear.

Deep, penetrating fear.

Senses on fire, she continued to move through the tunnel, holding her wand up to make her way through the dark passageway. Again the darkness seemed to swallow up most of the wand light.

She dropped.

Wind rushed past her face.

This time she landed on her ass and cried out at the sharp pain that shot up her spine. She still gripped her wand tightly in her hand and it illuminated the dank space. She was underground in another passageway, and she had the feeling it must lead to a larger cave.

Were those voices she heard? What about those dark shapes?

She blinked. Nothing was there.

The tunnel felt claustrophobic, as if it were closing in on her while she sat, the passageway becoming smaller and smaller. She scrambled to her feet and started making her way through the cramped tunnel, slightly bent over. She felt the scrape of rock and dirt against her skin and the smell of rotten fish nearly overwhelmed her.

Cobwebs caught in her hair and she brushed them away with her free hand, then wiped the sticky remnants on her jeans. Her copper earrings dangled against her neck. Holding the lit wand in front of her, she moved through the tunnel, pieces of rock crunching under her running shoes.

In the distance she saw something red, and the glow of her wand illuminated it.

She came to a complete stop.

Blood—so much blood.

It rushed down the passageway, coming straight at her.

Copper came awake with a start. She tried to sit up, but Tiernan's arm was draped over her waist, his leg casually flung over her thigh, pinning her down to the floor of the shelter.

She struggled against his hold. With a sleepy mumble he pushed to a sitting position and moved his leg from hers, freeing her so that she could scramble to her knees. She barely missed hitting her head on the rock ceiling. Zeph immediately came to her from his nook of the shelter and she felt his concern.

"What is wrong?" Tiernan rubbed his hand down his face, trying to wipe the remnants of sleep from his mind.

For a moment Copper couldn't talk. She trembled as she looked past him into the meadow that was now the misty gray of predawn. Not long and the sun would be rising. Sounds of crickets met her ears, and she thought she heard the clink of Drow pickaxes deep below the earth, although that was probably her imagination. The arrogant Dark Elves had a tendency to work at night and late into the morning. They still had her wand, damn them. No doubt Garran was keeping it, just waiting for her to come to him.

Tiernan caught her chin and brought her attention back to him. "Nightmare?"

She took a deep breath and rubbed her arms to drive away some of the cold. "I don't know. It could have been a dream-vision. It was so clear, so vivid, like I was *there.*"

He released her chin and dropped his hand to her shoulder and squeezed. "Tell me."

The dreams had been so strange, so intense, so real. But were they just that? Dreams?

Or were they all about something terrible to come?

Copper cleared her throat and told Tiernan everything. She could remember every last detail from all the dreams—the scent of damp earth, the sound of crunching rock beneath her shoes, the feel of cobwebs on her face and hand and the rough texture of her jeans when she'd tried to wipe the cobwebs off. She'd also been wearing a sweater and running shoes, and could recall how they hugged her.

When she finished, Tiernan was studying her intently, his hand still resting on her shoulder. "What do you make of this dream?"

She slowly shook her head. "I think it means we do make it home, because the clothes I was wearing were some of my things left in my apartment. But it also would mean that something bad is going to happen. Something really terrible will be set free—unless it can be stopped."

Copper frowned before she continued. "But the dream keeps changing. I think that could mean it's not set, it's something that could be kept from happening. Maybe it's a warning." She ground her teeth and clenched her hand before adding, "I've *got* to get us back home. I think it's more important than ever that we return. Especially with the threat of Balor."

His gaze remained fixed on her and for a moment the morning silence weighted them down. "Do you wish to sleep any longer?"

"I can't." Copper pinched the bridge of her nose. "Not after that."

He ducked out of their little shelter, and she scrambled out to stand beside him, Zephyr riding on her ear. It was the day following Tiernan's and Copper's "talk," about his situation with his fiancée. Since she'd agreed to still be friends with him, she'd allowed him to sleep in the shelter with her—but no sex. Except that when they first went to bed he hadn't been touching her.

A light smile came to her lips. She couldn't help it. She rather liked waking up with him engulfing her in his embrace.

Over the horizon, through the shimmering shield of their prison, faint pink tendrils of dawn crept through the trees. Mist swirled around her ankles, making her homesick once again. She missed the San Francisco fog.

She sighed. She missed everything.

At the same time, tension had taken hold of her body and she almost shook with the power of it. She *had* to get them home, and soon.

While Tiernan left to relieve himself, she walked to the apple tree and reached up on her tiptoes to snag one of the juicy fruits. It felt smooth and cool in her hand and made a small snapping sound as she pulled it from its branch.

Yesterday, after her talk with Tiernan, Copper had tried another spell to get them out of the meadow, but without her wand she felt off balance and insecure. She'd never been really good at hand-magic. She had to get her wand back from the damned Drow. Problem was, not a single one had come out of their underground home—at least not while she'd been awake—and she hadn't really wanted to make her way down there.

Of course, the mischievous Brownies or Pixies could've taken it, but she didn't think Riona would lead her astray by mentioning the Drow. The queen was a tease, but she wasn't mean-spirited.

When Tiernan had learned that her wand had probably been taken by the Drow, he'd been furious. Copper had simply said she intended to retrieve it and Tiernan went ballistic. He'd ordered her to stay away from the Drow, which had majorly pissed her off. No one, no man, told her what to do. She intended to retrieve it one way or another. She'd been to Garran's realm before. What was the big deal?

Tiernan had been damn lucky she let him sleep in the shelter with her last night.

Still thinking about their conversation, Copper wandered back to the rock outcropping holding the apple. Tiernan had left his dagger in its leather sheath in the shelter. After she retrieved it, she used the sharp blade to cut the apple horizontally. When he came back, she was looking at one half of the apple intently, the other half sitting on one of the rock shelves, the dagger resting next to it.

"Did you know," she said when she looked up at him, "the seeds of an apple are in the shape of a pentagram?" He cocked an eyebrow and she showed him the fruit. "The apple is blessed by the goddess. I have no doubt she put the tree here along with everything else for me."

She gestured around them as she continued, "Why would I have the conveniences of water, food, and Fae friendship for so long if it didn't mean something? I could just as well have been trapped with nothing at all."

He studied the apple half before looking up to meet her gaze. "You believe Anu planned all this?"

Copper sighed. "I've always believed that everything happens for a reason. But for the life of me, I can't figure this one out. Why would I have been placed here when I could have been home fighting beside my family? When I could be home now, trying to stop Balor from being freed. What's the *purpose* of all of this?"

He didn't answer. They leaned against the rock outcropping, ate their apple halves, and watched the sunrise without talking for a long time.

After a while, Copper said, "Are you afraid of anything, Tiernan?" She glanced up at him. "Or are you just the big macho warrior?"

He frowned as he looked down at her. Finally he said, "I have no fear of dying, of performing my duties, living up to my responsibilities, maintaining my honor. That all is a part of my life."

Tiernan looked away from her and continued, "However, I do fear for the lives of my comrades, my people, and yours. We are doing so little when so much more needs to be done." He sighed. "My brethren and my family need me, I fear you and I will never get out of this place."

Copper tossed her half of the core onto a rock for the Brownies. She looked to the sunrise. "I fear a lot of the same things you do. Not getting out of here, not being there to help, and I especially fear for the lives of my family and friends."

She glanced up at Tiernan as she said, "I know Silver struggles with using gray magic more than I do, and that worries me. I'm confident with mine. I have no problem using it, and I know I will never fall over that line into the dark. I just know it." Copper frowned as she thought about her sister. "But gray magic . . . it wears Silver out. I'm afraid for her when she uses it. I know she would never turn to black magic, but it's so hard on her."

Her heart crept into her throat. "I always fear losing someone important to me . . . again. If I had used gray magic when I was young, I would have been able to save my friend Trista's life." Her thoughts traveled far away as she remembered that dark night when her friend had been raped and murdered in a park near their Salem, Massachusetts, home. Copper had fought off the attackers using white magic, but by the time she had succeeded, it had been too late for Trista, who was human and unable to protect herself.

Copper balled her fists at her sides, seeing Trista's lifeless body in her mind. "If only I had used gray magic, Trista would still be alive."

"There was nothing you could do." Tiernan's calming voice broke into the memories of that horrid night. "And you will see her again in Summerland."

"I know we're supposed to believe that we go on to Summerland when we pass," Copper whispered. "But what if there is no Summerland? What if my loved ones aren't there waiting for me?" Her voice caught. "What if Mother isn't there now? And Trista?"

Tiernan caught her by the chin, forcing her to look up at him, and smiled. "That is one fear you can safely set aside. Summerland awaits us all, and those we love *will* be waiting."

"If you say so." Copper offered him a half-smile as his fingers slid away from her chin. "So what about your dreams?" She swallowed back the feelings of pain and loss. "Even though you've lived so long, are there still things you dream about doing, having, experiencing?"

He was quiet again. She could practically see the wheels spinning in his head as he contemplated her question. "There is not much I have not done, but one thing I have never had is a wife and children. Yes, I have dreamed of having a family, especially children of my own."

A lead weight settled in Copper's belly. "And now the woman you're supposed to marry is pregnant with another man's child."

Tiernan gave a great sigh. "Adopting a child is a special thing, but knowing that your wife is in love with another man, and knowing who the father is . . ."

Copper took his hand and squeezed it. When he looked down at her, she gave him a little smile. "You'll think of something. It'll all work out."

He looked down at her, his blue eyes, intense, focused. "I hope you are right, little fire."

The use of the nickname warmed Copper's insides and she had to force herself to drop his hand. "What if you don't figure something out?" she asked softly.

A weight seemed to press on Tiernan's chest. "Then I will raise the child as if he were my own and will treat him no different than any of my other children." He stared off into the distance. "Airell will bear my babes, and she will be forbidden to see Urien."

He looked down at her. "Do you wish for children?"

Copper shifted against the rock. "I've never been in any hurry to have kids, but I guess that one day I will, and I know I will love them as much as my parents have loved me and my sister." She tilted her head back and the stone felt rough behind her head. "As far as other dreams . . . I want to teach kids, I like kids a lot. Probably teach high school kids because I also want to coach the girls' softball team."

Copper pursed her lips before saying, "Like you, duty and honor is important to me, too. My duty is to serve the goddess Anu and my Coven. The hard part is that I believe strongly in using gray magic to fight evil, and my Coven and father don't. It's a really tough thing. I don't like doing something they don't feel is right, but I need to stay true to myself, too, you know?"

"Sometimes we have no choice but doing what is expected of us," Tiernan said quietly.

She looked up at him. "I think we do have a choice. We can't live our lives for others all the time. We have to do what we feel is right, too."

Copper gave a heavy sigh. "As far as dreams . . . right now I dream of home. Being back with my family, back where I belong."

He caught her hand in his and squeezed. It felt warm and reassuring and for some reason gave her hope that they would be able to return home soon.

♦ ♦ ♦

Tiernan was a grouchy ass as he again tried to find a way through the barrier. He snarled at any being that came near him, and he even snapped at Copper more than once.

She took great satisfaction in the frizziness of his hair and the number of Pixie designs springing from it. The green-skinned imps did something different with his hair every time he worked his way around the barrier, but always topped their creations with pretty blooms.

While Tiernan stomped around, Copper knew she had to take action to get her wand back. There was no way around it. She'd have to go belowground.

Her familiar was off playing somewhere with the Faerie children again. She thought about bringing the honeybee. His temper and his stinger could come in very handy.

"Zephyr!" she called, but the bee didn't come to her, even after a few calls. "Must be in the Faerie mound with the kids," Copper murmured. For some reason their connection didn't work so well when Zeph was with the Fae.

Riona fluttered down to land on Copper's shoulder. "Maybe you should take the D'Danann oaf," the Faerie said, nodding her dainty little head in the direction Tiernan was now cursing.

"I don't need him." Copper took a deep breath and stomped on the stone door. "I've been there and back before, so what's the big deal? I can handle this myself."

"If you think it is wise." Riona flapped her little wings and hovered above Copper. "But I am not the one Garran wants."

Copper gritted her teeth at the scraping sound of the door slowly easing open from Drow magic. "Are you trying to warn me or something?"

"Never." Riona gave a soft laugh and zipped away.

Torches sprang to life as she made her way down the staircase and the door closed above her. Once again when she reached the bottom of the stairs she was met by Naal, but this time a different warrior accompanied him.

Copper tipped her head up to look at Naal as they walked across the great hall. She liked his mischievous grin and his sanguine personality.

When they reached the throne room, Naal and the other Drow stood to either side of the doorway while Copper walked through the beautiful sparkling room toward Garran. He sat at an angle in his throne, his long legs stretched out and crossed at the ankles, with one elbow resting on the throne's arm while he rubbed his chin with his fingers. He was as handsome as ever with his silver-blue hair and powerful build.

"Copper, my love," he said with his rogue's grin. "Surely this time you have come to serve as my queen."

"Get real." Copper stared at him in exasperation, then glanced to the seat beside him where her wand rested. "You know exactly what I want."

Garran cocked an eyebrow. "So direct, Copper. I should be insulted by your lack of decorum."

She almost rolled her eyes. "I need my wand back. It's important to me."

The Drow king pushed himself out of his seat and was in front of her in a single step. Shock rocked her at the speed of his movement. She had to look way up to meet his eyes. His expression was fierce as he reached out, caught a lock of her hair, and wrapped it around his finger.

His voice came out low and gruff and his liquid silver eyes swirled with passion. "What price are you willing to pay, witch?"

Tiernan shouted and growled as he made attempt after attempt to breach the barrier surrounding the meadow. He did not like this helpless feeling, not at all.

When he'd had enough of testing the barrier, he kicked

off the six or so Brownies nipping at his knees, and batted the Pixies away from his hair. He slipped the leather lace from his neck opening.

He drew back his hair along with whatever creations the Pixies had managed to make in it. When his hair was tied, he plucked out pink and yellow flowers, hoping he got them all. This time he hadn't heard any laughter coming from the Faeries or Copper. No doubt the Fae had had their fun the last time and were just waiting to pull some other trick on him.

He frowned. Where was Copper?

Riona, the Faerie queen, zipped up to flutter before him. She had a small perfect body with full breasts and rounded curves. Her black hair tumbled down her back and her amethyst eyes held laughter, as usual.

He scowled at her. "What do you want?"

"More like, what do you want, great D'Danann warrior?" Riona flapped her wings, lavender dust glittering in the afternoon light.

Tiernan resisted swiping his hand at her to get her out of his way. "I am not interested in your games, Faerie."

She hovered in the air, tapping her tiny chin with her finger. "Perhaps you are interested in Copper?"

He frowned. She laughed.

"I don't think the Drow will give her up so easily." She zipped away, and then she was gone from sight.

"What?" Tiernan bellowed. When the Faerie didn't respond, he searched the meadow with his gaze. There were perhaps three places Copper could be. Behind the bushes of the Fae mound, behind the side of the rock outcropping they used when needing to relieve themselves, and the shelter itself. Ah, yes, a fourth—the side of the rocks that she avoided, where the Drow door was located.

To his increasing concern, she was nowhere to be found in the usual places. He stormed to the side of the rock outcropping he had only been by in passing when he was searching the barrier. He stared at the flat gray rock on the ground that was shadowed by a pine tree. It was, of course, a door leading to the Drow realm. There were similar doors all over Otherworld. No doubt the Faerie Riona hadn't been lying when she said something about the Drow not giving up Copper.

Shit. What in the name of the Underworld was she doing with the Drow? His chest burned. It was usually not an easy task to return from the realm of the Dark Elves.

He knelt beside the door that lay flat on the ground and rubbed his fingers around it, trying to find a catch. He felt nothing but smooth rock. The door was sealed tightly within its stone frame, which was as he expected. The more he searched, the more the knot in his gut grew. With all his strength he tried tugging and pulling at the frame, but it didn't budge. He sat heavily on the ground and wiped sweat from his forehead with the back of his hand.

"Perhaps you need my assistance now, D'Danann?" came Riona's tinkling voice as she fluttered before him. "Or are you too much the arrogant warrior to need help? You certainly have not asked the Fae or even Copper to assist you in any way."

Tiernan ground his teeth as he glared at the Faerie queen. "How do I get to Copper?"

She placed her hands on her thighs and leaned forward. "Pretty please?"

A low growl rose up in his chest. "Riona . . ."

She shrugged. "If not, then—"

"Pretty please," he shouted, and Fae giggles rose up from the other side of the rock outcropping.

Riona gave an amused grin. "Stomp on the door five times. Do not expect a warm welcome."

Tiernan pushed himself to his feet and ignored the Faerie as he raised his boot and pounded on the door.

The Faerie queen zipped in front of him as he backed away, and she gave him a small pout. "Not even a thank-you?"

"Thank you, Queen Riona," he snapped, then riveted his attention on the now moving door. Stone rumbled as it opened and a hollow sound rose up from below. When the door was fully open, he strode down into the darkness.

Copper resisted the urge to push Garran away as he tugged on her lock of hair. It wasn't that she found him distasteful. Actually, she found him quite sexy. But she wanted to put some distance between them.

She straightened her spine and tilted her chin, stretching to her full height, but she was still a good eight inches shorter than him. "What do you want, Garran?"

He drew her closer by pulling the lock of hair. He caught her off guard and she stumbled forward, and barely caught herself by bracing her hands against his bare chest. Muscles rippled beneath her palms. The king drew her close and wrapped his arms around her waist so that her body was flush with his. Heat rose to her cheeks when she felt his very large—obscenely large—erection pressing against her belly.

"You are the light to my dark," he murmured. "You have something magical in your spirit, a purity in your heart. I would give you everything."

Copper swallowed. "Just tell me what I have to do to get my wand back."

"A kiss." He lowered his head until she could feel his warm breath upon her skin. "I want a kiss and you shall have your toy."

Copper pushed harder at his chest and leaned back as far as she could. Not a Drow kiss! A kiss from one of the Dark Elves could make another being wish to stay below-ground with the Drow.

But it was only a kiss and she was a witch, immune to

much Fae magic. Yet she didn't know if she'd be able to resist the power. What if she fell under his spell?

His lips neared hers and she caught his earthy scent. "Just a kiss, my fair one," he murmured, a breath away from her lips.

Only a kiss. Only a kiss.

"You promise that I can have my wand?"

His mouth quirked into a grin. "Of course."

Copper's hands gripped his leather and gem-encrusted chest straps. "You promise you'll let me go?"

His gaze grew heavy-lidded, almost obscuring the liquid silver of his eyes. "If you still wish to leave."

She couldn't help but tremble in Garan's arms. "No magic," she managed to whisper.

He lowered his head. "Mmmm." The sound rumbled in his chest just before he pressed his mouth to hers.

When Tiernan reached the bottom of the staircase, Drow guards stood to either side of the doorway that led into an enormous great hall. One of the Elves had black hair, the other's was silver.

Tiernan glared from one Drow to the other. "Where is Copper?"

The silver-haired Drow's expression didn't waver. "Rudeness will not get you an audience with the king, if that is what you wish."

Tiernan blew out a long breath and tried to calm himself. If the Drow used any magic on Copper, it would be hell trying to get her out of here. "Please take me to your king," he said.

"Come." The Drow gestured to one of the archways across the hallway and then the two males began walking to either side of Tiernan.

Surprise filtered through him that they so easily granted him an audience with their king. Drow tended to be far more disagreeable and did not like Fae in their realm. They hadn't even requested he remove the weapons belt that secured his sword and dagger.

When they reached the crystal chamber, Tiernan strode into the throne room and came up short.

Copper was kissing the Drow king. Her arms were around his neck, her body snug against his, her eyes closed.

Rage rose up within Tiernan. That anyone, any being, would kiss Copper was enough to send molten fury rushing through his veins. He drew his sword. When the two guards grabbed his arms, he struggled against the power of their hold on him. *"Copper!"* he shouted as he fought to get away from the damnable Drow.

Her eyelids fluttered open and she jerked back from the Drow she had been kissing. Her face blushed crimson, and the Faerie kisses sprinkled across her nose stood out against the red of her cheeks. The copper pentagrams at her ears swung wildly with her movement.

The Drow king glanced up at Tiernan who still struggled to reach him. Amusement crossed the king's expression. "Copper may choose to leave or she may stay. You will not have a say in it, D'Danann."

Copper took one look at the fury etched across Tiernan's face and almost laughed. It was so obvious he was jealous, even though he might have to marry some other woman.

The arrogant ass deserved a little taunting. As did Garran, who was just as arrogant and just as much of an ass, so assured that his magic would bind her.

She turned back to Garran and ran her finger from his collarbone, over the crisscross leather straps to his belly and to the waistband of his breeches. Her tongue darted out to touch her lower lip. "What would you do with me if you had me?" she said in a husky purr.

A rumble sounded in Garran's chest. "I would fuck you

until you could not take any more, and then I would fuck you again."

Tiernan nearly roared. "And I will kill you where you stand, Drow!"

She tossed a look over her shoulder at the D'Danann and barely held back a grin. Her lashes fluttered again as she brought her gaze back to Garran's. His earth-and-moss scent was even stronger as she raised herself up on her tiptoes, nuzzled the line of his jaw, and moved her lips to his ear. She actually felt him shiver.

"Sorry, baby," she murmured, then drew back. "You got your kiss, and you promised me my wand and my way out of here."

Garran looked taken aback, but then smiled. "I didn't promise that the D'Danann could leave."

Copper frowned and tried to push him away. "No fair, Garran."

He cocked an eyebrow and his silver eyes glittered with amusement. "Who said I was fair, love?"

"Damn you." She pushed at his chest and this time he released her. He didn't stop her when she snatched her wand up from the chair beside him.

"What will you give me to set him free?" he said with a look to Tiernan and then back to her again.

Copper pointed her wand at his chest. "Release him or I—I'll spell your lips shut."

Garran pushed the wand away and cocked an eyebrow. "Do you think a human witch's inferior magic could harm me?"

The tips of Copper's ears burned. She backed up and pointed her wand again at Garran. "Let him go!"

Power rose up within her just as the ground began to rock.

A tremendous rumbling noise came from beneath their feet, like a massive hammer against stone.

The room shuddered. Copper lost her footing.

She stumbled backward and found herself in Tiernan's arms. Tiernan held her as great chunks of crystal rained down from the ceiling and one icicle-sized shard just missed grazing Copper's cheek.

Garran and the other Drow shouted and barely kept to their feet as they bolted from the room. Tiernan grabbed Copper's hand and they followed.

It was no better outside the royal chamber. Rocks, some the size of boulders, loosened from above and slammed into the floor of the great hall. From below came one thundering pounding noise after another. Other Drow were shouting and joining Garran and his guards. They disappeared through a far doorway, brandishing their swords.

Tiernan and Copper dodged the massive rocks as the boulders fell, and headed for the stairway that would lead them out and back to the meadow.

It was blocked by a wall of dirt and rocks.

The room continued to shake and shudder with the tremendous pounding noise. Tiernan still had a tight grip on Copper's hand as they ran toward the doorway the Drow had disappeared through. Dirt filled her mouth and her nose, and her body ached from the small stones that hit her.

When they made their way across the hall and through the Drow doorway, a great bellow came from below, and again another sound, like a massive hammer against stone. The passageway they were in must have been reinforced because only smaller rocks fell from above and tumbled down the walls, and dust filled the tunnel.

Even so, Copper didn't want to be in the tunnel. She wanted out, wanted to be able to breathe without choking on dust. It felt as if the walls were closing in on her. And it reminded her too much of her dreams.

When they finally made it out of the passageway, Copper and Tiernan came up short, and she gasped. Down in the mine pit Garran had taken her to, perhaps two stories below, was the biggest creature Copper could ever imagine seeing. Its skin was bark brown, it had long stringy brown hair, its eyes were brilliant green, and drool gushed from its mouth. It was hunchbacked with great jagged, mossy green teeth.

In one hand the giant beast held a shield as big as a garage door. In his other he wielded a club the size of a two-seater airplane, and was smashing it into the side walls. The arrowheads from Drow arrows were exploding on contact. The arrows stuck out of the giant's huge head like tiny toothpicks and blood poured from the wounds.

Heart pounding, she saw Garran in the midst of the battle, shouting commands. Naal, his brother and first in command, directed another troop of the Drow. Her heart leaped in her throat when she saw a Drow bashed up against the wall hard enough to sever his head. As his body dropped, it vanished in sparkles of obsidian.

Copper observed all this in just a fraction of time before looking back at Tiernan.

He was gone.

She whipped around to the other side of her and saw Tiernan holding his sword as he rushed down the cavern path to where the Drow were fighting the giant.

"No!" she shouted, her heart pounding so hard now she could hear it in her ears. He couldn't take on such a beast with a sword!

In the next moment Tiernan's wings unfolded from his back and he launched himself into the air.

Despite the pounding of her heart, Copper couldn't help but think how magnificent Tiernan looked, his great wings spread as he soared around the cavern like a great eagle. He held his sword at the ready, as if looking for the best angle to attack the giant.

The huge animal-like beast spotted Tiernan and swung its club at the warrior. Tiernan deftly dodged it, and flew even closer to the giant's face. The creature roared and swiped at him with his shield. This time Copper screamed

Tiernan's name as the giant came inches from hitting him.

At the same time Tiernan distracted the giant, the Drow continued their attack, more wounds bloodying its body as Elvin arrows exploded in its flesh. The giant stumbled as great rocks that were flung from the catapults slammed into him.

Copper tried to think of some kind of spell that would help. A thought came to her in a flash. She magnified the glow of her wand and pointed it so that the glare momentarily blinded the giant.

She barely saw Tiernan through the brilliance of the light as he dived toward the head of the giant. Her heart stuttered as he swooped down and drove his sword into one of the beast's brilliant green eyes.

The giant screamed and flailed. More rock rained from the ceiling.

Tiernan's blood boiled as he buried his sword in the beast's eye. No doubt this was one of the great giants of Underworld, of the kind Owain and his giant lion had fought to the death centuries ago. The giants were beasts, truly no more than animals, used as guards at crossing points to Otherworlds. What was such a creature doing this close to the surface of this Otherworld?

The beast started swinging its club toward Copper where she wielded such powerful light with her wand. Tiernan's blood pounded in his ears as he drew his dagger and flipped it through the air, end over end. The dagger buried itself into its target, the beast's other pupil.

The giant screamed and screamed, blindly spinning around with the dagger and sword jutting out from its huge eyes. It swung its club again and nipped Tiernan at his chest, the power of the momentum slamming Tiernan against a cavern wall. He caught himself before he tumbled to the cavern floor and soared back into the air, his chest aching and his breathing coming in harsh gasps.

With a great bellow, the beast dropped its shield and club to reach up to its eyes to pull out the sword and dagger.

The Drow attacked in full force, taking advantage of the giant's blindness and the fact that its hands were now empty of shield and club.

Copper's wand light dimmed, surely to keep from blinding the warriors.

Tiernan spread his wings and flew down to the center of the mine to join the rest of the Drow. He flew over a huge pit from which the beast must have emerged. Tiernan circled until he landed in a crouch. He drew his wings back in, and watched the beast at the same time his gaze searched the room for a loose sword.

The giant ripped both of Tiernan's weapons from its eyes and flung them to the rock floor with a clatter that was nearly lost in the roars of the Drow as they attacked. The beast tried to reach for its shield and club again, but was blinded from Tiernan's weapons' having pierced its pupils.

Tiernan spotted his sword gleaming in the rubble. He dived for it and barely avoided a swinging fist as he snatched up the weapon.

When his feet touched the soil, as one he and Garran bolted for the giant's feet. With a broadsword, Garran slashed one of the tendons above the giant's heel at the same time Tiernan sliced the other.

The giant bellowed again, the sound so loud the walls shuddered and more rock rained from the ceiling.

Both Tiernan and Garran rushed to get away from the flailing giant. Tiernan took to the air and Garran bolted with the legendary Elvin speed.

The beast wavered, its body swinging forward. Then back. Forward again.

With a bellow that rang through the chamber and caused more rock to fall, the giant slammed to its side on the rock floor.

Even as the blind giant tried to push itself up, the Drow slit its massive throat. It took several warriors to hack at its neck. Deep brown blood spurted and gushed from the wounds.

Copper's stomach churned and she held her hand over her mouth. She could barely hold back the bile rising in her throat.

All the while the giant struggled, knocking Drow from their feet with its huge arms and sending them flying. One of its fingers nearly hooked Tiernan, but he swung his sword down in a huge arc and cut the giant's finger off.

Finally, the giant gave one last shudder and stilled.

For a moment the Drow, Tiernan, and Copper were silent, watching blood flow from the giant's throat like a river gushing over a waterfall. Eventually the bleeding lessened until it was but a trickle.

Garran and Naal climbed over the rubble and approached Tiernan. The Drow king had a stoic expression on his face. When he reached Tiernan, Garran held out his arm, and they clasped one another's forearms at the elbow in the handshake of old.

"Thank you, brother," Garran said with a deep nod. "You are free to go."

"You better believe he is," Copper grumbled from above. "Let's get the hell out of here."

After the Drow helped to free the passageway so that Tiernan and Copper could leave, Tiernan was so angry with Copper he did not speak to her until they were through the Drow door and out into the sunlight.

He was sweating and covered in blood. Dirt streaked both his and Copper's clothing and faces. His breathing was harsh and his blood pumped in his veins like fire, from the rush of adrenaline that continued to flood him.

The moment the door closed behind them, Tiernan took her by the shoulders. "What in the gods' names were you thinking? First of all, you could have been killed by that giant, and secondly, you could have been bespelled by the Drow king."

Copper pushed his hands away and glared right back at him. "I was doing just fine till you arrived. I would have been out of there before that giant attacked if you hadn't come down and caused a freaking scene and delayed us."

Heat blazed through him. "You were kissing a gods-damn Drow."

He swore he saw the corner of Copper's mouth quirk, as if she were amused. "Jealous?"

Tiernan scowled. Jealous? Of course not, not with this maddening woman. Yet the sight of her kissing the Drow had sent fury through him, fury that he could not explain. Even the thought of it made him want to punch the bastard.

"Do you have any idea what could have happened to you?" he shouted instead of voicing the thoughts raging in his mind. "You could have been spelled. Then you could have been kept by the Dark Elves forevermore!"

"I was." Copper placed her hands on her hips. "Spelled, that is. At least a little. But I'm a witch and it had little effect on me. Not that it's any concern of yours."

Tiernan growled. He found himself wanting to shake her again.

That or kiss her.

The thought of kissing her again, the image of his lips on hers, chased every other word out of his mind. He was almost relieved when she whirled and strode back around the stone outcropping until he couldn't see her anymore.

He sucked in a deep breath between his teeth. Testing the barriers while trying to find a way out of this prison must have roasted his brains.

Twelve

By the time a couple of weeks had passed, Tiernan was certain he was stuck with the most illogical, maddening, impulsive, fiery being he had ever known. Worse than her sister by far.

From the beginning she had vexed him. Her impulsivity toward the Drow and not taking them and their actions seriously; her use of gray magic that far exceeded Silver's; the fact she would throw herself in the line of fire to save others, as she had when she used her shield to save him; the way she unintentionally teased him sexually, yet denied him what they both wanted; the way she argued with him about most everything.

And that damnable bee familiar had stung him no less than six times in the ass since he had been trapped with Copper.

His need for her was driving him out of his mind. To wake with her every morning in his arms, yet not actually be able to touch her the way he wanted to, was the most incredible torture.

His need to get back to help the other D'Danann became more intense every day. He wished he knew what was happening. He had to assist them and rid that world of the damned Fomorii before the demons and the warlock accomplished their goal and freed Balor.

And he sincerely wanted to unite Copper with her sister because it was so important to Copper.

This day he had just finished testing the barrier again and had tied his hair and Pixie creation back away from his face. It was close to noon. He was hungry—there was never enough food in this damnable place and he was heartily sick of apples—and had the desire to slam his fist into something. Gods, would they ever make it out of this prison? What he wouldn't give to be back in his home in Otherworld.

He frowned. His handfasting with Airell was not long in coming, and he had yet to determine a solution that would be to everyone's satisfaction.

It was not possible. No matter what choice he made, someone would suffer.

Yet, how could he wed a woman heavy with another man's child? But he would not allow her to be disgraced, marked, banished from the Fae realm.

Somehow, someway, he would work this out.

When he came back to the center of the meadow after tying his hair and braids back, he saw Copper climbing up and disappearing into the branches of the apple tree.

"What in the name of Underworld are you—" he started as he stood under the tree and looked up.

Tiernan couldn't speak anymore. He couldn't even think. He was directly under Copper and could see clearly beneath her vine-and-leaf dress.

As she climbed up the tree, her ass and her sex were bared for his eyes. Her smooth, curved buttocks and the copper-colored patch of curls between her thighs.

His mouth grew dry and his cock swelled against his leather breeches. His hands itched to touch her. His body ached to slide between her thighs again, to drive his cock deep inside her warmth.

He shook his head. Being trapped with this woman was definitely making him addled. Yet every minute he spent in Copper's presence made him want her even more.

Lust, he told himself, *it is merely lust.*

He forced himself to move away from beneath the tree so that he could no longer see her. "Get down," he commanded, folding his arms across his chest. "You could fall and injure yourself."

"Oh, get a grip," came her muffled voice from inside the tree.

He had to resist the urge to go back under the tree where he could watch her make her way farther up and then down again. He broke out in a sweat, unable to stop visualizing her buttocks, the tender flesh of her folds, and the soft red curls between her thighs.

He'd take her from behind, gripping those ass cheeks in his hands as he watched his cock slide in and out of her wetness. And then he'd turn her over, slide between her thighs so that he could suck her nipples as he fucked her until she climaxed over and over and over.

Tiernan's cock throbbed beneath his tight leather breeches, and he cupped himself, trying to ease the discomfort. His need to take her again had increased tenfold. He gritted his teeth. He did not know how much more he could take of being around this beautiful, sensual, maddening woman.

He heard a rustle coming from the tree, two thuds and a *damn* as two of the reddest, most perfect apples fell to the ground. A few more rustles and Copper swung down from a lower branch one-handed and landed easily on her feet.

She gripped her wand tight in one hand as she scooped up the two apples. She'd taken to carrying her wand everywhere with her, afraid that one of the mischievous beings in the bubble would make off with it. As she retrieved the apples, her dress hiked up and showed her upper thighs.

"Better eat these now." She straightened and presented Tiernan with an apple.

He scowled as he took the apple, focusing on his anger instead of his cock. "Do *not* climb the tree again. You could have fallen."

An annoyed expression crossed Copper's face. "Get over yourself, Tarzan."

She tried to brush past him, but he dropped the apple and caught her by her arms. "I am quite serious, Copper."

Annoyance turned into an outright glare. She yanked her arms away. "You don't tell me what to do. That's it. That's all there is to it."

She pushed past Tiernan, grumbling all the way to the shelter, and he heard the words *arrogant, controlling,* and *jerk.*

He didn't know what made him do it, but something burned within his body, something more than anger, more than concern for her safety.

In a few strides he reached her at the rock outcropping. She whirled around with fire in her eyes, but he backed her up against the wall of smooth boulders. He braced his hands on the rock to either side of her face. She dropped her apple and placed her free palm against his chest, as if to shove him away—

He took her mouth with a rough and angry kiss.

Copper caught her breath in surprise and her mouth parted, giving him the opportunity to slip his tongue into her warmth as he assaulted her with his kiss.

In the next second Copper was kissing him back with the same fiery intensity, putting her own anger, her own frustration into it. She slid her hands from his chest to his shoulders and wrapped her arms around his neck. Her wand poked him in the back of the head.

She tasted so sweet and smelled of apples, cinnamon, and woman. Whereas before his kiss was punishing, now it grew into something passionate, sensual, and needy. He groaned as she slipped her tongue into his mouth, demanding as much as he was taking.

Copper clamped her legs around his hips and pressed herself tight against him and his erection. His cock was raging to thrust into her right up against this rock wall, to take her now, to take her hard. To possess her. To own her.

He grasped her buttocks, turned them both away from the rock, moved to the center of the clearing, and sank onto his knees in the thick grass where he laid her on her back. She dropped her wand and it rested in the grass beside her.

He braced himself above her, his breathing hard, sweat dripping down his face, his erection pressed tight between her thighs. She was so beautiful beneath him, her mouth slightly parted, lips swollen from his kiss, her eyes heavy-lidded with desire, and her beautiful hair tousled.

A glint was in her cinnamon eyes as she looked up at him. "I can't help it, but I want you so bad," she said in a husky voice. "Is it really okay to do this? What if you can't find a solution and you have to marry Airell?"

Tiernan pressed his lips to her forehead. His arms trembled with the passion wound up within him and the force it took to control himself. He gently brushed his mouth over her soft skin, and she sighed.

"I will find a way, little fire." He pressed a kiss to her nose. "I will find a way."

He raised his head, and his gaze met hers. He saw nothing short of raw desire—and need. Need for him.

"All right." He was powerless to stop her as she took one of his hands, brought his fingers to the lower edge of her leaf-and-vine tunic, and pressed his palm against her bare mound.

All thought fled his mind as she moved her lips to his, kissing him with such intensity that he groaned into her mouth. She slipped her soft tongue through his lips and he couldn't stop himself from sliding his fingers deep into her wetness at the same time.

Copper moaned and moved her hips, riding his fingers as he rubbed her taut clit and then delved into her wet channel.

His head was spinning from the incredible kiss, from the feel of her soft body against his, the scent of her woman's musk. Had it been like this the first times they joined? This time seemed even more passionate, more fiery.

Copper grew wilder in his arms. She bit his bottom lip and he groaned again. She brought her palm to his shoulder and pushed him flat on his back. She ended up on top of him, straddling him. She pulled away from the kiss, rose up, and rode him, her bare folds pressed against his leather-clad cock. At the same time, she pulled her vine dress over her head and tossed it aside on the grass beside the apple tree.

He held her slim hips as she arched her back, her face tilted to the sky, her hands on her breasts as she tugged on her nipples. He'd never seen a more beautiful sight. Her breasts were small and firm, her body smooth and taut. Her copper-colored hair brushed her shoulders as she rode him through his breeches, and the sun made soft gold highlights in her tresses.

Copper lowered her face and looked at him, her cinnamon eyes devouring him. She released her breasts and braced her hands to either side of his head.

She kissed him again, a hungry kiss like she'd never get enough. He was certain he would not. He had to have her, all of her.

Copper stole her lips from his, dragging her mouth along his stubbled jaw, shimmying down his body as she gently bit the skin at the place where his neck met his shoulder, then licked the spot with her tongue.

She moved down farther, kissing the hollow at the base

of his throat, then the skin visible through the loose ties of his tunic. "Goddess, you taste good," she murmured, her voice husky and needy.

Tiernan wanted his clothing off, wanted bare skin against bare skin, but he sensed her need to be in control, and he would indulge her—this time.

Copper eased her way down to his breeches and began unfastening the ties. She released his cock, and her small fingers wrapped around it. Her lips slid over his erection.

"Gods," he nearly shouted as he felt the heat of her warm mouth sheathe his cock.

He grasped her hair in his palms, feeling the silky strands slide through his fingers as she moved up and down his erection and moved her hand in time with her mouth.

All blood, all thought, all awareness, was centered on his cock and the woman who was driving him out of his mind.

His orgasm began to build and build within him and her eyes urged him on. Gold bubbles rose up from her and floated down to seep into Tiernan's body to become flickering flames of desire that traveled straight to his cock. The intensity of the magic was too much. He gripped her hair, his bollocks tightened, and his hips bucked against her face.

He came in a long hard rush. His orgasm was beyond comprehension. Black spots danced behind his eyes along with the gold bubbles of Copper's magic. His body jerked against her face as she continued to suck him, drawing all of his seed into her mouth.

He grasped her head in his hands, forcing her to stop. "Are you trying to kill me, witch?" he managed to get out between each breath.

Copper raised her head and licked her lips, that mischievous spark in her eyes. "Is it working?"

Tiernan raised himself just enough to grasp her under her arms and draw her up so that he could kiss her. Gods, how he loved the way she kissed.

Another moan rose up in Copper's throat as she slipped her tongue between Tiernan's lips. He'd tasted so good when he came in her mouth. She'd wanted him and wanted him, and goddess help her, she had to have him.

Her mind whirled as he rolled over and she found herself on her back in the damp grass with Tiernan between her thighs, his hands braced to either side of her body. He smelled so good—of male musk and leather. She felt his still-free cock against her pussy. To her pleasure, he was hardening again. Damn, but these warriors had incredible stamina. And damn, how she ached to have him deep inside her.

Tiernan continued to kiss her, his leather-clad body rough against her naked skin, the stubble on his jaw chafing her face. It felt naughty and sexy that he was still clothed while she was entirely naked. She squirmed beneath him, needing him, wanting him.

He released her mouth to trail his lips along the line of her jaw to her ear. He flicked his tongue inside and she shivered when he bit her earlobe.

"My little fire," he murmured in her ear. "You drive me insane."

"Then take me." She gripped his soft leather shirt in her fists. "Fuck me."

"When I am ready," he said as he moved his mouth to the sensitive spot just behind her ear.

Copper shivered as he worked his way down and his tongue danced between her breasts.

She arched her back. "Suck my nipples. Now."

He gave a soft laugh and brought his hands to her breasts and squeezed them, causing her nipples to rise into high peaks, so close to his lips.

Instead of taking one taut bud into his mouth, he blew warm breath over her nipple. She gasped at the sensation and he moved to her other breast and released his warm breath over it.

Copper linked her hands behind his neck and tried to force him closer. The maddening man only raised his head and looked into her eyes. His gaze was hungry, fierce, and she bit her lower lip at his feral expression.

"If you don't behave I *will* make you wait, woman," he growled in that deep Irish brogue of his that made her so hot.

He commanded as if used to wielding authority. Well, she might let him this time, because she needed him so badly, but next time . . .

She couldn't think anymore because Tiernan started circling one of her nipples with his hot tongue. The rosy skin puckered beneath his touch and she dug her fingernails into his shoulders and squirmed beneath him.

"Please." She could barely catch her breath as she begged him. *"Please!"*

A growl rose up within Tiernan and he finally captured one of her taut buds in his mouth.

He sucked *hard,* causing her to cry out at the incredible feeling. That animalistic part of him that she had witnessed in his expression came out as he bit her nipple and pulled it with his teeth.

Copper pounded on his shoulders with her fists, wanting the pain and pleasure to continue. Goddess, how she liked it.

He tugged harder and her eyes watered at the exquisite feel of it.

Tiernan released her nipple and moved to the other. She sighed with disappointment that he had stopped, but hissed her breath out when he captured her other nipple between his teeth. She tilted her head back and wriggled her body beneath his, unable to stop herself.

He licked and sucked and bit her. She cried out again and dug her nails into his shoulders, feeling the leather beneath her touch once more, clenching so tight she was certain to leave her own mark on his skin, as he was leaving his mark on her body.

When he finally released her nipple, she relaxed on a sigh. The nubs felt incredibly sensitive and wonderful as he lightly flicked his tongue over one and then the other. The fact that he had made them so tender heightened the sensations beyond belief.

"Did you enjoy that?" he murmured as he raised his head and his gaze met hers.

"You'd better stop teasing me." She squirmed beneath him. "Or there'll be hell to pay."

"You are a wild one." He licked the space between her breasts again. "You need to be tamed, little fire."

He was an arrogant ass, but soooo good that she didn't argue. She wanted him to hurry and fuck her.

Tiernan moved slowly down her stomach, swirling his tongue in her belly button. The sensation made her suck in her breath. He trailed his firm lips down farther, until he reached the soft copper-colored curls of her mound.

More of those strange golden bubbles floated above her and then seeped into her skin.

Sex magic.

So, so much power filled her with every bubble that settled against her flesh. She felt like she could do anything—any spell, any type of magic she wanted to.

Not only did she feel magical power, but the golden bubbles intensified the feelings within her, making her nearly burst with her unbelievable lust for Tiernan. The bubbles had never happened to her before the first time she and Tiernan had sex. It had to mean something.

Sex magic.

As he slid lower down her body, she could no longer grasp his shoulders. She slipped her fingers into his thick blond hair and clung to him. Her thighs trembled as she waited for his mouth to slip into her wet folds.

Instead, he pressed her legs farther apart and licked and nipped at the soft skin between her thigh and her pussy. Copper almost cried with the need to have his mouth on her, to have him lick her clit until she exploded with an orgasm to rival all orgasms—even those he had given her that first afternoon and night. She knew that it would be even greater, knew it with everything she had. If only he would stop teasing her.

He moved his mouth again, this time stopping to draw in a deep breath. "By the gods, you smell of the sweetest nectar."

Just do *it!* she wanted to scream. Instead she begged him, "Lick my pussy, Tiernan, please."

He simply ignored her again and flicked his tongue along the inside of her other thigh.

Without thought she raised her hips, forcing her folds closer to his mouth.

He rose up and shook his head. "Behave, little fire."

This time she almost cried.

Tiernan sat back on his haunches, then hooked his arms under her knees and raised her up so that her thighs were against her chest. He moved close enough that his cock slipped between the folds of her pussy and stroked her clit. The entire time he kept his gaze fixed on hers.

"Do you want me to fuck you, Copper?"

She nodded in a quick, jerky movement. "Yes. Now."

He shook his head. "Not now."

"What?" she almost screamed.

He merely smiled and raised her up farther and moved himself lower so that his mouth hovered just above her pussy.

Copper remained still, tears of lust nearly blinding her.

He gave an arrogant smile, then delved into her wetness. Copper shouted out and her voice echoed across the meadow. He thrust two fingers into her channel at the same time he licked her clit with slow strokes that made tears roll down her cheeks. Tears of need, tears of desire, tears of frustration, tears of near fulfillment.

He slowly finger-fucked her at the same time his tongue

stroked her from her folds to her clit, up to her mound, and then repeated the process all over again.

Copper was close to climax, so very close. But the way he was stroking her, it held her just below that elusive peak. Barely keeping her from her orgasm.

Tiernan started driving his fingers into her, pounding his knuckles against her folds. The gold bubbles were all around her. He licked her harder, then sucked her clit and she screamed.

Her body spasmed and she swore the whole meadow lit up. Golden magical bubbles shot up above her, as if exploding from her orgasm.

It was truly the most incredible orgasm she'd ever experienced. It went on and on, her hips jerking against his face and his tongue and fingers relentlessly driving her on.

"Stop!" The exquisite pleasure was too, too much. "I can't take any more!"

He slowly raised his head and released her knees so that her thighs were no longer pressed to her chest and her feet were flat on the grass again. The shower of her magic, the golden bubbles that had filled the meadow, faded to nothing but a spark here, then there.

He moved up so that he was over her, his hands braced on either side of her head, keeping most of his weight off her. He was so big, so powerful. His cock again pressed against her folds, and even though her orgasm had left her boneless, she still wanted him to fill her.

She reached for him and he lowered his head and brought his mouth to hers in a slow, sweet kiss. The taste of her juices was upon his tongue. He was so gentle with her, not at all like the man who had just driven her to such incredible completion.

When he finally rose up, his gaze locked with hers, his blue eyes studying her almost like he had never seen her before. "I need you, Copper. Gods help me, but I need you."

"Then take me," she whispered.

Tiernan drove into her so hard, so deep that her channel convulsed around him again. Goddess, she had missed this. He was so big, so thick, and he filled her perfectly.

He kept his eyes on her as he drove in and out. He started slow, but his pace increased until he was fucking her at a fast and furious rate. His grunts of passion were as loud as her moans. She raised her head so that their mouths met and he thrust his tongue into her mouth, driving her crazy.

Copper was wild in his arms. She felt such incredible power, more than last time, power that she could barely hold back. It was unbelievable.

This time the fireworks around them were out of control. Gold bubbles, gold sparks. In her, outside her, throughout the meadow. And this time when she climaxed she was blinded by the flash of gold. Through the buzz in her mind and in her ears, she barely heard Tiernan's shout of release, barely felt the pulse of his cock inside her.

He was still breathing hard, bracing his hands to either side of her, and her body still trembled with her orgasm, when she knew. She *knew*.

"Come on!" She shoved at him and his expression was puzzled. "Hurry and get your pants back up!"

Tiernan frowned, but he rolled off her and tucked his cock back inside his pants.

The meadow was still filled with what looked like a meteor shower as Copper scrambled to her feet. She grabbed her dress and pulled it over her head. When she noticed all the Fae watching them, she didn't even care that apparently they'd had an audience.

Fine, they could help.

Copper felt incredible. Such amazing energy and power filled her. She had this wonderful feeling deep inside, like she was invincible. It had been magical, what she'd just shared with him—and it had been so much more. So very much more.

Sex magic.

A swell of warmth expanded in her chest. At this moment she knew she could accomplish just about anything.

Even get them out of this mess.

Scents of grass, apples, water from the stream, and flowers seemed so much richer and more vibrant, and the gold bubbles and sparks made everything glow. A sudden hard breeze rustled the branches of the tree and rushed over her bare skin.

When she was dressed and her eyes met Tiernan's, she saw that his frizzed hair was mussed, but still held back with the leather strap. He looked funny when his hair was sticking up, but he was quite sexy with his hair drawn back with the tie.

And right now he looked like male perfection, from his incredible blue eyes, to the sculpted muscles of his biceps, to the latent power he exuded. Like a panther, tensed and ready to pounce on her.

But not now. They didn't have much time.

"Zephyr!" she called as she scooped up her wand from where she had dropped it. Right away the honeybee buzzed to her from where he had been perched on one of the daisies. When he landed on the curve of her ear, she immediately sensed his disapproval over what she and Tiernan had done, but she only laughed. "If it's not one male it's another."

Copper motioned for Tiernan to join her when she reached the center of the meadow. "I'm going to try a spell that I've been thinking about for a while." She wiggled her toes in the soft grass, tugged her dress down, and took a deep breath of fresh air as the gold still rained down. "This magic we've created. I know we can do it."

Tiernan looked puzzled and as if he were starting to say something, when Riona flitted up to Copper, her lavender wings fluttering as her Faerie dust glittered around her. "Allow our magic to join with yours," the Faerie queen said.

"Definitely." Copper nodded to the other beings frolicking in the grass. "And theirs, too. I've just got this feeling that this time we can do it—set us all free. But we've got to hurry."

Riona had a solemn expression on her usually animated features. "We will."

Tiernan reached Copper and scrubbed his hand over his face. When he looked down at her, he smiled and her heart pounded a little harder. "This time?" he asked.

She nodded and clenched her wand tight in her hand. "My magic and my gut tell me it's going to work. If I have *everyone's* help, we can all be free."

He reached up and fingered a leaf of her vine dress as he studied her. "I believe you."

Immediately Copper and Tiernan were surrounded by Faeries, Pixies, and Brownies. The Undine had risen from her place in the stream, her liquid blue eyes focused on the circle. Even from a distance, Copper could feel the Undine's magic radiating from her, and knew the being would join the circle if she could leave the water. But certainly the power she offered would strengthen their effort.

The Drow—well, it was no surprise they hadn't joined the circle. Besides, it *was* daylight.

It was a surprise, however, that all the Fae were more or less solemn. Copper raised her wand and looked from the Faerie queen to the self-proclaimed leader of the Brownies, to the whole of the Pixies who had no leader, but usually followed the will of the Faerie queen. When they were in the mood.

Zephyr buzzed in her ear, giving his support, as Copper took a deep breath and exhaled. "I need you all to lend me your power as I perform the spell," she said, letting her voice carry across the meadow. "Together we will break through the barrier so that you may all return to your homes in Otherworld, and so that Tiernan and I may return to where we belong at this moment."

She paused, knowing the Fae weren't going to be happy about what she had to say. "I need you all to please join hands."

Copper was surprised how easily the Fae cooperated and focused their attention on her.

She gripped her wand tighter and took Tiernan's hand in her free one. She squeezed his fingers and felt his warmth and his D'Danann magic, followed by the magics of every single being around them. Zephyr's powers as a familiar seemed magnified and her confidence grew stronger.

Then she did what felt incredibly right. She summoned a huge dose of gray magic.

Copper closed her eyes and felt it all rise within her, blending with the gold. So much magic! So much power! This time she didn't need to cast a circle because she was surrounded by a very magical one with all the Fae.

Warmth, strength, and the magic filled her from her head to her toes and she nearly lost her breath from it. She needed the gray. That's what had gotten her here, that's what would get them out. The feel of it was so strong, so dark, but she knew she wasn't crossing the line.

Copper opened her eyes and began to chant:

> *What was made will be broken, what was imprisoned will*
> *   be free,*
> *Like the rage of fire and the surge of the sea.*
> *Into the power of Wind, Water, Earth, and Fire, we delve.*
> *Open the door for Fae, Undine, Brownies, and Dark Elves,*
> *Otherworld is where our friends must return,*
> *While San Francisco is what Tiernan and Copper yearn.*
> *Ancestors, goddesses and gods so gracious, hear our plea,*
> *Our will and desire fulfilled, we honor thee.*
> *As it was, as it is, as it will become, so mote it be.*

For a moment all was calm—too calm—like being in the eye of a hurricane.

Brilliant gold fire burst from around the circumference of their circle with a loud whoosh, and gray glittered in the air like dark fireworks.

The gray magic . . . it was working!

Gold flames slammed into the shimmering barrier. Sparks exploded and rained down like stars over all the Fae, Tiernan, and Copper.

The barrier flashed, wavered.

A loud crack echoed through the meadow.

The shimmer was gone.

Copper's heart leaped. Nothing stood between the Fae and the rest of Otherworld any longer. The barrier had vanished!

They had done it! They had set everyone free!

In the next moment, Copper felt an incredible pulling sensation, as if she were being stretched like taffy. She squeezed Tiernan's hand tighter in her own, but then found herself gripping nothing but her wand.

The gold light vanished and she was flying. Brilliant colors of a sunset flashed by. Around her, through her. She could see only pinks, oranges, purples. And then it became gray, then darker gray, and fear caused her heart to beat in her throat. Her head felt as if it were going to be ripped from her body. Her stomach clenched and unclenched and she was certain she was going to throw up.

Everything happened so fast, yet slow, too. Every sensation was vivid, intense. Surely she was going to be stretched in two!

Then she was flailing, floundering in the air.

She dropped. Slammed to a hardwood floor. Pain shot through her hands and knees.

Her arms buckled and her lips met the wood. Every part of her trembled as she tried to grasp a sense of reality. That she was no longer being flung through the sunset, then the darkened tunnel.

That she was no longer in the bubble of Otherworld.

A buzz from the tip of her ear let her know that Zephyr had made it with her, wherever she was, and she gripped her wand tight in one fist. Her dress was skewed around her waist.

A thud hit the floor beside her and she heard a loud groan. Without looking she knew it was Tiernan, especially when he began cursing in Gaelic. His warm masculine scent washed over her, mingling with smells that were familiar, yet things she hadn't smelled for a long, long time. Lemon oil? Wood? Old books?

Was she back on Earth? Back in San Francisco?

Still shaking, and more than a little dizzy, Copper pushed herself to rest on her haunches, her heart thundering in her ears. Using her gray witchcraft had helped, but for some reason this time it had drained some of her life force. She raised her eyes—

And found herself looking into Darkwolf's black gaze.

Chirteen

San Francisco

Darkwolf looked as shocked as Copper felt. "Watch out, Tiernan!" she shouted. Heart pounding, instinct led her to jab her wand in the air. Her glittering gold shield blazed from her wand, shot across the room, and surrounded Darkwolf and the desk he was standing next to.

The warlock snarled and raised his hands. Purple light bled from his fingers to the shield. His magic rebounded and slammed into him. Darkwolf stumbled back, almost losing his balance. A surprised and furious expression crossed his face as he regained his footing. The black stone eye against his chest began to glow crimson, and the eye stared right at Copper as if it could see through her to her very soul.

Copper's heartbeat moved up from her chest to thrum in her throat. Now she had him where she wanted him. If it weren't for Darkwolf she wouldn't have been exiled to Otherworld. Not to mention all that Tiernan said Darkwolf had done to the witches! It was his fault the Fomorii had invaded Earth and that one of them had killed her mother.

"You son of a bitch!" she shouted, her wand still raised.

"Release me, witch," he growled. "Now!"

Furious as she was, Copper's body still protested and trembled as she scrambled up, because of the journey from Otherworld. The wood floor was warm beneath her bare feet and her vine-and-leaf dress ruffled as it slid back down to her thighs. She kept her wand aimed at Darkwolf and her focus on maintaining the shield the entire time. She felt a draw on the gray magic she used, as if something were pulling it from her.

What was this pull on her gray magic? Did it come from Darkwolf and the eye?

It almost seemed to . . . drain her powers.

She shook her head. No. Her gray magic was powerful and she was in full control of it.

At the same moment she contained Darkwolf, she saw a beautiful, sophisticated-looking woman. She stood outside the shield on the other side of the desk, her hands clenched into fists and her eyes narrowed. "Shall I kill them now?" the woman asked without looking at Darkwolf.

"Wait." Darkwolf held up his hand as he studied Copper. He smiled, a confident smile. "We must contain her and use her when the time is right."

"*As if!*" Copper shouted.

Darkwolf and the woman were at least ten feet from Copper and Tiernan. She didn't have to look all around her to know that they were in some kind of enormous private library. It was filled with shelves and shelves of books, along with beautiful works of art. Behind Darkwolf was a floor-to-ceiling window with a view of the Bay Bridge and the surrounding city.

They were in San Francisco!

Elation mingled with anger and fear, causing her chest to tighten.

From the corner of her eye she saw Tiernan had gotten

to his feet, his sword drawn, and fury etched on his features. Zeph had hidden himself in Copper's hair, and she could sense the familiar's own anger.

"You might as well surrender," Copper said. "You're not getting away from us."

To her surprise Darkwolf began to laugh. He leaned his hip against the desk between him and the woman, and his expression was one of amusement. He folded his arms across his chest and kept his gaze on Copper, ignoring Tiernan. "You were almost mine before, you'll be mine now."

Copper felt her strength wavering, and the glitter of her shield grew faint before brightening again. "I owe you big time."

He glanced at the woman on the other side of the desk. As she started forward, he held up his hand. "I'll handle this, Junga."

Copper swore she heard a deep growl rise up from the woman's chest.

"Junga." Tiernan had drawn his sword and had it gripped with both hands as if prepared to slice the weapon through the woman. "That bitch is the Fomorii leader."

"Queen," the elegant woman said, and as she spoke her fingers started to change. They elongated, turned a shade of royal blue. The nails grew and lengthened into claws.

Copper's throat constricted. She stiffened and her control on her magic began to falter. "That's the demon that murdered my mother?"

"No." The woman's teeth began to lengthen and her voice deepened. Copper couldn't control a shudder. "Kanji, your mother's killer, died at my claws when I took my rightful place as queen."

"But you *would* have killed Moondust," Tiernan said to the demon-woman in a voice filled with rage. "If you had had the opportunity you would have."

"I had plenty of opportunity." The woman's face was beginning to turn into something hideous, and Copper heard the crack and pop of bone. "I intended to use the witch, not kill her."

Copper stared in horror as the being shifted into a demon with a blue hide, needlelike teeth, bulging blue eyes, and an earless head. The creature had long muscular arms that reached to the floor, like an ape's. The Fomorii's claws were tipped with something dark, yet filed sharp. The nails glinted like polished metal in the recessed lighting of the library. The demon was enormous, three times the width of the woman it had formerly been, and much taller.

Copper gagged as the stench of rotten fish filled the room.

Without warning, the Fomorii bounded across the library, straight for Tiernan.

At the same time Copper's witchcraft faltered enough that Darkwolf's next burst of magic shattered the shield's hold on him.

The Fomorii attacked Tiernan and his sword met the demon's tough hide. He whirled in the confines of the enormous library and sliced his sword at the creature's arm. Blood spurted, spraying Tiernan and everything around them. But the wound immediately began to heal even as Junga howled in pain and rage.

He dodged and parried, barely avoiding the demon's teeth and claws. Books flew across the room and shelves were ripped from the walls as they fought. Priceless works of art crashed to the floor and were crunched beneath his boots.

Copper wanted to help him, but Darkwolf stalked her, the eye against his chest pulsating a furious red. Mouth dry and heart racing, she pointed her wand at him and a golden stream of spellfire shot from its tip. He merely flicked his wrist and the bolt slammed to the wood floor of the library, causing sparks to fly and the smell of burned wood to erupt. Apparently his magic worked a lot better when he wasn't caught off guard.

"You'll need to do better than that," Darkwolf said, as if they were conducting a casual conversation. "Like Silver,

you ride that edge of gray and are so close to the black . . .
Your magic is actually darker than hers, yet Silver is probably closer to converting than you are."

"Silver would never turn to black magic!" Copper felt
the gray witchcraft building within her. It seemed more intense this time, far more powerful.

He smiled, a sensual yet chilling smile, and held up his
hand. Purple light began to emanate from him. "You have
no idea how close Silver is to becoming mine."

"Ooooh!" Copper gritted her teeth and focused on pouring her witchcraft into her wand. She felt Zephyr's power,
but then the familiar shot from where he'd been hidden in
her hair and straight toward the warlock.

Darkwolf focused solely on Copper and she readied to
counter his magic with her own.

Before she could spell him, he cried out and slapped at
his face, then his neck.

Huge welts—ten, fifteen, more perhaps—began rising
on his skin. Copper felt a rush of triumph as Zeph buzzed
back to her and landed on her ear.

Copper took advantage of Darkwolf's distraction and
blasted him with a bolt from her wand. Her power
slammed into the warlock and he flew back, his head striking the wall so hard he dented the paneling and slumped to
the floor. He shook his head as if to shake away the pain
and dizziness and wobbled as he tried to get to his feet. The
welts on his face distorted his features and made him look
hideous rather than handsome.

The entire time she and Darkwolf were going at it, Tiernan and the demon fought. Roars, shouts, and snarls continued to echo through the now decimated library.

Copper heard more growls coming closer from the other
side of the closed twin mahogany doors. With a flick of her
wand she bound the demon Junga with gold ropes of power
that caused the giant Fomorii to stumble forward and land
on its face. Copper whirled and pointed her wand to the

double doors and another rope of magic shot out of the tip and wrapped around the door handles to bind them shut.

Something hard crashed against the door and wood splintered. Breathing heavily, Copper hurried to Tiernan's side, where he stood beside the floor-to-ceiling window. Demons were attacking the doors with such ferocity that they would doubtless break in within seconds.

"Let me finish this bitch off." Tiernan started toward the demon that was bound on the floor by Copper's magic, his weapon raised to slice off its head—

The library doors burst open. Fomorii poured into the room.

Darkwolf got to his feet, his dark witchcraft blazing.

Copper threw up a magical wall between them and the warlock, and readied to create another in front of the Fomorii.

Tiernan rammed the hilt of his sword against the safety glass with enough force that it shattered outward but also showered down upon the wood floor. Before Copper could throw up the second wall, he caught her by the waist with his free arm and jumped through the window.

She screamed.

A demon's jagged teeth raked her bare foot just as they sailed through the window. Pain seared her like fire. Even the broken shards of glass that tore at her skin were nothing compared to the pain of the demon's bite.

Her stomach pitched as they fell from the top floor of the home.

Tiernan unfurled his wings as they dropped and then they were flying.

Flying over San Francisco.

Fourteen

Copper flung her arms around Tiernan's neck as he soared higher and higher, and she almost lost her grip on her wand. Wind rushed through her hair and ruffled her vine-and-leaf dress, and Zephyr buzzed in her ear, sharing his own delight. Copper's head spun with the magnitude of what had just happened, and the fact that they were back in her city.

She clung to Tiernan as she stared at the sights below. The Coit Tower! The Transamerica Building! Chinatown! She could see it all from the height he had taken them to. The Golden Gate Bridge, the foggy bay, Alcatraz, the Bay Bridge, Market Street, trolleys, Union Square—her hungry gaze took in everything.

And the air—it smelled wonderful! Even the pollution coming from cars and buses didn't bother her. It was home. She was home!

"Are you all right?" Tiernan held her tight as he pumped his powerful wings. He was heading in the direction of Golden Gate Park.

Copper laughed. "I'm wonderful. I'm home!" She didn't

care about the blood trickling from the glass wounds or the blood running down her foot or the burn from the demon's teeth. Adrenaline still pumped through her body and she felt high from it and from the excitement of being back where she belonged.

Tiernan gradually lowered, circling the Haight-Ashbury district, then began his descent. "Where are we?" Copper asked, as he came closer to what looked like a large apartment building.

"Headquarters is here," he said as he touched down. When their feet met the rooftop of the building he kept his hands on her waist, steadying her. The roof was made into a little patio with lounge chairs and a small garden area near the stairwell. The flagstone floor felt cool beneath her bare feet.

Copper's head felt as if it might float off, but she also felt supercharged, as if she could do anything. Even her foot that was bleeding from the demon teeth didn't feel too bad.

"You're injured." He frowned as he looked down at her. "I must get you to the witches immediately."

Tiernan scooped her up in his arms and she gave a surprised cry. "I can walk. Really."

"I think not." His tone told her this was one fight she wasn't going to win.

Instead she held on and pelted him with questions. "Is Silver here? What about the other witches? The Coven?"

He opened the door to the stairwell. "All your answers lie within."

Zephyr tickled the curve of Copper's ear as she let Tiernan carry her. She was so excited that had she been on her feet, she would have darted ahead of him—if she had had any idea where they were headed. Her heart raced, and as far as she was concerned Tiernan wasn't moving fast enough. He opened a door to a hallway on the second floor and her heart beat even harder against her breastbone.

Tiernan finally stopped in front of an apartment door at

the end of the hallway, gently set her on her feet, and reached for the door handle. He paused and met her anxious gaze. From the other side of the door she heard muffled voices that sounded like they were arguing.

He opened the door and she took a deep breath.

Silver!

Her sister was standing in the middle of the room, her hands on her hips, as she glared up at a man who stood well over a foot taller than her. The man was clad much the same as Tiernan, including a sword belt, but he had dark hair to his shoulders and a shadow of a beard. At their feet was Silver's python familiar, Polaris, and he seemed to be glaring at the man, too.

All Copper really cared about was her sister. Silver was as beautiful as ever with her long silvery-blond hair and her large gray eyes. She was wearing a silk blouse, short skirt, and high heels as usual. Her sister enjoyed dressing sexy when she wasn't working with the Paranormal Special Forces. Copper was a more down-to-earth jeans type.

All these crazy thoughts went through her mind in just a matter of seconds.

Silver was jabbing one finger at the man's chest as she was saying, "I *am* going and that's—"

She glanced at the doorway and her face went pale. For a moment she didn't speak.

"Copper?" Silver's eyes widened as she dropped her hands to her sides. "Copper?"

Tears came out of nowhere, rolling down Copper's face as she nodded. She couldn't speak. Instead, she ran toward her sister and flung her arms around Silver's neck, almost hitting her with the wand, and held her tight. Zeph buzzed his annoyance at just about being crushed between the two, but Copper couldn't begin to think about the little familiar.

She felt her sister's tears against her neck as Silver said, "I can't believe it! I can't believe it!"

"Goddess, I've missed you," Copper said in a choked

whisper. Silver still smelled of lilies, a scent that brought back so many memories and had a comforting effect. "I love you so much."

They pulled away but continued holding on to one another. "You're really here." Silver stared with amazement at Copper as tears continued to leak from her eyes. "I can't believe you're standing right in front of me! That I can touch you!"

"Me, too." Copper reached up and brushed Silver's tears from one cheek. "It's been so long. I'd begun to think I'd never get back."

Silver bit her lower lip and shook her head. "This is like a dream."

Copper rubbed her thumb along her sister's cheek, wiping away more tears. "It's real," she whispered. "I'm real. You're real."

While the sisters hugged and cried and laughed, Copper heard Tiernan explain about their ending up within the Fomorii lair and their escape. From the corner of her eye she saw the dark-haired man's face harden and his jaw tense. "We must gather our brothers and sisters and go at once. Perhaps we can catch them before they escape."

Tiernan nodded. "My thoughts as well."

"You stay with Copper," Tiernan ordered Silver.

"Well, *no kidding*," she snapped at him. Then, "Arrogant jerk," as he closed the door behind them. Silver hugged Copper again. "I have no intention of letting you go. Ever."

Copper laughed. "Not even to go to the bathroom?"

Silver rolled her eyes, then shook her head with a smile. "I've missed your sense of humor."

Polaris, Silver's familiar, wrapped his body around Copper's bare feet, just avoiding her injury, and she felt the mental warmth of his own pleasure that she was back. Zephyr buzzed from Copper's ear and landed on Silver's shoulder.

"It's good to have you back, too," Silver told the little bee familiar.

After another quick hug, Copper and Silver separated. Copper didn't bother to brush away her own tears.

Silver's expression of mingled joy and shock turned to one of dismay as she noticed all the blood and scratches. "What happened to you? Are you okay? We need to treat these wounds." Her expression was still one of disbelief as she looked into Copper's eyes. "I feel like you're going to disappear again."

"I'm fine, I'm here for good, and I'll tell you everything that happened." Copper stepped over Polaris and let Silver lead her to the kitchen of the apartment. It was bigger than the one Silver lived in before Copper ended up in Otherworld, but not by much. The furniture and the décor were the same and that told her Silver lived here now instead of in the apartment above Moon Song.

Zephyr landed on the edge of Silver's pewter cauldron, that was perched in the middle of a table. Silver pushed Copper onto a chair beside it, then immediately went to the kitchen.

Silver started rummaging through cabinets and pulling out small jars, a little bottle, and then grabbed a soft cloth and some cotton balls. "Where on earth have you been?" she asked as she returned with everything. The jars and bottle hit the table with a thump as she set them down.

Copper managed a smile as she set her wand next to the jars. "I haven't exactly been on earth."

Silver paused in the act of opening the bottle. "What?"

With a shrug that was more casual than she felt, Copper said, "It's a long story."

"I think we have time now for you to tell me everything." Silver finished opening the bottle and Copper caught the strong scent of tea tree oil. "Well, time enough to get started."

Silver tended first to the foot the demon had bitten. Silver took the bottle of oil and poured the contents over the slashes on Copper's foot. "This must hurt." She glanced up at Copper. "What happened?"

The tea tree oil burned and Copper flinched. "It was one of the Fomorii that Tiernan and I just ran into."

Silver looked stunned and horrified. "The Fomorii? Were you clawed by one of the demons?"

Copper shook her head. "It bit me."

Silver breathed an audible sigh of relief. "Thank the goddess it wasn't their claws."

Copper scrunched her eyebrows. "Why?"

"A lot of them have tipped their claws with iron," Silver said with a sigh. "Iron's deadly to Fae and Elves both."

"Huh?" Copper blinked. "Um, you're not making any sense. We're witches, not Fae or Elvin."

Silver bit her lower lip.

"Tell me, whatever it is." Copper hissed in pain as Silver cleansed one of the deeper gouges in her foot. "You're either scaring me or pissing me off. I'm not sure which."

"Mother . . . Mother . . ." Silver took a deep breath and more tears spilled down her cheeks as her gaze met Copper's.

Copper's own tears returned. "I know. Tiernan told me that she—that she passed on to Summerland."

"It was horrible," Silver whispered. She wiped away some of her tears with the back of her hand and tried to compose herself. "Did he tell you she was half Elvin?"

Confused, Copper stared at Silver with wide eyes. "What?"

"I couldn't believe it either." Silver repeated as she reached for a jar and opened it. Copper caught the scent of yarrow. "A *lot* has happened. After she died, Father told me that Mother was half Elvin. That's why you and I tend to lean toward gray magic."

"Really?" Copper blinked. "That means we're a quarter Elvin."

With a nod, Silver put the yarrow cream on her sister's

foot. It soothed the pain and some of the tension left Copper. "It's a long, long story," Silver said, "but I promise to explain more." She looked up at Copper. "First you've got to tell me where in the Goddess's name you've been. And where Tiernan disappeared to and how you came back here together."

Copper gave the condensed version of her story while Silver tended to her foot. She started with the attempt at the ceremony on the beach and her spell hitting a shield, and moved on to her time in Otherworld. She explained how another spell had brought Tiernan to Otherworld rather than help her to escape. She left out the part about the wonderful sex with Tiernan and moved on to how they were able to break the barrier, freeing all the captive beings, and how they ended up in Darkwolf's lair.

Silver had just finished wrapping Copper's foot when Darkwolf was mentioned. Polaris the familiar hissed, and Silver stilled, a strange look on her face.

Copper explained the battle with the warlock and the demon Junga, and their narrow escape. She told Silver about the library.

"I scried as much in my cauldron—except you weren't in the vision," Silver said. "We were on our way there just now. Hawk was trying to make me stay here."

"I'll bet they'll change their base of operations now that we've discovered their location," Copper said.

"No doubt." Silver gently set Copper's bandaged foot on the floor. "But we can hope the D'Danann make it before they do escape."

"Darkwolf said you walked the line, close to the dark," Copper said softly. "I didn't believe it for a second."

Silver took a deep breath, her chest rising and falling. "No, I would never turn to black magic. But I do have a lot to tell you."

Copper waited, but Silver said instead, "Your dress."

She touched a leaf and fingered it at Copper's shoulder. "It's all vines and leaves."

"The Faeries made it for me." Copper gave a wry smile. "I wasn't wearing a darn thing because I was going to perform the 'new moon' ritual, and that's when Darkwolf showed up and I was spelled into Otherworld." Copper brushed at the leaves and vines of the skirt. "All the Fae were so mad about being imprisoned—they blamed me— that I had to run around naked for days. Eventually I made friends with the Faerie queen, Riona, and she had the dress designed for me. It's magical—it never gets soiled." She gave a big sigh and a grin. "I'm glad I had something to wear all this time, but you don't know how badly I want to get into T-shirts and jeans!"

"I still have all your clothes and belongings." Silver hugged her sister. "I knew one day that you'd return. I just knew it!"

"Thanks for not giving up on me." Copper gave Silver a tight squeeze. "It's more than wonderful to be back home. It's *incredible. Unbelievable!*"

While all of Copper's scrapes, scratches, and cuts were being tended to, Silver and Copper spent time trying to catch up on everything that had happened in the fifteen months or so that Copper had been gone. Once Silver finished doctoring Copper's wounds—which had all nearly vanished due to Silver's magic—the sisters settled on one of Silver's overstuffed couches, within touching distance, neither wanting to be very far from the other.

When it was her turn, Silver explained who Hawk was and how he had appeared to her one night, warning her about the Fomorii being summoned by Darkwolf and his Clan of warlocks. Hawk told her she must perform a ritual to bring him and other D'Danann to San Francisco to battle the Fomorii. Silver had tried to convince their D'Anu Coven of the dangers they were about to face, but they re-

fused to believe her until it was too late and the demons
had taken all but Silver, Eric, and her apprentice, Cassia.
Eric had later been murdered by one of the Basilisks the
demons had brought with them.

While Silver continued to tell Copper the condensed
version of what had happened during the time Copper had
been gone, Zeph buzzed around Polaris's head and the
python playfully stuck his tongue out as if to catch the bee.
The two familiars had almost always gotten along well, and
had shared their magic with both Silver and Copper more
than once.

"What happened when the Fomorii and Darkwolf took
the D'Anu?" Copper asked with dread in her belly.

"A lot." Silver looked beyond sad. "Some of the witches
and apprentices were murdered, a couple turned to black
magic because they had no hope left—like Sara. Can you
believe she turned to black magic? The others . . . they
were traumatized and injured, but they're alive."

"Witches murdered and turning to black magic. I just
can't believe it." Copper laid her hand on Silver's arm.
"Where are they all now? What about Rhiannon and
Mackenzie—are they all right?"

Silver nodded. "They're okay. As a matter of fact
they're living here with the rest of us—Jake Macgregor,
the D'Danann, along with Hannah, Sydney, and Alyssa."

With a frown, Copper eased back on the couch, flinch-
ing when her foot hurt at the movement. "What about the
rest of the D'Anu? Surely the Coven hasn't split. That
would destroy the balance of white magic with the other
twelve covens in the U.S."

"I was banished." Silver's voice was soft as she spoke.
"I used excessive gray magic and the Coven saw me performing it." Her throat worked as she swallowed. "I killed,
Copper. I didn't mean to, but I killed a demon. And I also
used my gray witchcraft to aid the D'Danann in slaying
what Fomorii they could."

Copper stared at her sister in shock. "Surely you didn't turn to black magic. Darkwolf said—"

"No!" Silver's features darkened. "I walked a little too close to it, but I never turned to the black."

Relief flushed over Copper in a warm wave. She hadn't believed it, but when her sister said she had killed . . .

"When I killed the demon it was in self-defense," Silver said as if reading Copper's mind. "And my gray magic—I think the Ancestors blessed me in what I had to do. Otherwise I shouldn't have been able to summon the D'Danann, or banish many of the Fomorii back to Underworld. I think the Ancestors believe as I do that gray witchcraft is needed to fight these demons."

"What has happened to the Coven?" Copper fidgeted with the hem of her vine-and-leaf dress. "What about the balance?"

Silver crossed her legs at her knees. "Apprentices from other parts of the United States and the world have come to San Francisco to replace those who are gone."

"So Rhiannon and the others left our old D'Anu Coven, too?" Copper asked.

"Yes." Silver pushed her long silvery-blond hair over her shoulder. "They believe the D'Anu are far too conservative and will not use the power that is needed to defeat the Fomorii. So we have started our own D'Anu Coven of gray witches.

"But something surprising happened," Silver continued. "Janis Arrowsmith visited me a couple of weeks ago."

Copper couldn't help the surprise in her voice. "What did she want?"

"It was kind of surreal," Silver said, "finding Janis on my doorstep. She has appointed herself as representative from their Coven to ours. She is still angry with me for using gray witchcraft, but their D'Anu Coven is doing what they can with white magic. They are praying, chanting, and trying to heal whatever damage they find—taking the

cleanup end, because it's more consistent with their be-
liefs. They will come to heal after battles, restore plants
and so forth."

Silver still looked somewhat mystified, when she added,
"The part about helping us after battles surprised me, because that was almost like approval of what we're doing.
They just won't have any part of actually destroying the
demons."

"Interesting." Copper raised her brows. "Of all the
witches, Janis must have found that hard to do."

Silver gave a quirky smile. "You should have seen her.
She was looking down her nose at me as if I were the low-
est of the low, yet obviously giving an inch while we take
the mile."

She continued her story, explaining how their parents,
Moondust and Victor Ashcroft, had been taken hostage by
the Fomorii and warlocks. Her voice choked when she
mentioned their mother's name, and when she got to the
part about Moondust's death, Silver fell apart and so did
Copper.

They comforted one another the best they could. When
Silver explained her talk with their father, Copper had a
hard time believing that their hard-as-nails father had
opened up so much. Oh, he loved them, but he wasn't one
to show emotion. She couldn't wait to talk to him. The fact
that Moondust had been half Elvin was amazing, but when
Silver explained how they could move between Earth and
Otherworld because they too were part Elvin, Copper
shook her head in amazement.

"So it's only a matter of being taught by Cassia how to
use the entryways?" Copper asked.

"I've taken Hawk across several times to see his daughter, and to visit his home."

Copper noticed the way her sister looked every time she
spoke Hawk's name. She grinned and interrupted Silver.
"You and Hawk have a thing going."

Silver gave a radiant smile. "I'm in love with him. He can be frustrating and overprotective at times, but he's mine."

"So he has a daughter?"

"Her name is Shayla, and she is so precious." Silver's expression grew animated and her tears dried. "She chatters like a little bird. I adore her and she acts the same with me. When Hawk and I are bonded, we'll live part of the time in Otherworld, and part here in San Francisco."

Silver's smile disappeared and anger filled her voice next. "Once we rid this world of the Fomorii, that is."

The door opened with a crash that made both sisters jump in their seats and their gazes to shoot toward the door.

Hawk and Tiernan stormed in, both looking furious.

"They were gone." Hawk scrubbed his hand over his stubbled jaw. "They managed to escape before we made it there."

Tiernan looked like he wanted to kick something, and Copper was going to jump all over him if he did. Instead he rubbed his hand over his head and the tie holding back his hair slipped off.

His hair immediately sprang up into a blond Afro with braids, and for a moment Hawk and Silver just stared at him. Then Hawk snorted and gave a laugh. Silver started giggling. Copper couldn't help but laugh, too. The big, arrogant warrior looked like he'd been electrocuted. Well, he sort of had been.

Tiernan snarled and snatched the tie off the floor and drew his hair back again.

"The braids," Hawk said in a choked voice, as if holding back more laughter, "are an especially fine touch."

Tiernan glared at all of them. "I need to bathe."

"We have to make up some dandelion shampoo." Copper grinned at Silver. "Although back in Otherworld, the Faeries may have used some magic to help get rid of the frizzies."

"Maybe my shampoo will do." Silver left to go into the bathroom within her bedroom, then returned within moments and handed it to Tiernan. "Let me know if this works."

While Tiernan stomped out the door to his own apartment, Copper explained the electrified wall that had kept them prisoner and how the Pixies enjoyed teasing Tiernan whenever he tested the barrier. Hawk and Silver laughed out loud as Copper told them about the Brownies clinging to his boots and nipping at his knees while the Pixies added flowers to their hair artwork.

Hawk snorted again while Silver and Copper couldn't stop laughing.

"The big bad warrior with a Pixie Afro and an attitude," Copper said between giggles.

When they settled down, Copper talked about the Drow and King Garran, and how Tiernan had helped the Elvin warriors battle the giant. "It was thanks to Tiernan," she said, "that they finally brought him down."

Tiernan eventually let himself back into the apartment, his wet blond hair subdued but still wavy. He looked clean and refreshed, even if he was grumpy.

"Definitely need dandelion shampoo," Copper said with a grin and Tiernan scowled.

"I've got to take you downstairs." Silver smacked her forehead with the palm of her hand. "Everyone will be crazy to see you again. And we need to call Father!"

"I can't wait to talk to him." Copper looked down at her vine-and-leaf dress. "Can I clean up first? I'm dying for a nice warm bath and *real* clothes!"

Silver was all smiles as they went to her bedroom, and she brought out one of Copper's old chests from under her bed. The smell of cinnamon, spice, and cedar swirled through the air when Copper opened the chest. She smiled at her sister. Silver had put sachets in with the clothing to keep them from smelling musty.

After Silver left the room, Copper dug out her favorite pair of worn jeans, a cropped T-shirt, jogging shoes, a thong, bra, and socks. When those items were piled on the bed, she paused and drew out one of her thigh-high boots and a sexy silk mini-skirt. Wouldn't Tiernan just die to see her dressed to kill?

As she put the skirt and boots back into the trunk, Copper grinned at the thought of being out on the town with Tiernan. Now wouldn't that be interesting?

She stripped out of her vine-and-leaf dress, folded it, and put it into her trunk. She winced from the pain in her foot as she walked to the bathroom. The aged knobs squeaked as she turned on the hot water, and soon the room was filled with warm steam and the sound of water rising in the bathtub.

Copper climbed into the tub, careful to keep her bandaged foot raised on the side of the tub. She closed her eyes and reveled in the warmth of the water as it surrounded her skin. She'd had nothing but icy cold hand baths for so long. And this felt soooo good she didn't want to get out. She shampooed her hair with Silver's lily-scented shampoo, soaped her body, and scrubbed herself with a luffa sponge and lily body gel. She hadn't had a decent bath for ages. Well, over fifteen months according to how long Silver said she'd been missing.

When her fingers and toes started to wrinkle like prunes from being in the water so long, Copper knew she'd better get out. She let the water out of the tub, got up, then grabbed one of Silver's fluffy sea-blue towels and dried herself from head to toe.

It felt so weird putting on clothing. Everything seemed just a tad bigger after her sparse diet over the last year or so. And after wearing just that short little dress all the time, she felt as if she had on too much clothing. No matter, it still felt good.

It did hurt like crazy to pull her shoe over her bandaged

foot, but she was determined. She was a witch and she'd heal very fast, but right now she couldn't help but cringe.

The steam finally cleared from the mirror as Copper blow-dried her hair using her fingers as a comb. She paused. She hadn't seen her own reflection for so long. Her cinnamon eyes stared back at her, her hair was long now, not shoulder-length, and the freckles across her nose seemed lighter. She looked different. A little older. Maybe a little wiser?

She had to snort at that one. Wise—she didn't know about that.

As soon as Copper came out of the bedroom, Silver handed her the telephone. "It's Father. I broke it to him slowly—didn't want him to have a heart attack or anything."

Copper took the phone, her hand shaking. "Father?"

"By the goddess and the Ancestors." She heard the tears in Victor Ashcroft's voice. "I have missed you so much, my little witch. It seems but a dream that you are back. That you are real."

"It's me." Tears coursed Copper's cheeks. "I missed you so badly. I thought about you and Silver and Mother every single day."

"As you have never left my thoughts, daughter." She heard a honking noise and knew her father was blowing his nose. "I must fly out there at once."

Panic welled up within Copper. She didn't want to take the chance of losing her father—the Fomorii were still in San Francisco. "No. I'll catch a flight and come home. Just give me a week, okay?"

Victor finally gave in, obviously respecting her need for a few days to gather herself before she joined him in Salem.

After her conversation with her father, she found herself being swept down to the new shop, Enchantments, and into the kitchen where she was hugged, exclaimed over, and bombarded with thousands of questions.

She was fed *real* food—cooked by a part Elvin witch named Cassia, and plied with fruit drinks. Everything smelled so good and tasted even better—dumplings, ambrosia salad, asparagus with toasted pine nuts, honey-nut bread, and so much more.

By the time she had finished eating, her head was spinning and she was so exhausted she could hardly keep her eyes open. Cassia seemed to be the one in charge and she told Tiernan to take Copper upstairs and put her to bed. Tiernan scooped her up and she gave a squeal, then insisted she could walk on her own. But with Silver leading the way, she was taken from the shop to the apartment building and into a vacant apartment with a wonderfully soft bed.

When Tiernan left for his own apartment next door, she wanted to fall facefirst onto the bed and pass out, but Silver insisted on helping her get out of her clothes first. She was wrapped up in a nice satiny robe and then put to bed like a child and tucked in.

The last thing she heard was Silver's voice saying, "Don't you dare leave me again, Copper."

Copper snuggled into her pillow and murmured, "Don't worry, I won't," before everything faded away.

Fifteen

She was in the passageway. Walls crowded in on her as she moved. Smells of damp earth, sulfur, and the stench of rotten fish crawled up her nose. She sniffed again. Wolfsbane, too.

Down, down, down the tunnel she walked. She kept waiting for the blood to come rushing toward her, but all her wand light showed was more of the passageway ahead.

Confidence rose within her. This wasn't so bad. Nothing she couldn't handle. She was a witch.

She frowned. Ahead of her was a corner, red light bleeding around the turn, blending with her golden wand light and turning her light to a foul shade of crimson. Was that—was that a being with flames for hair?

No. That was crazy. Nothing was there.

Yet her confidence drained away, and her heart jumped back into her throat.

When she rounded the corner she came up short. She was on a narrow pathway. Below her was a massive cavern with stalagmites and stalactites jutting from ceiling and floor. She'd never seen such an incredibly huge place.

The walls were hewn of rough stone that glistened in the now red light of her wand. The entire cavern was bathed in red light.

She started down the pathway. The trail was smooth and her jogging shoes didn't make a sound as she crept forward.

This place was old. So very, very old.

Her journey seemed to last forever. She walked. Walked. Walked.

Goddess, why was it taking her so long?

And there! Those dark shapes again. She knew what they were. *Knew* it. So why couldn't she quite grasp it?

The shapes blended with the darkness and she pressed ahead.

Finally she came closer to a massive stone door. An ancient door that had stood for thousands and thousands of years—she didn't know how she knew, but she did.

Red light seeped from cracks around the door, the same red light that filled the cavern and blended with her wand light.

Intense pressure emanated from the door—as if something were fighting against it and trying to get out. The mere thought made her skin crawl. Whatever it was, she couldn't allow it to be freed.

She gripped her wand tighter. Her heart pounded faster. What could she do?

Her gaze moved to the floor and she saw that she was standing in a circle. A circle ringed by a larger circle. Within the two, crude runes were etched into the stone floor. Familiar runes, but nothing like the spiritual language of the trees, the *Ogham*. Nor were they as beautiful as Elvin or Fae runes.

No. These were evil.

And then her gaze dropped to see what was beneath her very feet. She was standing on an eye. A lidless eye. It was moving, glowing a deep red.

Her breathing came shallower. Her limbs weakened. She wavered, felt herself begin to lose consciousness. Through her hazy gaze she stared at the eye . . .

The red of the eye was blood.

And the eye was draining that blood from her.

Copper screamed out loud. When she stopped, her breathing came hard and heavy and the darkness seemed oppressive. The dream—it had been even more terrifying than the times before.

Dazed, she expected to see the rock of her shelter above her, feel rock beneath her along with the dried grass, vine, and leaf bedding.

But no . . . she was in a soft bed, wrapped in clean sheets that were twisted around her as if she'd tossed and turned in her sleep.

Relief flooded her. She was home! She was in San Francisco.

Yet that knowledge did little to push away the fears still gripping her from the dream.

She was in the strange apartment that Silver had arranged for her to live in. Even though she was happy to be back where she belonged, she felt so alone. A strange thought occurred to her. It was the first time in a long while that she had woken without Tiernan's body fitted snugly around her like she had every night in the shelter in the Otherworld prison.

A knock sounded at the front door, startling Copper. She sat up in bed and her heart beat a little faster. The clock beside the bed said two A.M. Who could it be?

The knock again, this time louder.

Copper stumbled from the bed, almost tripping in the tangle of sheets, and hurting her bandaged foot a little. She managed to rid herself of the sheets and sleepily staggered from the apartment's bedroom to the front door. She peeked out the peephole and saw Tiernan in the lighted hallway.

A rush of pleasure came out of nowhere, and she quickly unlocked the door.

He pushed his way through and grabbed her by the upper arms. "Are you all right?" he asked, the dim light from the hallway showing concern on his features. "I heard you scream."

Instinctively, Copper wrapped her arms around his waist and she pressed her face to his hard chest. He was wearing a black robe that was open down to his waist and she felt his warm skin against her cheek. He smelled so good. Of male musk and shampoo, and the clean scent of crisp linen sheets. With his mussed hair, he must have been sleeping.

Tiernan pushed the door closed behind him, enveloping them in near-darkness. The only light came through a window from one of the streetlights outside the building. He wrapped his arms around her and gave her a hug. "Are you all right?" he repeated, his voice husky with worry.

She nodded against his chest and sighed. "It was just the nightmare again."

He slipped his large hand into her hair and pressed her tighter against him. "Do you want to talk about it?"

"Okay." She started to draw away, but then she gave a little cry and her world spun as he scooped her up into his arms and carried her to the bedroom. He'd been doing that a lot lately.

Save for the bedroom, the apartment was empty of any furnishings, because it was new and because Copper had just arrived. There had been no time to get anything out of storage.

When they reached the bedroom, the streetlight peeked through the blinds, leaving stripes across the bed, giving them enough light to see by. He stepped over the pile of sheets she'd left tangled on the floor. He laid her on the middle of the bed, then scooted himself next to her so that they were facing one another.

"I felt lonely when I woke up without you." Copper reached up and stroked his stubbled cheek. "I missed having you wrapped around me while I slept."

"I missed you, as well," he said softly. He turned his face to her palm and kissed it, sending a shiver through her. "Tell me about this dream."

Copper sighed and moved her hand from his face to his chest to stroke the satiny material of the robe he wore.

"It started out similar to the other dreams, but it went further and was different." The memory of it made her throat dry. "This time there was a huge cavern, and on the other side of it a door and a circle with evil runes. And an eye made of blood beneath my feet."

Tiernan pressed his mouth to Copper's forehead, his lips firm yet soft at the same time. "Whatever it is—if this is truly a vision—we will face it together. You will not be alone."

She smiled, feeling a sense of warmth and comfort at his words. She clenched her hand in his robe. "Thank you," she said just before she reached up to kiss him.

Immediately, his mouth took hers in an expert kiss, biting her lower lip and causing her to sigh. They slipped their tongues into one another's mouths and Copper savored the masculine taste of him. The day they left Otherworld—was it only yesterday?—she'd reveled in being with him, and she wanted more. So much more.

She moved her hands up to his neck and pressed her body against his as her kiss grew more frantic, more needy. Tiernan matched her movements, his soft groans mingling with the tiny mewling sounds she made as they kissed.

To her satisfaction, his cock was hard against her belly while she grew damp between her thighs. She desired him so badly she wanted to pull apart his robe and take him now. No matter what, he was hers for tonight.

"You are so beautiful." He trailed his lips along her jawline to her ear. "What do you do to me? It is as if you are seducing me with your magic."

She laughed softly. "I'm willing to seduce you any way I can, but I think what we're doing is making magic together."

"If you say so, little fire." His brogue drove her mad with desire and she tried to keep her voice steady as his lips reached her throat. He found her pulse at the curve of her neck, licked and kissed the skin. "Right now you are the beat of my heart, the blood rushing through my veins."

Copper sighed and melted at his words. "You really do know how to sweet talk a girl."

He raised his head and kissed her soundly before saying, "I do not think I am the one who started this seduction."

"Okay, I did." She gave him a playful grin and slid her fingers over his cock that was covered by the satin of the robe. "And I'm not finished with you yet."

Tiernan groaned at the feel of Copper's hand on his erection. His thoughts turned only to pleasuring her, to being deep within her. Once again he could think of nothing save Copper.

He palmed her breasts that were like ripe peaches in his hands. She took her fingers from around his cock and pulled apart her own robe so that her breasts were bared. He sucked in his breath and pinched her nipples between his thumbs and forefingers.

"Yes." Copper could barely catch her breath. "Squeeze them harder."

Tiernan had no problem complying and pinched each hard nub tighter. He would do anything for this beautiful witch.

She sighed and slid her hands into his hair. "Suck my nipples."

He was used to being in command, in control, but at this moment he could only obey her orders. He scraped his stubbled cheek down her soft chest to the sensitive place between her breasts.

She clenched her fingers tighter in his hair. "Suck them hard."

He laved his tongue over each nipple and she gasped and arched toward his face. When he slipped one nub into his mouth and sucked, Copper pressed him tighter to her breast. "Harder, Tiernan. Harder!"

While applying deep suction to one of her nipples, he flicked his tongue over it, then bit down.

"Yessss!" Copper hissed with pleasure. "Goddess, that feels good."

With his fingers, he squeezed her other nipple hard. Then he bit down on the nipple in his mouth and Copper cried out. "Ohmigoddess!"

Tiernan scraped his stubble across her soft skin as he moved his mouth to her other nipple and sucked it as hard as the first one. He couldn't believe how good she tasted, how responsive she was to his touch. She was squirming beneath his mouth, holding his head tight to her breasts with her hands in his hair.

"I could come just from the way you suck my nipples." She cried out again as he bit her. "Don't stop."

He kept his mouth on her while slipping his other hand into her robe, down her taut belly to her mound. He bit her nipple again, just as he slipped his finger into her wet folds.

Copper saw bubbles of magic the moment he touched her clit, just like what had happened in Otherworld. Gold bubbles that lingered between the two of them.

Sex magic.

Somehow her hurt foot didn't even bother her. If sex made the pain go away, she was all for it.

While he nipped first one nipple, then the other, he thrust his fingers deep into her pussy and she rode his hand.

"That's it!" She rocked her hips against him and the

gold bubbles around them seemed to grow in number. "You're so good. I want all of you again and again."

"Come for me," he said in a growl against her chest. "I want to feel your climax, little fire."

Copper writhed. So close to orgasm, so close. When he pressed his thumb against her clit she gave a small cry and shuddered in his arms. Her channel clenched around his fingers and she rubbed her mound against his hand. Her nipples were raw from his rough attention to them and that added to the pleasure of her climax.

Her head swam a little as she pushed herself up to a sitting position while Tiernan reclined on one elbow. Glittering gold magic still sparkled around them and she batted a couple of bubbles away from her face.

Slices of yellow light spilled across Tiernan's face through the blinds. His look was intense, fiery. His robe had come undone and his cock jutted out from the opening of the cloth.

Copper slipped her own robe off so that it slid down her shoulders and arms to the bed, and she was bared to him. The memory of the times they'd been together was heady, only making her want him more and more.

Tiernan's mind was filled with the vision before him. Her long copper-colored hair was mussed, her eyes heavy-lidded with lust, and the curls between her thighs moist with her juices. Gold bubbles glittered in the air between them. As they had before, they added to the intense need he had for her and made it difficult to restrain himself. Was she using her magic to make him feel such an incredible need for her?

He pushed himself up to sit facing her. He shrugged his robe off and tossed it onto the floor.

"*You* are beautiful," she said, her voice breathy and her eyes wide. She reached up and caught a lock of his blond hair, twirled it around her finger and smiled. "Still a little wavy, but I think Silver's shampoo got the worst of it. Although your hairstyle was quite, er, interesting before. I especially liked the Pixie artwork."

Tiernan gave a low rumble, grabbed her beneath the arms, and started tickling her.

"No, no, no!" Copper squealed and squirmed, trying to get away from him, but he was far too powerful.

He chuckled as he found other ticklish spots. The insides of her thighs, her knees, and the bottom of her uninjured foot. Copper was giggling so hard tears rolled down her cheeks and he could tell she was having a hard time catching her breath.

She threw a pillow and it landed square in his face. He growled as he tossed it aside and she tried to throw another one at him. Before she could, he pinned her naked body beneath his weight.

"Let me go, you big barbarian," she said between gasps as he tickled her some more. "I swear I'll get revenge on you!"

He only laughed and braced his arms to either side of her head. When he looked down at her his laughter died away and so did hers.

"Fuck my breasts." Her eyes met his as she pushed the mounds together. "And let me lick your cock."

Surprised, but more than pleased to comply, he rose up and straddled her chest so that he was kneeling, his thighs clamped against her sides. He pushed his erection between the softness of her breasts and began pumping his hips. Every time his cock met her lips, she swirled her tongue around its head and he groaned at the incredible pleasure of it.

He continued to thrust his hips, sliding between her breasts and feeling their softness around his length, and her tongue laving him. Sweet goddess, her tongue on the head of the shaft only made him want to pound into her wet core harder and harder yet.

"I want to taste you now," Copper said. When he drew back, she eased down so that her face was directly beneath his erection.

"You little witch." He braced his arms against the headboard and eased in and out of her mouth as she sucked him. "Ah, gods. Your mouth is like hot satin around my cock."

She fondled his balls and gave a soft humming sound that vibrated throughout him. He came so close to the peak that there was almost no turning back. With effort, he withdrew from her mouth, his cock and balls aching so badly that he clenched his teeth to hold back his orgasm.

Copper's entire being was in flames. She was ready for him, and she was ready for him now.

"Fuck me, Tiernan." She ran both hands up his firmly muscled chest. "Drive yourself deep inside of me."

A rumble rose up from his chest and he straightened so that he was resting back on his haunches between her splayed thighs. He looked like a Viking of old with his wavy blond hair, his finely crafted body, the fierce expression on his face.

"Turn over," he commanded, to Copper's surprise and excitement.

She turned so that she was on her belly, then rose up on her hands and knees with Tiernan's hands grasping her waist. Her stomach flip-flopped and her body shook in anticipation.

"Lower your face to the bed and rest your arms above your head." He rubbed his cock against her folds. "I'm going to fuck you deep and hard."

Copper's body was on fire as she obeyed. She rocked herself back so that his erection rubbed against her folds some more.

Tiernan positioned his cock right at the entrance to her pussy. He grabbed her hips with both hands and slammed himself deep inside her.

She cried out at the incredible sensation. He was so thick and long and filled her so much she could swear she felt it all the way to her belly.

The gold bubbles began floating around them again as Tiernan began thrusting his hips, his strokes achingly slow. Copper moaned as she rocked back to meet every plunge of his cock. The magical bubbles were adding to the sensations she was feeling. Her skin felt so sensitive. She'd never felt so alive and free yet captive all at once.

He palmed the firm globes of her buttocks, massaging them as he pumped his hips. "I like to see my cock sliding in and out of you, little fire. So slick with your juices." He slammed into her harder. "Your sheath is tight and hot."

Her extra-sensitized nipples rubbed the bed sheet with every movement as her face was pressed to the bed and her arms stretched out above her. It was so erotic how he had positioned her, the way he was taking control. The sound of flesh smacking flesh filled the room, and their combined scents were heady.

She wiggled her hips, hardly able to catch her breath with her orgasm building within her. The power of it was incredible. She knew the golden bubbles were intensifying everything she was experiencing.

He gripped her hips tighter and slammed his own hips harder against her ass. "Are you about to come?"

She could barely speak, but managed to get out, "Yes . . . just a little more."

Tiernan slipped one hand from her hip down into her folds and flicked her clit.

Copper shouted, "Ohmigoddess!" as her orgasm exploded within. Some of those golden bubbles seeped into her skin, causing her climax to go on and on as Tiernan continued to fuck her. She couldn't believe the fire in her body, the way her channel kept clenching and unclenching around his cock. It was like that one orgasm would never end.

He drew his cock out, rubbed the cleft of her buttocks with it, and then he slipped a finger inside the tight bud. "Have you ever been fucked in the ass, Copper?"

The sensation was amazing. Barely able to breathe,

much less think, she shook her head. The idea of being taken like that, filled in another way that she'd never been filled before, made her pussy spasm again.

"I will." He pumped his finger in and out of her tight rosette and his words were definitely a promise. "But not right now. Now I'm going to take you on your back."

He slipped his finger out and rolled her over. He was between her thighs, his chest against hers, his cock pressed up against her pussy, his arms braced to her sides so that his complete weight wasn't on her. For a long moment he looked down at her and in the dim light from the windows and the golden bubbles of magic she was able to see the untamed look in his blue eyes, his lust, his desire. Sweat glistened on his forehead and his hair was damp.

She didn't know how he was controlling himself, not driving into her until he had pumped his come deep inside her.

He lowered his head and captured her mouth in a wild kiss that she equaled. His mouth was hot and he tasted of male and of her juices from when he'd gone down on her earlier.

Tiernan's senses were reeling. It was an act of incredible self-control to keep from plunging again into her warmth and reaching his climax.

He kissed her salty skin, flicking his tongue out, starting at her jawline, down her neck to her breasts where he bit each one in turn.

Copper cried out. "Goddess yes, Tiernan. You do that so damn good." He lifted his head to see his fiery angel. Her hair was tangled and mussed from their wild bout of sex. She was breathing hard and her eyes were dark and heavy-lidded.

He rose up and hooked his arms under her knees, pushing forward so that her thighs were against her chest. She wrapped her ankles around the back of his head and he grunted as he took her deep.

If Copper had thought he filled her when she was on her

knees, facedown on the bed, it was nothing like what he was doing to her now. The position he had her in allowed him to go deeper than ever and she felt him straight to that sweet spot that no one but him had ever been able to reach before.

"Jeez, Tiernan." She slid her hands down so that she grasped his thighs as he moved in and out of her. "Don't go so damn slow!"

He gave her a wicked smile and didn't pick up his pace. His slow thrusts made her crazy. She looked between their bodies and saw his cock moving in and out of her and she gripped his thighs tighter so that her nails were digging into his muscled flesh. If he was going to tease her, then she was certainly going to leave her mark.

Gradually, he picked up speed, his thrust coming harder and faster. His body was so slick between her thighs from sweat and the moisture created between them. The magical gold bubbles grew in number, and she was vaguely aware of them penetrating his skin as well as her own.

Harder, harder, harder, he fucked her. Closer, closer, closer, she came to climaxing again. Just a little more, and she'd be there. But she wanted to wait for him, wanted to feel his release at the same time as her own.

She dug her nails deeper into his thighs. "Tell me when you're going to come, big man."

Tiernan grunted and he pumped his hips so hard she knew he was close. His jaw was clenched, his eyes wild, and his body rigid.

"Now," he growled. "Right now!"

"Do it!" she cried as her own orgasm burst through her.

Tiernan shouted, his voice echoing through the room. His cock pulsed inside her pussy and the walls of her channel contracted around him. He continued thrusting his hips, drawing out every bit of his fluid, and her body took from him all that he offered.

When they both stopped shuddering, but continued to

gasp for breath, Tiernan released his hold on her and with-drew his cock. He rolled to his side, taking her with him. Her thigh was nestled between his. He felt hot and sweaty and the room smelled of sex.

Gradually, the gold magical bubbles drifted away as if carried on a gentle breeze. The intensity of feelings in her body began to subside and she relaxed in Tiernan's arms.

Copper sighed, completely sated. She snuggled into his embrace, her head resting on his arm, and easily fell into a deep sleep.

Sixteen

Copper woke with Tiernan's arms and leg wrapped around her from behind, just as she had every night in the cave. Only this time they were naked. She snuggled deeper against his warmth and felt his morning arousal pressed against her backside. His musky scent and the smell of sex lingered in the air.

Tiernan's large hand moved to the nape of her neck and she felt him twirl a lock of her hair around his finger; he tugged, drawing her head back a bit. "Mmmm . . ." He nuzzled the curve of her neck. "You smell like apples and cinnamon. You feel so good in my arms. I could make love to you forever, little fire. I don't think I can get enough of you."

She grinned and wiggled her ass against his cock. "What in the world are you waiting for?"

"I wait for nothing that I want." He slid his leg off hers and moved it between her thighs, opening her so that he could take her from behind. He positioned himself so that his cock slipped into the wetness of her folds. "And I want you. Now."

Copper barely held back a moan, not wanting him to

know just how badly she needed him right at this moment. "You can't *always* have what you want, you know," she managed to get out, but just barely.

He pumped his hips just enough to slide his erection between the lips of her wet slit. "I can, and I will."

The way he was rubbing his cock against her clit—back and forth, back and forth—Copper had a hard time thinking at all. "Um, ah, jeez . . . What, oh . . . um, what if I say no?"

"You won't." His cock was now at the entrance to her core. "You're mine, little fire," he growled just before he slammed his cock inside her.

Copper gave a loud cry of excitement as he thrust in and out of her pussy with an even greater frenzy than he'd showed the night before. He was so damn big and his thickness and length filled her up.

He reached over her shoulder and grasped one of her nipples and squeezed it hard. Goddess, her nipples were so sensitive from last night that the sensation drove her wild. He reached farther and pinched her other nipple even harder, and she couldn't hold back another cry.

"Damn, you are so freaking good." She moved so that her ass met his hips with every thrust. Her words seemed to drive him even wilder as he pumped his hips impossibly harder.

Those bubbles began floating around them like soap bubbles blown from a plastic wand. Some floated, others seeped into their skin. Like before, they made her wilder, more needy for him.

He fucked her hard, his hips slamming against her ass, his big cock plunging in and out, filling her, leaving her, filling her, leaving her, filling her. His fingers continued to squeeze first one nipple, then the other, and he did it so hard that she cried out with every pinch.

His hand left her breasts and he eased it slowly down her belly. The sensation of his callused hand against her flat stomach added to her excitement. He moved his big, long fingers to her folds and began teasing her clit at the same time he drove in and out of her.

It was too much. The feel of his cock inside her, his hand on her clit—Copper came in a hard rush that sent heat throughout her body. The bubbles floating around them grew in number, tickling her nipples and joining his fingers in her pussy. Her body wouldn't stop shaking. The tremors kept on coming and coming. She reached for his hand, trying to still him, but he kept drawing out her orgasm as he thrust deep inside her.

"Tiernan, stop. Tiernan!" she shouted, going beyond wild in his arms. "Goddess. Oh, goddess!"

"Little fire," he said in her ear. "You belong to me." He gave one last pounding thrust of his hips and a loud groan of release. She felt him pulse inside her and her own contractions squeezed down on his length.

When he finally let up on her clit and they were breathing hard, their skin hot and sticky with sweat and sex, Tiernan kissed her nape. "Good morning, little fire."

Copper laughed and snuggled back more deeply into his arms. "What a way to start the day."

After Copper fell back asleep, Tiernan dressed in his robe. He paused to look down upon Copper's beautiful face and brushed a stray lock of hair from her cheek. The Faerie kisses across her nose made her even more beautiful. While sleeping she still had a mischievous expression that made him shake his head and grin.

A great weight seemed to tug at his heart and his smile turned into a frown. If he did not come up with a satisfactory solution, he would have to leave for Otherworld to wed Airell. That thought sat heavier with him now than it ever had.

As he drew his hand away from Copper, Tiernan wondered why she did not appear so young to him, the way Airell did. Copper was headstrong, impulsive, maddening . . . and yet he found himself captivated by her like no other woman whom he had shared pleasures with. It had seemed as if their physical joining were more than simply fucking.

He straightened his spine and hardened his expression.

Impossible. Illogical.

Then he remembered his own words mere moments before he had climaxed: *"Little fire,"* he had said. *"You belong to me."*

What had he been thinking?

He had been thinking with his cock.

After one final look at Copper, Tiernan turned and quietly strode to the front door and let himself out of the apartment.

Copper woke to an empty bed. She slipped into her robe and headed to Silver's apartment. Of course Copper didn't have her own soaps and supplies in her apartment bathroom yet. She'd also have to hit the store and buy herself an honest-to-goodness real toothbrush, along with other supplies.

When she went to Silver's apartment, Zeph joined Copper, riding on his favorite place, the upper curve of her ear. Copper knocked on Silver's apartment door and Copper heard a cheery "Come in!"

The minute she walked in, the smell of breakfast washed over her at the same time Silver met her at the door and hugged her.

"I just have to touch you again to make sure you're real!" Silver gave her another big squeeze before releasing her.

Copper grinned, then closed her eyes at the heavenly smells coming from the small kitchen. "If I'm not mistaken that's Mother's recipe for breakfast casserole that I smell. Eggs, potatoes, broccoli . . ." She opened her eyes as her stomach rumbled. "I've missed real food so much. I know I said that last night about ten times, but I don't think

I'll be able to eat enough. I doubt I could look at another Faerie seedcake or grass-and-berry tart again."

Silver laughed and headed back to the kitchen. She was all in royal purple, wearing heels, a short skirt, and silk blouse. "There's plenty of casserole." She grabbed a pair of pot holders, then headed to the oven. "As long as you eat before Hawk comes back. That man is never satisfied. He'll probably have Tiernan with him. I'd bet he's had his fill of Faerie food, too."

The thought of Tiernan caused a delicious warmth to sweep over Copper. The memory of her incredible night and morning with him made her smile. It had been sheer heaven. She felt sore all over, especially her nipples. And damn, but it felt good.

Silver caught Copper's attention again when she said, "You have a kind of dreamy look to your eyes, little sister. I don't suppose you have a thing for a certain Tuatha D'Danann warrior?"

"I'll never tell." Copper teased her sister with a wink. "Mind if I use the shower and grab more of my clothes?"

"Of course not." Silver brought the casserole out of the oven and set it on the stovetop. With her oven mitts still on, she made shooing motions with her hands toward the bedroom. "This can cool a bit while you shower. Make yourself totally at home."

Copper paused in mid-step. "By the way . . . All my stuff and my bank account . . . ?"

"Your furniture and everything but your clothes are in storage." Silver picked up an orange from the counter, sliced it in half, then grabbed a juicer. "I do believe your mutual funds and bank account have been growing quite nicely over the last fifteen months or so."

"I figured you'd take care of all of it." Copper smiled at her sister. "Thank you for everything. It'll be great to have money again. And to go shopping!"

"I knew you'd be back." Silver's expression became

solemn. "I never doubted it for a moment. It was just a matter of *when* you'd return."

Copper gave her sister another smile before heading to the bedroom, and Zephyr zipped off to go hang around Silver and Polaris.

She was too hungry to take long at her shower and getting dressed. Her foot felt lots better, but she still flinched when she unwrapped it before her shower. The wounds looked *much* improved, and had mostly healed, so she decided not to wrap it again. It was good being a witch.

When she dried off, she slipped on one of several pairs of her jogging shoes from one of the trunks of clothing Silver had kept in the room for her. These shoes were a pretty shade of sea blue. She put on a royal-blue crop-top T-shirt, faded blue jeans, and stuck her wand in her back pocket— she'd been so tired last night that she'd left it on Silver's vanity table. All the time she'd spent in Otherworld, she'd worn her jewelry constantly, never taking it off, and last night she'd slept in it all as usual. It had become a part of her, even more than it was before.

She dried her hair magically with her fingers again and studied herself in the mirror. She preferred shoulder-length hair, but long hair didn't look too bad on her. Wanting to keep it out of her face, she braided it into a long single plait. She brought the end over her shoulder and tied it with one of Silver's blue hair ties. Copper's pentagram earrings swung at her neck and the pentagram on her thick bracelet sparkled against her wrist with her movements.

In no time she was out of Silver's bedroom and in the kitchen, thankfully before the D'Danann men showed up. She and Silver scooted up to the table and started spooning out the casserole, Copper taking an entire plateful from the giant serving pan. Goddess, was she ever hungry.

She took a big bite and closed her eyes in heavenly bliss. "As good as Mother used to make," Copper said when she finished chewing. She saddened and opened her eyes to look at Silver. "I just can't believe she'll never make it again."

The sparkle left Silver's eyes and she squeezed Copper's hand. "We just have to believe that she's happy and well in Summerland. One day we will be with her again."

After what Tiernan had told her, his confidence that there *was* truly a Summerland made Copper feel a little better. Since he was of Otherworld, and a former god, he no doubt knew what he was talking about.

Silver released Copper's hand to pour them each a big glass of fresh-squeezed orange juice. Copper loved the citrus scent, and the taste was just as heavenly as everything else had been.

When he came in with Hawk, Tiernan was wearing black leather as always, and a different long black coat. He'd left his other one in Otherworld. Hawk had a long coat on, too, and she figured they wore them to hide their daggers and swords.

Tiernan's hair was damp, obviously from taking a shower. His blond hair hung to his shoulders, still a little wavy, and his deep-blue eyes made her squirm as he looked at her, and her nipples grew taut.

Hawk looked from Tiernan to Copper and frowned as if he disapproved, which surprised Copper. But the big warrior said nothing as he scooted up to the table and began spooning giant scoops of casserole onto his plate.

By then Silver and Copper had finished eating, so after she took her plate, cup, and fork to the sink, washed them, and put them away, Copper wandered around Silver's living room. She ran her fingers along the back of the delicate couch and touched the blue lampshade and crystal lamp. She noticed a huge overstuffed recliner that Silver must have gotten for the big D'Danann warrior who no doubt felt uncomfortable on Silver's furniture.

Copper loved Silver's oil paintings of various sites around San Francisco, like the Golden Gate Bridge and the most crooked street in the world, Lombard Street. She paused at a crystal vase of fresh white lilies and yellow daisies and touched the blooms, which were soft under her fingertips. From one of the chairs, Polaris, Silver's python familiar, watched Copper's every movement. And if snakes could smile, she thought he did.

Copper went to one of the curtained windows, Zeph riding on her ear, and drew aside the lacy white curtain. Down below, the street was fairly quiet but would soon be swarmed with tourists and locals. The Haight-Ashbury district was always filled with colorful people.

She turned away from the window and spotted Silver's huge mahogany desk with its mess of papers, a flat-screen computer monitor, what looked like a state-of-the-art printer, and a cordless phone. She felt like a kid at Christmas as she went to investigate. She couldn't wait to get her own stuff. Sure, it was materialistic, but she found joy in the modern world, especially after being exiled for so long.

In the background she heard the rumble of male voices, both men speaking in their strong Irish brogues. Silver was talking with them, and since she wasn't really paying attention, Copper vaguely heard the words *plan, location,* and *search.*

She walked to the desk and the first thing she picked up was a picture of their family. Her heart felt crushed by a heavy weight as she studied Moondust's ethereal beauty, her precious smile. Copper could see the Elvin in her now. Her gaze traveled to their stern father, who had a proud expression on his face, and on to her sister and herself. The picture had been taken in Ireland on one of their excursions a couple of years ago.

Copper set it down and picked up a crystal-framed picture of her and Silver. The picture made her feel both happy and sad. Happy to see both their familiar expressions, and sadness that she had missed so much over the last months.

She sighed, set the framed photo down, and noticed a picture of herself alone. She scrunched her nose. Did she really look like that? All those bright freckles, a pert nose, and a grin that made her look like she was up to no good.

Copper had to smile. She usually was up to something.

A paper lying next to the picture caught her eye and she frowned. It was a piece of parchment with strange symbols on it. When she picked it up, the parchment felt heavier than paper and rough between her fingertips, and smelled of ancient books and dust.

As she studied it, her stomach clenched and she felt blood drain from her face. Her hand shook, and so did the parchment.

The drawing was of the door from her nightmare last night. And below the door was the double ring containing the evil runes.

Seventeen

The parchment slipped from her fingers and floated to the floor like a fallen leaf drifting from a tree. She couldn't move. Her mind raced and her heart thudded.

"Copper?" Silver grasped Copper's shoulder. She looked up into her sister's worried expression. "You're so pale. What's wrong? Does it have something to do with this?" Silver had picked the parchment up from the floor and her fingers trembled enough to make the paper shake. "You're scaring me."

Before Copper realized it, Tiernan and Hawk were surrounding her.

"You know of this?" Tiernan asked, his tone both concerned and harsh—not at her, but for how it had upset her, she was sure.

Copper cleared her throat. "Last night—in my nightmare, that was the door." She pointed to the rectangle. "I dreamed that I was standing in the middle of a circle just like that one, except that at the center was a giant eye, like a big flat version of the one Darkwolf wears around his neck." She looked from the parchment back to Silver. "It was bloody. And it was my blood beneath my feet, as if the thing were sucking the blood out of me."

Everyone remained silent as they looked from one to another. Silver's face had gone beyond pale.

Copper went on to explain that she'd had various versions of this dream, each time traveling a little farther, and each time it got more frightening.

"I'm certain now, very certain, that these are dream-visions, not just nightmares." Copper glanced at the parchment, but didn't want to hold it—the evil in her vision came strongly and forcefully just from staring at it.

Tiernan put his hands at her shoulders and massaged some of the tenseness from her. She was surprised at his consideration and she leaned back into his touch, enjoying the way he loosened up the muscles of her neck, shoulders, and upper back. He was very, very good.

Hawk gave Tiernan a look of disapproval, and Copper wondered what Hawk's problem was.

"Maybe I can scry again, and learn more from your vision." Silver took the parchment to the table reluctantly, as if she were afraid of what she might see.

Copper began clearing away the now-empty casserole pan and juice pitcher, and the men took their dishes from the table into the kitchen and to the sink. Apparently these men had manners—or Silver had trained them well. Before Silver dragged out her pewter cauldron and the jug of purified water, Copper washed and dried off the table.

Everyone had crowded around Silver by the time she'd filled the cauldron and was ready to scry. Polaris was up on the surface of the table now, his body wrapped around the cauldron, obviously to add his own magic.

Silver held up her hands and glared at the men. "Back off. I can't do this with you hanging over my shoulders. It's probably better if you leave."

Both men scowled. "I will not," Hawk said.

Silver jabbed her finger at the big man's chest. "You

will if you want me to get anything out of this. Last time you two watched, it made me nervous. Copper and her familiar can stay, but the two of you have to go."

Their scowls deepened, but Hawk and Tiernan strode from the apartment, and Hawk closed the door just a little too loudly.

"Phew." Silver pushed her hair over her shoulder so that it didn't hang into the cauldron. "It's not easy getting rid of those two."

Copper smiled, but her insides were still chilled from the sight of the drawing on the parchment.

Zephyr buzzed from Copper's ear to perch on the lip of the cauldron. She felt his magic, along with Polaris's. The honeybee might be small in comparison to Polaris or other familiars, but his magic was just as strong.

Silver braced her palms on the tabletop, to either side of the cauldron. Copper waited two steps away, not wanting to distract Silver. Sometimes Silver could see visions in the water itself, while other times images rose up in misty fog and played themselves out in a three-dimensional scene.

Copper forced herself to pick up the parchment, her hands still shaking, and focused on the crude drawing. At the same time she lent her own magical support to Silver's.

Wisps of fog dragged her attention from the parchment to the cauldron. The strands coalesced, slowly combining to form figures that Copper immediately recognized. The forms were Copper and her sister. Both were at a lonely pier at the bay, a pier that wasn't familiar to Copper. No one else was around and light from a waxing moon glistened on the water that barely moved against the shore.

In the foggy image from the cauldron, both Copper and Silver crept through the darkness to one of the huge pilings, telephone-pole-sized legs holding up the wooden pier. They peeked around the pilings, obviously taking care not to be seen.

Three figures stood beneath the pier. Darkwolf, Junga in

her human form, and someone who was standing too far into the shadows for Copper to make out. The figure had long hair that glistened in what little moonlight there was, and something struck her as familiar.

In the next moment purple light blazed through the darkness—

And the foggy images vanished.

Both Copper and Silver stared at the cauldron, willing the images to come back.

"No!" Silver shouted, and Zephyr flew off the lip of the cauldron and returned to Copper's ear. "Bless it, that wasn't enough! I *hate* when that happens."

Silver looked to Copper, frustration on her features as she continued. "I recognize that pier. That's where the D'Danann and some of our group of witches battled the Fomorii. We won the battle, but we lost one of the D'Danann and McNulty."

"McNulty?" Copper's heart fell. "I really liked her." Then she added in a growl, "Fucking demons."

Silver sighed. "I was so full of rage when she died, that I helped the D'Danann kill the demons," she said as she looked to her sister. "I came so close to turning to the dark that time that it was frightening."

Copper wrapped her arm around Silver's shoulder and said in a matter-of-fact voice, "That would never happen. You did what you had to. I'm sure I would have done the same in your place."

She released her sister after one last squeeze and met Silver's gray gaze. Silver cleared her throat. "Darkwolf . . . he has some kind of pull on me. It's like we're connected on some wavelength, and he uses that to try and manipulate me. I've fought him off before, but I'm afraid one day I might fail."

Copper rubbed Silver's shoulder, the purple silk sliding beneath her palm. "You're strong. He can't hurt you."

Silver sighed and said nothing.

"Do you think we're meant to go there?" Copper turned back to stare at the now quiet cauldron. "Or is it a warning?"

"I think we are supposed to go to the wharf." Silver pushed away from the table and pursed her lips. "The only one dangerous magically is Darkwolf. The other Balorite warlocks are not even close to being as strong as he is, and the Fomorii have no magic other than being able to shift into human form and back. We probably wouldn't have any problem binding those other two with our witchcraft before they knew what was happening." She tapped her chin with her finger as she looked thoughtfully at the cauldron. "The third figure, though, I'm not exactly sure what it, he, she, is."

Copper's gaze returned to the cauldron. "That blaze of light—where was it coming from?"

At that Silver paused. "I don't know for sure, but I think from us. Sometimes my magic takes on a purple hue—when I draw from the gray."

Copper frowned at that. The gray caused Silver's magic to change hue? "When do you think this vision will happen?" Copper asked.

"Late this evening," Silver said with conviction. "I have no doubt about it. The waxing moon will be in that phase tonight."

With a sigh, Copper said, "I think you're right. We'll need backup."

Silver rubbed the snake bracelet that wound from the back of one hand and up her wrist. "Yeah, and the D'Danann will want to go barreling in there with swords and fists, and we'll never find out what's going on."

At that Copper had to grin. "Men. They have no subtleties."

Silver smiled. "At least not ours."

Ours. The word gave Copper pause, and she thought of her relationship with Tiernan. He'd been so possessive last night, yet he was possibly going to end up marrying a woman who was pregnant with another man's child.

The thought of him being married made her stomach pitch and she had to push it away.

A knock on the door startled them both and Silver rolled her eyes to Copper. "No doubt they've been trying to listen in while we've been talking."

Silver let the warriors into the apartment. After she closed the door behind them, she and Copper explained the vision they had seen and what they were positive they must do tonight.

"I will *not* allow you to go to the pier, Silver," Hawk said in a growl as he banged his fist on the table, causing water to slosh from the cauldron. "Especially not so close to the warlock and the demon."

"Get over it," Copper said to Hawk, causing the warrior to pause. "You'd better get used to us in the thick of things."

Hawk looked to Tiernan. "Is she as difficult to contend with as Silver?"

Tiernan sighed. "Worse."

Copper sniffed. Silver glared at Hawk and said, "After all we've been through together, you know I am more than capable of handling myself. I've kicked more ass than you can count. Our relationship is based on trust, isn't it?"

Hawk took Silver by the shoulders, and he looked so concerned and genuinely afraid for her. "I know, *a thaisce*. But I worry so about you. And with our babe—"

"You're pregnant?" Copper nearly shouted as she looked at Silver in amazement. Happiness rushed through her for her sister, yet frustration, too. "You guys are having a baby and you didn't tell me?"

"A babe?" Tiernan echoed, looking from Silver to Hawk.

"I was waiting for the right time." Silver's cheeks turned pink. "It's just been so crazy. I've been so thrilled that you're here, and with everything that's been happening—I just wanted some quiet time to sit down with you and share the news."

Copper folded her arms across her chest like she was

mad, then grinned. She pushed Hawk out of the way and hugged Silver. "We're having a baby." She bounced up and down on her toes. "We're having a baby!" She pulled away, still grinning like an idiot. "I'll have a niece or nephew!"

"A son, I think." Silver pressed her hand to her still flat belly and smiled. She glanced up at Hawk and the love in their eyes made Copper ache inside. "A boy who is the spitting image of his daddy."

"Or a girl." Hawk kissed the top of her head. "As beautiful as her mother."

"As beautiful as Shayla." Silver smiled. "I'm sure Shayla will love either a brother or a sister."

Hawk kissed her and the next thing Copper knew, Silver and Hawk were in a serious liplock. Copper glanced up at Tiernan, who looked slightly uncomfortable, and Copper couldn't stop smiling. "I'm going to be an aunt," she said, feeling incredibly giddy.

Copper turned her attention back to the smooching couple. "Hey, get a room already."

Silver and Hawk separated. She had a lovely flush over her features and her lipstick had been thoroughly kissed off.

Hawk held Silver by her shoulders and looked directly at her. "You know that I fear for both of you."

Silver sighed. "I understand that. But the baby will be fine. I'll be fine." She reached up to cup his cheek. "You can't treat me like a fragile piece of blown glass."

Resignation was in the big warrior's eyes. "Nothing I can do will change your mind?"

Silver shook her head. "Nothing."

Copper glanced up at Tiernan, who was looking at her as though he was ready to argue, too. "Don't even think about it," she said. "Just zip those lips."

Adrenaline heightened Copper's senses as she and Silver moved silently through the night along the narrow strip of rocky shore with Copper leading the way. To the right was a high concrete wall, to the left was the bay.

The pier extended far from the shoreline, out into the bay on its sturdy, water-stained, wooden pilings. A white and blue boat was moored at the end of the pier and the boat gave creaks of age as it moved with the gentle swells of the water. The waxing moon cast silvery ripples on the water's surface through the breaks in the clouds.

Both sisters were wearing all black—bomber jackets, jeans, and T-shirts. Silver wore her special boots that had sheathes for her stiletto knives. She'd clipped back her long silvery-blond hair with a silver Celtic-knot pin, and had a black stocking cap pulled over her head. Copper wore black jogging shoes and had her copper braid up under her stocking cap.

Tiernan, Hawk, and two other D'Danann hovered somewhere nearby. They were able to cloak themselves in invisibility when they were winged. Unfortunately, they could not maintain their invisibility when they fought, whether it was in the air or on land.

The not-so-distant sound of traffic and the gentle waves of the bay washing ashore were the only sounds Copper heard until a foghorn blared in the distance, causing her to jump.

She just couldn't get enough of the scent of brine and wind off the bay. So what if the fishy smell was a little pungent? She didn't care. She was home.

They continued stealthily through the night toward the pier. Copper had her wand up her jacket sleeve so that the moonlight didn't glint off its surface and the crystals didn't sparkle to give them away. Silver had done the same with one of her stiletto knives while her free hand was at the ready to do her magic. Her other knife was in her boot.

Copper often wished she could do the kind of magic that Silver did with her hands. But from the time she was a young girl, Copper had always relied on her wand as a conduit for her witchcraft.

Voices floated on the salty breeze, along with the scent of wolfsbane, moss, and rich earth. Copper and Silver stilled and glanced at one another. The sounds were coming from beneath the pier. Copper's blood throbbed through her veins as they moved silently forward. The voices grew louder the closer the sisters got to the pilings. They finally reached the pier and eased up to it, each standing behind one of the pier's large wooden piles.

Copper tried to control the nervousness and her breathing as she peeked around the curve of the thick wooden leg. She had to blink until her eyes adjusted to the darkness. The moonlight didn't fully reach below the pier.

"You will ensure her safety and deliver her to me," said a man's familiar voice, but she couldn't place it. It was as if that man didn't belong here, not at all. The man was so concealed by the darkness that she couldn't make out anything but the slightest shine from the hint of moonlight on his long hair. Perhaps he was one of the Fomorii demons and that was what gave her the sense of wrongness.

Junga folded her arms across her chest, her glare focused on the shadowed man. "First you must continue to aid us in our search for the door. How close are the—"

"Quiet, woman," the familiar voice ordered Junga, and Copper saw the demon-woman's body go rigid at the same time she flexed her fingers.

Darkwolf shot her a look, as if in warning. Junga clenched her fists and for an instant Copper caught a glimpse of the demon inside warping the stunning woman's features, but then it was gone.

The Balorite warlock opened his mouth as if to speak, but stopped and raised his chin, his nose slightly to the air, like a wolf scenting the wind for prey. Copper's skin chilled. Did he sense them?

Darkwolf gave a smile as his gaze returned to the man

whom Copper couldn't see. "All you need to know," the warlock said, "is that I will deliver what I have promised when you and your . . . *people* have reached the door."

The door! Copper thought. *They have to be talking about the same door from my dream-vision. The same one from the parchment.*

She moved back against the pile, no longer looking at Darkwolf, Junga, or the mystery man. She glanced at Silver, who was also leaning with her back against the pile, away from the trio under the pier.

Copper's heart pounded harder as she saw the rapid rise and fall of Silver's chest and heard her breathing growing harsher. Copper's alarm grew at the expression on Silver's face, the way she turned her head from side to side, as if saying *no* and as if she were fighting something internally.

Silver let her stiletto slip from her jacket sleeve and into her hand so that she was holding the hilt tight. The metal glistened in the moonlight as Silver clenched her teeth. She seemed to be at war with something inside.

Fear grew rampant in Copper's heart. What was happening to Silver? Copper eased her wand from her own sleeve and gripped it in her fist, prepared to fight. Was Silver struggling with her gray magic, walking dangerously close to the dark? Or did it have something to do with Darkwolf?

Copper peeked around the corner and a glimmer of light lit the features of the mystery man.

Garran. Oh, my goddess, it's Garran!

Every piece of the puzzle came rushing to her and her head spun with it. The dark familiar shapes in her dreams had been the Drow. Their continuous digging. The giant that had made its way to the Drow cavern, obviously woken from its post in guarding things better not reached. The human-made clock in Garran's chamber that showed the date and time—probably telling him when to meet with Darkwolf.

"But for now . . ." Darkwolf's voice reached through her fear for Silver and her shock at discovering Garran's betrayal. "Two of our treasures can be found."

Alarm bells went off in Copper's head, but not before brilliant purple light flooded the pilings, just like in the vision.

Instinctively, Copper threw up a golden bubble, intending to surround both herself and Silver. But to Copper's horror, the dark purple magic wrapped around Silver first, separating Copper's shield from her sister. Purple ropes immediately bound Silver to the pile. She couldn't move!

The stiletto slipped from Silver's hand and clattered on the rocky shore. She shouted, "No!" and struggled against the magical ropes.

Blood thrumming through her veins, Copper dropped her own protective bubble and pointed her wand at Darkwolf's shimmering purple barrier. She released a powerful blast of witchcraft, trying to break through the warlock's shield.

His shield wavered.

Adrenaline surged through her as she sent another blast of power at the barrier.

It dissolved into a million purple sparks.

But Silver was still bound to the piling with the magical ropes.

At the same time Copper struggled to fight Darkwolf's magic, D'Danann cries had rent the night.

Darkwolf appeared at Silver's side almost instantly. Copper's heart raced as she aimed her wand at him and muttered a chant under her breath. Golden spellfire shot from the end of her wand, but Darkwolf held up his hand and deflected her magic with his own. It struck a piling and the acrid stench of smoke and burning oil filled the air.

Hawk charged for Darkwolf, sword raised.

His sword arced through the air at the same time the warlock wrapped his arm around Silver's waist.

The bonds dropped.

Darkwolf's lips moved as if he were speaking.

Silver struggled and shouted.

She and Darkwolf vanished.

Vanished.

For a moment Copper was so shocked, so horrified, she couldn't move. No sound would come from her mouth. Filled with fiery rage, she whirled to fight the demon woman and Garran who had been beneath the pier, intending to capture them to find out where Silver had been taken.

But they were both gone.

Gone.

She ran into the darkness, her wand light flooding what was once dark. All she saw was the wall of earth and concrete beneath the dock and no sign of the demon or the Drow.

Tiernan stood beside her with his sword raised and utter fury on his face.

Copper swung her gaze back to look at Hawk, whose features were twisted into a devastated expression. He roared and slammed his boot into one of the pilings and Copper heard the massive wooden leg crack.

"Godsdamn!" Hawk shouted, a mixture of rage and fear for his mate in his tone. "I will find that bitch of a demon," he said just before he bolted out from beneath the pier and took to the skies. The other D'Danann warriors followed close behind.

"I can't believe Darkwolf took her." Tears wet Copper's cheeks as she clenched her wand in her fist. "The bastard took her!"

The wand lit up Tiernan's harsh features. He'd stayed with her, no doubt for her protection. "We will retrieve your sister," he said in a low growl.

"It happened so fast." Copper couldn't keep the tremble from her voice. "I was in shock at seeing Garran—"

"Garran?" Tiernan grabbed her by the shoulders, surprising her. "The Drow king was here?"

She nodded. "Apparently, he's been betraying us all along."

In the light from her wand she saw Tiernan's jaw tighten before he released her. "I shall throttle the Elvin bastard."

"Get in line." Rage and pain coursed through Copper's body. "*I'm* going to kill the son of a bitch. After I finish with Darkwolf and get Silver back.

"I tried to throw up a shield to protect us both, but his got to her first." Copper's voice cracked. "And Silver—" Copper continued, her voice trembling. "Before she was captured, I saw her face. It was like she was fighting something inside her mind. I was so concerned about her, and so in shock about Garran, that I wasn't prepared when Darkwolf attacked."

Copper rubbed her jacket sleeve over her eyes. She couldn't stop the tears. "I should have protected her."

Her legs gave out and she found herself on her knees, rocks digging into her flesh. Tiernan knelt beside her and wrapped his arm around her shoulders as she choked back sobs. She leaned into him, needing his comfort.

Copper trembled so badly she didn't think she could get to her feet. Tiernan took one of her hands and helped her rise, then caught her in his arms when her knees wanted to give out again. "We will find your sister." He sounded as if he was grinding his teeth. "We *will* find her."

Without responding, Copper went to where Silver had dropped her stiletto knife and picked it up. The hilt was slightly warm where Silver had gripped it. Pain cut through Copper's chest as if the stiletto had knifed her.

Goddess, why hadn't she been able to protect her sister? And Garran . . . how could she not have put all the clues together before?

When she finally gathered herself enough to go back to HQ, she drove Silver's beat-up yellow VW Bug to the apartments, barely able to think clearly.

On their way to the pier, Silver had explained how

Hawk had saved her after she'd collapsed from a summoning. He'd driven the car, taking her back to her apartment above the Moon Song café. Hawk had managed to trash her new car, because he was from Otherworld and had never driven before. At the time Silver had told Copper the story, it had been funny enough that she'd giggled almost all the way to the wharf. Silver did have insurance, she just hadn't had the time to have the Bug fixed.

Copper didn't even know why she was thinking about that as she drove up and down the steep streets of the city. Her chest burned with fear and anger, and her head ached from crying. Damn, but they should have listened to the men and not gone to the wharf. But why did the scrying cauldron show them doing just that? It didn't make sense.

She clenched the steering wheel tighter and tried to focus as she came up on a four-way stop.

It also hadn't made sense that all those months ago she had felt compelled to go to the beach alone, that her dream-vision had insisted she do so, only to meet Darkwolf and to end up in Otherworld.

What was going on?

She brushed the back of her hand over her wet eyes again. She'd been home *two* freaking days, and had managed to let her sister be kidnapped.

As she continued to drive through the city she racked her brain to figure out how to find Silver. She couldn't scry like her sister. Copper's dream-visions were her only divination talent.

Her heart leaped as she remembered Rhiannon. She had the sight! Then there was Cassia, who could discover clues through her rune stones. Mackenzie used tarot cards that could give additional hints, not to mention all the divination talents among the rest of the witches. With all their skills, they were bound to figure out where Darkwolf had taken Silver.

And the D'Danann. She couldn't forget them. Hawk

wouldn't stop until Silver was found. She was sure Tiernan wouldn't, either.

Until now, the witches, the D'Danann, and even the Paranormal Special Forces led by Jake Macgregor had failed to catch Darkwolf, the Balorites, and the Fomorii that had escaped on Samhain. But now so much more was at stake.

Silver and her baby.

Eighteen

Darkwolf dropped the bonds from around Silver. As he snatched her around the waist, he steeled himself for the familiar sensation of transference. With the power of the god Balor and his stone eye, Darkwolf had the ability to transfer himself and up to three people at a time. All it took were two words spoken in the god's ancient tongue.

"Balor bahamenor."

Silver cried out. He heard the shouts of Copper and the yells of the warriors as he and Silver vanished from witch and D'Danann sight. He was leaving Junga to fend for herself, and the Drow king, as well.

Transference was a rush like no other. Exhilarating. Filled with power. As if he were flying through the sky with wings. His brilliant purple magic flowed around him and his prize. He finally had her. He sensed Silver's fear and that pleased him.

Although it seemed longer, it took mere moments to transfer from the pier to the new lair where the Balorites and Fomorii now resided. In order to be large enough to ac-commodate the Fomorii and to house the number of remaining Balorites, they had selected a penthouse suite that encompassed the entire floor of one of the high-rises. Again they had settled into the lap of luxury. After a taste of wealth, Darkwolf would have no less.

Of course Elizabeth Black had been wealthy when Junga took over her body, but when she was forced to go into hiding they didn't dare touch her funds. The police no doubt would be investigating her disappearance.

Unfortunately there were no servants, but the Balorites and Fomorii now had hefty bank accounts that Darkwolf controlled. This was thanks to the wealthy man who had owned the manor they had formerly inhabited. One of the Fomorii still controlled the man's body, however. And now another demon had taken over the shell of the exceedingly rich woman who had owned this penthouse.

All this shot through his mind during the transference. When they reappeared in the penthouse's large office, Darkwolf gripped the witch Silver tighter to him to ensure she didn't collapse from what would have been an unfamiliar experience for her.

He shook off the rush of the transference. At the same time, Silver raised her knee and her hand darted to her boot. She jerked out a stiletto knife, and had it buried in his thigh before he had the chance to blink.

Not again.

Pain ripped through him and he lost his grip on Silver. She spun away into a corner of the office near the computer. She gathered a blue spellfire ball, flung it at him, knocking him on his ass. Damn, the thing burned like white-hot heat. Not wanting to hurt her, he flung a shield around her and it glistened purple in the office lighting.

"Scum." Silver was so lovely when she was furious that he could almost forgive her for the pain he now endured. Not that long ago, during the battle of Samhain, she had buried her knife into his thigh in nearly the same location.

He gritted his teeth, reached down and yanked the knife

from his thigh before he pushed himself to his feet. Blood
flowed freely. A fresh bout of pain would have caused him
to drop to his knees if it weren't for the power of Balor that
filled him.

Instead, thanks to his magic as a warlock and to the god
Balor, the wound had already begun to heal, the flesh
slowly knitting itself together beneath his now ripped and
bloodied jeans.

He kept his expression as calm as possible as he tossed
the bloody knife aside where it landed on the white carpet
beside a pair of finely crafted wooden file cabinets. Silver's
gaze followed the knife, then shot back to meet his eyes.
Her eyes were a beautiful gray. When she'd torn away from
him, her long silvery-blond hair had fallen from beneath
the black cap, which now lay on the floor beneath the computer desk. A silver Celtic-knot hair clasp also lay on the
floor. Her black jeans hugged her slim figure, but disap-
pointingly, the jacket hid her lush breasts.

"Again in the thigh, Silver?" Darkwolf raised an eyebrow and gave what he hoped was an amused expression.
"Why not in the gut?"

"Next time," she growled and folded her arms across
her chest.

She was magnificent. With the most primal urges, he
had wanted Silver from the moment he had sensed her gray
magic and the power she wielded. And when he had first
seen her, he had wanted her even more.

There was something . . . special about Silver. His inter-
est in her bordered on obsession. And in the back of his
mind he felt as if somehow she could save him.

He couldn't help the sensual smile that curved his lips
as he studied her. For some reason she looked even lovelier
than ever, but he couldn't say why. By Balor, he wanted to
take her now, to fuck her as he'd planned to from that first
moment of his awareness of her. But he wouldn't take her
until she was ready for him.

Soon she would want him as much as he wanted her. Time . . . simply time.

And perhaps their joining could do more, could rid him of the evil that consumed him . . .

The eye warmed at his chest and a sharp pain burst in his mind, but he was certain Balor had not heard his thoughts. That was one thing the god had not been able to do—break down the barriers in Darkwolf's mind when he chose to raise them.

He attempted to mind-speak with Silver, as he had when they were at the pier tonight. He had caught her off guard, invading her mind with his thoughts, and rendering her helpless with his power.

But now she had blocked him from her mind as if with steel shields. He couldn't help but scowl as the power of his thoughts bounced away from her. Yet somehow it aroused him, too.

Darkwolf placed one palm facing Silver and slowly moved it from left to right. His glimmering purple shield strengthened around her, ensuring that she was his prisoner.

Silver's throat worked and she raised her head a notch. "Afraid, Darkwolf? Afraid that if you drop your shield I'll have you flat on your ass again and in my control?"

He chuckled. "You're a powerful witch, Silver Ashcroft, but you couldn't begin to outdo me."

"Oh, really?" Silver cocked an eyebrow. "Was that why you vanished on Samhain? You certainly didn't stay for the fight like the rest of us."

Darkwolf dismissed her question with a smile.

"Why do you want me this time?" Silver asked, her voice now cold and cutting. "Does it have anything to do with a certain door that you're looking for?" Silver gave him what amounted to a smug expression. "We know a lot, and you won't get away with your scheme. We even know about your helpers."

"What do you know of the Drow?" he asked, anger lacing his words.

She just smiled.

For a long moment he studied her, trying to break into her thoughts. The witches and D'Danann may have found the missing parchment with the drawing, but they couldn't possibly use it. No one could decipher the runes other than a servant or a child of Balor.

"What we've planned has nothing to do with you." He paused, thinking for a moment. "You'll simply be at my side when we release the demons . . . and Balor's body."

"We'll never let it happen," Silver said with absolute conviction in her voice.

Darkwolf shrugged. "How could you possibly stop us?"

"We will." Silver's gaze scanned her surroundings, then returned to Darkwolf. "What do you want with me?" she asked again.

Darkwolf slowly walked toward her until he was close enough to touch his own shield that surrounded Silver. The shield hummed beneath his fingertips and stroked him like a lover's caress. "What I want from you, Silver Ashcroft—I want everything. Your magic, your submission, your body . . . your heart and soul. As I always have desired."

"You're sick." The look of disgust that crossed her features was like a slap in the face and he nearly recoiled. "You'd better get over your obsession with me and fast. I'll never have anything to do with you, and I'll never turn to black magic."

Balor sensed Darkwolf's rage and the eye warmed against his chest. The power of Balor was palpable throughout the room and the pain in Darkwolf's head intensified. Silver's gaze dropped to the eye. She uncrossed and lowered her arms, straightening them at her sides. She clenched and unclenched her hands, her jaw tight.

Fear. Good, she feared him. She feared Balor. Once he broke through her hatred of him, he would strip everything away from her, layer by layer by layer, until even her soul was bared to him.

Darkwolf turned away, flicked his fingers, and the office door sprang open. On the other side of the door, guarding the office, were two Fomorii in their human shells.

"Watch her," he said in a snarl to the man-demon and woman-demon. "Inform me the second she tries to break through my barrier."

He didn't bother to look back or to close the door.

Darkwolf stalked from the office, which adjoined the elegant front room of the penthouse. Sara was standing in the room, slightly turned away from him. Her head was cocked to the side as if she were listening to something. Perhaps she was having another vision.

She looked delectable. Again she wore a low-cut shirt that revealed her cleavage. This time she wore a short skirt and high heels that accented her lovely legs.

He wondered if she had dressed that way for him. He knew how much she wanted him to fuck her.

As if feeling the flames that burned within him, she turned to Darkwolf and gave him a sensual smile. He strode directly to her, and she turned to face him completely. His cock was on fire from being so close to Silver and he had the need to fuck like he never had before.

Darkwolf grabbed Sara by the shoulders and he saw her expression of lust. His gaze raked her body, starting at her flushed features, descended to her breasts, where her hardened nipples were already pushing against her shirt, and moved on down to her tiny skirt. His eyes met hers again. She would do. Yes, she would do. He had promised to fuck her the moment he recruited her from the D'Anu, and now it was time. She wanted him, and right now he needed her.

He loosened his grip on her shoulders and began to knead them, working at the knots in her shoulders. "You are beautiful, my lovely Sara," he murmured then brushed his lips over hers.

She gave a soft moan as he slipped his tongue into her mouth. Sara's kiss was hungry, matching his. He demanded more from her, crushing her lips and tasting the sweetness of her mouth. She smelled of jasmine, and the scent suited her. As he rubbed her back, her answering kiss grew deeper, almost frantic. She braced her hands on his biceps, her fingers digging into his flesh.

Darkwolf brought his hands between them and squeezed her beautiful breasts that fit his palms perfectly. He pulled her low-cut shirt down, along with her bra, so that it caused her breasts to jut up high as if on serving platters.

His mouth moved to one of her breasts and he flicked his tongue over the taut nub. Delicious. His cock throbbed harder beneath his jeans. He didn't know how much longer he could wait to be inside this woman. He suckled at her other nipple, then moved his mouth between her breasts, rubbing his face against her softness.

"Sweetness," he murmured as he kissed his way up the curve of one breast. "I want to fuck you here. Right this minute."

He wanted to rip her clothes off and drive his cock deep inside of her. But he had to hear the words from her mouth. He never took an unwilling woman, not that he'd had one refuse him yet—other than Silver Ashcroft.

It both pissed him off and excited him, making him want Silver even more. A challenge. He liked a good challenge.

"Yes, my lord." Sara gave a moan as he laved her nipple again. "Fuck me."

That was all Darkwolf needed. He pressed her back against a leather couch and she braced herself with her hands to either side of her, a wild look on her face. She looked luscious with her shirt and bra under her breasts, causing her nipples to jut out at him. He jerked her skirt up to find that she wore only a tiny lace thong. With a yank he tore it away and she both gasped in surprise and gave a needy moan. More roughly than he probably should have, he whirled her around so that she was facing the back of the couch.

She started to look over her shoulder, but he placed his palm flat against her back and forced her down so that she was completely bent over the back of the couch. She looked absolutely delicious with her skirt pushed up above her ass, her thighs spread wide and exposing the folds of her pussy. Her buttocks were presented high and beautifully, and he debated whether to fuck her in her pussy or her ass.

In seconds he had his jeans undone and his cock and balls free to take her. He positioned his erection at her slick entrance and, without waiting a moment longer, drove his cock into her pussy.

Sara cried out at the initial thrust. Her cries became moans as he drove himself in and out of her tight channel. She was hanging upside down over the back of the couch, her brown hair over her face, with just his hands on her hips to steady her. Her nipples and her pussy were against the leather couch, likely adding to the sensations she was experiencing.

"You are a sweet little bitch, Sara." He palmed the taut globes of her ass as he fucked her. "I love your ass. Nice and round." He was aware of the demons in human form behind him, still guarding the office door, and he was certain they were getting off by watching him fuck one of the warlocks.

She moaned and thrashed against him. "That feels so good, my lord," she said in a voice rich with pleasure. "Fuck me so hard that I'll feel it in my throat."

Sara's words sent a rush of heat through him. He pounded harder and deeper into Sara as he brought his hands down to her breasts and palmed them, enjoying how they felt in his hands. "We're being watched, Sara. Do you enjoy being watched?"

"Yes!" She gave a louder moan. "It makes me even hotter."

Darkwolf smiled. A cry tore from her throat as he began smacking his hips against her backside in long hard thrusts. The scent of her musk was strong and turned him on even more. He was certain her pussy would taste sweet.

When he was close to reaching his climax, he palmed the globes of her buttocks again, only this time he sent a burst of his magic radiating throughout her.

Sara shouted, her voice muffled against the couch. Her body bucked and shuddered beneath his and he heard her cries of, "Balor, Balor, Balor," with every pulse of her channel around his cock.

Darkwolf threw his head back and nearly howled with his release as sensation burst through his cock. It throbbed within her channel and his come spurted inside Sara's pussy. He continued moving in and out of her, feeling the walls of her channel squeezing down on him with every contraction of her orgasm. He continued pumping, drawing out her climax and his own until he was entirely satisfied.

After slipping his cock from Sara's pussy, he assisted her from where she was sprawled over the couch, turned her around, and took her mouth in another kiss. His cock was hard again, and he grabbed it to rub Sara's folds with its head.

A low growl caught both his attention and Sara's, and his gaze leveled on Junga who had apparently just walked into the room. She was in Elizabeth Black's elegant form, but her face was twisted with fury and obvious jealousy. She had her hands fisted at her sides and her cheeks were flushed.

Sara smiled at Junga and ran her tongue along her lower lip as Darkwolf intentionally began playing with her nipples, squeezing them harder and harder as Junga's expression grew even more furious.

His cock ached beyond belief, and he debated whether to take Sara again, while he forced Junga to watch. Or perhaps he would command the demon-woman to submit to him in front of Sara, or perhaps he'd have them both submit to him at once.

Yes, he was ready for another good fuck.

Nineteen

Copper sat in the kitchen of Enchantments, barely able to concentrate on what the witches were discussing. They were all talking at once about Silver's capture by Darkwolf.

The usually warm and friendly room seemed to be closing in on Copper, and not even the scent of fresh-baked bread and cinnamon coffee cake took away the chill in her heart. Zeph perched on the curve of her ear, offering what comfort he could as a familiar.

"How'd we miss that Garran was working with Darkwolf?" she murmured to the bee that buzzed his unhappiness.

The D'Danann had all taken to the skies to search for clues—they had hopes that some of the Fomorii might have retained their demon forms and the D'Danann could then catch their rotten-fish stench. Unfortunately, when not in demon form, the Fomorii carried the scent of their host bodies, masking their demon smell.

Rhiannon had called the Paranormal Special Forces, led by Jake Macgregor, but they were out investigating a paranormal crime. As soon as they were finished, Jake promised he'd be back to help search for Silver.

Copper barely resisted burying her face in her arms on the kitchen table and bawling her eyes out. Her eyes ached from crying and she felt as though she were going to throw up. She still couldn't believe she hadn't been able to protect Silver.

But there was no way in all the Underworlds that she was going to give up. Whatever it took, she was going to get her sister back. And whatever it took, she was going to find a way to stop those demons that were ultimately responsible for her mother's death. The world was already an emptier place without her mother. She *would not* lose Silver, too.

Trying to compose herself and take control of the situation, Copper sat straighter in her seat. She projected her voice and said, "Listen to me!"

Rhiannon, Mackenzie, Cassia, Hannah, Alyssa, and Sydney all stopped talking and looked to Copper. The six other women were the members of the gray magic D'Anu Coven Rhiannon and the others had formed when Silver was banished from the D'Anu. All of the witches who belonged to the new Coven had left the D'Anu because they believed in Silver, gray magic, and what Silver had done to save everyone from the Fomorii.

Copper rubbed her forehead with her fingertips, her elbows on the table. "We've got to take this a step at a time. Somehow we have to figure out where Darkwolf has taken Silver and how we're going to get her back."

"Something's been blocking us every step of the way." Rhiannon slipped into a chair and scooted up to the large, rectangular Formica table. The white and brown flecked table was scarred and gouged, but it served its purpose. "With all of our divination talents, with the D'Danann, and the PSF—we should have been able to find the Fomorii and the Balorites by now."

The remaining witches took their chairs like Knights of the Round Table—only it wasn't, er, round, Copper thought and then wondered why her thoughts were straying when something much more important needed attention.

Copper studied each witch's face. A vivacious beauty, Rhiannon had chin-length, auburn hair that swung forward as she braced her arms on the table, her fiery green eyes flashing. Petite, blond, blue-eyed Mackenzie was worrying her lower lip with her teeth. The gorgeous raven-haired and lavender-eyed Sydney thoughtfully adjusted her chic glasses. Alyssa, with her soft light-brown curls, had her brown eyes focused intently on Copper. Hannah had dark brown hair that hung straight to her shoulders and beautiful chocolate-brown eyes. A single chunk of blond hair swept over her brows to frame the other side of her face. Hannah was the only one who looked accusingly at Copper. Then there was turquoise-eyed, blond Cassia, with her ethereal Elvin beauty, who had no judgment in her gaze whatsoever.

Copper took a deep breath before she spoke. "No one could possibly feel worse than I do about Silver's capture. She's my sister." It was all Copper could do to hold back more tears. "I should have been able to protect her from Darkwolf, but he was too fast, and I was caught off-guard."

Cassia placed her hand over Copper's and squeezed. Something about Cassia's Elvin touch calmed Copper and she was able to continue.

"Of course, we each have divination skills." Copper pulled off the black stocking cap that she'd been wearing at the pier. Static electricity made wisps of her hair rise as her braid fell down her back. She stuffed the cap into the back pocket of her black jeans. "We can use those gifts to give us clues to answer some questions. One: where is Silver and how can we rescue her? Two: who or what has been blocking our powers? Three: why were Silver and I given visions that ended up in disaster, rather than helping us?" She took a deep breath before adding, "Unfortunately, my only divination talent lies in dream-visions, but I don't think I'll be taking a nap right now."

Hannah, a computer software engineer, looked coolly down her nose at Copper, no warmth in her chocolate-brown eyes. "We've combined our talents before and our clues have been minimal. We've barely been able to keep the Fomorii and Balorites on the run. And even then we had Silver and her scrying cauldron."

Zephyr gave a buzz of annoyance in Copper's ear at the tone of Hannah's voice. "Maybe we just need to ask the right questions." Copper held Hannah's stare. "Maybe something *is* blocking us, and if we work together to get past that block, our talents will aid us better."

Mackenzie glanced around. "Who should start?"

"I'll go last." Rhiannon tucked her chin-length hair behind her ear as her familiar, a large cat named Spirit, jumped into her lap. "Hearing what you all come up with may help make my vision stronger."

"Hot tea would do us all some good." Cassia scooted away from the table and made her way to the other end of the kitchen. She brought out a huge copper kettle and filled it with water. Within moments it was whistling, obviously heated by Cassia's magic. Copper wondered just how powerful the Elvin witch was.

Sydney's chair legs squeaked against the linoleum as she pushed her chair from the table. "I need to gather candles." She gracefully stood and slipped away from the table. Sydney was the CEO of an advertising agency on Market Street in downtown San Francisco.

"I need one, too," Alyssa said as she got up and then disappeared through the swinging door and into the darkened shop behind Sydney.

Mackenzie went to her backpack that hung from a hook on the wall and brought out a scarf-wrapped bundle. When she returned to the table, she reverently unwrapped the deck to reveal her well-used deck of tarot cards. She laid the iridescent scarf in her lap and began shuffling the cards

Hannah went to the cabinet and brought out the sea salt crystals. She dug her scrying mirror out of her briefcase, which was hanging on another wall hook.

When everyone was seated at the table again with the tools of their divination skills, Alyssa lit a purple stick of incense at the center of the table. She had chosen a pewter Faerie holder with the Faerie clasping the incense stick in her little hands. Gradually the lilac-scented smoke drifted Copper's way—purple and lilacs were used for psychic work and clairvoyance.

At the same time, Cassia poured hot water over home-made tea bags in an odd variety of porcelain cups. The women passed the filled teacups around the table and the scent of citrus and cloves rose up with the steam.

After everyone had their cup of tea, Copper turned to Cassia, who sat next to her. "Want to start?"

Cassia answered by reaching into the pocket of her flowing skirt and bringing out a black velvet bag. She closed her eyes and fingered the rune stones through the cloth, projecting her Elvin magic. When she opened her eyes, she drew apart the bag's drawstring and let the stones tumble onto the table. They were black with golden runes etched upon them.

For a long moment Cassia studied them. Copper was about to take a sip of her tea, but found her hand was shaking too much to bring the cup to her lips.

Finally, Cassia said, "I see communication—I believe Silver will find a way to get word to us, although I don't see it freeing her. She has protection, which I read as her magic, and that will help her hold evil at bay. Family will be involved." At that she glanced at Copper, then back to the stones. "The situation is unpredictable and deals with more than simply saving her from Darkwolf and the Fomorii. There are other threats." With that, she gathered her stones into her velvet bag, tied the drawstring, and slipped it back into the pocket of her skirt.

Copper swallowed and looked to Alyssa, who sat on the
other side of Cassia. Alyssa nodded, her soft brown curls
bobbing with the movement, as she struck a match and
raised it to the silver candle before her. The taper was held
in a serpent candleholder, the base of the candle held taut
in the serpent's jaws.

The smell of sulfur, then burning wood of the match-
stick met Copper's nose, followed by the lily scent of the
candle. Or was that her imagination—that she caught Silver's perfume?

"Obviously I chose the serpent since it's Silver's
totem," Alyssa said in her quiet voice. "And I chose a silver
candle to represent her."

Alyssa placed her palms flat on the table and stared un-
blinking at the candle flame. Her eyes unfocused and
glazed over. The soft sound of the other witches' breathing
seemed magnified in the silence, as did the ticking of the
clock over the stove, and the drip of water from the sink's
faucet.

It seemed to take forever, but it was mere moments before Alyssa pulled herself out of her trance. She blinked
several times before blowing out the candle, leaving only a
thin trail of smoke rising to the ceiling of the kitchen.

While she waited Copper managed to get her cup to her
lips before she heard what Alyssa had to say. The citrus-
clove flavor of the tea was both sweet and tangy. Her
teacup rattled on its saucer when she set it down.

Alyssa frowned at the now unlit candle, her eyebrows
pinched together in concentration. "Silver's pissed more
than anything. She does know she won't be harmed because Darkwolf doesn't plan to hurt her. He has other intentions for her, which I couldn't get a grasp on. I believe
she's somewhere on the other side of the city, possibly
close to the pier, but she's not certain where she is."

Alyssa turned to Hannah, whose mirror was lying
faceup on the tabletop. The mirror had an ornate frame of

two dragons, each biting the tail of the other so that they formed a never-ending circle. The mirror itself was black and cast no reflection to anyone but Hannah.

She didn't bother to look at anyone. Instead she poured rock crystals into her palm from a clear jar and set the jar back down. She let the salt crystals tinkle and bounce onto the mirror. Not a single crystal fell off its surface, even onto the frame.

Hannah had her answers within seconds. She looked directly at Copper. "Darkwolf doesn't want Silver hurt. Like Alyssa said, he wants her for reasons that are unclear. But she's in danger, and even he doesn't realize the danger he's going to put her in. She's going to be used in a way that could mean her death."

Chills rolled over Copper and goose bumps pricked her skin. "You don't see us finding her soon?"

Hannah shook her head, her single lock of blond hair a stark contrast against the darkness of her brown hair. "I don't see it. But then, nothing is set. The future is always in question."

Copper's neck was stiff as she gave a single nod and turned her attention to Sydney, whose lavender eyes were focused thoughtfully on the fat pillar candles she had chosen for her divination. In front of her was a medium-sized, engraved silver bowl filled with consecrated water. The three short pillar candles positioned beside the bowl were silver, black, and green.

"Like Alyssa, I chose a silver candle to represent our Coven sister." Sydney struck a match and lit each candle. The tang of sulfur was stronger this time. "The silver candle also represents the goddess, mysteries, the moon, and intuition. In addition I chose a black candle for protection and removing bad luck, and green to invoke the goddess."

As all of the witches watched Sydney, she raised the silver candle and let the wax begin to drip into the bowl of consecrated water. The silver wax looked like blobs of mercury at first before they chilled into patterns in the water. Again Copper caught the perfume of lilies.

Sydney frowned, and Copper's stomach clenched. The black-haired witch selected the black candle next and tilted it so that its wax slowly dripped into the bowl, on and around the silver wax. The scent of patchouli was strong.

This time Sydney didn't pause after she set the black candle down. She immediately picked up the green candle and tilted it to allow its wax to dribble into the bowl, too. This candle smelled of pine.

When Sydney had set the green candle on the table, she let them continue to flicker in the still air of the kitchen as she studied the wax patterns in the bowl.

She finally raised her head. "The goddess had nothing to do with your dream-vision that told you to go to the wharf, Copper." Flickering candlelight reflected in Sydney's eyes as she spoke. "Anu also had nothing at all to do with your vision of the wharf. A dark force was involved, and I believe it was Balor."

"Balor?" Rhiannon said, her face flushed in anger.

Sydney nodded in response, but continued to speak to Copper. "However, the goddess did protect and provide for you in Otherworld. When Darkwolf would have taken you, she sent you to Otherworld to learn something that will aid us in our task."

"Garran. Of course." Copper's mind raced as she wondered if anything else concerning her exile could be related to these events.

Sydney brought her attention back to the present when she said, "Silver's captivity will somehow be to our benefit, as well."

"How can you say that?" Rhiannon snapped, nearly upsetting her teacup as she placed her fists on the tabletop. The cat, Spirit, hissed from her lap. "She's been kidnapped by that bastard Darkwolf, and is in the clutches of the Fomorii!"

Sydney simply looked at Rhiannon and said, "I am only relating to you what the goddess and Ancestors have shown me."

Rhiannon clenched her jaw and sat back in her seat with her arms folded across her chest. "I'm not liking what I'm hearing."

"I don't think any of us are." Copper's voice was on the edge of shaking. "There are only two of you left. Mackenzie, you're next."

Mackenzie's knuckles were white from clutching her tarot deck so tightly. She looked at Copper, quickly shuffled them again, and began to lay the cards out in the Celtic-cross spread, which consisted of ten cards.

"Copper, this spread is for both you and Silver," Mackenzie said. She took a deep breath before she began. "The first card—Queen of Swords. It means that you will be rational and logical in this situation." She frowned. "It's crossed by the Emperor reversed, which tells us that more powerful people or beings are in control of your and your sister's destinies." She moved on to the next one. "The third card is for strength and this means that you could triumph over the enemy and will fight on others' behalf."

Unlike how she'd appeared when she'd been white-knuckling the tarot deck, now Mackenzie's voice held no hint of hesitation. "Next is the Moon reversed, meaning you both are dealing with insincere people and may find it hard to distinguish between fantasy and reality." She touched another card. "Five of Pentacles reversed. You both need to work hard, but your faith and confidence will grow."

Throughout Mackenzie's tarot reading, Copper's palms were sweating and her scalp itched. Everything she was hearing was confusing, frustrating, and not what she *wanted* to hear. She wanted to know exactly where Silver was and that they would rescue her, and *now*.

"Future events," Mackenzie continued. "Your hard

work may be well rewarded, bringing new friends. The seventh card is the Five of Cups reversed. This means an unhappy time could come to an end, but pain and struggle will have left their mark. The card also represents happiness coming back to you both in the shape of a friend or lover returning. New opportunities will allow you to make up your differences and restore a relationship."

Copper blinked. What could that mean?

"Six of Swords reversed." Mackenzie tapped the card. "Continuing difficulties are of a temporary nature. There are still battles to be fought; courage and strength are required now." She moved on to the next card. "Nine of Wands. I see that your efforts may pay off, and problems may be overcome. However, there will be one last challenge and you'll both need significant strength to overcome it."

Mackenzie took a deep breath, her chest rising and falling with the movement. "And last, the tenth card—the Wheel of Fortune. You both are approaching moments in your lives when fate takes a hand in your affairs. If fate deems it, the wheel may turn in your favor and a new cycle may begin. Although the problem may be difficult to live through, when the dust settles, you will discover a whole new set of friends."

Everyone at the table was quiet as they looked to one another. Copper was trying to digest everything she'd heard tonight, and was having difficulty wrapping it into a neat, understandable package she could use to take action. Zephyr buzzed his confusion in her ear, too.

So far she was hearing that she and Silver had battles to be fought, that their cause might be the same, but that they might not be fighting them together.

Did that mean they wouldn't find Silver yet?

Finally, Sydney said, "It's up to you now, Rhiannon."

Sparks lit the fiery witch's eyes. Rhiannon was sitting next to Copper and grasped her arm. She wasn't surprised, as Rhiannon normally needed something to channel her energy through.

Spirit, the cat familiar, rose up in Rhiannon's lap and rubbed his head against Rhiannon's chest in a show of support and probably to lend his magic. Rhiannon closed her eyes. Her chest rose and fell as she took a deep breath. For a very long moment she was so quiet that Copper began to feel dazed and light-headed.

"I see Silver and she looks uninjured, just angry," Rhiannon said slowly when she finally began to speak. "She's in a room like an office, but she's caged in one corner by Darkwolf's magic shield. It looks like she's checking to see if the guards are paying attention. She's reaching into her pocket and slips out her cell phone . . ."

The ringing of the telephone cut through the air and everyone looked up in shock. Copper was the first out of her chair and dived for the kitchen phone. "Silver?"

"How'd you—never mind." Silver's voice was low and breathless. "Darkwolf *is* looking for the door and he wants to release Balor's physical body. They think they can do it tomorrow!" Silver's voice held fear and concern. "I tricked Darkwolf into mentioning his allies. They are the Dark Elves, the Drow."

"I know." Copper rushed to interrupt her sister. "Where are you?"

Silver hesitated. "I don't know, but I think I'm safe for now. I—"

The connection went dead.

"No!" Copper shouted into the phone even as the dial tone rang in her ear. She slammed the phone down on the countertop and whirled to look at her friends. She rubbed her forehead with the heel of her palm. "It was Silver. She doesn't know where she is, but she confirmed everything we've suspected." She eyed her sister witches. "And she thinks the Balorites and Fomorii are going to be able to open the door tomorrow night with the Dark Elves."

"The Dark Elves?" Cassia moved closer to Copper. "It would have taken them a while, but yes, they could have tunneled to some kind of cavern deep below the surface where a door to Underworld would be. They've tunneled deeper than they should have before—once they tunneled so deeply they released the earth giants. It would take much time to tunnel even deeper than that."

"I know the Drow king who leads the Dark Elves who are working with Darkwolf." Copper met the other witches' gazes. "His name is Garran and he was trapped in Otherworld like I was, except belowground. Rather I thought he was trapped. Apparently, all this time he's been able to travel between worlds while he left the rest of us to live in a prison." She clenched her fists because her gut told her it was true. It made sense. Darkwolf needed the Drow to tunnel, and no doubt that's what they'd been doing all this time. They certainly couldn't have done it in the two days she'd been free. "I knew he could be an ass, but I never thought he'd . . . *betray* all the Fae trapped in that bubble."

The sound of the front door to the shop opening, the warding bells tinkling, and the sounds of boot steps alerted the witches to the presence of others in the shop. Copper's wand was out in an instant and all the witches were ready with their hands or whatever form of magic they used.

Tiernan burst through the door of the kitchen, followed by Hawk and a host of D'Danann warriors, until nine of them occupied the now very crowded kitchen, along with the seven witches. Fortunately, it was a large kitchen, but even so it was filled to the brim and the body heat made it stifling.

Most of the D'Danann wore black trench coats over their leathers, to hide their swords and daggers when among humans. Tiernan and Hawk had not put theirs on this evening.

"We searched the city and found nothing." Hawk's face

was twisted with fury and agony at the same time. "There is no trace of my mate."

Tiernan raked his blond hair from his face. "No sign, no stench of the creatures."

Hawk looked to the witches. Copper said, "Silver managed to call us, but only briefly." She explained what Silver had said.

Hawk looked to Copper, the fury on his face no less than before. "The Drow are in league with Darkwolf and the Fomorii. I will kill them."

Copper tossed her braid over her shoulder. "Tiernan and I know the Drow king who's behind this, and after I'm through with him you can do whatever you want with the bastard."

Cassia began bringing big trays of food to the table and the other witches got up to help. Copper remembered from what Silver told her yesterday that the D'Danann were always hungry, even in a crisis. Tiernan had eaten so many apples in Otherworld that she'd worried their never-ending supply of them might just end. Thank goodness the Fae had been kind enough to leave more food than they normally did.

Copper couldn't have touched a morsel of food if she tried, her stomach was so tied in knots. It was all too much. Anger at Darkwolf kidnapping Silver, all that had been said during the divinations, and fury at Garran for helping Darkwolf.

She stood away from the table with Hawk and Tiernan. Hawk had one hand braced against the wall while Copper leaned against it. Tiernan stood just to her right, making her feel caged.

Before the men even had a chance to ask, Copper started explaining all that they'd learned from each witch's turn at divination. There were common themes—Silver would not be rescued yet, but she was safe for now; both Copper and Silver would be used in some way that would put them in danger; and Balor had been manipulating them all this time.

Tiernan rubbed his temples and Hawk shook his dark head. "I refuse to believe we will not rescue my mate before she is put into further jeopardy."

"The future is never set." Copper laid her hand on Hawk's arm. "It's still possible you can find her before she's in danger."

She took a deep sigh and looked to the clock above the stove. "It's nearing four A.M. We all should get some rest so we can figure out what we need to do next."

"I will not sleep." Hawk rested his hand on his sword. "I will comb this city for my mate."

Cassia took that moment to present a mug of beer to Hawk. "If you wish to continue your search, you may as well do it well fed and with your thirst quenched."

Hawk took the mug and knocked back the entire contents of the glass.

But Copper knew he'd been had. Among the yeast and hops smell of the beer, she'd caught the scent of valerian root and a couple of other things that didn't belong in beer. Yup, it was going to be nighty-night for one very large warrior.

Hawk frowned as he handed the mug back to Cassia who smiled. "That brew was fouler than normal," he grumbled.

"That's because I put valerian root into it, along with an Elvin sleeping powder of patchouli and poppies," Cassia said calmly. Before turning away, she said, "Sleep well."

"What—" Hawk started, but then began to shake his head as if trying to stay awake. He took a few staggering steps away from the wall.

"You and one of your friends better grab him." Copper gave Tiernan a gentle shove toward Hawk. "He's going down in a hurry."

Twenty

She was in the tunnel again. It was cold, dank, and very dark, and she couldn't stop shivering. Her wand grew warm in her hand, helping to ease some of the chill as she used her magic to light the wand and illuminate the way.

Her heart was pounding in her ears as she crept along the narrow passageway she'd been down before. She stumbled over loose rocks and dirt and almost dropped her wand.

She eased up to the corner where the red light crept, holding her breath, knowing that the cavern waited for her. When she could breathe again, she slipped around the corner and caught her breath.

The cavern was just as beautiful this time. Her golden wand light glistened off the crystal formations hanging from the ceiling and jutting up from the floor of the cavern.

But at the other side of the cavern was the bloody glow that squelched any admiration for the cavern. Something so evil shouldn't be in such a place of beauty.

She stumbled down a rough-hewn trail to the floor of the cavern, knowing she had no choice but to go to the red light.

Her feet grew leaden as she walked across the cavern toward the great stone door. It was as if heavy weights had been tied to her legs. Her wand light dimmed so low that it was almost useless.

When she finally reached the door, she once again stood in the circle of runes, except this time there was no great eye. The crimson glow seeped around the door's edges, creeping toward her like bony, bloody fingers.

Chills rolled over her at the evil emanating from behind that doorway and she stumbled backward. Whatever was behind that door was bad . . . very bad.

Her heart thrummed.

Her throat closed off. She needed a spell to counteract the black witchcraft that surrounded her, filled her with intense fear.

She tried to find the words. Only a rusty croak came out when she opened her mouth.

She tried again.

Nothing!

She couldn't do it! She wouldn't be able to keep the door closed. But she had to! Goddess, why wouldn't the words come?

But they wouldn't. This time she tried to move forward to face whatever was behind that door.

Shock jarred her as her feet sank into the stone to her ankles, like quicksand. Then the quicksand molded around her feet as if they were encased in concrete.

The pounding of her heart grew faster and faster as she fought for freedom, fought to save her own life in order to save her family, her friends, her city, her world.

She couldn't let that door open!

Using her wand, she tried to cast a spell that would free her, but her mind remained blank. It was as if something blocked her, like a steel wall she couldn't see through.

She went completely still.

And then it slammed into her with the force of a boulder careening down a mountaintop. *She* was a sacrifice. A sacrifice to the gods who had been waiting for millennia to be freed.

And to feed.

The cavern began shaking. Dirt and stones rained down on her. A rock struck her in the temple and she swayed from the force of it.

The red light brightened as the door scrubbed stone and began to open.

Silver screamed Copper's name.

Copper's eyes flew open to see only darkness. She tried to sit up, but a heavy weight pinned her down. She fought against the weight, fought to free herself. She banged her fists on the mass trapping her—

She was shoved flat on her back, her arms pinned above her head, the great weight suddenly on top of her, between her thighs.

"Little fire," a familiar voice said. "It was a dream. You are safe, with me."

Tiernan. It was Tiernan.

Relief rushed through her in one large sigh.

Copper was breathing hard as her eyes came back into focus and her nightmare bled away. She was in Tiernan's room and had slept with him, while he had simply held her all night. They were both naked, but they had fallen asleep almost immediately. She wondered what time it was. The blinds were drawn tight, so she had no idea.

She was still beneath him as he released her arms. "Sorry," she murmured. "The dream—it was worse this time."

Tiernan brushed his lips over hers in a whisper of a kiss as he eased beside her. "I am here, little fire. Whatever it is, we will face it together."

She cuddled closer to Tiernan, needing his warmth, his

comfort. Goddess, how she needed him in so many ways. Ways that she couldn't even begin to fathom.

He stroked her head and she relaxed in his arms. "Everything will be all right," he said as he caressed her. "I am here for you."

Yes, he made her feel as if all would work out. That they could do anything together.

Something gripped Copper's belly so tightly she almost couldn't breathe.

No, it wasn't possible. No, no, no. Not possible.

Love.

She couldn't have.

She had.

She'd fallen in love with Tiernan.

Oh, goddess. A man who might soon be married, and she was in love with him.

Copper pushed herself from his arms and swung her legs over the side, letting the covers drop away from her. She took a deep gulp of air as the sensation in her belly became more intense.

"Copper?" He moved behind her and placed his hand on her shoulder. "Are you all right?"

"I—I . . ." Copper swallowed. "I can't do this anymore. I can't be with you."

She shoved his hand from her shoulder, stood, and moved away from the bed. He studied her with a puzzled expression and a look that tore her gut apart.

Hurt. He looked hurt.

Before she could embarrass herself by proclaiming her love, she grabbed her clothing from last night and dressed as quickly as she could. She avoided his gaze and turned her back on him.

"What do you mean, Copper?" he said softly as he came up behind her and pressed a kiss to the nape of her neck.

Copper bit her lower lip. She wouldn't cry, dammit. She would *not* cry. This whole thing had been about sex from

the start. She'd known it. She'd gone into it with her eyes
wide open. She'd figured they'd have sex and go their
merry ways.

She never considered the possibility she would fall in
love with the man.

Copper ducked away from him and grabbed her socks
and jogging shoes in one hand and reached for the bedroom doorknob with her other. She cast one tortured
glance back at Tiernan. "I can't be with you. I can't have
sex with you. It's over."

And with that she let herself out the door and hurried
out of the apartment.

Tiernan felt as though he'd been punched in the gut. His
heart and soul had an ache he couldn't define.

He sat where she left him for a long time. They had enjoyed pleasures together. He could not imagine a woman
he wanted more. But it was a physical need. Nothing beyond that.

Then why did her reaction tear him apart?

Tiernan's logical mind churned over possibility after
possibility. He analyzed his feelings for Copper. A word
struck him so fast and hard that his heart clenched and he
was rocked to his core.

Love.

He was in love with Copper.

Being over two thousand years old, Tiernan had never
really believed in love, at least not for himself. That was
usually a fanciful notion that two people occasionally held
for one another. Lust was another thing. Sharing pleasures
with others was common in Otherworld, and nothing more
was expressed beyond satisfaction of slaked desires.

But he could not deny the pounding of his heart, the
feelings welling up inside of him for Copper.

In the D'Danann hierarchy, none of the lords and ladies
of the court joined for love. They wed to make their houses

stronger, for prestige. His arranged joining with Airell was to make the Houses of Cathal and Torin two of the strongest among the D'Danann.

He had felt no emotion when he had agreed to join with her, he had simply acquiesced to his parents' wishes. No emotion whatsoever had been involved.

Tiernan blew out a long breath. He had yet to come up with a solution that would satisfy all parties involved. His heart told him he could not marry Airell when she carried Urien's babe. Yet how could he not without humiliating her? The consequences were too dire to consider.

And Copper . . . gods, how could he let her go?

The thought of never being with Copper again tore him open like a sword through his belly. And the thought of never seeing her teasing smile again, or the fire in her cinnamon eyes when she was angry, and how dark those eyes grew when they shared sexual pleasures, of never touching her again—it was as if that sword in his belly had been heated in a forge and it burned hot and heavy in his gut.

He felt dazed as he stared at the apartment's front door, his thoughts consumed by Copper. How had this happened? But there could be no denying the thumping of his heart, the way his skin grew hot, then cold, the way blood thrummed in his ears.

Tiernan continued to stand frozen in one spot. A battle raged in his mind, but he could not negate the truth. He was in love with Copper.

Tiernan inhaled deeply and let out a long exhale. How could he solve this situation to everyone's satisfaction, including his own and Copper's?

Possibilities churned through his mind as he fought to find a solution. He raked his fingers through his hair. If he went against his parents' wishes, he could damage their relations with Airell's house and he would humiliate the young woman once it was known she was pregnant. There was no suitable D'Danann with enough wealth to take her hand in marriage.

Tiernan's thoughts turned to Urien. The man was as young as Airell but was from a D'Danann lesser court. Airell had proclaimed her love for Urien, and carried his babe. But Urien did not have the means to raise his station.

Tiernan stumbled into the shower, needing to feel the heat of the water pound on his body. As he cleansed himself, his head ached from the enormity of his thoughts, but it was nothing compared to the ache in his chest and the feeling of the fiery sword in his belly.

Gods. He stepped out of the shower, dried himself, then strode back into the bedroom. It was so, so empty without Copper.

He paused for a moment and looked up at the ceiling with its yellowed paint and cobwebs in one corner. He felt as trapped as one of the insects tightly snared within the spider's web. There had to be some way to rectify the situation. His analytical mind continued to consider possible solutions as his heart ached and that sword twisted within his gut.

A thought came to him that he tried to reject, yet it was the only possibility he could think of. If he chose that path, he would be disowned from his own family, tossed from the court, but Airell . . . gods. If he left, he would never again know the life he had lived for centuries. He would be throwing away the responsibilities that had been shouldered upon him.

Responsibility. Duty. Honor.

Yet there was no other answer that would come to mind. He could not bear those responsibilities and have Copper, too.

Head aching with the thought of what he must do, Tiernan left the apartment and walked into the early morning air. He went straight to Enchantments, past the witches working in the store and into the kitchen. The door swung shut behind him as he went up to Cassia. The only other person in the room was Hawk, who was leaning back against the table, his arms across his chest.

The Elvin witch gazed at Tiernan thoughtfully, but did not say anything.

He gave a heavy sigh. "I need you to help me cross over to Otherworld."

"As do I," Hawk said, coming up beside Tiernan. "I must enlist the aid of more of the D'Danann in finding Silver."

Tiernan nodded. "You will have my assistance, brother, when we return. It should not take us long to deal with what business we have."

When Cassia said, "Come," Tiernan simply nodded and he and Hawk followed her through the store and out into the foggy day.

They walked silently along the streets until they reached a great wooded area that he had gone to with Cassia before, the massive Golden Gate Park. Hosts of people strolled the sidewalks and the streets, some on bicycles, others on a series of spinning wheels beneath their shoes that he had been told were inline skates.

The air carried to him the scents of water, pine, and grass, but Copper's apples-and-cinnamon scent, too. Tiernan frowned. Could she have come this way?

When they reached the small footbridge that ran over the stream, he paused and looked at Cassia. His long black coat flapped around his boots that sank into mud at the base of the bridge.

"I'll need to take you across one at a time," Cassia said, avoiding the mud and moving onto the bridge. Her full skirts swished as she passed by him. She was a third of the way over the bridge when she turned and looked over her shoulder. "Stop wasting time."

Tiernan followed her, mud sloughing off his boots in clumps as he walked up to stand by her side.

"You wait," Cassia said to Hawk, and the warrior gave a swift nod. "Remember to concentrate on your home so that you will arrive in the correct location," she said to Tiernan.

Again Tiernan gasped and tried to breathe when they

reached the top of the bridge. He could not see and his chest was afire. Then he was in his world where he took deep gulps of air. Cassia was gone, only the mound of earth behind him. But then Hawk and Cassia appeared out of the earthen mound. Hawk seemed to have fared no better than Tiernan when he crossed, and the large man shook his head as if to shake away the strange feelings of the transport.

Cassia focused her eyes on Hawk. "When you have concluded your business, go to the Great Guardian and ask her to use the transference point to return you to where you belong."

With that, the Elvin witch turned her back on them, walked straight into the mound and vanished.

Tiernan heard the Dryads tending to their trees and the Pixies playing among the star flowers.

Pixies. He'd never think of them the same way again.

Silently Hawk accompanied Tiernan, obviously lost in his own thoughts. When they reached the village, other D'Danann warriors greeted them with smiles and slaps on the back. Hawk gave them orders to meet him in the training yards, and the men and women warriors simply nodded their understanding.

When he parted from Hawk—who had left for the D'Danann training yards—Tiernan strode to the gates behind the Chieftains' chamber and through the black gates. His thoughts were clear as he neared his home. Surely this was the right thing to do—for himself and for Airell. Gods, he hoped so.

His insides burned even hotter at the thought of what he must do.

After he entered the manor, he waited for one of the servants to summon his mother. Lady Cian hurried from the parlor, a flurry of pale blue silk and a smile of delight on her pretty features. "You have returned early!"

Tiernan forced a smile and kissed his mother's knuckles. The sight of his mother brought warmth to his chest. As well as guilt, along with the desire to not disappoint his parents. But he had no other options.

"Where is Father?" Tiernan asked, his voice gruffer than he intended.

Cian's hand fluttered in the direction of his father's study. "In there, as always."

Tiernan glanced at his mother as he took her by the arm and escorted her to the study. His chest tightened and his gut burned. How could he disappoint the people he loved? How could he turn his back on his responsibilities, on honor and duty?

How could he not be with Copper?

Tiernan's father appeared delighted to see him, his smile wide and his handshake firm. Tiernan wished he could return the smile.

Artan stepped back and frowned. "What troubles you, son?"

Tiernan drew his sword from his sheath, knelt, and laid it at his father's feet. With his head bowed he said, "I have come with much to discuss, Father."

The symbolism of Tiernan's laying down his sword could not have been lost on Artan.

"Rise." His father's voice was gruff.

Tiernan stood and met his father's gaze head-on. Tiernan was taller, but not by much. His father wore a brown shirt with bloused sleeves and brown breeches.

The ache magnified in Tiernan's chest over what he must now do. He was negating all of his duties as his father's son. He was disregarding the responsibilities that had rested so heavily on him. That still did, even though he must now renounce them.

He was forsaking his honor.

Tiernan cleared his throat. "I cannot wed Airell."

The silence following his statement made his ears ring.

"How could you even say such a thing?" Cian stared at

him with horrified eyes. "This marriage has been planned since Airell was a babe."

Artan's face turned a ruddy red that nearly matched his tufted hair. "You will join with Airell. There is no further discussion."

"We *will* discuss this, Father." Tiernan's voice held a note of finality. "I am in love with a witch of human and Elvin blood, and if she will have me, it is her I will wed."

Artan slammed his fist on his desk, upsetting a bottle of red ink so that it toppled and began to bleed across pages on his desk. "You will wed Airell or you will be disowned, never to be taken back into our family."

"No!" Cian gave a little cry. "You must join with Airell. Her family would be devastated by the loss. Airell will be humiliated. There is no other man of stature that she may marry. And our house? What of the House of Cathal?"

Tiernan swallowed and raised his head. "Airell is in love with Urien."

"She *what*?" Cian said, disbelief in her voice.

Artan's expression darkened. "Urien does not have the gold to raise his stature within the court. He must equal you in wealth for him to join with Airell."

"I realize this." Tiernan raised his hand indicating that his father hear him out. Artan sputtered but let Tiernan continue. "I will go to the sum-keeper and transfer all my gold to Urien. That will provide him with more than enough to buy his way higher in the court and to provide for Airell, and make the House of Brend one to contend with."

Artan straightened, his face impossibly redder. "You will *not*."

Cian gasped. "We will not stand for it." She clenched her hands in her skirts. "Neither will Edana and Faolan."

"I understand Airell's parents will not be pleased, but Urien is a good man." Tiernan looked from his mother to his father. "The gold is mine to give. I do not care that it shall make me a pauper." He sighed as his gaze returned to his mother. "I know you have expected much of me, and it is with a heavy heart that I must disappoint you. But what matters now is the woman I love."

Artan bellowed, "What you propose now is unaccept-able. These responsibilities have been given to you for cen-turies. You have been trained to accept them from the time you were born."

"You are usually levelheaded," Cian said, panic in her voice. "Has someone made you ill, or perhaps used magic against you?"

Tiernan sighed again. He felt tired, as if the weight of worlds rested on his shoulders. "No, Mother. I am in my right mind. I know what it is I must do."

Artan gritted his teeth, then said, "I warn you, you will be disinherited. You will get *nothing* from your mother or me."

"I am sorry to disappoint you, Father." Tiernan gave a low bow. "I have sought only to please you and Mother all my years. But I have no choice. I cannot leave behind the woman I love."

He knelt and retrieved his sword, then sheathed it as he looked at his parents. "I love you both as well, and it is to my sorrow that I have hurt you so." He paused, looking from one horrified face to the other. "This maid is far more important to me than anything in Otherworld. If she will have me, then my life is hers. If she will not, then I will continue serving as a D'Danann warrior and live with my comrades in the village."

"Out!" Artan pointed to the door, his entire body shak-ing. Tears rolled freely down Cian's face. "Do not return."

"As you wish, Father." Tiernan bowed again to Artan, nodded to his mother, then walked out of the only home he had ever known.

His insides twisted and his head ached. A strange sensa-tion pricked the backs of his eyes. What he had proposed was the only solution, but the responsibilities he had for-saken weighed heavily on him.

Honor. Duty. Responsibility.

Was it not honorable to make Copper his life mate? Was it not his duty to provide and care for her? Was it not his re-sponsibility to share his heart with the one he truly loved?

Tiernan went to the sum-keeper's house next. Crevan, a bald, jovial man, seemed delighted to see him and escorted Tiernan into the study where he did his sum-keeping. "Lord Tiernan. What may I do for you?" the man asked.

Tiernan did not sit. "Transfer all my gold, every last bit of it, to Urien's account."

Crevan's jaw dropped. "P-pardon?"

"Urien is to receive all my wealth." Tiernan gestured to a stack of blank parchment. "Please draw up the papers now."

"But—"

Tiernan braced his hands on the sum-keeper's desk and met his watery-blue eyes. "Draw up the papers," he re-peated slowly, with enough authority in his voice to make the sum-keeper blink rapidly.

Obviously flustered, Crevan brought out sheets of parchment and began to scratch words feverishly across the pages.

Tiernan drew away from Crevan's desk. "May I send your servant to bring Lord Urien and Lady Airell to your quarters?"

The sum-keeper did not look up from his work, but waved one hand toward the doorway. "Yes, yes."

Tiernan spoke to the servant, a beautiful blond woman dressed in a simple gray frock. She nodded her under-standing and curtsied as she said, "Yes, my lord," and scur-ried from the manor.

By the time the sum-keeper had finished making three copies of the document—one for Tiernan, one for Urien, and one for his own records—both Airell and Urien had ar-

rived. They appeared confused, and Airell seemed somewhat flustered to be in the same room as Tiernan and Urien
at once. Her gaze darted from one to the other, and then
she looked at her hands that were clenched before her.

Airell wore apparel befitting ladies of the court. Her
blue gown was snug down to her tiny waist that would soon
blossom with child. The gown had voluminous sleeves and
the skirt that reached her toes was so wide and full that it
was a wonder she had been able to pass through Crevan's
front doors. Urien, as one of the younger D'Danann, wore
the black garb of the warriors.

Tiernan ignored them for a moment as he took a quill
from the sum-keeper, dipped it in ink, and scratched his
signature across one of the documents. He proceeded to do
the same with the other two.

When he finished, Tiernan cleared his throat, drawing
everyone's attention to him. "Airell, I cannot wed you. We
both are well aware of the circumstances."

At that the blond, blue-eyed beauty's cheeks flamed, but
Urien had gone pale.

"Let me continue," he said, raising his voice. He took
two of the documents from Crevan and handed one to
Urien.

"I am turning over my entire fortune to you, Urien."
Tiernan watched the man's eyes widen. "This will be more
than enough to increase your stature and the House of
Brend within our courts so that you may wed Airell."

The pair of them stared at him, shock and confusion on
their features.

Tiernan smiled, feeling as though at least one burden
had been lifted from his chest. "I have fallen in love with
an Earth witch. I do not know if Copper will have me, but I
know I cannot wed another."

Both Urien and Airell looked stupefied. Then Airell
seemed to come alive. She flung her arms around Tiernan's
neck and hugged him, enveloping him in her powdery

scent, before releasing Tiernan to wrap her arms around Urien. "This means we can truly be together!"

Urien seemed hesitant, but then hugged Airell back. They held on to one another as they drew away enough for Airell to look up into Urien's gaze. Airell had tears in her eyes, and Urien appeared to be choked up.

"This gift . . ." Urien stared at the document that gave him instant wealth. "It is too much . . . I cannot—"

Tiernan interrupted him. "You can and you will."

Urien shook his head, more in disbelief than in argument. "Why would you do such a thing?"

Tiernan smiled. "As I said, I love another." He looked to Airell. "I could not leave you with nothing and I would never dishonor you."

The front door to Crevan's home opened with a slam against the wall, causing Airell and Urien to spring apart from their embrace.

Airell's mother, Edana, and her father, Faolan, stood in the entryway as the servant shut the door behind them. Edana's head was high, her pinched features taut with anger. Faolan's mouth was an angry slash across his face, his hands curled into fists at his sides.

Both of Airell's parents looked accusingly at Urien and Airell, who each had a high blush on their cheeks. Then Edana's and Faolan's gazes riveted on Tiernan.

"How dare you attempt to break your vow to our daughter?" Edana clenched her hands together and her hands were completely white from gripping them together so hard. "You cannot break your betrothal."

"I have given my wealth to Urien," Tiernan said calmly, looking from Edana to Faolan. "It is done. The sum will give the House of Brend the stature in the court that he may wed Airell."

Faolan shook his finger at Tiernan and bellowed, "No! It is your house that is to be joined with ours." His burning gaze turned on Urien. "Not someone bred of a lesser court."

The power of Faolan's prejudice sparked Tiernan's anger and he gritted his teeth. "Urien is a good man. He and Airell love one another, and will make a perfect joining."

Spit flew from Faolan's mouth as he turned on his daughter. "You will not wed the likes of this—this lesser man."

Airell straightened, her shoulders thrown back and her chin high. "I choose Urien." A blush tinged her cheeks as she glanced at Tiernan.

Edana's mouth opened in surprise and Faolan looked taken aback.

"What—you—how dare—" Faolan sputtered.

Urien put his arm around Airell's shoulders, holding her tightly to him, and stood tall before her parents. "We love one another, and have since we were children. It is a blessing that Tiernan has given us."

Edana and Faolan looked too shocked to speak.

Airell turned to Tiernan and gave a deep curtsy, spreading her sapphire skirts before standing straight again. "I owe you much, Tiernan." Her gaze turned to Urien's. "*We* owe you much."

Urien reached out and grasped Tiernan's hand. "Thank you, brother. If there is any way I can repay you, I will do so gladly."

"Your happiness will be my reward," Tiernan said with a small bow to Urien and Airell.

To Faolan and Edana, Tiernan gave another bow. When he straightened he said, "Urien will make a good match and a good son-in-law. They will bear many children and carry forth the name of both your houses."

Tiernan folded his copy of the document and then slid it into his black trench coat. He gave the stunned sumkeeper, Urien, Airell, and her parents each one last nod and strode out the door.

Now that he had forsaken all that he had ever known, he would return to Copper and tell her of his love.

Twenty-one

After realizing she'd fallen in love with Tiernan, Copper needed to get away for a while. Not to mention she had to have time to *focus*. To figure out where the door was and to come up with a spell she could use against the opening of it. The time was nearly at hand. She knew what had to be done.

She had jogged from the Haight-Ashbury district to the opposite end of the three-mile-long Golden Gate Park. Jogging cleared her mind and got her blood pumping and her thoughts churning. She'd gone all the way to Ocean Beach, where she'd sat on the sand for a bit to catch her breath. She stared at the water for a while, contemplating spells that could work to keep the door to Underworld closed.

When Copper felt she had worked out a strong enough spell, she brushed the sand off her butt and made the jog back.

If her dreams were true at all, then that door was going to be opened tonight, and somehow she was going to be there to see it happen. It would be up to her to either make sure it stayed closed, or to close it if it was opened. It made her feel a little better to have a plan and a spell readied before she arrived at that door. She just hoped it wouldn't be too late by the time she got there.

Too late for what? she asked herself. *What if you're wrong about this door? What if you can't find it?*

What she had been experiencing were dream-visions, and whether Balor was influencing them or not, she was destined to face whatever was coming next.

She had no doubt now that this was the answer to her question of why she'd been stranded in that small part of Otherworld. She'd had firsthand experience with the Drow, had been inside their realm, and had even seen the massive tunnel the giant had come up through.

That was the key to it all. She had to return to Otherworld, and one way or another get through that tunnel and to the door. There was no doubt in her mind that the Dark Elves had been working side by side with Darkwolf to find the door, and that was her ticket to stopping whatever was going to happen.

Except, unlike in her dream-visions, she wouldn't be alone. She'd damn sure take reinforcements.

She'd had time to think about a lot of things during her mind-clearing six-mile jog, and plenty of time to plan what she would do next. The fact that her sister was missing, and that she'd been unable to help Silver, was like molten lead in Copper's belly. Somehow, someway, she had to get to Silver. It didn't matter that all the divination readings had said otherwise, she couldn't just wait.

She refused to let her thoughts stray to Tiernan. She kept him pushed well to the back of her mind.

Copper's whole body and mind ached by the time she made her way up the stairs to Silver's apartment. Fortunately the key was still in the pocket of the black jeans she'd been wearing since yesterday. She felt sweaty, sticky, and grimy after her long jog and her time on the beach.

She let herself into the quiet apartment and choked back the knot of emotion in her throat. Goddess, she felt alone. Silver wasn't there. Her absence could be felt in every way. Polaris was curled up in a chair beside the door, as if waiting for Silver to walk through it. Copper went to him and stroked his head. "I'm sorry, big guy. If I could carry a big ole python like you, I'd take you with me to find her."

When she turned away from Polaris, Zephyr zipped up to her with an angry sound. She'd left him in Silver's apartment last night, and he obviously wasn't happy at her for spending most of the day away without him.

"Give me some time to get myself together," she said, and the familiar buzzed in her face. She felt his anger die and his sorrow for her flooded her being before he flew up to rest on the curtain rod.

Once she was out of the shower, she jerked on her bra and thong, a pair of well-worn jeans, a soft sweater, and comfortable jogging shoes. After she dried and then braided her hair, she stuffed her wand in her back pocket, grabbed her jacket, and got the hell out of there. She had things to do. For now she had to push aside all the pains in her heart and concentrate on Silver.

Zephyr zipped to his normal place on her ear. When she entered the shop, smells of sandalwood, berries, and patchouli wafted over her from the displays of incense beside the front door. Scents of cinnamon, vanilla, blueberry, pine, and apple met her nose next as she passed the candle display. Enchantments was arranged differently, yet the shop was much the same as Moon Song.

Enchantments was perhaps even more homey and comforting. It was filled with colorful robes, a huge variety of wands, chalices, cauldrons, books, wind chimes, charms, pentagrams, and other types of jewelry, and much more. It was a place where one could get lost in enjoyment for hours. One customer wandered around stands of bookmarks, shelves of pretty boxes, and displays of handmade shawls, and another was perusing the Faerie figurine section. Alyssa manned the register and Mackenzie was in the café.

Copper made her way into the cozy kitchen and barely acknowledged Hannah and Rhiannon, who were in a heated discussion about who the hell knew what. The moment they saw Copper, though, Rhiannon went to her.

"The time is now. Darkwolf has taken Silver to the door," Rhiannon said, her eyes wide. "The one on the parchment."

"You don't know that." Hannah scowled. The brunette brushed the single chunk of blond hair from her eyes and it fell to the side of her face to frame her features. Even when she scowled she looked beautiful.

Rhiannon stared at her. "You just scried it with your mirror and salt crystals!"

"Balor could be influencing all of our divinations." Hannah placed her hands on her hips. Her taupe slacks fell in straight lines to her taupe-colored heels. Her creamy blouse was unwrinkled, sleek, and as sophisticated as the rest of her. Copper wondered why she wasn't at the software company where she was director of development. "We don't know what to believe now."

"Just as I finished telling you, this time I was prepared." Rhiannon's cheeks had gone pink, her chin-length auburn hair a little wild. "The goddess blocked out all outside influences when I had my vision. Silver is there, or will soon be. We *must* go after her."

"Wait!" Copper shouted, and both women looked to her. "You saw Silver at the door?"

"I saw Darkwolf carry her to the center of the circle surrounded by those evil runes." Rhiannon swallowed, fear evident in her features. "She was unconscious and bleeding."

Copper thought her legs would give out from under her.

She grasped the back of a chair beside the kitchen table to steady herself. Zeph gave a distressed buzz.

"Like I said, she may not be there yet." Rhiannon took Copper's free hand. "This could have been a future vision."

"Either way, we have to go after her." Copper took her hand from Rhiannon's and pressed her fingertips to her forehead. "I'm certain I know how to get there. Through the Drow tunnels."

"Now how are we going to get past a bunch of Dark Elves?" Hannah's chocolate-brown eyes snapped along with her voice.

"I have a lot of Fae friends there now," Copper said, then furrowed her brow. "At least I hope so. Anyway, Garran won't hurt me, I'm certain of it. At worst he'll take me there as a prisoner, and then I'll have a chance."

Rhiannon raised a brow. "And what about us?"

"You'll go, too." Copper began to pace the kitchen. Zeph climbed her ear to the top curve. "My dream-visions may or may not have been influenced by Balor. But your vision—if the goddess blocked out all outside influences, then we know it's true!"

"It is true," came Cassia's soft voice from behind them. She was pulling a large tray of sugar cookies out of the oven. The air smelled of the warm cookies, and the heat of the oven whooshed over Copper before Cassia shut the oven door.

"But I can't allow you to go." Cassia's turquoise gaze met Copper's. "You must be protected at all costs."

"I *will* be going." Copper gritted her teeth. "I won't go alone, but I have to get to the Drow king. I have to get Garran to stop this madness and to help me find Silver before it's too late."

Cassia held her hands at her sides, her features still composed. More than ever she had the Elvin look about her. "I was sent to protect the bloodline—yours, Moondust's, and Silver's. I have failed them. You are the last and I cannot permit you to go."

Copper just blinked at her. "You were sent to protect our bloodline?"

Cassia gave the faintest and slowest of nods. "It is my duty."

"Screw *your* duty." Copper felt blood rush to her face. "*My* duty is to my sister, and I *will* go after her."

She turned back to Rhiannon, her face heated and her body tense. "Who will go with me?"

"You can damn sure count on me." Rhiannon gestured to the doorway leading to the shop. "I'd bet that most would join us."

"If you insist." Cassia came up to Copper and held her gaze. "If there is nothing I can do to persuade you otherwise, then I'll be going, as well."

"You all need to change." Copper looked them over. "Jeans, sweaters, good walking shoes, and jackets. I think it might get chilly down there."

Copper went to Sydney—who for some reason was also home from her job—Alyssa, and Mackenzie, and they all automatically said they would go. After Enchantments' patrons were encouraged to leave the shop because it was closing early, all the witches hurried off to their apartments to change, and Copper went back into the kitchen.

Cassia had taken off her oven mitts, removed her apron, and had started making sandwiches. "I know you're hungry—I doubt you've eaten anything all day. You need to in order to maintain your strength."

Copper hadn't imagined she could eat anything today with all that was tearing her apart, but her stomach rumbled at the thought of the food. "You're right," Copper said as Cassia handed her an egg-salad sandwich. "Thanks."

With Copper's help, the Elvin witch made enough sandwiches for each witch and bundled them in paper towels. They retrieved seven oranges, seven packages of raisins, and seven plastic bottles of water. Cassia also bagged up a dozen and a half warm sugar cookies in a brown paper bag.

Cassia grabbed Copper's earth-brown backpack off one of the hooks on the wall. She stuffed her pack with her share of the food along with the whole bag of cookies. Copper helped Cassia pack each witch's belongings so that they were all ready by the time the women returned. Cassia went off to change while Copper and her friends made plans.

"Should we take any of the D'Danann with us?" Alyssa asked.

"None are here." Rhiannon shook her head. "They're all out patrolling the skies for signs of Silver. I have no idea when they'll be back."

"We can't wait for them to get around to coming with us," Copper said, slinging her backpack over her shoulders. Zephyr moved down to her earlobe, close to the swinging pentagram earrings.

"What about the PSF?" Sydney's gaze met Copper's. "Jake will be pissed if we don't include him."

"Can't," Rhiannon said. "They're all human and can't pass through the veils like Fae, Elves, and witches, except when escorted by one of the full-blooded Elves."

When Cassia was back, dressed in jeans, too—which looked really strange to Copper since she'd only seen Cassia in skirts—they left. Without waiting or saying anything to the witches, Cassia led the way through the swinging door of the kitchen, out into the shop. The other witches were talking in excited and nervous voices. Copper just stuffed her hands farther into the pockets of her bomber jacket and stared at Cassia's back. She was in no mood for any kind of chitchat.

As they headed through the front door, the warding bells gave a merry tinkle that annoyed Copper. Why should anything be merry when so many horrors had happened and were happening? After Cassia locked the door behind them, they hurried up the street.

Tendrils of Copper's hair not held back by her braid ruffled in the breeze that met them head-on as they walked along the sidewalk. The light wind cooled Copper's cheeks. She snuggled into her jacket as she followed Cassia who was setting out uphill.

"So you can get us exactly where we need to go?" Copper asked.

"I can take you to the location where we'll need to cross," Cassia said softly as Copper caught up to her. "Because you're part Elvin, you'll be able to travel to Otherworld without my assistance. Most of the others I will have to escort."

All of Copper's emotions had settled in her belly and she couldn't think of anything to say as Cassia took them to Golden Gate Park, right back to where Copper had been all day. She couldn't stop thinking about her mother, her sister, and Tiernan.

An occasional cyclist whizzed by, a couple holding hands, and a panting jogger or two, but those were the only humans Copper saw. The air smelled of cypress and freshly mowed grass.

It seemed to take forever, and Copper's body was already sore thanks to jogging from one end of the park to the other that same morning, not to mention all she'd been through the past couple of days. Her foot still hurt a little from the Fomorii bite.

Finally Cassia took them over a rise into the trees where they could no longer be seen from the road. They went over another rise, and Cassia led them to a small bridge that spanned a little stream Copper had never seen before. That in itself wasn't surprising—the park was somewhere around a thousand acres and had over a million trees, nine lakes, and a lot of ponds.

But she had a feeling this was a magical place. She was certain the footbridge was no ordinary bridge despite the fact that it was weathered, its green paint curling, peeling, and chipped away. At the base of the bridge large boots had sunk into the muck. Dried mud from the boots was tracked up on the bridge, then disappeared from sight at the midpoint.

"Someone else was taken across earlier," Copper said as she looked to Cassia. The witch nodded but didn't offer any explanation.

Copper hitched her pack up higher on one shoulder and Zephyr settled on the curve of her ear again.

Cassia looked at her solemnly, her Elvin features ethereal in the waning light. "This is a door to Otherworld. At the midpoint of the bridge you will feel a barrier. Picture the exact location you wish to arrive at, and when you cross that barrier you will be there."

"That's it?" Copper gestured to the bridge. "I just walk across and that's all there is to it?"

The witch nodded. "If you didn't have Elvin blood, I would need to escort you across. But you'll be able to travel alone with the faith that you will end up where you need to be."

Cassia took two steps back. "Remember. Focus on the *exact* location you wish all of us to arrive at. We will be able to follow your energy."

It felt as though Pixies were creating havoc in Copper's belly as she looked away from Cassia and her friends, and gripped the backpack on her shoulder with one hand while grasping the roughened bridge rail with her other. She started forward, one foot in front of the other. The dried mud from the large boot prints crunched beneath her jogging shoes.

The moment she reached the center of the bridge, everything around her was silent. It felt like she had earplugs stuffed in her ears, and her skin went numb. She couldn't feel anything, hear anything, and her mouth was completely dry.

Her heart raced faster as the air in front of her wavered

like the shimmering surface of a pool of water. She stepped through it, still feeling muffled and numb—

And found herself in bright sunshine, Zephyr riding on her ear. Copper blinked as her eyes adjusted to the sunlight. She was in the middle of a meadow.

Her meadow.

Her chest seized. Not again! She couldn't be trapped again! She'd wanted to be just outside the meadow, not in the freaking middle of it—just in case.

She turned to run back across the footbridge . . .

And found herself face-to-face with the rock outcropping. No bridge, just rock. She had walked through the massive stones!

She backpedaled, knowing that she needed to get away from the rock wall to let the others through, so that they wouldn't bump into her.

Copper waited.

Nothing. Not a blur, not a whisper of movement. Nothing.

She waited some more.

A little longer.

And longer yet.

She walked back to the rock and placed her palm against it. Solid. As if she'd never walked through it.

"Crap." She bit her lower lip before saying aloud, "Where is everyone?" Her stomach clenched, she bit her lip again, and gripped the strap of her backpack tightly.

Zeph answered her with an unhappy buzz.

Slowly she turned in a slow circle. It was warm, and felt and smelled like spring. Her body was no longer numb and she could hear the happy chirp of birds and the *gruuup, gruuup* of the ferret-toad things, who were apparently mating again. They were sure horny things.

Apple-tree leaves, grass, and dandelions ruffled in a gentle breeze and a huge forest lay beyond, a forest she hadn't been able to see too well when she lived here, because of the barrier. Her shoes sank into the soft earth as her gaze and senses explored the meadow. Last night it must have rained because the air had a rain-washed scent. She caught other familiar scents, too, including apples and wet earth.

It was hard to believe she'd left this place only three days ago. She thought she'd never be back.

This time the grass was beneath her jogging shoes instead of her bare feet as she walked up to the apple tree. She pressed her hand up against the trunk. It felt rough against her palm, yet surprisingly comforting at the same time. Birds twittered from the tree as if telling her to leave their home alone. When she looked up she saw among the leaves and apples a nest with two bright red birds perched on its sides. She had never seen birds in the meadow before. That had to be a good sign.

Even though she was in the one place she thought she'd never want to be in again, somehow it felt like home. At least one home that she had come back to visit, but definitely not to live in again.

She continued to look around her. The rock outcropping was there—well, she'd just walked out of it, *duh*. The water from the small waterfall tinkled into each basin before flowing back into the ground.

So much emotion swirled through her.

Her throat ached and she felt the pain of her mother's death as fresh as when she had first learned of it. This was where she had been told her mother had passed on to Summerland. The rush of pain was harsh and the back of her eyes felt as though they were being singed from the hot tears that wanted to flood her cheeks.

And this was where she first met Tiernan.

Copper swallowed and tried to turn her mind to other things. Her gaze rested on the meager shelter that she had shared with Tiernan before they left, and her chest seized. This place was where she had fallen in love with him.

Copper forced her thoughts away from him. She stared

at the part of the rock outcropping she had just walked through. Her friends. Where were they? Zephyr buzzed his concern, too.

The bushes at the Faerie mound were still, no Faeries were collecting nectar, and no Faerie children were playing tag among the flowers. No Pixies, no Brownies, not even the Undine was there to greet her.

It felt so incredibly lonely.

Copper sighed.

She dropped her pack beside the apple tree and walked to where she knew the shield had always been. Holding out her hand, she took a step forward, then another step, then passed right through where the barrier had stood. She continued to walk around the meadow, testing the air for the barrier. It wasn't there!

A huge rush of relief left her chest and she grinned. She bounced up and down on her toes, her earrings jangling. She'd done it! Before she left she really had set them all free!

She whirled around to head back to the tree and came to an abrupt stop. The Faerie queen, Riona, along with several other Faeries, a few Pixies, and a couple of Brownies, all of whom she recognized, were gathered around her backpack. They were all looking at her as if expecting something. To her side she saw the beautiful Undine rise from the water.

Riona flitted away from the others, the lavender dust from her wings sparkling in the sunlight, and the scent of roses accompanying her. "Welcome back, Copper." The naked Faerie perched on Copper's shoulder, crossed her legs, and swung her foot. Zeph gave a buzz of greeting from Copper's ear.

She smiled at the Faerie queen. Copper went over to the odd group of creatures that normally didn't have a patient cell in their bodies, but now were uncommonly still— maybe Riona had cast a spell on all of them. With the

Faerie queen on her shoulder, Copper knelt and settled on her haunches in front of them.

"It's good to see you," she said and did her best to smile. It was so hard when the situation was so dire.

The Faeries bowed, the Pixies jumped up and down and clapped their little hands, and the Brownies made little grumbling noises. It occurred to Copper that she could offer them all a little treat as they'd done for her so many times.

"I've got something for each of you." Copper retrieved her pack from between a Pixie and a Brownie who had been shoving one another, then dug out the paper bag of sugar cookies.

The cookies were slightly warm, and huge compared to the Pixies and the Faeries, but the Brownies handled them all right. As a matter of fact, they munched down on the treats so quickly that in mere moments all that was left of their own cookies were crumbs. They even made sure to lick the crumbs from their fingers and to snatch them up from the grass. Copper gave them each another cookie, which they took with greedy little hands.

Copper kept glancing at the rock outcropping, hoping to see her friends walk through. Had they been transferred somewhere else?

Riona fluttered to Copper's hand and broke off a small handful of cookie and delicately ate an itty-bitty piece of it. "This human food—delicious," she said. "We will take our portion back to our Sidhe to share with the others of our kind." She waved her hands like a maestro conducting a symphony and all of the Faeries' cookies disappeared, along with the Faeries who had greeted Copper. Queen Riona stayed.

Riona stood on Copper's backpack as they watched the Pixies vanish into the greenery with their own cookies. The Brownies trundled away, looking pleased and full.

Copper pushed herself to her feet and carried a sugar cookie to the Undine who graciously took it with a bow of her head. "It is good to see you again, dearest Copper," she said in a voice like water trickling over stones. She sank down into the shallow basin of water and disappeared, cookie and all.

When Copper made it back to the apple tree to wait for her friends a little longer, it was just her, Zephyr, and Riona. While Zeph went to pollinate a few flowers, Copper sat cross-legged on the grass beside the Faerie queen. Riona was perched on the smooth rock that Copper had sat upon so many times before.

"So everyone was able to go back home?" Copper asked.

Riona was still delicately nibbling on the remaining cookie. "The barrier went away the moment you went back to your world. We still live nearby, but we are free to come and go as we please."

Copper smiled and felt another swell of relief in her chest. "I'm so glad."

But then that smile and relief disappeared as it hit her again that she was alone. None of her friends were coming through the barrier. And worst of all, Silver was in danger.

Riona braced her hands on the rock to either side of her and looked up at Copper. The queen's black hair was lying over her shoulders, covering her perfect little breasts. Her amethyst eyes were wide and serious.

"Your friends . . ." Riona started slowly.

"You know what happened to them?" Copper said. "Why didn't they come through with me?"

The queen delicately cleared her throat. "Balor blocked their way. He wants you alone, without the defenses of your companions."

Copper's body went limp and she slumped against the apple tree. "Oh, goddess."

"Although your sister is in trouble, you cannot go by yourself," Riona said softly. "It could mean your death, as well."

Copper dropped her hands to her lap. "Excuse me?"

"Our seer . . ." Riona shifted on the rock. "Suffice it to say that we know some of what would lie ahead of you if you made this journey alone. I wish we could be of assistance, but as you know, the Fae cannot tolerate being deep within the earth. It would kill us."

This time it felt as if Brownies were nipping at the inside of Copper's belly, *hard*. "Are you saying that Silver is in danger, but that you don't think I should go after her?"

Riona sighed. "She will soon be at the door. We do not know if she will be injured enough to die, or if she will survive."

"What the hell are you talking about?" Copper jumped to her feet. "You're telling me my sister could *die* and I'm not supposed to do anything about it?"

The Faerie queen stared solemnly at Copper. "You could die, as well."

"It doesn't matter what happens to me." Copper got back down on her knees and grabbed her backpack. "What matters is that I save my sister."

"There is no one who can help you." Riona's voice was pleading. "The Mystwalkers cannot live far from water, the Shanai and the D'Danann are too far away for us to contact in time. I can send word, but the only way they could make it is if they use the Elvin transference point, and the D'Danann and Elves do not speak to one another. As for the Elves assisting you, those of pure Elvin blood cannot go belowground or they will become Dark Elves. And as I said, none of the Fae can help. Only the D'Danann could if they were near enough. But as it is, I doubt they will be here in time."

Riona fluttered beside Copper while Zephyr zipped to

her ear as she stood and slung her backpack over one shoulder. She headed to the side of the rock wall that she had always dreaded going to.

"Please." Riona's voice was urgent. "Do not do this alone."

"I don't have a choice." There was no one to help her, and there was no way in hell that she was going to let her sister die. "I've got to find her, and I have to save her. I *will* save her."

When Copper reached the Drow door, she took a deep, deep breath. Then without any further hesitation, she stomped on the door five times.

While Copper waited for the door to open, Riona gave her a feather-light kiss on her cheek, then moved to hover in front of her and sighed. "I will send word to the D'Danann, but I do not know if it will make a difference."

Copper sucked in a breath. "A girl's gotta do what a girl's gotta do."

"Good luck, Copper Ashcroft." Riona fluttered her wings so that Faerie dust sprinkled over Copper's head and shoulders. "May the goddess be with you."

The door began to screech open at Copper's feet. The Faerie blew her one last kiss, then was gone in a blink of an eye.

That horrible nails-scratching-chalkboard sound grated along Copper's spine as the stone door moved. She shuddered when it finished and the door was finally open. The steps leading deep into the darkness were barely visible. She withdrew her wand from her pocket with her free hand and the crystal at the end began to glow its golden light. She hitched the pack up a little higher and started down the stairs.

Twenty-two

It was dark by the time the messenger arrived to tell Darkwolf that he had met Garran at the pier. The messenger, a demon in a young man's shell, handed Darkwolf a parchment filled with magic. Darkwolf closed his eyes and took a deep breath. Yes . . . the magic-infused paper would lead him directly to the door.

Triumph filled Darkwolf as he opened his eyes, but much of that triumph was forced through him by Balor's eye. Part of him was reluctant, because of what he would have to do with Silver. He would ensure she would not be killed, but he feared harming her.

He pocketed the parchment, which was of no use save for the transfer. He dismissed the messenger just as Junga approached. She had changed out of Elizabeth's elegant suit and was wearing functional jeans, a gold jersey with SAN FRANCISCO 49ERS emblazoned across it, and walking shoes. The shirt was all she'd been able to find at the last minute that would fit her while she was in her human shell. The jeans were tight as hell on her, and they made her ass look good enough to fuck.

When Darkwolf walked into one of the guest bedrooms to retrieve Silver, he stopped for a moment at the doorway. She was holding one palm against her belly, and she looked vulnerable and tired. Very tired. It was something he had never seen in her before.

In that moment, he was Kevin Richards again, the former white witch who longed to be human again. A human who might have been able to win the spirit and the love of such a woman. This woman.

What if she could save him? Return him to the life he once knew?

The moment she sensed his presence, she straightened her spine, dropped her hand from her belly, and raised her chin. The hatred in her eyes brought him back to reality. He belonged to Balor now, and this woman would never love him. He could keep her, always his captive, but she would never love him.

Silver looked beautiful despite her day of captivity. She had bathroom facilities within the room she had been relegated to, and she had eaten all that he'd placed in front of her through the powerful shield. Although it had looked like she was forcing herself to eat. Her hair hung long and loose around her shoulders and she had a soft flush to her cheeks.

He loved that fire in her gray eyes, her spirit, her beauty. Something about the unguarded moment he had just caught her in concerned him. Something beyond being held captive was disturbing Silver.

Sara walked into the room and sidled up to Darkwolf as she met Silver's gaze. Sara had once belonged to the same D'Anu Coven as Silver, before Silver was kicked out and before Sara had been seduced into the Balorite fold.

With no hesitation, Sara reached up and kissed Darkwolf, slipping her tongue into his mouth. She tasted sweet and when she rubbed his cock through his jeans, he wanted to fuck her, right in front of Silver, to show her what she was missing.

He heard a low growl behind him that he knew was Junga. After deliberately extending the kiss, he physically separated himself from Sara. She gave him the sensual pout that she was so good at. Her nipples were taut beneath her low-cut blouse and he was certain her pussy was wet, waiting for him.

Junga growled again, but he ignored her. He tweaked one of Sara's nipples and she gave a satisfied smile. "No time now." He pinched her other nipple and she moaned a little louder. "I'll give you a good fucking when we get back."

Sara smirked at Junga and looked down her nose at Silver, who had a horrified expression on her face. She obviously was shocked at how easily Sara had embraced being a warlock, and her relationship with Darkwolf.

"Let's get the witch and go," Junga said in a harsh voice that sounded much like a command.

Darkwolf turned to Junga, ice in his eyes. It was not her place to give him orders. He wore Balor's eye. He had the power of the god. However, the demon queen would never quaver before him, despite the fact he was certain he could kill her through Balor's magic. He brushed aside his irritation. He looked from Junga to Sara. "Prepare for the transfer."

His gaze returned to Silver and the shield around her that had been multiplied by the strength of Balor. She hadn't been able to penetrate this shield no matter how many times she'd tried. He had watched her, amused at her attempts. The shield was in front of the bedroom door and covered the curtained window so that she could not break through it, and she had no means of communication.

He frowned. Unlike the fraction of time she'd had to use her cell phone. Her guard had been down, though, and he'd been able to use his magic to retrieve it from her.

Just how much did she know and how much did she tell her friends? The D'Danann and witches had not appeared at his door, so he was certain she hadn't been able to relay their location. No doubt there was nothing to worry about.

When Silver had noticed Darkwolf, her hands were immediately prepared to fight him the second he removed the shield. Instead of releasing it, he wrapped the shield snug around her, like a lover, the way he wanted to wrap his arms around her.

"It's time." He stepped closer to her now that she was confined to one small space with his magic.

She reached up to touch the barrier, then snatched her hand back. "Time for what?" She dropped her hands to her sides and clenched them into fists.

Darkwolf sighed. He truly didn't want to do this, but he saw no choice. They would need only a little of her blood—Balor had promised this when he'd spoken to Darkwolf through the stone. He would have to take her to the door itself, now that the location of the door had been made known.

He slipped his hand into his pocket, pulled out a small vial, and opened it. Careful not to breathe in the contents, he pushed the open bottle through his shield and splashed it on Silver before she had a chance to react. He briefly caught the scent of poppy seeds, chamomile, and his own special ingredient.

Darkwolf let the shield drop just in time to catch Silver before she collapsed and fell into a deep sleep.

Twenty-three

Copper's heart pounded as she descended the stairs. She had no doubt this was what she was supposed to do—this was her destiny. The Drow were trying to open that evil door, and she had to stop them.

She wished she had her witch friends with her, or the D'Danann, or the PSF—well, all of them—but everyone and everything had been blocked from her for one reason or another. She was forced to do this alone. And she was determined to save her sister and her unborn child.

Unlike the other two times Copper had walked into the recesses of the Drow stairway, torches did not automatically flicker to life as she made her way down. Once the door screeched shut above her, the light of her wand was all that lit her way.

Her shoe slipped and she barely kept from falling by bracing her palm against one rough wall. She steadied herself and held her wand tightly in her other hand. The journey seemed to last much longer, and her heart was pounding harder by the time she reached the foot of the stairs.

"How am I going to confront Garran about this, Zeph?" she asked, more to herself than the familiar. She wasn't afraid of Garran, she knew in her gut he wouldn't hurt her. He wanted her and he wouldn't let any harm come to her.

She believed that, despite the fact he had betrayed her and all the Fae in the meadow by not telling them he could travel in and out of their prison, belowground. Not to mention the fact that he was apparently in league with Darkwolf and trying to open the door that separated evil from Otherworld, and perhaps her own.

Oh, goddess. Was she a total freaking idiot to trust him at all?

Surprisingly, in the absolute dark, no guards were there to greet her at the foot of the stairs. Or rather, it would have been completely dark if she didn't have her wand light. She was in the main chamber with its polished granite floor. All the debris that had fallen when the Drow and Tiernan had battled the giant had been cleared and the floor shone once again.

The entrance chamber was completely silent. "Where is everyone?" she said and her words echoed throughout the huge chamber. Other than her own voice, she didn't hear the slightest sound of speech, clink of armor, rustling of clothing. It was hollow, achingly empty. Her familiar flew to land on her wand. Zeph buzzed his wings, showing his nervousness.

Feeling as though she were sneaking into someone's home without them knowing—which she more or less was—she crept forward, her jogging shoes not making a sound on the smooth floor. Her wand light cast a bright golden glow that played off the carvings in the walls and made shadows seem to move and writhe, sending a crawling sensation up her spine.

When she reached Garran's chamber, her heart pounded as she peeked in. No one was in the room. The glow from her wand sparkled off the thousands of crystals, creating a dazzling scene. The one blight on the crystal was the obsidian door that seemed to suck up all the light from her wand.

She'd bet her last dollar that obsidian door was the doorway to Otherworlds.

Her stomach felt queasy. "Why would Garran leave his chamber unprotected?" she mumbled, and Zephyr moved down her wand from the tip to her hand, tickling her a little.

A noise behind her caused Copper to whirl around. Her braid flopped over her shoulder and her earrings swung. She moved out of the chamber and held her wand out, prepared. But she saw nothing.

Zephyr buzzed back to her ear and she felt his increasing agitation mingling with her own.

For a moment she paused, looking from one exit to another leading from the circular area. "Well, Zeph, which exit should we follow?"

But her gut knew exactly which one to take—the one that led to where the Drow and Tiernan had fought the giant.

It was obvious to her now that the Drow had been digging far below the surface to find the door that would release all manner of evil. The giant had come from deep beneath the ground where its kind stayed unless disturbed.

Copper crept across the large room to the exit leading to the chamber where the battle had taken place. When she reached the tunnel she took a deep breath. It smelled of dry dirt and she sneezed when she inhaled some of the dust. Her wand light lit the way through the tunnel.

It wasn't long until she reached the landing overlooking the pit. She raised her wand and it gave off just enough light to illuminate the expansiveness of the pit. From this very point she had watched Tiernan and the Drow fight the giant.

In her wand light she was able to make out the huge hole in the floor of the pit. One large enough for the giant to have climbed through.

Her shoes skidded on the dirt path when she took a step forward, she stumbled over a rock, and almost lost her balance. "Oooookay. Let's not do that again." Holding her wand out, she peered over the side of the path and swallowed when she saw just how sheer of a drop it was. Heart beating just a bit faster, she continued down the trail that led around and around the pit, slowly making its way to the stony floor and the enormous hole.

It took so long she should have been tired by the time she reached the bottom of the pit and the hole itself, but she wasn't. Between that and her six-mile jog today—from one end of Golden Gate Park to the other and back again—anyone else would probably have been nearing exhaustion. But thanks to all of her workouts during her captivity, she could more than keep up, and she was only a little sweaty. Wisps of hair clung to the perspiration along her neck and brow. She felt sticky beneath her bomber jacket and she shrugged out of it and set it aside with her backpack while she checked out the hole at the center of the pit.

The hole was enormous. It was blocked off by dirt and boulders lying all around it, as if something had exploded upward. The dirt pile was open on one side, and through that opening she could clearly see the hole. She moved past the boulders and dirt, closer to the hole and peered over its edge. It was very deep by the look of it, and as wide around as the kitchen at Enchantments—or rather the giant that had come through to attack the Drow. Her wand light didn't reach the bottom.

Copper had no doubt this was the tunnel the Drow had used to reach the door that was to be opened to free Balor. It all made perfect sense. Why else would they have been tunneling here? The giant being disturbed from its guard post far belowground and coming up through the tunnel to attack the Elves clinched it.

Of course, that meant she needed to follow the tunnel that was bound to lead her to the Drow, to Silver, and to the door itself. Why weren't there any ladders, or ropes? Something that could be used to climb below? After all, the Drow couldn't fly. Well, she didn't think so, anyway.

She raised her wand so that she could see better and saw that there *was* a rope tied around one of the boulders and it disappeared into the depths of the giant hole. She hadn't noticed it at first because it was so thin and almost transparent. It glistened in the wand light.

Unfortunately, it was several feet away from her. Copper stuffed her wand in her back pocket, keeping the lit end up. It threw just enough light around her to see, but she would have preferred its full light in front of her. Carefully, she climbed over piles of rocks and dirt, grasping handholds and finding footholds, as she worked her way to the rope. Dirt was under her fingernails and she scratched the insides of her arms on the rocks.

Her pulse elevated every time pebbles slid beneath her shoes or fingers and into the darkness below. Stones would bounce against the walls of the hole, but the fact that she didn't hear them hit bottom added to her feeling of urgency to reach that rope.

"Not gonna fall. I'm *not* gonna fall." Sweat coated her forehead and she took shallow breaths as she worked her way around.

When she finally reached the boulder that the rope was tied around, she sagged against the rock in relief and gave herself a moment to catch her breath.

"I can do this." She worked to convince herself as she reached for the strange-looking rope that glittered in the faint wand light that came from her back pocket. She hugged the boulder and reached as far as her arm could go, and made a frustrated sound when her fingers came just short of it.

"Damn." Her arms trembled from the strength it took to hold on to the boulder and keep her footing. Just a bit farther and she'd have it.

Any farther and she was likely to plunge into the hole.

She was about to try to stretch a little more when Zephyr buzzed off her ear and toward the rope. He zipped straight to the other side of the rope and landed hard against it—hard for a honeybee.

Surprisingly, the rope moved closer to Copper's finger-tips. He flew off it and then back to it—harder this time— swinging on it as it came even closer to Copper's hand. Familiars were stronger than their forms, and obviously Zephyr had more strength than she'd realized. "A little more, Zeph," she said.

He buzzed off, then rammed his little body into the rope, causing it to swing close enough for her to grab.

With relief she gripped the rope. "Thank you, Zeph."

The fingers of her other hand slid across the boulder's surface.

She lost her hold.

Her feet slipped out from under her.

Copper cried out as she fell.

She clenched her fingers tightly around the rope. It burned her palm as she slid a few feet down. She grabbed the rope with her free hand and with a jerk and a cry she brought herself to a halt.

Copper clung to the rope, tendons stretched tight, her arms aching. She brought her knees up around the rope and crossed her feet at the ankles as she'd done in gym class all those years ago when she was in high school. Her whole body was coated in sweat now and her heart beat like crazy. She wanted to rest, but her muscles burned and her body cried for relief. Good thing she'd been doing all those pull-ups during her imprisonment.

"Okay." She sucked in her breath as her familiar landed on her ear. "Here we go, Zeph."

She started to slowly ease down the rope. One hand under the other. One hand under the other.

How much farther? she asked herself.

The tension in the rope vanished.

The rope dissolved in her fingers.

She dropped.

Copper screamed as she fell. Wind rushed past her face. She braced herself for the impact she knew was coming.

She fell. And fell. And fell—

With a *thud* and a *whack* she landed on her ass. A snapping sound. She fell back. Her skull struck the hard-packed earth. She swore she saw little lights sparking in her mind. Her entire body ached, from her head to her back to her tailbone.

Groaning, she pushed herself to a sitting position. It was pitch-black . . .

Copper's pulse jumped as she realized she'd just landed on her wand. Her hand shook as she reached back and withdrew her wand from her back pocket. Already she could feel that it had been flattened in the middle since it was only made of copper. Heart sinking, she brought it in front of her, focused her magic on it. Rather than a quick illumination, it slowly grew just faint enough that she could see. She looked closer at her wand—

The quartz-crystal point had cracked. The tip had fallen off.

"Nooooooo!" She shook it, as if that would possibly fix it, and peered at it again. "Fuck, fuck, fuck!"

Again she tried to make it work, but nothing helped.

She crouched on her knees and wrapped her hands around her belly. "Now what am I going to do?" she whispered. "Now how am I going to help Silver?"

Zephyr buzzed up to her ear and he sounded more than sympathetic, he sounded incredibly worried.

She had to have her wand to do magic. She wasn't any good at hand witchcraft like her sister was. When she became proficient with her wand at a young age, she had completely relied upon it.

Copper held the wand up and the meager light glinted

on the broken crystal quartz on the floor of the cave. She scooped it up from the dry dirt and her stomach pitched as she stared at the piece in her hand. Maybe a spell could fix it. The round crystal at the other end of the wand was unscathed, so maybe it would help.

Her hands trembled as she tried to fit the shard to the broken crystal at the end of the wand. Ignoring the pain in her back, neck, and head, and the burn from the rope on her hands, she sat cross-legged on the floor of the tunnel and held the shard between her thumb and forefinger as she said her spell.

> *What was broken will be remade,*
> *For this crystal is needed to aid.*
> *In fighting the evil this way come,*
> *With this wand good shall be from.*
> *By the earth and fire will this be forged,*
> *So that all that is evil may be scourged.*

Copper held her breath as the broken part of her wand glowed. A soft gold, not the brilliant light she was accustomed to. The glow reflected through the broken shard, casting fractured light throughout the huge tunnel. Her fingers that held the shard felt a horrible burning sensation. Tears of pain prickled at the backs of her eyes.

When she didn't think she could take any more, the wand light went out. The crystal shard fell from her fingers and into her lap. "No, no, no, no!" she shouted and her voice bounced against the walls of the cave.

This time a tear did roll down her cheek, and with one fist she pounded the earth beside her in frustration, anger, and fear. This hadn't happened in her dream-vision. She'd had her wand, *dammit*!

How could she get out of this mess? Then her chest seized. She had to get to Silver. She had no choice. What if her sister lay dying at this very moment? What about Silver's baby?

Pain shooting through her body, Copper eased to her feet and stuffed the shard in her pocket. She raised her stupid wand high enough that its minimal glow let her see that she was in a huge tunnel—big enough for the giant to travel through. That was different from her dream, too.

She wiped her hands on her jeans and started down the tunnel, which led in only one direction. The other side was blocked. Rocks crunched beneath her feet and the smell of freshly dug earth was strong. No doubt the giant had widened the Drow tunnel when he'd made his way to the top.

It seemed as though she had been walking for an hour before she finally saw an opening into some kind of chamber—and heard noises. She got down on her hands and knees and crawled toward the opening, certain her wand light was too dim for anyone to see. Her thumb and forefinger still stung from when she'd tried to repair the wand, and the dirt beneath her fingers and palms magnified the pain from the rope burn.

When she reached the edge of the chamber she blinked in the darkness. Her eyes had become adjusted to seeing with very little light, and her heart caught in her throat as she saw four giants. Two lay dead in the center of the chamber, their bodies riddled with arrows and holes the arrowheads had made when they exploded in the giant bodies. Their throats were slashed, too. Copper recognized those arrows. They belonged to the Drow.

Like the other giant Tiernan and the Drow had fought, these giants were hunchbacked, had skin of bark brown with stringy mosslike brown hair. Their eyes were all a brilliant green and their teeth mossy green and jagged.

Scattered on the floor were shields the same size as the one the other giant had used, as big as a garage door. Two clubs the size of a commuter plane lay haphazardly near the giants.

The two living giants carried nothing. However, they were making grunts and other sounds of fury as they looked upon what must have been guards to the gates—gates that surely led the Drow closer to Underworld.

Each of the enormous beasts grabbed a dead giant by the foot and began dragging it across the floor of the chamber to a huge tunnel on the other side of the room. Big ponds of blood remained behind and some streaked the floor as the bodies were hauled away. The smell of the giants and the blood was like garbage left out in the sun too long.

The blood looked fairly fresh, so the Drow must have passed this way not long ago. That thought actually gave her some hope. Maybe she'd still reach them before it was too late.

Adrenaline rushing through her body, heightening her senses, Copper scrambled from out of the tunnel and onto the dirt floor of the giant chamber. She bolted across it, dodging the pools of blood, and running toward the opposite wall where she saw another large tunnel. Goddess, it was so far!

When she reached the midpoint of the chamber, she heard the rumble of a giant nearby. She cast a look in the direction the two giants had gone through and her blood rushed in her ears when she saw that one of the giants had come back. Thanks to being a track star when she was in high school, she was able to double her speed.

Earth pounded and it shook dirt and rocks loose from the ceiling of the chamber as the giant rushed toward her, its huge steps giving it an advantage she didn't have. Terror knifed through her as the beast drew closer.

Copper was almost to the tunnel. She pushed herself harder, faster, and slipped through its entrance. The barely glowing wand kept her from smacking into walls as she ran, and she prayed there wasn't a wall that ended this passageway.

The only problem was that the tunnel was large enough for the giant to crawl in after her. Chest heaving and sweat pouring down her brow, she continued to run. Her thighs burned, her lungs burned. She ran straight into a cobweb and wiped it out of her face as she heard the grunting and panting of the giant still behind her. It was a tighter squeeze for the giant, but it was gaining on her.

She felt Zeph leave her ear and she didn't have time to stop to call him back. What if he got caught in the cobweb? Did he have enough magic to free himself?

In the next moment she heard the giant bellow. The pounding behind her ceased as the giant cried out in obvious pain and fury.

Zephyr! The familiar had attacked the giant, probably stinging it in the face multiple times. Goddess, how she loved that little guy.

Even though she could barely breathe, and her body ached, she kept running until she was positive nothing was behind her.

She bent over, hands on her thighs, her head dizzy, legs and arms trembling. Her braid flopped over her shoulder. She straightened and tipped back her head, trying to control her breathing and slow down the racing of her heart. Just like when she'd raced in track meets in high school, she knew she had to walk off the run. Her face was hot and her chest still burned.

Copper braced her hands on her hips and walked forward, barely able to see because her damaged wand was peeking out from her clenched fist at her side.

She took a step forward. Her shoe met nothing.

With a scream she tumbled into darkness again.

Twenty-four

Hawk met up with Tiernan outside the brown gates of the court with Keir at his side. Keir was Hawk's bastard-born half brother and held little love for Hawk. Keir was a formidable warrior, had a scar across one cheek, and fought like the hounds of Underworld. He had returned to Otherworld after Samhain to attend to the training of additional D'Danann warriors who were to join them in Copper's world.

"I have enlisted more of our brethren. They will join us shortly," Hawk said to Tiernan. His features were still twisted with anger, his hand clenched around his sword hilt. "I shall kill Darkwolf with my bare hands when we meet. And if Silver or our babe is injured, I shall kill him again."

Keir's arms crossed his chest and his look was thunderous. He might have no love for his half brother, Hawk, but he obviously respected and cared for Silver.

Tiernan felt the same way about Silver. And Copper . . . he couldn't find the words to express himself.

Hawk gave Tiernan a long measured look as they waited

for the warriors. Tiernan could hear the men and women coming in the distance.

"You have been trifling with Copper's heart," Hawk said. "If you hurt her, D'Danann brother or no, I shall have to flay you."

"I deserve that beating. I have already hurt her." Tiernan gave a great sigh as Hawk's eyes darkened. "However, I hope she will have me once I explain—and now that I have freed myself from my responsibilities of the court." He raked his hand through his hair and scrubbed his scalp in frustration. "I broke my vow to Airell. I gave all my wealth to Urien so that he may rise in stature within the courts to wed her. My parents have disowned me, but what is important to me is Copper."

Hawk raised one brow. "All your wealth? Your stature?"

"My responsibilities. My honor." Tiernan pushed his fingers through his hair. "If Copper does not take me, then I will choose to live the warrior's life with the rest of the D'Danann."

Tiernan was just about to ask Hawk how many D'Danann would be joining them when Urien came tearing through the gates, a Faerie riding on his shoulder. "Tiernan! This Faerie has news for you."

"Riona?" Tiernan's belly churned when Urien reached him. For the Faerie queen to bring tidings herself, the news she carried would not be good. "What brings you this way?"

The Fae cousin to the D'Danann used her tiny hand to push her black hair from her face. She looked as if she were winded from a long flight. Lavender Faerie dust sprinkled Urien's shoulder with every movement her wings made.

"Copper—" The Faerie sounded tired, which surprised Tiernan further. "Balor has blocked Elvin entries and exits from Copper's world to Otherworld. Cassia, the other witches—no one was able to follow. Copper has gone alone to face Darkwolf and the Drow to save Silver. Her sister is in mortal peril."

Shock arrowed through Tiernan's chest.

"Speak, Faerie," Hawk commanded, obviously impatient for news of his mate.

The queen gave him a haughty look and flew straight from Urien's shoulder to buzz in front of Hawk's nose. "I will answer your questions only because Copper is friend to the Faeries and we fear greatly for her safety."

The other warriors arrived and the situation was quickly explained to them. "How shall we get to this place? Is it a long journey?" Tiernan asked.

Riona nodded. "It is far, and it was only due to magical flight that I was able to arrive as quickly as I have."

"Then how shall we reach her?" Tiernan said between gritted teeth.

The queen looked from Tiernan to Hawk. "You will need to go to the Elvin transference point and ask the aid of the Great Guardian."

Immediately shouts of agreement and disagreement broke out among the D'Danann warriors. Tiernan watched for a moment as Hawk started forward with no hesitation. His first wife, who had passed to Summerland, had been half-Elvin, and Hawk had maintained his ties to the Elves despite the animosity between Fae and Elves.

"I will speak with the Great Guardian." Hawk unfurled his wings and immediately began his journey through the forest.

"You can count on me to aid you, as well," Urien said, his gaze resting on Tiernan. "I owe you much."

Tiernan gave a quick nod. He and the other warriors took to the sky and followed Hawk as he made his way through the forest, away from the D'Danann village. Riona settled on Tiernan's shoulder, looking queenly, though somewhat tired.

"Godsdamn!" Tiernan could not contain the emotion

raging through him. "I promised Copper I would be there for her. She cannot face this alone!"

Riona crossed her legs at her knees and bounced her dainty foot. "You will be there for her. If you hurry now."

Fear for Copper raged through Tiernan's mind, like nothing he had ever felt before. His heart pounded against his ribs, his skin felt hot, then cold. She had described her dreams to him vividly. What if they were true? Every last detail?

Tree branches scraped his face, and even through the smells of rich earth and fresh flowers, he felt the air closing in on him, as if he were trapped in the bubble again.

They eventually came to an ancient Elvin transference point and each D'Danann landed and folded away their wings. Elvin runes had long ago been carved around the circular platform made of a stone like gray marble, only far stronger, far more enduring. Beyond the platform was a small bridge and a stream tinkled merrily beneath it.

"Veils can only be crossed by the Elves during special times throughout the year, such as the solstice or equinox," Riona said. "However, Elves can also travel through doorways—over ancient bridges, or beneath great mounds of earth. Since there are such a great number of you, we will need the transference point along with the aid of the Great Guardian."

Some of the D'Danann grumbled. Prejudices ran deep between Fae and Elves.

"Quiet!" Hawk bellowed, and complete silence from the warriors reigned instantly. "We will wait and see if the Great Guardian will bless us with her presence."

The sounds of birds chirping, the low music of Dryads singing, the whisper of wind through leaves, and the tinkling stream could be heard as they waited.

For a long moment all warriors remained quiet, their eyes fixed on the bridge. The wind picked up and a sound like bells filled the air.

Tiernan could barely contain himself, his need was so great to aid Copper. He could tell Hawk felt the same way about Silver just by the clenching of his jaw and his fists.

An Elvin woman of incredible grace and beauty appeared on the footbridge.

She was as tall as most of the D'Danann warriors. Her pointed ears peeked through strands of her white-blond hair that hung straight and silkily, all the way to her feet. Her hair and her skin were perfect. She appeared young, but with such incredible wisdom in her eyes.

The sound of metal scraping against a scabbard was loud as Hawk removed his sword and laid it at the foot of the transference point. Tiernan followed suit, and they both knelt.

"Rise and sheathe your weapons." The Great Guardian's voice could be called nothing less than musical. "You must hurry if you are to save the ones you love."

Tiernan and Hawk looked at one another and quickly obeyed the Guardian. They shrugged out of their coats and tossed them aside on the grass as one, both apparently needing to be free of anything that might hinder them.

"I can allow two of you to cross at a time." She gestured for Hawk and Tiernan to stand on the stone. "You must hurry through the Drow door and into the tunnels." She focused on Tiernan. "Remember the encounter with the giant."

How she had known about the fight with the giant, Tiernan had no idea, but he was not about to question such an intelligent and wise being.

"Battle well," she said as Hawk and Tiernan stepped upon the stone, and Riona fluttered onto his shoulder.

Tiernan braced himself for the transference. Again that feeling of suffocation, of his eyes bulging, of wanting to claw at his throat, nearly overcame him. But in mere moments they were free and stood within the meadow Tiernan knew only too well.

◆ ◆ ◆

Copper was tumbling through a hole. Again. She screamed, but it was lost in the rush of air whooshing by her cheeks. She couldn't think past her fear.

Her feet slammed onto hard ground. Pain screamed through her as her right ankle wrenched. She heard a popping and grinding sound, and she fell to her hands and knees.

"Oh, goddess!" she shouted, unable to hold back another cry.

The pain in her ankle was so excruciating that tears leaked from her eyes and sweat broke out on her brow. She scrubbed her face on her arm, wiping away the moisture before gently lowering herself so that she was sitting on her butt.

No matter how carefully she moved, the pain in her ankle was so intense she could barely breathe. She held her knee up and her foot off the floor of wherever it was that she'd landed. She was afraid to put any pressure on her foot. The slightest touch would send her screaming, she was sure.

She was gripping her damaged wand, but its light was out again, and it was pitch-black once more. "Dammit! Stupid ass thing." Instead of slamming the wand onto the ground like she wanted to, she raised it and focused her magic on the shattered tip. A soft golden glow fractured from it, giving her barely enough light to see by.

She moved it like a flashlight with dying batteries, shining it around the place she was now in, while trying to ignore the throbbing agony in her ankle. Once again—surprise, surprise—she was in a passageway. Only this one was much smaller, only tall enough for a Drow to walk without bending his head, and wide enough for two to walk side by side. No giant had made this tunnel.

Copper wondered if destiny had screwed up, or if Balor had been fucking with her dream-visions again. Here she was, things happening like in her visions, only in them she hadn't broken her wand and hadn't broken her ankle, too.

"Crap, this is *so* not good." Her voice sounded hoarse. "And, wasn't that the understatement of the year?"

Her head, back, and butt still ached from her first fall, her hands from the rope burns, but that was nothing compared to the all-consuming pain in her ankle. She swore she'd never felt anything so intensely painful in her life. It was the same foot that the Fomorii had scratched when she'd arrived in San Francisco, and even that wound seemed to flare up worse than before.

Maybe a little witchcraft would help—at least a bit. She'd helped her sister witches before, why couldn't she help herself? She pointed her broken wand at her swelling ankle, and said a small chant meant to help numb the pain. Sparks sputtered from the end of her wand, not the glittering glow she was accustomed to. She held her breath, hoping the charm would work and that her pain would ease.

No such luck.

If anything, it hurt worse.

She clenched her wand tighter. "Fuck."

Goddess, how she wanted to hurl the wand through the tunnel. If she didn't need what little light it offered, she would have ditched the stupid thing already.

Bracing her hands on the floor first, then the walls, she eased herself to a standing position, putting all of her weight on her good foot. It didn't help to keep more pain from shooting through her like an explosion in her ankle.

She cringed and moaned and couldn't help a few more tears.

Yeah, this is just peachy.

The tunnel only went in one direction. It sloped downward, just a slight decline. Gritting her teeth, Copper started hobbling, balancing herself by bracing one hand against the wall while she moved. It didn't matter how careful she was, the pain just wouldn't stop. She smelled fresh dirt, and the earth felt cool and rough beneath her palm as she steadied herself.

"Where's Zeph?" She paused in mid-hobble and looked over her shoulder. "Zephyr!" she called, panic edging her voice. Her stomach clenched. Had the giant squashed him? "Zephyr!"

She waited a few heartbeats, but when he didn't come to her, she saw no choice but to continue.

She didn't seem to have a whole lot of choice in anything.

Copper made her way slowly down the tunnel and she was relieved when the pain in her ankle slowed to a dull, throbbing ache as if going numb from the injury. No doubt when she had to put pressure on it again, she was going to be in for some serious agony. She had a nagging headache from her first fall, and her back was killing her.

"How am I going to do this?" Her voice sounded small and lost in the tunnel. "I need you, Zeph!"

No comforting buzzing sound met her ears.

Why had this all happened? Hadn't she and her sister been through enough?

No time for a freaking pity party, Copper. Get your ass in gear. There's no choice but to go forward.

The tunnel seemed to go on forever and ever. She was aching, filthy, she had a broken wand, and a broken ankle.

And a broken heart. While she moved down the tunnel she had time to think of lots of things. The constant void the passing of her mother had created and the pain of her death that would never go away. Silver was now imprisoned with Darkwolf. Was she safe? What about the baby? How was Copper going to get her sister back?

Or did Darkwolf plan to use Silver for some obscene ritual that had to do with the door?

The thought made Copper shudder and she tried not to let her mind go *there*. She would get to her sister before anything happened to Silver. She *would*.

She forced her thoughts away from her fears and found

herself thinking about Tiernan. How could she have fallen in love with him? She wasn't sure the pain of loving him, since he probably had to marry another woman, would ever go away.

Time heals all wounds.

Now wasn't that a load of bullshit.

Copper continued to limp-hop down the passageway until finally a red glow mingled with the dull light of her wand.

The red light crept around a corner of the tunnel and grew as the passageway turned. Copper's heart rate picked up. This was it. This was where everything would come to a head.

Goddess, how she wished she had *someone* to help her. Her witch friends had been shut out, the Fae and Elves couldn't help. And the D'Danann were on the other side with the witches in her world. They had to have someone with Elvin blood to take them across, so how could they get to her if no one else could?

Copper took a deep breath. She hobbled forward until she reached the corner and peered around it.

She didn't need her wand light anymore. The horrible red creeping from a door across the cavern covered everything in a crimson glow. She stuck her wand in her back pocket and gripped the wall with both hands as she took a moment to take in her surroundings.

Like her dream-visions, she had entered an immense cavern filled with stalactites and stalagmites. Like blood-red rubies, crystals sparkled throughout the cavern. The cavern had an eerie red glitter about it that made her feel sick to her stomach. Everything seemed bathed in blood.

It was hot, so very hot, like the heat of a furnace.

As far as she could tell, the chamber was empty. Where were the Drow? Darkwolf, the Fomorii, Silver?

Copper took a deep breath as she clung to the corner of the tunnel that led into the cavern. Unlike in her dreams she didn't smell that rotten fish stench, and she didn't catch the scent of wolfsbane. The earthy, mossy scent of the Drow was there, although she didn't see them.

She did smell something she couldn't quite identify. It was a sickly sweet odor that made her stomach churn. It smelled like—like burnt sugar.

Over and over in Copper's mind, she ran through the spell she'd been thinking of all day when she'd jogged the length of the park and back, and while she'd sat and watched the ocean for a while.

With that spell, she would be prepared to keep that door closed, unlike her dream. She rubbed her back pocket where she'd stuck her wand. The only difference was that in her preparation for this spell, she'd been counting on her wand.

Now she'd have to count on hand magic instead. At that thought she bit her lip. She'd always relied on her wand. She should have practiced hand magic rather than having to rely on a tool.

Silver needed her. She would not fail.

Shoring up her courage, Copper hobbled fully around the corner, and then beside the rocks that barricaded one side of the path that led down to the cavern. When she reached the cavern floor, she was surprised to find a path through the flat rock floor that was fairly smooth and worn, as if traveled upon by many feet over centuries.

No longer having a wall of any kind to brace herself with, Copper had to skip-hop from stalagmite to stalagmite, pausing to catch her breath and ease the pain of her ankle. More sweat broke out on her forehead and her body felt even hotter. The pain in her ankle constantly made her want to vomit.

The closer she came to the door, the harder her heart pounded. The crimson glow made it easy enough for her to see, but she couldn't quite make out everything ahead of her.

She hop-skipped a little closer. Closer. Closer. Until she

was a good twenty feet from the door. She'd almost reached the last stalagmite, and would have nothing else to hold on to once she took another step forward.

Copper came to an abrupt halt. The red glow from the door was bright enough that she had to blink to become accustomed to it. The smell of burnt sugar was much stronger now. She scanned the cavern and saw no one—no sign of the Drow, the Fomorii, or warlocks.

She dropped her gaze. On the floor was the circle with the runes—

At the center of that circle was her unconscious sister, blood trickling from the corner of her mouth.

The moment Copper saw her sister at the center of that circle of runes, she couldn't help the scream that tore from her throat: "Silver!" The word echoed throughout the cavern, bouncing from wall to wall, stalagmite to stalactite. "Ohmygoddess, ohmygoddess, ohmygoddess!"

Her heart raced as it had never raced before. Adrenaline surged through her, giving her the strength to push herself away from the last stalagmite and hobble to Silver as fast as she could. Copper didn't care about anything but getting to her sister. Silver was lying on her back spread-eagle. Her head was turned, facing Copper, her eyes closed, a dried trickle of blood coming from her bottom lip where she'd apparently bit it hard enough to draw blood—or where she'd been hit.

Through her fear and the haze of her pain, she had the presence of mind to look about the cavern again. Where were Darkwolf, Junga, and the Drow? Other Fomorii or warlocks?

When she reached Silver, Copper dropped to her knees, the pain in her swollen ankle bringing a rush of agony through her body that made her feel faint, yet she did her best to ignore it. She reached for Silver's wrist and found that it was bound tight to a metal stake in a witch's knot. With her fingers, Copper felt her sister's pulse. It wasn't as strong as it should be.

And Silver was still. So unnaturally still.

What was wrong with her? And was the baby all right?

Tears squeezed from Copper's eyes and splashed onto Silver's arm. Copper's sister's silvery-blond hair was loose around her head like a halo. She was wearing the same black clothing she had been wearing the night she was taken.

When Copper glanced at Silver's other bound wrist, she saw it had been sliced open. From a small cut, blood slowly seeped from Silver and into the connected runes engraved into the stone. The blood wasn't drying; it was creeping into the etchings and making its way through them, from one rune to the next.

"No!" Copper crawled on her hands and knees to the other side of Silver, her mind consumed with saving her sister. She had to perform a healing spell to stop the flow of blood. But she didn't have her wand!

Gritting her teeth, she held her hands over the small cut through one of Silver's veins. Obviously someone had meant to bleed her slowly. A faint golden glow began to seep from Copper's fingers and she let out a low growl as she pushed her magic further.

Nothing. Blood still trickled into the rune below Silver's wrist.

Copper's whole body wound tight as she focused her magic onto that one small cut. The glow from her fingers grew brighter, like gold flames licking Silver's wrist.

She pushed harder. Harder yet.

A sense of elation filled Copper as the wound began to cauterize. The stream of blood from Silver's wrist stopped flowing. A scab formed where the cut had been, and then vanished.

The little bit of hand magic she'd performed had worked!

Copper gave a sigh of relief that at least Silver was no longer bleeding. But knew she had to free her sister fast—

Something slammed Copper upside her face.

Stars exploded in her head.

She cried out as the force of the impact caused her to topple and land on one cheek. More flashes of light burst through her mind as her head struck stone. The wand dug into the side of her butt cheek and she heard another snap of crystal.

Before she could react, a large boot pressed against her cheek, pinning her head to the stone. Copper froze, looked up with one eye, and saw Darkwolf standing over her. It was his boot on her face. The eye on the chain around his neck swung away from his chest and was glowing a brilliant red. A red as bright as the light seeping from the door.

"Let me go, asshole." Her words came out awkward with her face mashed.

"I was beginning to think you'd never show up." He gave her a grin that was nothing short of evil. His gaze turned to Silver and surprisingly his features softened. "We can't have your sister bleeding to death." His eyes met Copper's again. "You're the one I've been waiting for. Balor promised to deliver you."

Riona had been right. Balor had interfered with the veils and with their divination, sending Copper here alone . . . for this. Like in her dreams, she was to be a sacrifice to Balor. Right now that wasn't important. *What's important is that Silver lives.*

Copper noticed Darkwolf glancing to her right, and with her side vision she saw the demon in human form, Junga. Of all things, the demon-woman wore a 49ers jersey, and Copper had the strange desire to giggle. But then the emotion caught in her throat. Was that Sara beside Junga? Sara formerly of the D'Anu? By the amused look on Sara's features and the evil glint in her eyes, Copper had no doubt Sara was in the clutches of the blackest, blackest magic.

"Cut Silver's bonds," Darkwolf commanded with a nod toward Junga.

The demon-woman scowled. "We should bleed them both. Together their blood will make the ritual more powerful."

"As I have told you—" Darkwolf's voice cut the air like a blade—"Silver is *mine*."

Sara cast a disgusted look in Silver's direction.

Junga gave a low growl. "This obsession you have for the witch will be your ruin."

Darkwolf raised his hands and purple sparks dripped from his fingertips as his gaze fixed on Junga. She gave him a haughty expression, but at the same time her fingers extended into claws, just like they had when Copper and Tiernan had appeared in Darkwolf's library. Junga knelt and with a swipe of one clawed finger she sliced the bindings at one of Silver's wrists.

Pain from the boot on Copper's face matched the pain in her head from the stone floor. The agony in her ankle was enough to make her sweat double—from the heat emanating from the door and the intensity of her injury. She thanked the goddess that Silver was going to live. Copper would gladly take her sister's place, if it meant Silver wouldn't die.

Yet Copper wasn't about to give up. Somehow she'd get them both out of this mess. She'd get Silver away from Darkwolf, keep herself from being sacrificed, and make sure the door stayed closed.

Yeah. No problem.

Darkwolf took his boot from her face, giving her head some relief. He bent and grabbed one of her hands and jerked her to her feet.

Copper screamed and her legs buckled as the momentum twisted her broken ankle. Tears of pain and fury coursed down her cheeks.

The warlock brought her to her feet again, held her beneath her armpits, and she was able to keep pressure off her ankle. His dark eyes had an unnatural red glow about them.

"Soon you will not feel any pain, Copper." Darkwolf adjusted her so that she had her weight on her good foot and so that he could hold her with one hand. With his other he pushed from her face her sweaty hair that had escaped her braid. He looked human—not like the evil warlock he was. His eyes no longer gleamed that awful red, and instead were dark, almost black. He pressed his lips to her forehead and drew back. "Know that your sister will be safe with me, and your blood will allow us to release the door to Underworld—already Silver's blood has opened it a fraction."

Darkwolf smiled, his eyes glowing red again, and he no longer looked human. It chilled her to her gut as he brought his hand to the eye lying against his chest. Red light bled from between his fingers as he continued. "Balor's body will be freed to join his essence bound in this eye. His wife, Ceithlenn, will be able to walk the shores of our world as she once did, and Balor will rule again."

Copper swallowed. Even that slight movement hurt her aching body. She glanced down at the double circles and saw Silver had been freed and her body was being tossed none too gently to the side by Junga. Silver's head lolled so that one cheek was on the smooth stone of the cavern floor, her body lifeless.

"Be careful with the witch!" Darkwolf's eyes glowed redder yet. "If you injure Silver, there will be great consequences."

Copper's heart beat faster and fear rode her in waves as she looked back to the warlock. "What's wrong with her? Why is she so still?"

He gave a slight shrug of one shoulder and the red in his eyes dulled a bit. "She's drugged. Long enough to bleed you and open that door."

Copper's mind raced. With her wand she could throw up a shield around herself, but without it . . .

She focused on her hands, felt some warmth at her fingertips and imagined shielding herself with her magic.

Darkwolf laughed and her eyes locked with his. The pressure of his grip on her increased. "You have no power without your wand, Copper Ashcroft. I can read it in your mind, feel it in your thoughts."

Copper reacted, too fast for thought.

With all her might she slammed her fist into his nose. She heard the crack of bone followed by a gush of blood.

Darkwolf gave a cry of rage and pain. Blood flowed over his mouth, down his chin, to his black shirt. He slapped her so hard he flung her body from his and she landed hard in the center of the circle.

Copper cried out as her body struck stone and her ankle wrenched yet again. Despite every bit of pain, she willed herself to sit up, willed her hand magic to work, but only the faintest golden glow came from her fingers and her body wouldn't move.

Sara stood at Copper's feet. The pretty witch looked normal for a moment, like the friend she had once been to Copper. But then her lips twisted into an evil smirk.

Copper's eyes widened as the former witch raised her foot. With a satisfied smile, Sara slammed her shoe onto Copper's broken ankle.

Copper shrieked.

She'd never felt such excruciating pain. It flooded every nerve ending in her body. It forced a flood of tears from her eyes and cries for mercy from her lips. "Stop, Sara!" she begged. "Please stop. Please."

Sara responded by grinding her foot onto Copper's ankle.

The agony was so great she saw spots before her eyes. Black spots. Red spots. Black spots.

Then blessed nothingness as Copper slipped into the depths of darkness and she felt no more.

Twenty-five

Tiernan didn't wait for the rest of the D'Danann to cross from the transference point. Once he and Hawk were in the meadow, he immediately strode around the rock outcropping to the Drow door. With Riona still on his shoulder he stomped on the damned door five times.

"I will guide the others," Riona said before she fluttered off Tiernan's shoulder and back to where the other D'Danann warriors would be appearing.

Tiernan and Hawk remained silent. The chirp of birds and hum of insects were drowned out as the Drow door opened with an annoying grating sound.

As Tiernan stepped down the Drow stairs, his eyes easily adjusted to the darkness, which was one of the abilities of the Tuatha D'Danann. He did not expect the torches to flicker to life, and in that he was not disappointed. He headed down the stairs silently. Behind him he sensed Hawk and the other D'Danann, but they made not a sound.

When he reached the enormous round chamber, he expected to see guards, but found no one awaiting them. He strode across the great room to Garran's chamber, and again found nothing but darkness.

"Shit. Where is Copper?" Tiernan's gut tightened as he rested his hand on his sword and stepped back into the huge hall.

Hawk made a low growling noise. His features were constantly twisted in an expression of fury and of fear for his mate. "By the gods, we must find her and Silver."

By then all the D'Danann warriors had gathered around them. Thirteen had made the trip to this part of Otherworld, counting Tiernan, Hawk, Keir, and Urien.

Remember the battle with the giant, floated through Tiernan's mind in the Great Guardian's voice.

"This way," Tiernan commanded as he drew his sword and headed toward the passageway that led to the mine where he and the Drow had battled the giant. In the short tunnel, with his night vision, he examined the dirt floor for signs of Copper. He easily spotted a pair of prints made from shoes such as Copper wore, on top of boot prints made by the Dark Elves.

Satisfied he was headed in the right direction, Tiernan continued until he made his way out of the tunnel and onto the pathway that led deep into the pit mine of the Drow. With his keen scouting abilities, he noticed where Copper had skidded and then continued on down the path.

"As I suspected, she has gone after the Drow, fool witch." Tiernan moved away from Hawk and the other D'Danann and began to shift. His great wings unfurled from his body and he flapped them once before leaping from the ledge and soaring down into the pit. The mine's cool air swept his hair from his shoulders and slid over his wings. He easily reached the center of the pit and the enormous hole that was obviously the location where the giant had torn through the ground to reach the Dark Elves. Next to a rock were Copper's backpack and her jacket.

After sheathing his sword, Tiernan looked into the hole. It was deep. So deep he could barely make out the bottom. He raised his head, and with his gaze he quickly scanned the dirt and rock surrounding the hole. His heart began to pound as he saw Copper's shoe prints where her feet had met dirt, and handprints where she had clung to handholds in yet more dirt. He furrowed his brow as his gaze swept the area that she had worked her way around.

"What was she doing?" he said aloud. And then he saw something that made his blood chill. Beside a boulder her shoe prints slid off the ledge. She had fallen.

"Shit!" Tiernan threw himself into the hole, feathers sleeked back, and arrowed into the darkness. "Wait for my instructions," he called back over his shoulder.

With his night vision, he saw the bottom and that Copper was nowhere in sight. Before he hit, he unfurled his wings, and brought himself to a soft landing.

Tiernan crouched and examined the dirt around him. Copper had landed on her backside, and the deep indentation indicated she had also landed on her wand. And was that the tip imprinted in an awkward position? Had it broken? At the thought of her losing one of her defenses, Tiernan's blood chilled.

He could make out where she had fallen back and where her head had struck dirt, and even the imprint of her braid. There was a little scuffling, as if she had crossed her legs at the ankles and had sat before getting up and starting down the tunnel.

"Clear," Tiernan shouted, and moved out of the way so that his brethren could follow. While the other D'Danann silently flew down the enormous tunnel, Tiernan walked along the passageway, following Copper's prints for a few feet. The tunnel was large enough to fly in. He spread his wings and flew as fast as he could through the darkness.

When they reached a massive chamber he came to a light landing at its opening and heard his brethren touch down behind him. By the markings on the walls, the enormous prints on the dirt floor, and the huge shield and club, this place belonged to the giants.

"How did such creatures make it into Otherworld?" Hawk asked, obviously noting what Tiernan had.

"I have no doubt the Dark Elves have been delving too far below the surface," Tiernan said.

Congealed and drying blood lay thick and heavy on the floor of the chamber, and arrows littered the dirt. He saw Copper's shoe prints cross the great room, and then they appeared smudged, as if she were running—and a pair of giant footprints were following hers

Tiernan flapped his wings and darted across the chamber, following Copper's shoe prints to another large tunnel, and then he resumed flying. Often the giant's prints obliterated Copper's, but at times he saw hers.

Long before he reached it, he caught the smell of rotting garbage. He hurried even faster until he reached the giant that lay sprawled on the dirt floor of the passageway— motionless, stiff, obviously dead.

Tiernan landed, folded back his wings, and held his hand up to indicate to his comrades that they should halt. "Wait here."

The tunnel was still large enough for him to fly, and his wings carried him from the feet to the head of the giant where he touched down just inches from its matted, mosslike hair. Its eyes were open, its expression one of excruciating pain. Its face had swollen so that its head looked three times larger than that of the giant he and the Drow had slain.

That was when he noticed the red marks all over the giant's face. "Bee stings," he said aloud. "It had to have been Zephyr." The giant had obviously been allergic to bee stings, and had died from them.

"Clear." Tiernan motioned for the other warriors to follow, then continued down the passageway.

He hadn't gone far when he heard a distressed buzzing noise. Puzzled, he halted and listened. He followed the sound until he came to a large spiderweb. The buzzing was louder now, and as his gaze raked the web, he saw a honeybee caught in its strands. There was no reason for a honeybee to be down below the surface. It had to be Zephyr.

"Halt." Tiernan held up his hand again to indicate the others were to wait for his orders.

"Hello, old man," Tiernan murmured, turning his attention to the bee. "How did you get yourself into this mess?"

Zephyr gave an angry yet urgent buzz. A movement just to the side caught Tiernan's attention and he saw a very large, very wicked-looking spider headed toward the bee.

It was one of the most poisonous spiders known to Otherworld, a spider that even wasps and bees feared.

With a quick movement of his hand and a flick of his wrist, Tiernan had the spider pinned to the wall with his dagger. The creature waggled its legs against its own web as poisonous green fluid drained from its body. After a few moments the creature went still.

Not one to take a chance that the fluid might burn through his scabbard, Tiernan plucked the blade free of the spider, knelt, and wiped each side of the metal on the dirt floor, making sure the poison had been cleared from the blade. When he finished, he rose, wiped the blade on his leather breeches, and sheathed it again.

Zephyr gave a buzzing sound like a sigh and Tiernan almost smiled before he realized that Copper was without her familiar and he was certain her wand had broken. Trusting that the bee wouldn't sting him, he lifted his fingers to the web and worked to free Zephyr. The sticky web stuck to his hands, and even as his urgency increased to help the familiar, that urgency also rose at the thought that this was holding him back from reaching Copper.

Finally the bee was separated from the web. Bits still

clung to his tiny body, but he was able to climb onto Tiernan's hand and then fly to his shoulder. He moved slowly, as if exhausted, then gave a tired buzz when he landed.

"You will be all right once you catch your breath." Tiernan turned back toward the direction that Copper had gone and motioned for the other warriors to follow. "Now we have to find that fool witch."

In the darkness he could see that Copper had still been running, probably to put as much distance as possible between her and the giant. He followed at a jog and saw by the look of her footprints that she had come to a stop, and then begun a slow walk.

His gut lurched when he saw something that Copper obviously hadn't—a hole in the middle of the tunnel's floor. "Damnation!" With the warriors behind him, he hurried to the hole. Her footprints disappeared, only the heel of one shoe catching the edge.

Tiernan knelt beside the hole, judging its width and its depth. He could see the bottom—a far drop—but no sign of Copper. He had to thank the gods for at least that. It meant she was still alive and moving.

"Too narrow to fly." Hawk knelt beside Tiernan.

He nodded and looked at his comrade. "We can jump."

D'Danann had the ability to jump great distances without injury. Tiernan boosted himself into the hole and dropped. When he reached the floor of the small tunnel he landed in a crouch, bracing himself with one hand in the dirt.

In just that moment, as he quickly scanned the ground, he saw that Copper had been injured. By the way she moved along through the tunnel, he could see that she was limping and favoring one leg.

"Damnation." It was bad enough that she was down here alone, that she was without her familiar, and her wand was probably damaged. But now she was injured, as well.

Zephyr gave an angry buzz and shot down the passageway ahead of Tiernan.

◆ ◆ ◆

Copper blinked, unable to focus her eyes for a few long seconds. Stalactites glowing like red rubies came into view. Confusion slipped through her mind for only a fraction of a moment before she remembered all that had happened. How long had she been unconscious?

Her ankle screamed with pain, making the aches in her body feel like nothing in comparison. To no surprise she was spread-eagle on the stone floor as her sister had been. She tugged her arms even though she knew she'd be bound. She tried her good leg and it had been secured, as well. She didn't dare test her bad ankle.

She felt weak beyond the pain. Light-headed. As if her life force were being drained from her.

She glanced at first one wrist, then the other. Both had small slits in them, and her blood dribbled into the runes as Silver's had. And from what she could see by slightly raising her head the blood was moving along more freely now, filling the interlocked runes.

Her vision was hazy again. She blinked. Then blinked once more. Her face was turned so that she saw her sister sprawled where she'd been left before Copper had passed out. But hadn't she been lying in a different position? Could she have moved on her own?

Grimacing from the pain, Copper turned her head to the other side, looked toward the door, and squinted. The red light was becoming brighter now. The door was open a fraction more. She couldn't have been unconscious for long.

To the side of the door stood Darkwolf with the glowing eye of Balor around his neck.

On one side of him was Sara, who had her hands on her hips and her back to Copper as she stared at the door. On his other side squatted the large blue beast that Copper knew to be Junga in her demon form. Apparently she had shifted while Copper was out of it. Junga had her back to Copper, too.

Copper kept her eyes shuttered, not wanting them to know she was awake if they looked at her. Not that it mattered. How was she going to get out of this mess?

"Slice her wrists so that blood spills from her body faster," came Junga's rough demon voice. She cut her gaze to Copper who went completely still. "We need the Balor-damned door open, now."

"I don't like repeating myself." Darkwolf scowled at her and they both turned their attention back to the door. "Balor insists this must be done slowly, or we will fail."

Hopelessness flooded Copper, a feeling she didn't like at all. She turned her head in the other direction and saw Silver still lying on her side—only her position had changed again. A low moan came from her sister. Copper's heart rate picked up. Silver was waking!

A scraping sound brought Copper's attention back to the door. *Shit.* It was opening wider! Not wide enough to let anything through, but now she could hear growls and snorts coming through the crack and a rank stench like rotting meat. And barking—like the hounds of Underworld.

As blood continued to trickle from the cuts at her wrists, Copper fought to keep tension from her body. Tensing up would only cause the blood to flow faster. She took a deep breath, tried to focus, tried to come up with a plan.

She almost laughed. Sure, a plan. Spread-eagle in the middle of a sacrificial circle, bound, blood being squeezed from her body. Where was the cavalry when you needed it? Goddess. If only her Coven had been able to join her. If only the D'Danann hadn't been blocked from traveling to Otherworld, as well. If only the Paranormal Special Forces could travel worlds.

The scrape of stone was harsh to her ears as the door opened another fraction. The pounding of her heart doubled. She looked to her wrist and raised her head as best she could to see that the flow of blood was steady and the runes were filling, blood snaking from one rune line to the next.

"Soon," Darkwolf said in a voice unlike his own, a voice so deep and evil that it resonated through the room. It was as if the voice were being channeled through him, as if Balor himself spoke through the warlock. "Soon I will bring together all my children and rule them once more."

Copper rested her head back against the stone and willed her heart to slow its beating. She had never been allowed by the D'Anu to donate blood to the Red Cross because of her witch heritage, so she didn't have that experience. But she couldn't imagine that more than a pint had been drained from her so far in this circle. No doubt it wouldn't be long until she'd be too weak to do anything. Already she felt as if she'd had the crap beaten out of her—which she more or less had.

Another scrunch of stone against stone had Copper's teeth grinding and her focus moving toward the door. The red glow was brighter. This time claws crept around the stone, and snouts of what were sure to be hideous beasts were visible—Fomorii. More growls, snorts, and roars met her ears. The stench coming from the door mingled with the smell of blood, dirt, and stone from the cavern.

Copper felt sudden warmth at her right arm and she cut her gaze to it.

Silver was on her knees, her hands held over Copper's wrist.

Copper's heart leaped to see her sister awake. Dark circles were apparent under Silver's eyes and she looked beyond exhausted, but she was alive.

Silver's blue magic poured from her fingertips, healing the cut in Copper's wrist almost instantly. Copper started to open her mouth, but she snapped it shut when her sister held one finger to her lips.

Silver looked even more bleary eyed and as if she might faint again, but she crawled over to Copper's other wrist.

Before she could do anything, the door scraped a fraction more and this time bodies squirmed in the opening. More Fomorii! They were trying to get out but the opening just wasn't big enough for them.

"We'll get out of this," Silver whispered. Again her blue glow eased from her fingertips and the slice in Copper's wrist closed and healed.

Silver's strength gave out and she crumpled to the stone floor, her eyes closed.

Wounds healed, Copper found the strength to struggle against her bonds. Even though no more blood dripped from her veins, what had already left her body was still moving slowly through the etchings.

The door scraped open a tad more. The stench of rotten fish mingled with the burnt-sugar smell.

A shadow fell across Copper's face. Her heart leaped in terror as she saw someone dark and foreboding above her, wielding a long, thick blade.

It was Garran, King of the Drow.

"No. Garran, please," Copper whispered. Disbelief coursed through her veins like ice water. It wasn't possible. He wouldn't kill her.

He clenched his jaw, swung the blade down, and Copper closed her eyes, prepared for the death blow.

She heard a scrape against the rope, a sharp tug at her wrist, and the binding was suddenly free. Her eyelids sprang open. He had sliced the tie from one of her wrists. Shocked, she watched him free her broken ankle and she bit her bottom lip until she tasted blood as she tried not to scream from the pain. In quick movements and even quicker strokes, Garran cut the bonds from her other ankle and wrist.

When he finished, he carefully brought her to her feet. She couldn't help but want to cry out before she had a chance to put all her weight on her left ankle. For a moment she sagged against Garran, unable to stand on her own, and he gently held her. His earthy scent was almost comforting—if it wasn't for the fact that he was a traitor.

She separated herself from Garran's arms and glanced at where Darkwolf, Junga, and Sara stood, and was relieved that they were solely focused on the door.

"The blood." Copper kept her voice low as she looked down at the fluid still moving through the etchings. "We have to stop it."

"I am not here to hinder the opening of the chamber." Garran sheathed his dagger, his silvery eyes reflecting the red light seeping from the door. "Balor has promised that all the Dark Elves may again tolerate light and live aboveground in your world when his body is freed. Once the door is open that promise will be fulfilled." He gripped her arm tighter, his eyes meeting hers. "I wish only for you to live." He glanced at the floor. "You have bled enough."

Open-mouthed, Copper balanced on one foot in the center of the circle. "You don't understand. To allow these creatures out would devastate my world."

He placed his callused palm against her cheek and his earth-and-moss scent flowed over her again. "Come with me, Copper. I have wanted you since you came to Otherworld. I have waited only for you to come to me willingly."

She would have backed up if she could have. "You're a traitor, Garran. You could have let us all out of the bubble prison long ago, but you didn't."

"In order to free my people from darkness, I could not." He glanced up at the door that was a fraction wider. When he looked back at her she saw regret, yet caring for his people in his eyes. "Come with me now. I will protect you."

She shook her head. "No."

For a moment he looked like he was going to take her against her will. His muscles flexed and his jaw tensed. He glanced at the doorway and back to Copper. "Come!" he commanded in a low voice filled with urgency and passion.

"I can't." Copper looked to her sister who was still on the cavern floor, but stirring again. "I have to help my sister and I have to stop that door from opening."

Garran brushed his knuckles across her cheek and pressed his lips to her forehead. "May the gods and goddesses be with you, Copper." He gave one last look at her, released her arm, and slipped away into the darkness.

Shock filled Copper over her exchange with the Drow king, but she couldn't think about Garran.

Her heart pounded as she glanced down at her sister, and Copper thanked the goddess Silver was moving, pushing herself up from the floor. The red glow from the opening door cast a crimson sheen across her sister's silvery-blond hair. Silver shoved her hair out of her face and over her shoulder, then braced both hands on the floor and took a deep breath. She didn't seem to have the strength to get to her feet.

Copper's gaze shot back to the door. Now it was open just enough that bodies were closer to squeezing through. Growls, snorts, and cries were so loud Copper wanted to clap her hands over her ears. Now she could smell something like really bad dog breath mixed with rotten fish and burnt sugar.

Junga's, Sara's, and Darkwolf's attentions were focused solely on that door. The way Copper was standing now, she could better make out the side of the warlock's face. A triumphant smile curved the corner of his mouth. The demon Junga gave a growl of approval, and Sara made a sound of delight.

Copper felt her useless wand in her back pocket and ground her teeth. She would do this using hand magic. She *had* to do it.

Keeping her weight off her right leg, while trying to ignore the screaming pain, she mentally prepared herself for

the spell. She raised her hands, palms facing the door, and
began to chant the spell she'd practiced all day when she'd
jogged the length of the three-mile-long park and back.

> *Goddess, hear our words, our plea*
> *In this time out of time,*
> *In this place out of place.*
> *Goddess, we raise our hands to thee*
> *In this dark beyond darkness,*
> *In this world beyond worlds.*
> *We await your grace.*
> *We await your power.*
> *We stand at the threshold.*
> *Goddess, please protect your children*
> *And banish evil to the Underworld realm.*

A faint golden glow emanated from her palms, but that
was it.

Copper's whole body tensed. She focused. Repeated the
spell louder this time, certain she wouldn't be heard above
the sounds the beasts were making.

Only a brighter glow came from her fingertips and no
more.

Crap. She ground her teeth harder.

This time she took all the pain in her body, all the rage,
all the frustration, and poured it into her gray witchcraft.
Dark gray magic filled her so powerfully that her vision
turned almost black. She could feel the darkness calling to
her, calling to her. Her body started to shake and her mind
began to fill with black thoughts.

She could control all the beings that would escape
through the door. She could rule. She could make everyone
who had hurt her family, killed her mother, pay. She would
use black magic for good, and all that was evil would answer to *her*.

Intense pain filled Copper as shock slammed into her like ice water.

No. No. No! How could she even be thinking this way?

With everything she had, she jerked herself away from the dark.

Ohmigoddess, how could I have taken gray magic so lightly? I risked my soul, my life—risked everyone's life so arrogantly, like it would never cost me and those I love.

It came to her, in that flash of time, that no matter what, she wouldn't have been able to save her childhood friend, Trista. And at such a young age she might have lost herself to the dark.

Copper shoved away the gray and chanted the spell louder yet, using only white magic. Safe, pure white magic was all she needed to close that door.

Just a second before she finished the chant, the door opened another crack and beasts began to pour through the opening.

Copper could hardly breathe and could barely continue the chant.

Sara broke away from Junga and Darkwolf to stand in front of them, just a few feet from the doorway.

She spread her arms wide.

A brilliant red glow suffused her body, followed by what looked like black fog.

Shock registered on Darkwolf's face as his gaze swung to Junga, and Junga roared.

Copper's terror magnified the spell as she yelled the last lines of the chant.

Brilliant golden light poured from her body.

Shot across the room.

Rammed into the door.

Slammed it shut.

The crunch of stone crashing against stone rose above the snarls and shrieks of the Fomorii, Basilisks, and

Hounds of Underworld that had escaped. Screams cut the air from two Fomorii smashed between the great stone door and doorway as they tried to squirm free.

"No!" Darkwolf shouted and whirled to face Copper. The red light in the cavern had dimmed, but she could see rage twisting the warlock's features. The red of his gaze matched the unholy red of the eye at his chest.

But Copper's gaze was torn from him to Sara.

Oh, my goddess. When Sara turned, her eyes blazed even redder than Darkwolf's. Her hair looked like it was living fire, flickering red, orange, yellow. She was the fire-haired being from Copper's dream!

And Sara's clothing—it was as if the being that possessed her changed everything about her, down to the black leather she now wore.

Sara spread her arms and bent her back. Great wings sprang from her arms, anchored at the middle of her back—like bat wings. She gave a hiss and a cry that was louder than the roars and snarls in the cavern.

Copper's attention whipped back to Darkwolf. The warlock raised his hands as Fomorii charged Copper.

Purple light shot across the room from Darkwolf toward Copper as Junga charged. At the same time the Sara creature took to the air. Terror rode Copper and she tried to throw up a shield.

Her hand-magic didn't work.

Just before Darkwolf's spell slammed into her, a blue bubble of protection surrounded Copper. Her gaze cut to her sister who was on her knees, blue light flowing from her hands and forming the shield around them both.

Instead of rebounding Darkwolf's magic, Silver's shield absorbed his power, strengthening the protection around them. The bubble shimmered bluish-purple, and Copper knew Silver was using her gray magic to protect them.

In that instant she saw the struggle on her sister's face, saw the connection between her and Darkwolf.

"No, Silver," Copper shouted. "Use white magic to battle him or he'll pull you over the edge!"

Copper's heart beat frantically as she channeled her energy through her hands. To her shock gold magic poured from her palms. Her magic joined with Silver's blue and the purple, causing it to have an iridescent sparkle. Copper still felt shakiness in the bubble of protection as the Fomorii crashed against it.

With all her might, with all her focus, and with all the love she had for her sister, Copper thrust more energy from her body into the shield.

Golden bubbles began pouring from her body to join with the other magic. Gold bubbles that had appeared the times she and Tiernan had made love.

Love.

That soul-deep connection that she had with her sister, on another level she had with Tiernan.

She shoved the thought from her mind and focused on the warlock and Sara, who flew around the cavern like some great flame-haired bat, assessing the situation. Copper didn't know who was more dangerous at that moment.

What had Sara become? What was she capable of?

Darkwolf's nose was slightly crooked now from the punch Copper had dealt him earlier. Although it no longer bled, she couldn't help a bit of satisfaction at the bloodstains left behind on his shirt. It was the perfect reminder . . . he *wasn't* invincible.

Shock registered once again on his face when he glanced to where Sara now perched on a huge stone, her red eyes and hair blazing. She crouched, her feet on the rock, her hands between her knees as she gripped the edge of the boulder. It was surreal—like looking at a kind of comic-book gargoyle.

Even as she took everything in, Copper didn't let up on her magic. To her surprise it didn't drain her. If anything it made her feel almost omnipotent. She no longer felt pain, no longer felt anything but the power of her witchcraft. She no longer had to hold up her hands; her strength radiated from her in waves and in the golden bubbles.

Silver rose to stand beside Copper. A healthy glow had risen in her cheeks, and her eyes weren't marred with dark circles beneath them.

Copper glanced around them at the countless Fomorii, the snarling red-eyed hounds, and the Basilisks that had slipped out of the door. Some were vanishing into the darkness, and others were attempting to attack the shield surrounding Copper and Silver. So many beings had escaped!

Copper felt vibrations every time a demon slammed its body into the shield. Thank the goddess it held.

Junga slowly paced back and forth before the bubble, her eyes focused on Copper. Spittle dripped from the corner of the demon's mouth, and Copper knew that the queen Fomorii was just waiting for the opportunity to strike. If the shield fell, the demon was going for the kill.

"Now what?" Copper said, her voice trembling. Her eyes darted to where the Sara being crouched. "Goddess, what has Sara become?"

Silver's eyes were focused on Darkwolf's as if she couldn't break the connection. "I don't know what to do next," she said. "There are too many of them for us to fight alone. And our magic—how long can we hold out?"

A tiny dot of anger buzzed past Silver and Copper.

Zephyr!

Battle cries rent the air.

Forms shot past the sisters. Copper caught the flap of wings, the glint of metal.

The D'Danann!

Twenty-six

Rage filled Tiernan as he darted through the air. He tasted battle-lust and blood on his tongue. The stench of filth, of rotting things, and a sickly-sweet odor filled the air.

He charged the blue demon that he knew to be Junga. He reached her and hovered over her within fighting range. With an angry slice of his blade, his sword connected with her shoulder. Blood spurted and the queen Fomorii shrieked. She swung her long arms up and swiped her claws at him, attempting to rip him from the air.

Blood poured from the wound in her shoulder, but it was already healing. There were only two ways to kill a Fomorii: rip their hearts out or behead them. Otherwise their bodies healed almost immediately.

Tiernan flapped his great wings and dodged the demon's deadly iron-tipped claws. He prayed to the gods that none of the other Fomorii released from Underworld had coated their claws in iron like Junga and the Fomorii already in Copper's world.

He dodged and feinted as he attempted to gain position in order to behead the demon. She was too strong, too fast, and her apelike arms were too long. She was one of the most powerful and formidable Fomorii he had ever battled.

Tiernan darted up and out of Junga's reach to give himself a chance to assess the situation. His gaze swept the cavern. With his heightened senses and keen vision, he quickly took in what was going on around him.

D'Danann battle cries filled the air along with the shrieks, roars, and snarls of the beasts they fought. The air was thick with the rank Fomorii odor of rotten fish, the Basilisks' odor of feces, the filthy stench of the hounds of Underworld, and the smell of bloodlust.

The thirteen Tuatha D'Danann warriors were outnumbered by the creatures that had been released from Underworld, but they were better trained at the art of battle. Thus far not one of the D'Danann had succumbed to any of the beasts they were fighting. Already a couple of the Fomorii had been beheaded, their bodies turning into silt the moment their heads were sheared off. A Basilisk and one of the red-eyed Hounds of Underworld had been destroyed, as well.

Although the D'Danann remained relatively unscathed, Tiernan saw one of the hounds rip open Urien's leg with its tremendous jaws. Urien seemed oblivious to any pain, flapped his wings, rose up, then dived into the fray once again.

Darkwolf barely had time to throw a shield up around himself before Hawk touched down and arced his sword through the air straight at the warlock's neck. Instead of connecting with flesh his blade rebounded off the protective shield, just as it had happened during the battle of Samhain. Hawk stumbled back.

"That is getting old," Hawk grumbled and barely regained his footing before he was forced to face one of the Fomorii, a red beast with at least six arms.

Keir tore into the fray with the roar of a madman. His dark eyes were like a falcon's as he ripped through one Fomorii after another.

That fiery-headed woman-creature watching the scene from the rock—it was as if the being were waiting for something. Waiting to attack?

Tiernan darted back to Junga, his sword high. As he prepared to swing, a one-eyed purple demon joined the queen, and Tiernan was now fighting two beasts. Sweat poured down his face and his veins roared with the lust for battle.

As he took the two demons on, he was thankful Copper and Silver were behind a protective shield.

He glanced their way. His heart nearly stopped and he almost faltered when he saw their shield vanish.

The two witches began to fight the demons with their magic.

From behind the shield, Copper and Silver looked at one another as the battle raged. As one they nodded, raised their hands, and faced the demons.

They dropped the shield.

Immediately, blue ropes of power whipped from Silver's fingers to wrap around a red demon charging Hawk. She jerked the demon off its hind feet. Hawk took the opportunity to slice the beast's head from its shoulders. The demon's head and body turned to silt. Silver wasted no time in snaking her witchcraft around another demon.

Copper had a hard time keeping her balance on one foot, but she was intensely focused on her witchcraft. Her confidence had risen and she knew she could perform hand magic with the strength of her belief and the power that had grown within her.

Between her palms she instinctively gathered some of the golden bubbles that floated from her body and formed them into a large ball. Winding her arm, she prepared to use her best softball pitch. She released the spellfire ball. It bulleted toward one of the two demons attacking Tiernan and struck one of them. The purple demon's head burst into fire. With the skill of the finest swordsman, Tiernan beheaded it.

The stench of burning flesh joined the malodor of rotten fish. Copper tasted blood in her mouth and realized she was biting the inside of her cheek.

No sooner had she released the first pitch than she flung another one, this time straight at the demon queen.

Junga saw it coming. She leaped through the air, the spellfire barely grazing her back.

Flapping his wings, Tiernan started to go after her, but was waylaid by a great Basilisk that rose up between them.

The Basilisk looked like a giant snake, but the thing had a fan of bone and skin that was like a crown at the back of its head. It was so damned tall—at least two times the height of one of the D'Danann, and as thick around as the circle of runes that Copper still stood in the middle of.

Tiernan's sword bounced off the Basilisk's armorlike scales. Copper's heart pounded when she saw the green poison dripping from the beast's fangs as it gnashed them at Tiernan. Copper didn't know if the poison was deadly to the Fae, but she wasn't taking any chances.

Nearly without thought, she had another ball of spellfire in her hands. Gray magic threatened to consume her. She couldn't let the beast hurt Tiernan!

At the same time she couldn't let the gray magic turn her to the dark. How could she have so carelessly used gray in the past? How could she have been so cocky? She needed to be more careful. To not use it so blindly.

With all the white magic she could muster, and keeping a tight rein on her gray witchcraft, she pitched the spellfire straight at the Basilisk's mouth.

A tremendous flash blinded the beast, giving Tiernan the opportunity to lop off the Basilisk's head.

That was the second time she'd saved Tiernan's ass. But who was counting?

A green demon roared and leaped at her, diverting her

attention. The Fomorii's several eyes flashed with the red glow in the cavern. *Shit*. She pitched a spellfire ball at it, but this one bounced off.

The demon was close now. Too close. Still she drew back to pitch—

A blade sliced the demon's head from its body. As the Fomorii fell to the cavern floor in a pile of silt, she saw Tiernan standing on the other side of it, his blade covered in blood. Their eyes met for just a fraction of time before they turned back to the battle.

Copper pitched again and again. Her magic slammed into two hounds of the Underworld, and she saw Zephyr attacking the hounds, as well. They howled at her magic and his powerful stings. The beasts snapped their jaws at him, but he easily dodged their mouths and stung them again on their faces, their eyelids, their snouts. He traveled from one to the other like a tiny whirlwind. The hounds howled continuously and rubbed at their heads with their paws. They were distracted just enough that two of the D'Danann were able to kill them with ease.

With two more pitches, Copper brought down another Fomorii that was immediately beheaded by a D'Danann warrior.

She whirled to fight another demon and came nearly face to snout with Junga. The demon lunged at Copper. She dropped, rolled, and screamed as she wrenched her ankle again and the pain caused stars to burst behind her eyes.

Copper didn't let the agony slow her down. She continued to roll away from Junga at the same time she gathered a spellfire ball in her hands. Her heart slammed against her breastbone as the demon leaped into the air.

She wasn't going to have enough space to throw the spellfire ball. Her magic would consume them both. She'd be damned if she'd die without taking the demon out. Resolution filled her and she held the ball in front of her . . . prepared to die.

Just as the queen demon made her descent over Copper, an arrow caught Junga in the shoulder. The impact and resulting explosion was so powerful it flung the demon away in mid-leap. She slammed into a stalagmite.

Instantly Copper recognized the shaft. A Drow arrow!

In the next moment she was yanked to her feet by a strong hand. Again she almost passed out from the pain of the pressure on her ankle. Before she had time to process the pain or the hand on her arm, she was flung over a great naked shoulder. Whoever had her had the bluish-gray skin of the Dark Elves.

In no time the Drow warrior deposited Copper on her backside off to the side of the battle. Her gaze shot to her protector. Garran!

She tried to push herself to her feet, but he put his hand on her shoulder and forced her back down. He gave her an intense look. "I never meant to jeopardize your life, Copper." His features were grim. "This evil—we thought only to release Balor to allow the Drow to walk in daylight once again. Not this. We never wanted to free such creatures."

His long silvery-blue hair was wild about his shoulders and his gem-studded metal and leather straps that crisscrossed his broad bare chest glinted in what red light was now in the cavern. He turned away from her and faced Junga.

She saw that the other Drow had joined in the melee against the beasts. Drow arrows were piercing demon flesh, the diamond heads exploding. Where the arrows ripped the flesh apart, the wound immediately healed in the Fomorii—unless it reached the demon's heart, and the arrowhead exploded within that pulsating organ, killing the demon.

The Sara-creature scowled and began pacing back and forth, glancing at the closed door with fury on her features. Drow arrows exploded in the air around her, not a single one reaching her flesh. The D'Danann who tried to attack her simply rebounded backward as if the being were shielded.

Copper took this all in within a moment. Much of what she realized came from her witch's intuition.

When her attention snapped back to Garran, his jaw was clenched as he turned, nocked another arrow in his bow, and aimed it at Junga.

The demon leaped into the air again, this time directly for Garran. Standing firm, no emotion on his face, he shot his arrow straight toward her chest. Junga twisted her body while in flight. The arrow entered the flesh beneath her forearm and blood splattered as the tip exploded in her flesh.

But it had missed her heart.

Junga pounced on Garran.

Slammed him to the floor.

His head struck with such power that Copper heard a crack. His head fell to the side.

Junga raised her claws to dig into his flesh.

A Drow arrow exploded in her hip.

Naal! Garran's brother was behind Junga.

Junga screamed and toppled off Garran. She was to her feet in a fraction of a moment.

She whirled on Naal and flung him to the cavern floor, his head hitting a huge cone of stalagmite. Before Naal could react, Junga raised her powerful arm.

Dug her claws into his chest.

Ripped his heart out.

And ate it as it still pulsed in her claws.

Naal's body disappeared like sparkles of obsidian.

Horror widened Copper's eyes and she screamed, "Nooo!" Such fury raged through her, hot and molten, that she gathered the biggest spellfire ball yet. She poured all the magic she could into that ball without tipping too close to the dark, wound her arm, and flung it at the demon.

From her position on the floor she wasn't able to pitch accurately. The spellfire hit Junga on her side, but it was powerful enough to knock her a good twenty feet away from where Naal had died. The demon slammed into a large stalagmite. This one cracked and a huge chunk of it fell onto Junga, striking her temple.

Junga shook her head as she rose and stumbled as if dizzy.

Copper pushed herself up and balanced on her left foot. She readied another ball of spellfire, but the demon glanced away from Copper, toward the battle. With one more look of demon hatred at Copper, Junga leaped toward Darkwolf.

Twenty-seven

Intent on retrieving his prize, the witch who belonged to him, Darkwolf dropped his shield a second after Silver and Copper released theirs. The pain in his broken nose was forgotten as he focused on Silver. Despite the smell of blood, Fomorii, and other stenches, he could swear he caught Silver's sweet lily scent.

Her power snaked around a demon and she saved her lover, and then she wrapped another Fomorii with her power.

Her lover. Darkwolf ground his teeth so hard his jaw hurt. By Balor, how Darkwolf wanted to destroy the D'Danann bastard.

As she battled, Darkwolf had no doubt Silver's consciousness was partly focused on him. He reveled in the fact she had to keep giving a part of her attention to him, even if it was to keep her guard up. She knew what he could do to her.

He glanced to the being that had once been Sara. The creature watched. Waited. Then its flaming red eyes met Darkwolf's and fear slammed into his chest as the eye

hanging around his neck told him who or what the being
was. The pain in his head was so intense he almost dropped
to his knees.

The being was Ceithlenn. Balor's wife.

No more were Ceithlenn or Sara simply seers, they had
united, joined with some evil essence from Underworld,
and had become something fierce. Dangerous. Deadly.

Just how dangerous and deadly? And to whom?

One thing he was certain of, one thing he felt in waves
from across the room—Ceithlenn was furious that Balor's
body and soul had not been released from Underworld.

But the battle was going awry. He would have to leave
the demons to fend for themselves. The Ceithlenn-Sara
creature remained untouched by Drow arrow, witches'
magic, or D'Danann talons.

When he ripped his gaze away from Ceithlenn's, he focused on his target.

He *would* have Silver for his own.

For the moment, not harried by any of the D'Danann or
the Drow traitors who had joined against him, Darkwolf
stalked Silver, who was a good fifty feet away. He raised
his hands. The power of Balor filled him as he prepared to
destroy all that stood in his way.

Silver whirled to face him. Her features were a mask of
hatred. No fear whatsoever.

Jaw clenched, she gathered a huge ball of spellfire and
flung it at him.

He waved his hand, casually causing the ball to flick to
the side. It bounded toward a stalagmite. The cone of minerals exploded on contact.

Shock flickered across Silver's face, immediately replaced by determination.

Junga bounded toward Darkwolf, drool and blood dripping from her fangs.

"Prepare for transference!" he commanded Junga as she
joined him.

Just as Junga transformed into Elizabeth's shell, a ball of Copper's golden spellfire came straight for Junga.

"You bitch!" Copper shouted as she flung the spellfire.

The demon-woman dodged, but the magic grazed her cheek, cutting her open like a knife. With a scream she dropped to her knees.

Copper gathered another ball of spellfire, but held up when Silver shouted something Darkwolf couldn't hear.

Darkwolf readied his ropes of magic to once more bind Silver so that he could use the power of transference to take her away with him, when instead she stunned him into a momentary stupor.

She flung up a bluish-purple net of power.

A net.

It looked like a fisherman's net, thick strands crisscrossing one another like a checkerboard. He barely had time to throw up a shield of protection around Junga and himself before the net encompassed the shield.

He and Junga were trapped.

If he released his shield, they would be covered by the net. Captured by a witch's inferior power.

Darkwolf growled, the sound pouring from his chest like one of the demons. He had no options left. Not this time. He glanced at Junga, who was on her knees. She held her hand to her bloody human cheek. His own broken nose ached and blood began pouring down his face again.

Darkwolf grabbed Junga's upper arm and prepared himself for transference as he said, *"Balor bahamenor."*

The last thing he saw was the glow of Ceithlenn's narrowed eyes.

Twenty-eight

Copper's heart ached at Naal's death, and fury rocked her as Junga and Darkwolf disappeared.

As soon as they vanished, she hobbled back to where Garran lay still. Her heart stuttered until she saw him move and groan. The bloodied warrior shook his head, then seemed to come to his senses. With a shout he pushed himself to his feet at the same time he grasped his bow from the cavern floor.

Relief poured through Copper. She started to turn back to the battle.

"Stop!" A tremendous voice boomed through the cavern loud enough to cut through the growls, shrieks, and shouts. The voice shook the room so that rocks and chunks of stalactites rained from the ceiling. Copper whipped her head in the direction of the red-eyed, bat-winged, fire-haired being where it had been perched or pacing during the entire battle. "I am Ceithlenn, wife and soul of Balor. When the time comes, you will all be extinguished."

Due to the power and loudness of the booming voice, more rocks and silt fell from above, one rock grazing Copper's shoulder. The being obviously had everyone's attention, but the Drow and D'Danann didn't falter in their attacks, the consummate warriors. "Come, my children," Ceithlenn said. "We will destroy these beings when the time is right. Very soon."

With that, the creature held out her arms. Red lightning crackled from her fingertips, creating an arc over everyone. A flash like fire engulfed the cavern and Copper flung one of her arms up to protect her eyes. To her surprise there was no heat. When she lowered her arm the D'Danann, Drow, and witches were staring at one another. All the living Fomorii, Basilisks, creatures she hadn't recognized, and a three-headed dog had vanished, along with Ceithlenn.

Garran shouted something. What the Drow said, Copper wasn't sure because it was in some strange language, but it sounded pretty much the way she felt.

Fucking demons.

Her gut churned. That creature . . . That being who called herself Ceithlenn . . . What the hell had been unleashed?

Copper grimaced as she skip-hopped back to where her sister stood. She couldn't believe Darkwolf, Junga, and that Ceithlenn creature were gone. The battle was over. For now.

"Oh, my goddess." Silver's eyes widened as Copper hobbled up to her and she looked at Copper's ankle. "It's twice the size of a softball." Her gaze shot back up to meet Copper's. "What happened?"

"I broke it way back in one of the tunnels," Copper managed to get out through gritted teeth. "Long story."

Zephyr buzzed around and around the two of them as Silver knelt at Copper's feet and held her hands to either side of the swollen ankle. She closed her eyes and blue magic began to flow from her palms, sparkling in the air as it moved toward Copper's ankle and then seeped through her jeans and into her skin.

Copper's relief was so great she sagged and might have

fallen if Tiernan hadn't grabbed her arms from behind and then folded her into his embrace. She immediately caught his scent of leather and wind. It was mixed with the added smells of blood and sweat. She recognized the strength of his embrace and the way he held her.

She wanted to melt against him, but instead she pulled herself away. Her heart ached too much to let him hold her. The movement caused more pain to rip through her ankle and she saw a few stars again.

That was getting *reeeeaaalllly* old.

"Be still." Silver frowned up at Copper, then went back to pouring her healing magic into Copper's ankle. Silver wouldn't be able to repair broken bones, but she could ease the pain at least a little.

And that was enough relief that Copper felt she could manage until the bones could be set.

At the same time Silver was addressing Copper's ankle, Copper was completely aware of the man who held her. Tiernan rubbed her upper arms in a soothing manner. He spoke soft words in Gaelic, but she didn't even care what he was saying. She had to shield her heart from him.

When the swelling had reduced so that her ankle was only the size of one softball instead of two, Silver rose to her feet and hugged Copper. "If I had known, I would have eased your pain earlier."

Silver drew away and Copper gave an uncomfortable smile. Uncomfortable because Tiernan was still holding her from behind, and his nearness was heady, almost causing her to forget that he may have to marry another woman.

"There was no time," Copper said. "You healed my wrists and stopped the flow of blood. That's what was most important."

Silver frowned. "But still . . ."

Copper found the strength to put her weight on her good ankle and balance herself. She hop-skipped out of Tiernan's arms and over to a stalagmite where she balanced herself and turned her gaze from him, trying not to let him see the pain in her eyes.

At the same time, a battle-worn Hawk came up to Silver and swept her into his embrace. She wrapped her arms around his neck, and Hawk pressed his lips hard against her forehead. He closed his eyes and held his position for several seconds before his gaze met Silver's. "*A thaisce*, I shall never let you out of my sight again. No more battles for you."

Copper knew her sister better than that, but Silver just kissed him firmly on the lips. She drew back and smiled. "I love you."

"Gods know I love you more than anything in any of the worlds." He hugged and rocked her, her feet completely off the floor of the cavern.

Copper sighed as she stared at the pair and tried not to look at Tiernan. She'd thought she could have that same happiness one day. But it probably wasn't something she would ever have. She'd never get over Tiernan. It was her own fault, of course. She'd known where she stood from the beginning.

"Copper." Tiernan's voice startled her from her thoughts and from watching her sister and her future brother-in-law.

"I can't," she whispered, avoiding him.

Maybe she could help some of the injured D'Danann.

With that thought she pushed herself away from the stalagmite she'd been resting against. She hobbled past Silver and Hawk, blindly moving away from them all. She wasn't sure where she was going.

Drow arrows littered the ground and she avoided the ones with diamond heads that hadn't exploded. The mood of the Dark Elves was somber after the loss of their prince, Naal. Somehow they had known about each of the losses of their kinsmen, no matter that their bodies had vanished in sparkling obsidian. Garran's expression was so tortured that Copper's eyes stung with tears for both him and his brother. Before she could say anything to him, he'd turned away.

The stench of burnt sugar had all but vanished with the closing of the door, but the horrid smells of rotten fish, blood, and really, really bad dog breath still filled the cavern. One thing she was grateful for was that the bodies of the beasts vanished or turned to dirt when killed.

Copper ended up where the D'Danann were seated or standing, tending to injuries or talking of the battle. A young man tried to get up, but a female D'Danann warrior forced him down. "You are no good to any of us if you die. Let me at least stop the bleeding," she was saying.

She didn't recognize all the warriors. She didn't know how Hawk and Tiernan had been able to cross over, but she was so glad to see them, as well as the new warriors they had recruited.

The warrior who had tried to get up was seated on a rock, his leather pants torn open at the leg and jagged fang marks in his flesh. The teeth that had made these wounds must have been poisonous to the Fae because they were still bleeding profusely.

Copper held back a groan as she tried to kneel and then sit by the young man's leg without twisting her ankle further. She didn't have a whole lot of luck, but she did manage to get her butt onto the cavern floor beside his leg.

"We need to get him to our healers," the D'Danann warrior woman with long blond hair said. "But we can only do that if the Great Guardian takes us back to our Sidhe."

Copper focused her attention on his leg. "What's your name?"

"Urien," the man ground out. He was a good-looking, brown-eyed and brown-haired warrior. He looked pretty young compared to the rest of the D'Danann.

"Well, I'm Copper. Let me see what I can do to help at least a little." She cast a look over her shoulder and saw

Silver, Hawk, and Tiernan across the chamber. Hawk and Tiernan were apparently discussing something. Silver had a strange look on her face.

More confident now with her hand magic, Copper put her palms a few inches above Urien's wounds. She closed her eyes and concentrated until she felt warmth pulsating from her body, the ebb and flow of her magic and her essence.

When she opened her eyes, she stared with pleasure at the golden bubbles of magic flowing between her and the D'Danann. The flow of blood slowed and then stopped, but the flesh still lay open.

"He'll need stitches," came Silver's voice from beside Copper. "We've got to get him either to the shop or to someplace in Otherworld and take care of that." Silver gave Copper a big smile as she knelt, and hugged her shoulders. "I think you got all the poison out with your magic, and that was without your wand."

"Really? The poison is gone, too?" Copper blinked, then looked closer at the wound. It did look clean, as if it just needed to be stitched up.

"It feels a hell of a lot better," Urien said with obvious relief.

Silver frowned and cocked her head at Copper. "What happened to your wand, anyway?"

With a grimace, Copper pulled the mangled wand from her back pocket. It was now completely lifeless, smashed, and both crystals broken off.

Silver gave a pained expression. "Ouch."

"You can say that again." Copper sighed and almost tossed the wand aside, but pocketed it. "I was pretty freaked out. I've never been any good at hand magic."

"I think you can safely say that was all in your head." Silver laughed, a sound that felt good to Copper. "You saved all of us by closing that door. And you really kicked ass out there."

"I guess I did." Copper's smile faded as her thoughts turned to Naal, who had died saving her and Garran. "With a lot of help."

"Tiernan loves you, you know," Silver said softly.

The words made Copper choke up and tears threatened to fall. "It doesn't matter. He's probably going to marry someone else."

"Is this the woman?"

Both Copper and Silver startled at the voice of the young man whose leg wound they had treated. Copper had pretty much forgotten about Urien.

Copper raised her brows and Silver cocked her head. "And you are probably the guy he gave it all to."

The young warrior's cheeks reddened and he nodded. "He insisted . . . and he has given Airell and me the means to be together."

"What is going on?" Copper looked from Urien to Silver. Her eyes widened. "Wait. Isn't Airell the name of the woman Tiernan is supposed to marry?"

Urien and Silver looked at one another, back to Copper, and nodded in unison. "His family arranged the marriage," Silver said.

"But Airell is in love with me," Urien said, his face turning bright red.

Copper looked at Urien and grabbed his gaze with hers. "So what good is it for you to love her when she can't get out of it, either?" She raised her brows. "Wait. Silver said he gave it all to you, and you said he gave you the means to be with Airell. What the hell does that all mean?"

"He broke the arrangement between his house and Airell's," came Hawk's voice from above them. The big man had his arms folded across his chest. "He gave all his wealth to Urien so that Urien's house might rise to the station necessary to wed Airell. Tiernan's family has disowned him and he has no doubt been thrown from the court. If he returns to our Sidhe, he will live with the D'Danann warriors and will start out in poverty."

Copper looked from Hawk to Urien and Silver. "Why would he do something as stupid as that?"

"Because I love you."

Tiernan's voice shocked Copper so badly she almost fell backward and had to brace her hand on the cavern floor to balance herself.

She raised her gaze—up, up, way up—to see him standing beside Hawk. In the next moment he was on one knee before her. His face was close enough for her to touch.

His features were worn, haggard, beyond what he might have experienced in battle. It was as if he'd fought another battle, too. He seemed tentative as he reached up to brush several loose strands of hair from her face. He cupped her cheek in his warm hand and she leaned into his touch. Her belly flip-flopped.

He brushed her cheek with his thumb. "I love you, Copper. It is you I wish to join with, to be with always."

Copper was so overwhelmed her head was spinning.

He'd given everything up because he loved her.

Loved her.

For a long moment she looked at him. Everyone around them was completely silent as if waiting for her response.

She raised her chin a notch. "You're arrogant, demanding, and bossy."

"This is true." He nodded. "And you are impulsive, reactive, and stubborn."

Her lips twisted. "Made for each other, eh?"

"Aye." His expression lightened and he gave a hopeful smile. "Will you join with me?"

Copper brought up her own hand to cup Tiernan's against her cheek. "Okay."

His hand slipped roughly from her cheek to grasp the back of her head and brought her to him in a rough, hungry kiss. Copper's head was still spinning and she wanted him so badly. Wanted everything he had to offer her.

She wrapped her arms around his neck and he rose up, taking her with him, and she hiked her thighs up and around his hips. Their lips never left one another's and she couldn't think past Tiernan. Couldn't think past the taste of him, the feel of his body pressed to hers, the strength of his embrace. Couldn't think past her love for him.

When he finally drew away from her his breathing matched hers, heavy and ragged.

"I love you, Tiernan," she said.

He grinned. "I know."

She slapped him playfully. "Arrogant jerk."

Applause broke around them and Copper's cheeks heated as she was brought back to reality and the fact that they were surrounded by a cavern full of warriors, the Drow, and her sister.

"Let's do what we have to do and get out of here," she whispered against his lips.

Twenty-nine

Darkwolf and Junga arrived in the same location they had left from, the room in which Silver had been held captive. Junga dropped to her knees, her hand holding her face where it had been sliced open by Copper's spellfire.

His nose was bleeding all over his shirt and his hands. Using his magic he spelled himself clean, then did the same for Junga. His nose stopped bleeding and he felt the healing begin, from the power of Balor's eye. He wasn't confident that his nose would be straight again.

"I must shift in order to heal," Junga said in a voice filled with pain.

Darkwolf turned, left the room, and strode into the home's great room.

And came to a dead stop.

His gut clenched and blood pounded in his ears.

In the room stood Ceithlenn-Sara. She had retracted her wings so that they had vanished, and her hair was no longer made of flames. It was punk-red, though, not natural. Her eyes didn't glow that vivid crimson color. Instead they were ever-changing—blues, grays, greens, and browns shifted like wind ruffling the swells of the sea. She wore a black skin-tight leather catsuit. The look on her face was a mixture of Sara and some other being. Her features were sharper, yet she was beyond beautiful.

It was Ceithlenn—possessed by some kind of great evil that had been buried deep in Underworld.

With her hands on her hips and a cold, cold look in her eyes, Ceithlenn stared at Darkwolf. For the first time since he had become a warlock high priest, he felt the urge to kneel before someone else, as if he were being forced to—a great pressure weighted his back and his legs trembled. He struggled. Fought against the force. But even Balor's essence was telling him to bow, and pain shot through his head.

Ceithlenn narrowed her eyes and Darkwolf felt powerful magic slam into him.

He dropped to his knees.

Junga, in her demon form, loped into the room. She hesitated when she saw Darkwolf on the floor as if she were shocked. The blue demon Queen of the Fomorii then moved to Darkwolf's side and went down on her knees, her long arms out in front of her as if she were worshipping this goddess-being.

Ceithlenn smiled, the expression just as cold as the look in her eyes. "You serve me now." Her voice was Sara's, yet not. It was confident, powerful, and beyond arrogant. "Until my husband, Balor, is released, I will serve in his stead. Is that understood?"

Darkwolf didn't want to, but the magical power forced his head down so that he was no longer able to look at Ceithlenn.

"Warlock." The moment she spoke to him, Darkwolf's head snapped up to look at her once again. "Bring me the eye."

A wave of ice-cold panic washed over Darkwolf and his skin prickled. Again magical power forced him to move.

He rose, and with leaden steps he approached Ceithlenn. When he reached her, his eyes were locked on hers, and he smelled the overpowering odor of burnt sugar along with a hint of Sara's jasmine scent.

Ceithlenn reached up and slipped her fingers into his hair before drawing him into a tight, painful kiss. She bit his lower lip so hard he tasted his own blood along with her taste—which was strange. Off. Like her burnt-sugar smell.

When she drew away, she smiled, and he saw that her canines had lengthened and she looked like a vampire—a very dangerous vampire. "You will do." She slipped her palm down his throat to the stone eye hanging from the thick chain. Gently she caressed the eye and spoke to it before lifting the stone and pressing her lips to it. "Soon, my love, soon."

Ceithlenn raised her head and she pushed Darkwolf out of her way. No words came to him. Fury boiled inside him, that this being, that any being, should attempt to rule him. Yet there was no doubt she was far more powerful than he.

Darkwolf ground his teeth.

Ceithlenn moved closer to Junga and raked her gaze over the prostrate demon. "Rise."

Junga pushed herself to a standing position, the demon's great apelike arms hanging at her sides, her lips closed over her needlelike teeth. Ceithlenn slowly walked around Junga. When she came back to face the demon, she said, "I shall need you to command the Fomorii and other beings. You will answer to me."

A growl rose up in Junga's throat and the look on Ceithlenn's face turned murderous. "You will obey me. Or you die."

Junga bowed her head. Whether by force or of her own choice, Darkwolf didn't know.

Ceithlenn smiled coldly as she looked from Darkwolf back to Junga. "For now the Fomorii and our other friends will reside in the sewers." She glared at Junga. "Where they belong." She placed her hand on her hips and turned to Darkwolf. "You will again seek out the strongest of witches to serve both me and Balor."

With a faraway look in her ever-changing eyes, she added, "The time will come, and it will be soon."

Thirty

Tiernan could barely believe that Copper had agreed to join with him. It gave him a feeling of completeness, of power, that he had never felt before. It made it difficult to concentrate on the tasks that must now be performed.

Copper cuddled against him as he carried her and he caught her wonderful scent of apples, cinnamon, and woman mixed with the smell of sweat and battle. He could feel her bone-deep exhaustion. What she had been through . . . A lesser being could not have accomplished what she had. She was truly a warrior in heart and spirit.

"Let me down," she said, as they neared the circle of runes where dried blood now resided in a portion of the etchings.

Reluctantly he allowed her to slip from his embrace, but he made sure her weight was on her good ankle when her feet touched down. She still winced as she gripped one of his arms while standing beside her sister, who was studying the runes.

The other D'Danann gathered around, silent as they watched the witches. The Drow stayed back in the dark-

ness, all except Garran, who stood beside Copper and
Tiernan.

"We have to destroy it." Silver's gaze met Copper's as
Silver continued. "This is the key to opening this door to
Underworld."

Zephyr landed on Copper's ear and she felt his unease
mix with her own as she nodded. "Between the two of us I
bet we can do it." She looked to the door where red light
still seeped from the cracks, bathing the cavern in its eerie
glow, and still lending the cavern the look of blood dripping from its crystals. The creatures that had been stuck in
the doorway had vanished, destroyed by the D'Danann
during the battle. "Not only do we need to take care of the
runes, but we need to deal with the door," Copper added.
"It's got to be sealed."

"First let's tackle the circle. Using our magic we can
wipe these runes away so that they no longer exist." Silver
moved closer to the etchings and studied them. "I bet a little hand magic would do it. We can burn it away."

Copper balanced on her good leg as she stood side by
side with Silver. They were just outside the circle and
looked at one another, then back to the runes. Both sisters
raised their hands at the same time. As one they took a
deep breath.

Blue light immediately flashed from Silver's hands and
Copper's golden bubbles chased the blue blaze. Their
magic was like laser beams and began burning the runes at
once. Everywhere their power touched, their magic seemed
to melt the runes away until nothing but black soot remained. The air filled with a strange burning smell, like
metal filings or a shorted-out electrical wire.

With Copper hop-skipping, she and Silver slowly paced
the circumference of the circle, their magic continuously
burning into the runes. As they went on, a more rancid
stench, like the foul smell of evil, rose up.

A black substance like thick blood or tar rose up and began to bubble at the center. It started out the size of a pin-prick, then expanded as it began to spread to the borders of the inside circle. It crept closer to the runes as if to protect the etchings.

The sisters backed up a little, but continued to burn away the runes. Zephyr lent his magic to theirs. Copper's and Silver's blue and gold magic worked in tandem to destroy the etchings.

The black blood rose higher and covered some of the runes, making it more difficult to destroy them. The tarlike substance splattered when their magic hit it and Copper felt a yank and a shove at her power, as if something evil in the blood was fighting them—drawing out their gray magic and trying to yank her across the line and into the dark.

"More," Copper said through gritted teeth, keeping a tight rein on her gray magic. This time she knew it wouldn't be wise to delve into the gray. "We're almost done."

Copper poured as much white energy as she had left into her witchcraft at the same time she felt more resistance. Her golden light took on a brighter shade.

"We're almost to the end." Silver backed up and Copper followed with a hop-skip.

The moment they burned away the last of the runes, Copper nearly collapsed with relief. The drain on her magic vanished.

A liquidlike figure rose up in the middle of the blood, in a shape that was almost human. It gave an unholy scream that echoed throughout the cavern.

It dropped with a splash and vanished into the thick blood.

Copper swallowed and watched as all the tarry blood rolled to the center of the circle. Every bit of it moved back to a spot the size of a quarter, then a pinprick, and then vanished. All that remained was the destroyed circle.

Silver and Copper looked at one another. "Phew." Copper pushed away damp hair from her sweaty forehead. "That was freaky."

"No kidding." Silver sighed and massaged her temples. She looked just as sweaty and battle-worn as Copper felt.

"Now for the door." Copper searched her mind. One thing she'd always been good at—until she'd been stuck in the meadow—was coming up with spells. Of course she'd always had her wand then. She sighed, then felt a burst of warmth in her chest. Tonight her spell to shut the door had worked with her hand magic!

"Any ideas?" Silver braced her hands on her hips and looked at Copper.

She cocked her head to the side and then it came to her. A little adjustment to the spell she'd used to shut the door might just do it. She murmured it to Silver who nodded her agreement. They both chanted together.

> Goddess hear our words, our plea
> In this time out of time,
> In this place out of place.
> Goddess, we raise our hands to thee
> In this dark beyond darkness,
> In this world beyond worlds.
> We await your grace.
> We await your power.
> We stand at the threshold.
> Goddess, please protect your children
> And forever seal this door of darkness.

At the same time they chanted, their magic flowed from their hands and Zephyr's powers joined theirs. The brilliant blue and gold of their witchcraft battled the evil red glow seeping from the cracks around the door.

Nothing happened.

They shoved harder with their magic.

Copper and Silver raised their voices, chanting louder

and louder and poured more and more of themselves into their magic.

The door shuddered. The power of its movement caused rocks to rain down from the ceiling of the cavern. Copper felt dirt scatter on her hair.

Again Silver and Copper chanted, this time shouting the words. The brilliance of their gold and blue magic intertwined, working as one. The light that flowed from the sisters had grown as tall and as wide as the door. The power that Copper felt was unlike anything she'd ever experienced. She felt high, capable to take on anything.

"On three, push with everything you have!" Copper shouted. From her side vision she saw her sister give a quick nod.

"One . . . two . . . *three!*"

Their combined magic exploded against the door. The power of the impact sent Silver and Copper flying backward. Copper slammed into one of the D'Danann, and she saw someone catch her sister as well.

The cavern lit up, the light so bright that Copper could barely see. She shielded her eyes with her arm. Blue and gold glittered throughout the cavern, sparkles that floated through the air before they fell to the floor like falling stars.

When the brilliance faded a bit, Copper squinted at the door. The red glow was gone. It was sealed!

Just as she turned to grin at her sister, the cavern went dark.

Immediately Silver filled the cavern with her blue magical glow, which she easily made with her hand magic.

Everything started to rock, to buck, to shake—far worse than when Ceithlenn had caused a shower of rocks to fall.

This time a tremendous amount of rock and dirt rained down on their heads and a stalactite loosened and landed between Copper and Silver, its cone shattering at their feet. The cavern was coming down around them!

Before Copper had time to react, or to try to form her

own glow to help light up the room, she felt Tiernan's strong arms around her and he leaped into the air. The next thing she knew they were flying toward the tunnel and the now open passageway.

"What if the tunnel collapses all the way?" she cried out.

Tiernan's arms tightened around her. "We have no other options."

D'Danann warriors swooped ahead of her and at their sides, and Drow darted through the cavern along with them.

In no time Tiernan landed with Copper in his arms. He folded his wings and bolted into the tunnel, running faster than she could have imagined in the darkness. She clung to him as he ran. If it wasn't for her ankle—and the fact that it was too dark to see—she would have insisted on being perfectly capable of running on her own. Her lips twisted into a smile. She *was* stubborn.

That smile vanished as she heard the roar of the cavern collapsing in on itself. Dirt flooded the tunnel and she choked and coughed as dust went up her nose and into her mouth. She couldn't see anything in front or behind her, but apparently Tiernan could. Goddess, had her sister made it into the tunnel with the rest of them? Had they all made it?

Copper's concern about Silver lessened when she saw her sister's blue magic illuminating the tunnel, allowing her to see a little through the dust. Not that there was a lot to see. Dust ahead, dust behind, and nothing but tunnel.

The ground rocked, but Tiernan didn't stumble. It seemed like no time and forever before they reached the place where Copper had fallen through the hole and broken her ankle. How were they going to get back up there?

Duh, she thought the moment Tiernan unfolded his wings. He didn't have much room to spread them, but somehow he was able to propel them up and into the giant's tunnel.

He didn't stop once they were in the enormous passageway. He was able to fully unfurl his magnificent wings. He shot down the tunnel like an arrow from a bow and she clung to him tightly, feeling safe and secure.

When they had made it up the Drow stairs, through the door, and out into the growing dark, Copper thought she'd never seen anything so beautiful as her meadow. She smiled at the thought while she wrapped her arms tighter around Tiernan's neck. It was only three days ago she had freed everyone in the meadow from captivity. She grinned when it occurred to her that she'd probably fallen in love with the arrogant ass the day the Pixies made designs out of Tiernan's hair and tied flowers at the ends.

"Okay, you can let me down now." Copper looked up into his dirt-streaked, sweaty face. She wanted to push his long blond hair away from his eyes.

He just shook his head. "Not yet."

Copper swatted his chest and Zeph buzzed at her ear. "We're out of danger, okay?"

Tiernan gave her such a sexy grin that it melted her on the spot. "But I do not *want* to let you go."

Garran followed the D'Danann and two witches out of the Drow door. It was almost dark, so Garran was able to remain aboveground. His features were proud and fierce as always, but Copper could see grief in his eyes for his brother.

Riona fluttered up to them, a delighted shimmer to her amethyst eyes and countless sparkles of Faerie dust sprinkling from her wings and glittering in the evening. "You have done it," she stated, and gave one of her beautiful smiles.

Copper smiled back and Riona drifted over to lay a soft, tiny kiss on each of Copper's cheeks. Zephyr even climbed onto the queen's arm, the honeybee looking huge in comparison to her hands. Riona hovered before Copper and Tiernan as she stroked the familiar. When she removed her hand, he buzzed his wings in appreciation before flying back to Copper's ear.

"Remember your friends here in Otherworld," Riona said to Copper. "We will think fondly of you."

Tears pricked the corners of Copper's eyes. Her voice shook a little, but she managed to get the words out. "I could never, ever, ever forget you."

Riona smiled, swooped up to kiss each of Copper's cheeks again, and then kissed even Tiernan's. The Faerie queen gave a little wave, then left in a puff of lavender Faerie dust.

Tiernan and Copper looked at one another and smiled before he strode away from the Drow door, still carrying her.

The moment they rounded the rock outcropping, all the D'Danann and the two witches came up short. Before them stood the most beautiful, ethereal being that Copper had ever seen. She almost seemed to *glow* in the growing darkness. She was tall, no doubt pure Elvin from the look of her pointed ears peeking through her long white-blond hair that dropped all the way to her feet. She had such an air of wisdom about her, but she looked so young.

"The Great Guardian," Tiernan said quietly but with reverence.

This time Tiernan did set Copper on her feet, still taking great care with her. But the moment she was steady, he bent on one knee and bowed his head before the Elvin woman who Tiernan had called the Great Guardian. All of the other D'Danann bowed, as well as Garran, the Drow king.

Copper and Silver shot looks at one another, Silver looking as bewildered as Copper felt.

"Rise." The Elvin woman had a musical voice and it almost sounded as if she was amused.

The D'Danann and Garran obeyed. As Copper looked to each of the warriors, she saw reservation in their expressions, but utmost respect.

First the Great Guardian turned to Garran. "You have lost much." Her voice was hard, definite.

"Aye." Garran's eyes showed his pain, but his stance was

tall, proud. "My brother is dead, as well as several of our comrades."

Her features remained impassive. "You and your brethren have set free what was never meant to be released."

Garran lowered his gaze. "We erred in our judgment."

"As you have aided the D'Danann and the witches," the Great Guardian said, "and helped to reseal the door, your transgressions will be forgiven." Her eyes glowed along with the rest of her, and Copper shivered as the Great Guardian continued. "Return in peace to your Sidhe, my Elvin brother."

Garran bowed, then inclined his head to Copper, giving her one last, long look.

"Goodbye," she said softly to Garran before he turned away and disappeared around the rock outcropping.

Copper heard the Drow door scrape as it closed. Copper shuddered one last time. She never wanted to hear *that* sound again.

"You will now cross over and return to where you belong." The Great Guardian drew Copper's attention and held her hand out toward the rock wall that Copper had come through when she'd arrived back in the meadow. "You will go first, Copper Ashcroft and Tiernan."

Copper started because the Great Guardian knew her name, but she grasped Tiernan's hand and gave a little bow of her head. It was instinctive, as if it were the right thing to do.

The Elvin woman swept her hand out in a motion that Copper took to mean, "Get going."

Clutching Tiernan's hand tightly in hers, Copper took a leap of faith, stepped facefirst into the rock wall. It shimmered like a curtain of rain and she passed through it.

Like the time Cassia had taken her across the footbridge, Copper's skin was numb and her ears felt like cotton had been jammed into them. She couldn't hear a thing.

Two steps more and she could breathe again. She could

hear again. And she could see exactly where they were. On the footbridge in Golden Gate Park, sunshine filtering through tree leaves.

Still gripping hands, Tiernan and Copper glanced at one another, smiled, and stepped forward. Well, Copper hobbled, but she moved nonetheless.

Hawk and Silver appeared behind them. Even though she was obviously exhausted, her face streaked with dirt, and her clothing filthy, she ran up to Copper and hugged her tightly.

"We made it, honey." Silver squeezed her tighter. "We made it."

Copper relaxed in Tiernan's embrace as he and Hawk flew with Copper and Silver in their arms, under their cloaks of magic. None of the other D'Danann had followed them to this world, so the Great Guardian must have sent them elsewhere. Probably back to their Sidhe.

When they arrived at the store, there were exclamations of surprise and concern from all the witches, but Copper just wanted to collapse into bed with exhaustion. The shop was empty of customers and Mackenzie turned the sign at the front door over to CLOSED. The four battle-worn men and women were ushered into the shop's kitchen.

The news that they had returned spread quickly among the D'Danann stationed in the apartments, all the Coven of D'Anu witches, and even Jake from the PSF. The kitchen of the store and café was so crowded that soon Cassia was chasing most of them out.

Mackenzie, Rhiannon, and Sydney stayed to help Cassia, one witch per returnee. The other witches opened Enchantments again, keeping busy and holding back all their questions until Hawk, Tiernan, Silver, and Copper had been cared for.

Copper was in Tiernan's lap for the moment, his arms around her as she leaned her back against his chest. Every ache in her body made itself known, and she couldn't move on her own for the life of her.

"Put her in this chair so that Sydney can tend to your wounds, Tiernan," Cassia ordered.

Copper tilted her head back and looked at Tiernan with concern. For the first time she noticed a small gash along his jawline. "You're hurt!"

He smiled and kissed the top of her head. "I'm fine, little fire."

Nevertheless, Tiernan reluctantly let Copper go, and she allowed Cassia to help her up so that she could hobble to her own chair. Copper collapsed into it, and then Cassia brought up another chair for Copper to rest her swollen ankle on.

Next Cassia placed her hand over Silver's belly to determine if the baby was okay. When she smiled, and said, "The baby is fine," everyone breathed a collective sigh of relief. Hawk got down on his knees to hug Silver. Copper reached over to her sister and squeezed her hand.

"I agree with Hawk," Copper said. "You need to take it easy for a while."

Silver placed her hand over her belly. "Our baby is a strong one." She looked up at Hawk. "Like his father."

Hawk's features showed his shock. "A boy. You are certain?"

Silver smiled. "He let himself be known. Now we have to think up a name for our little warrior."

Hawk was forced into a chair where his wounds could be attended to, but his eyes never left Silver's.

At everyone's insistence, Silver told them all about her captivity, and how Darkwolf had used transference to bring her, Sara, and Junga to the cavern. "I was mostly out of it since I'd been drugged by Darkwolf. I passed in and out of consciousness, so I got the gist of what was happening from their conversations," Silver said, and then groaned as Mackenzie cleansed a long cut on her arm.

Apparently Garran had been at the cavern, waiting. The Drow had finally discovered the place and the warlock had been informed. The Drow had been stationed around the cavern behind great rocks and stalagmites, blending with the darkness and waiting for the door to open.

"Darkwolf gave me a little more of the sleeping drug when he saw that I was waking," Silver said as she shoved her dirty hair out of her face. "I was out, and then the next thing I knew, I was bound in the middle of the circle and bleeding into the runes. I passed out of consciousness again, but woke up to find myself off to the side, and Copper tied down instead of me."

Hawk growled his displeasure and leaned over to kiss Silver firmly on the lips. "I should never have let you attempt such a foolish thing as you did at the pier, *a thaisce*," he said.

She rolled her eyes. "Like you could stop me."

He growled again.

Tiernan and Hawk took turns relating their trip to Otherworld. Hawk had gathered a group of D'Danann warriors while Tiernan took care of some business. At that Copper looked at him and couldn't help a smile at the way he studied her.

They explained everything from Queen Riona coming to them, to following Copper's trail, to fighting the demons and beasts that had escaped through the Underworld door before it had been shut.

Copper went last. "I had no choice but to go alone. No one crossed with me, and I had no idea that Tiernan and Hawk were in Otherworld. Riona told me that Balor had closed all entrances from our world to Otherworld."

She told her story, even pulled out her mangled wand and tossed it on the table. Tiernan's look was thunderous when she came to the part where Sara had smashed her ankle even worse than it already was.

Copper winced. It hurt just to think about it.

The entire time the four shared their stories, Cassia, Mackenzie, Sydney, and Rhiannon took care of their wounds—their scrapes, cuts, and bruises—using witch magic, herbal creams, and healing oils. Copper was filthy, exhausted, and so ready for sleep that she could barely keep her eyes open.

"You know we'll have to set the bones in your ankle," Cassia said, her blue eyes meeting Copper's. "It's not going to be easy. Some are shattered."

Copper flinched. "I can't do it awake. There's no freaking way I can take it."

Rhiannon came up to Copper, who opened her mouth as Rhiannon tilted a brown bottle so that bitter drops landed on Copper's tongue. She swallowed the fluid more than willingly.

Her body relaxed and she felt Tiernan pick her up and settle her on his lap so that he could hold her as her bones were set.

She gave a sleepy smile as her eyelids fluttered closed. She felt as if she were floating on a breeze, flying in the darkness. Everything slipped away and she fell into the deepest of sleeps.

Thirty-one

When Copper woke and opened her eyes, she found herself snug in Tiernan's embrace, in his bed. She smiled at the feeling of rightness, the feeling that their hearts and souls were as one.

The room was fairly dark, the only light pouring into the room from the bathroom. What light there was made the furniture in the room less ghostly-looking. She didn't know why the light was on, but for some reason she was glad for it. Maybe she'd had too much deep darkness to last her a while.

Her ankle throbbed and when she adjusted her leg she felt a cast on her foot, with only her toes free and the cast covering her leg up to her shin. Oh, joy, wasn't this going to be fun. At least she was a witch and would heal faster than a human would.

Copper felt clean and refreshed, and figured she'd been given some kind of bath as she slept. Even her hair was clean and silky. She gave a long, catlike stretch and sighed. The feel of satin surrounded her skin and she knew she'd been wrapped in a robe before being put to bed. How long had they been sleeping?

Tiernan stirred behind her, but she wasn't sure he was awake despite the fact he had a huge erection pressed up against her backside. But then he nuzzled her hair and she heard his deep inhale.

"My little fire," he murmured against her nape and she shivered. Her need for him was so great she wanted to push him on his back, slip his cock into her pussy, and ride him hard.

An idea came to her and she grinned at the thought. She slipped out of his embrace and swung her legs over the bed and stood with a clunk of her cast. Oh, good. Cassia had given her a walking cast so that she could at least try to get around without crutches.

He propped himself up on one elbow and his black robe fell open to reveal his muscled chest. "Come back to bed."

She curled her finger in a "come and get me" motion. "I have a better idea." She whirled and hobbled to the front door of the apartment. Her ankle throbbed and her body ached, but she was ready for a little fun.

When she reached the front door, Tiernan came up behind her and grasped her by her shoulders. He slowly rotated her to face him and she looked up into his incredible blue eyes. Goddess, he looked so sexy with his tousled blond hair and stubbled cheeks. "What are you up to?" he said in his deep Irish brogue. "I am of a mind to take you straight back to bed."

She playfully pushed at his bare chest, and almost melted against him at the contact of his warm skin against her palm. But no, she wanted to have her fun. "Come on. This'll be great."

He shook his head in a sign of exasperation and she moved back to the door. The knob squeaked when she turned it, and the door hinges gave a rusty sound as she and

Tiernan slipped into the corridor. After they shut the door behind them, Copper grabbed Tiernan by the hand and tried to tug him down the hallway to the stairwell.

Before she could take a step, he swooped her into his arms and she gave a little squeal. "Whatever it is you have planned," he rumbled, "I will not have you walking on a broken ankle."

She wrapped her arms around his neck and snuggled against his chest. "Take us all the way to the rooftop."

His muscles flexed as he carried her up and onto the flagstone floor of the roof garden. Only streetlights illuminated the greenery, along with the chairs and lounges in the small garden area near the stairwell.

Tiernan set her down carefully, her earth-brown satin robe sliding against his in a sensual motion. His erection pressed against her belly as he brought her into the circle of his arms. "You desire me to take you here and now?"

Copper grinned up at him. "You're getting closer."

He cocked an eyebrow as she took a couple of steps away from him. His palms slid down her satin-covered arms until he reached her hands and released her.

With her eyes focused on his, she untied the robe and the belt fluttered to the flagstone. His gaze darkened as she let the robe slide down her shoulders to her feet, leaving her completely naked.

Copper's nipples immediately tightened in the light breeze that caressed her skin and caused her hair to lift from her shoulders.

Tiernan's hungry gaze took her in. "You are beyond beautiful," he said, his brogue deep and husky.

When he tried to reach for her, she took a step back. "Your turn."

He ripped his belt from his waist, shrugged out of his robe, and flung them aside. For a moment she studied his muscular form. She'd always thought of him as masculine perfection, but tonight he looked even more incredible to her. His blond hair stirring about his broad shoulders, his well-cut body leading to tapered hips, powerful thighs and calves, and even handsome feet. She'd never really thought of feet as handsome before.

Copper's gaze rested on his cock jutting from its nest of curls and the large sac hanging beneath. Her breathing increased and she held herself back from getting on her knees and slipping him into her mouth.

Tiernan looked like such a fierce warrior as he restrained himself from taking her down to the floor of the rooftop. Copper stepped forward, holding her hands out to him, and he took them within his larger grip. She was close enough now that his cock nudged her belly and her nipples brushed his chest. Everywhere they touched was like a furnace against her body.

"I cannot wait much longer to have you, little fire." His grip on her hands tightened. "I can see by that look in your eyes you are up to something."

She laughed, slid her arms around his neck and reached up for his kiss. He crushed her body to him as he took her mouth as hard with his kiss as he certainly wanted to take her. His lips were firm against hers, and she groaned with every nip of his teeth on her bottom lip and every plunge of his tongue into her mouth. Her body was on fire now as they pressed hard against one another.

Tiernan cupped the back of her head with one hand and he clenched her hair tight in his fist. His stubble was rough against her jawline as he moved his moist lips from hers and kissed her soft skin along her cheek to her ear.

"What do you want, little fire?" he said in a voice rough with passion. "I will give it to you."

Copper's lips found his mouth again and she murmured against them, "I want you to take me up. I want you to make love to me while we fly."

Tiernan groaned. "By the gods, you are incredible."

Before he could shift, she said, "Wait. I want to watch."

"But I don't want to let you go." His grip on her tightened. "I want to be inside you now."

She kissed him hard again, then traced the line of his mouth with her fingertip. "Just let me watch."

With an air of reluctance, Tiernan released her, took a few steps back, and then turned away from her.

It was the most incredible sight. His large brown wings slowly unfurled from his body. The muscles across his back rippled as the wings grew through his skin, from his shoulder blades down to his waist, and she heard the sound of bone popping. When he finished, he flapped them and it caused a strong breeze to caress her naked body.

Tiernan faced her again and she was in his arms in a fraction of a moment. "Wrap your legs around my waist," he said, his jaw taut with hunger as he cupped her buttocks and raised her.

Copper obeyed, doing her best to clamp her thighs around his hips and cross her broken ankle with her good one. If she wasn't so hot for Tiernan, so ready for him, she would have laughed at her awkwardness in a time of such passion.

She wrapped her arms tight around his neck and his eyes took her in while he used one hand to place his erection at the entrance to her core. He grabbed her hips with his palms and propelled the two of them into the air at the same time he drove his cock deep inside her.

Copper let loose a cry of fulfillment and exhilaration as Tiernan made love to her at the same time they flew. It was incredible. Beyond incredible. Beyond description.

City lights swirled around them as Tiernan dipped and rolled and even held her on top of him. Wind that should have chilled her skin felt warm as her body flushed with heat and passion.

The smell of the ocean mixed with Tiernan's pure male scent and she could still taste him upon her tongue. She pressed her lips to his, needing to taste him again. His mouth was so very hot, and she slipped her tongue inside as he pumped his cock into her pussy.

Their lips parted when he twisted so that he was flying with her directly beneath him, their arms tight around one another. Goddess, every movement of his hips drove him deeper inside her, bringing her so close to climax that she cried out with every thrust.

Golden bubbles sparkled in the night sky around them, and Copper felt them bind him closer to her, binding her closer to him. The magic slipping from her surrounded them as if they were a comet sailing through the atmosphere.

Their hair whipped around their shoulders and into their faces. In the golden illumination she could clearly see Tiernan's blue gaze. He focused on her eyes with such intensity it brought her even closer to the peak.

His hands gripped her hips tight, driving into her as he brought her to him in the same motion as he flew higher above the city. He reached that perfect spot inside her and she knew she couldn't hold back any longer.

"Tiernan!" Copper shouted as her orgasm whooshed through her, like the air past her body. Her magic brightened, making everything around them light up. Her climax was like an explosion in her mind, city lights swirling with gold.

He thrust and thrust and thrust, harder each time, making her body throb even more. "I'm going to come, little fire."

"Do it." She could barely get the words out. "Come inside me."

Tiernan gave a shout as he climaxed and she felt the throb of his orgasm inside her. He held her tight and groaned loud and long.

He stayed inside her as they flew through the sky. They clung to one another, their breathing hard and their bodies pressed tight.

Too soon his feet touched down on the apartment building's rooftop.

Copper's head was still spinning from their wild flight and lovemaking. Tiernan smiled down at her as his cock slipped from inside her and he lowered her to stand on her feet.

Her arms were still wrapped around his neck and she didn't want to let go. She reached up and kissed him again, refusing to break the contact between them.

When they finally parted, Copper was amazed at the warmth that flowed through her at the look of love in Tiernan's eyes.

She sighed and pressed her head to his chest, his skin warm against her cheek. "I love you so much, Tiernan."

Copper tilted her head back to see his arrogant grin as he said, "I know." She gave him a playful slap on the arm and he laughed. "I love you, little fire. Now if you will only learn to do what you are told . . ."

She laughed. "Yeah, like that's going to happen."

And coming soon, a sexy new
romantic suspense novel from
Cheyenne McCray

Chosen Prey

St. Martin's Paperbacks

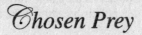